O9-BSA-543

THE WISDOM OF
FATHER DOWLING

THE WISDOM OF
FATHER DOWLING

RALPH MCINERNY

FIVE STAR
A part of Gale, Cengage Learning

CENGAGE Learning™

Detroit • New York • San Francisco • New Haven, Conn • Waterville, Maine • London

GALE
CENGAGE Learning™

FICTION

LIBRARY OF CONGRESS CATALOGING-IN-PUBLICATION DATA

McInerny, Ralph M.
     The wisdom of Father Dowling / by Ralph McInerny. — 1st ed.
         p. cm.
     "Fifteen of the best Father Dowling mystery short stories."
     ISBN-13: 978-1-59414-679-4 (alk. paper)
     ISBN-10: 1-59414-679-9 (alk. paper)
     1. Dowling, Father (Fictitious character)—Fiction. 2. Catholics—Fiction. 3. Clergy—Fiction. I. Title.
     PS3563.A31166W57 2009
     813'.54—dc22   2008039753

Published in 2009 in conjunction with Tekno Books and Ed Gorman.

Printed in the United States of America
2 3 4 5 6 7 12 11 10 09

For Marika and Thomas Gordon Smith

CONTENTS

ANATHEMA SITS

1

The first time Norman Shield showed up at the St. Hilary parish center, no one recognized him. A game of shuffleboard went on and a small slam was made at the serious table where little was said and bridge was played with the utmost dedication. Of course Madeline Young knew who he was, but she said nothing. She was sitting with the women who brought their sewing or knitting and occupied a corner, only their hands and their eyes moving as they followed the activities of the other seniors. Madeline had taken a chair next to old Mrs. Williams, whose arthritis did not seem to affect her skill with a crotchet needle.

"I don't see how you do it," Madeline said with genuine admiration.

"Neither do I."

"Oh come on."

"If I think of it, I can't do it. It's like tying your shoes. Who is that tall man with all that silver hair?"

"Father Dowling brought him," one of the knitters said.

"Is he a priest?"

Gloria Walsh, the youngest in the group, looked over the circle of wood that held her work, round eyes above round glasses; her mouth too formed a little circle. She shook her head. "He's not a priest."

Madeline stood then and drifted away, not toward the silver-haired man who was the object of this curiosity, but out of the former gym and up the stairs to what had once been the school principal's office to see if she could be of any help to Edna Hospers.

The next day, Madeline was again helping Edna when Gloria Walsh came in, waited just inside the door for effect, and, when she had gotten Edna's attention, said, "We have a celebrity in our midst!"

"Who?" Edna asked.

"The tall man with silver hair we thought was a priest? He's Norman Shield, the famous artist!"

Madeline listened to the breathless account of Norman Shield's career and could not help thinking how dissatisfied the artist himself would be with it. Fame is relative, of course, and to have achieved it in Chicago was no small thing, but like most artists Norman had dreamt of global renown. Once perhaps he would have settled for what he had achieved, the most sought-after portrait painter in the Chicago area, certainly for a time, but that success had come to seem ashes in his mouth—his very words.

Gloria took Edna's hand and tugged her toward the door, wanting her to come to the gym and take part in all the excitement. Madeline followed the two other women down the hallway. Norman stood tall among the people who surrounded him to ask questions, talk to one another, or just admire. Surely few men received such adulation. The artist wore an expression that flickered between pleasure and displeasure. Only the serious bridge players went on with what they were doing.

Father Dowling came in when the excitement was at its height and asked Madeline what was the cause.

"Norman Shield."

"I told him he'd be recognized."

"You knew he was coming?"

"Do you know him?"

"Long ago. He wouldn't remember."

"He has agreed to give an art class."

"That's where I met him."

"He said he had never taught before."

"We were students together."

2

Father Dowling had been astounded when Norman accepted the therapeutic suggestion that he run a beginning art class for the seniors at the parish center.

"I always avoided that, even when I needed the money."

"What would you charge?"

The artist smiled. "The benefit will be mine."

The sort of benefit penitents had once derived from taking long pilgrimages or mounting the *scala santa* in Rome on their knees. Norman had come to the parish house because he had lived in St. Hilary's as a boy.

"I attended the school."

"It's become a parish center."

"I'm almost surprised that the parish is still in existence."

Norman Shield was more saddened by the changes in himself than in his old neighborhood. There had been three marriages, and messy affairs as well. The artist had recently been in the news when Karen Jaeger, an irate client, took a shot at him.

"Just a flesh wound, Father." His brows went up as his eyes widened. "In every sense."

To the media, Shield had joked that his client must have been dissatisfied with her portrait. But she was a woman scorned.

"I should have scorned her from the beginning. Oh, I don't blame her. She might have killed me though." He was serious now. "Suddenly I saw what I had become, an aging satyr."

He had come back to find the boy he had been long ago

11

when he attended the parish school.

"Would you like to go see it?"

He would, so Father Dowling had taken him over. Norman was more interested in the memories evoked by the place than the current activities, but when they returned to the pastor's study Father Dowling suggested the art class.

"It won't interfere with any work of my own," he said somberly.

"Maybe it will bring back your muse."

Norman was experiencing what in a more spiritual man might be called the dark night of the soul. Life had lost its savor for him; he no longer cared to paint, and as he looked back over the years all he saw was futility.

"The nuns would have told me to offer it up."

"That's still good advice."

He started the following day. Standing next to Madeline Young, Father Dowling listened out of sight in the hallway as the artist explained his method of instruction. "I will show you by doing. I will paint a portrait. You will do the same. We will need a model. Any volunteers?"

Gloria Walsh offered to sit; three others decided that they would attempt a portrait, fortified by Norman's assurance that he would guide and coach them in the process. Father Dowling went back to the parish house thinking that Norman was already out of the doldrums.

"Madeline Young says she knows you," he said when the artist stopped by the parish house.

Apparently the name meant nothing to Norman. "That's her married name," Marie said, looking into the study from the hallway.

"What a remarkable face," Norman said, getting to his feet. The housekeeper backed away as he approached her. He stopped and held out his hand, so she would not run off. "I wish I were doing *your* portrait."

"This is Marie Murkin," Father Dowling said. "That's her married name."

Flustered by this unfamiliar attention to her appearance, Marie scampered off to her kitchen.

"Perhaps when you finish Gloria's you can do Marie's portrait, for the parish."

"I would keep it if I did it." He looked at Father Dowling. "Coming back to St. Hilary's is the smartest thing I've done." At the door, when he was leaving, he paused. "I did know a Madeline Hart once."

3

Three days later only one student, a determined Jim McGrade, a retired detective, former colleague of Phil Keegan, remained beside Norman, trying to follow the master's instruction as they both painted Gloria's portrait. Jim's canvas was a mess of muddied colors from which something like a human face tried to emerge. The kibitzers moved closer when Norman stepped back from his canvas to look at Jim McGrade's.

"What on earth is that?" He pointed with the handle of a brush at a place on Jim's canvas.

"Her hair."

"I mean what color."

"I'm still trying to get it right."

Norman stared at Jim, then took his canvas from the easel and leaned it against the wall. He handed Jim a pad and a soft lead pencil. "Draw," he advised.

This might have been more embarrassing for Jim if the onlookers had not moved closer to Norman's canvas. From her vantage point just inside the door of the gym, Madeline could see that Norman was producing a flattering version of Gloria. Thus far. He returned to his canvas, moving the spectators back, and looked with narrowed eyes at what he had done.

"Can I see?" Gloria asked.

"No."

Someone told Gloria she would love her portrait, and Norman glanced at the speaker. Madeline saw in his eyes the promise that the real Gloria would eventually appear on his canvas. These preliminary stages gave him the opportunity to study his model, to surprise the hidden aspects of her personality until finally he would capture it all in a slight downturn of the mouth, a partly lidded eye, or the beginning of a frown on the forehead. For the moment, however, Gloria looked like a debutante, years younger than her age. She did get a glance at it before Norman covered his canvas and carried it off to Edna's office, where it would remain until the following day. That day Madeline waited until he came to the office.

He recognized her immediately, and for a moment it seemed that a quarter of a century had not gone by since they had last confronted one another.

"Madeline."

"Hello, Norm."

Neither of them knew what to say next. So much time had passed since the night she left his apartment for the last time, years in which they had ceased to be part of one another's lives. Sometimes Madeline thought how easily she might not have discovered what he was until it was too late. Their friendship had given her the right to just sail into his apartment. The woman with him in his bedroom would later become his first wife, as if he had been trying to justify his betrayal of Madeline. Their eyes met now as they had all those years ago when they both realized that he had destroyed the love that had grown between them for more than a year.

"Norm?" Edna repeated, taking the canvas and looked quizzically at Madeline. "Do you two know one another?"

"We're old friends," Norman said, looking at Madeline.

"Oh, you're not so old," Edna said, and that enabled Madeline to exit on a laugh. Seeing Norm without being seen by him was one thing; it was very different to be looking him once more in the eyes.

4

"Matthew Walsh." Marie formed the name soundlessly, then had to say it aloud to get the pastor's attention.

"Gloria's husband?"

"He's in the parlor."

"Tell him to come in here."

"He says he wants to speak to you in the parlor."

Well, parlors are for parleys. Father Dowling still had no intimation of trouble when he went down the hall to the front of the house. Matt Walsh was obviously waiting for him, body tense, legs apart, arms held away from his body, hands formed into fists.

"My wife says she's getting her portrait painted over at the school." Walsh spoke as if his jaw was wired.

"I thought she might want to surprise you."

"Surprise me! She can't talk of anything else. Giggling like a schoolgirl. How long's this going to take?"

"It's not as if she's posing in the nude." Marie had followed the pastor soundlessly down the hall and spoke from the door of the parlor. Matt's mouth fell open as if the outrage Marie assured him had not happened had. Marie's intervention in pastoral matters often had equivocal effects.

"He wants Marie to model for him next," Father Dowling said, giving the housekeeper a look.

"Nude?"

The sound of Marie stomping back to her kitchen provided momentary distraction.

"Light your pipe," Father Dowling urged. Matt had been nervously shifting a pipe from mouth to hand.

"I quit smoking."

"Why the pipe then?"

"To prove I've quit."

"That could be dangerous."

"As dangerous as setting Norman Shield loose among those birdbrained women?"

Matt Walsh, it turned out, had done some elementary research on Norman Shield at the *Tribune,* where he worked.

"We kept most of the lurid stuff out of his obituary."

"Obituary!"

"We write them in advance, at leisure, so we'll have them when they're needed."

Father Dowling thought that it might unnerve Norman Shield to learn that his final send-off had already been written.

"I want to see that picture."

"I doubt that it's finished yet."

"I don't want it to be finished. I want it stopped."

Gloria had come to the parish center with an older neighbor and gradually had become a regular although she was much younger than the others, and her husband was obviously far from retiring. Nonetheless, they were beyond the age when one would have thought that jealousy would plague their marriage. Matt was clearly jealous, and ashamed to be, yet unable not to fear his wife's reaction to the unwonted attention of an artist whose record with women was anything but encouraging.

"Go over to the school and watch."

"Gloria's not there. She's at home."

He said no more. Apparently he had forbidden her to come to the parish center.

"Is Shield over there?"

"Would you like to go see?"

"No! I'm surprised you let a man like that hang around here."

"We're all sinners, Matt."

"No irate woman ever took a shot at me."

Watching Matt Walsh shuffle out to his car, round shouldered, a natural tonsure on the crown of his head, a forlorn Othello on a suburban scale, the priest's heart went out to him.

"What was that all about?" Marie asked.

"He objects to Norman Shield being set loose in the henhouse."

"What is that supposed to mean?"

"He wouldn't elaborate."

"Good Lord. He doesn't think that Gloria . . ." Marie ran out of breath before she could express the inexpressible.

Matt Walsh decided to speak his mind to Norman Shield on the phone, and the painter called to tell Father Dowling he wouldn't be coming the following day.

"Because of Walsh?"

"After what I went through with Karen Jaeger I'm a little jumpy."

The charges brought against Karen had been dropped when Shield said her story that the gun went off accidentally was plausible.

"It was about as accidental as the bombing of Hiroshima, but I wanted it over with."

"What happened to her?"

"What usually happens to little rich girls who don't get their way? She went on a world cruise."

"How long does that take?"

"Oh, she's home by now but I haven't heard from her. Maybe a shipboard romance turned her mind away from revenge." Shield paused. "How absurd that would have been, to die because of the pique of pampered brat."

"Lives end in odd ways."

"Well, Father, mine is not going to end as farce if I can prevent it."

5

"The painting is gone!" Edna said to Madeline when she came into the office.

"Are you sure?"

As if wanting to doubt herself, Edna entered into a joint search of the closet where she had put the unfinished portrait of Gloria Walsh.

"Has Norman asked for it?"

"Nooo. Madeline, do you think he took it away?"

"I don't see why he would have."

"Couldn't he continue working on it in his studio?"

"He doesn't work that way. He wants the one he is painting sitting before him whenever he is working on a portrait."

"Someone had to take it."

"Tell Norman that."

"He isn't coming in today."

"Oh?"

"Father Dowling called to tell me. That's when I checked on the painting and found it was gone."

Edna poured a cup of coffee, trying to calm down. The missing portrait obviously disturbed the orderliness her life exemplified.

"Would you tell him, Madeline?"

"Father Dowling?"

"Norman Shield."

"Me?"

"But you know him, don't you?"

"I did."

"Tell me about it."

"There's nothing to tell."

"The way you two looked at one another? Come on."

"It was a thousand years ago."

"That's a good beginning."

Madeline did go on and it was as if she were remembering for the first time the year during which her life had seemed to take on its fated direction only to be abruptly altered the afternoon she walked unannounced into her fiancé's apartment and found him with another woman. An effect of her love for Norman had been a lessening of interest in her own art. She had told herself that Norman had far more talent, that she would support and encourage him in his career. She longed to sacrifice herself for him. After everything blew up in her face, she found that she could not recapture the ambition that had brought her to art school. Even so, the art she knew had gotten her a job as art instructor on the high school level. Chuck Young had been a history teacher and coach, as different from Norman Shield as a man could be. He was athletic, in top condition, carefully tending his health as if he were preparing for some great athletic feat. And he had died on the golf course of a massive coronary at the age of forty-two. There had been no children; they were involved in a prolonged effort to adopt when Chuck died. Madeline withdrew the application. She found herself well provided for, did only part-time teaching for a year, then stopped altogether. She was as young as Gloria Walsh when she began to frequent the St. Hilary parish center. Sometimes she wondered if she couldn't wait to be old.

"How you must have hated him," Edna said.

"Norman? No. He just ceased to exist for me."

"Didn't he try to explain, ask your forgiveness, anything?"

"I wouldn't let him."

"Men are men, Madeline."

"Would you tolerate that in your husband?"

Too late she remembered that Earl Hospers was a prisoner at

Joliet. Madeline had never gotten a clear account of why he was there, but it was obvious that Edna was remaining true to him for however long it took. That's what love ought to be. That's what Madeline had thought she had.

"From him? Did he have that kind of love from you?"

Madeline looked at Edna and realized she could not have sacrificed her youth for a husband locked up for God knows how long. Still, Edna's question was unsettling. What if she had tried to forgive Norman all those years ago?

"I guess not."

"Maybe you'll get a second chance."

"Do you know how many wives he's had?"

"I'll bet you do."

This was not the conversation Madeline would have expected to have when she sat down to have a consoling cup of coffee with Edna over a missing painting by Norman Shield. Over the years, she had thought of the way she had turned away from Norman after the great discovery as a principled act, the only thing a decent woman could do. Suddenly it seemed something else, almost selfish.

They were sitting in silence when Father Dowling came in with the dreadful news. Norman Shield had been found dead in his studio.

6

Norman Shield lay on his back, a fallen warrior, his face smeared with paint by someone with a weak sense of color harmonies. The bullet had entered his forehead, a nice round aperture, though its exit at the back was a messy affair. Phil Keegan stood in the center of the lofted studio while the crime crew went through its ritual. The artist would never have dreamed that these technicians and their procedures had awaited him all along.

"They found the bullet," Cy Horvath said.

"Any sign of the weapon?"

Cy shook his head. "A twenty-two."

"Rifle?"

"I'd say handgun."

Neither said what they both knew. Their last professional encounter with Norman Shield had been when he suffered a flesh wound from the handgun of a distraught woman. A .22.

"What was her name, Cy?"

"Karen Jaeger. I'll pick her up."

That proved impossible. Karen Jaeger had flown out of O'Hare that morning, but not before she could have shot Norman Shield. Her flight had arrived in St. Petersburg half an hour ago.

"She has a condominium down there."

"Extradition will take time."

"Should I get started on it?"

Phil nodded. "I'd like you to go down there and talk to her right away."

It would have been impossible to tell from Cy's expression whether or not he found the prospect of a quick trip to Florida pleasant.

Meanwhile, Phil drove out to St. Hilary's to talk to Roger Dowling about his artist-in-residence. The priest was visibly shaken by the news.

"Did you call a priest?"

"It was too late, Roger."

"Never assume that, Phil. Experts continue to wrangle as to when death actually occurs."

"We had a choice of former wives to notify. I've never been sure whether it is the first or the most recent wife who gets priority."

"He had become a much more serious man of late."

"After his girlfriend shot him?"

"That did concentrate his mind."

"Wasn't it pretty unusual, him giving beginning lessons to the old people?"

"It was more a demonstration of his skills."

Roger suggested that he talk with Edna Hospers, and when she told him of the missing portrait Phil understood why. He looked into the closet where the painting should have been.

"Who would have stolen it?"

"It wasn't even finished."

"I guess it never will be now."

But Phil was thinking of the paint smeared over the dead face of Norman Shield. "What was it a painting of?"

"Gloria Walsh."

"Maybe she didn't like it."

"Oh, she loved it. Everyone did."

"She here today?"

"She hasn't been here for several days."

When he went back to the rectory, Roger Dowling told him about Matt Walsh's visit. Jealousy? Apparently.

"How old is she?"

"Is there an age limit on jealousy?"

The Walshes lived in a large brick house with a tiled roof and high windows flanked by green shutters. The driveway curled past the front entrance and then continued around behind the house. Phil parked on the street and sat for a moment looking at the house. It seemed solid and peaceful, a place where a professor might live. Was it possible that anyone living there had anything to do with the death of Norman Shield?

A timid Gloria Walsh answered the door.

"I know," she said when he told her who he was. "He didn't take it. I know he didn't."

It made it easy that she assumed he was here about her missing portrait.

"He tell you he didn't?"

"No! I didn't *ask* him, but I've looked everywhere."

She meant in the house. But why would he bring it home? From Roger Dowling's description of him, Phil thought the man was more likely to pitch it into a dumpster.

Walsh's office was in a corner of a vast floor in which the bustle and hum of people working against deadlines in cramped conditions seemed guaranteed to produce chaos. The office was partitioned off and was a little island of orderly quiet.

"Norman Shield is dead."

"We already sent a reporter over there."

"Good."

Walsh waited and so did Phil, hoping silence would make the man uneasy, but Walsh was more than calm.

"Did you know him?"

"I know who he was."

"I just talked to your wife."

"What about!" The calmness was gone.

"In a murder case, we like to talk to as many people as we can, people who knew the victim and might have some knowledge of why anyone would want to kill him."

"Captain, leave my wife alone! I mean that. I won't have you harassing her over this. She knew that man no better than I did. No better than dozens of other people at the St. Hilary Parish Center."

"No better than you did?"

"What are you getting at?"

"Your wife's portrait is missing."

"I don't know what you're talking about."

Walsh had been good at calmness and then at indignation, but lying was not in his repertoire.

"Where is it?"

The try at indignation was unsuccessful. He looked abjectly at Keegan.

"What did you do with it?"

"I didn't steal it." Walsh sat back and took a deep breath. "It's still in the school."

"Where?"

"I put it in the cloak room of one of the first-floor classrooms."

"Can I use your phone?"

Edna Hospers sent Madeline Young to the classroom and Phil kept the line open. It gave him a chance to study Matthew Walsh. Would a man who forbade his wife to go the parish center and who relocated her portrait where no one might find it be capable of more? Keegan had been at it too long to think there is a single type of killer. Anyone could become a killer given sufficient motive and opportunity. How jealous had Matt Walsh been?

"It's there," Edna said.

"Thanks."

"I'm putting it back in my closet where it belongs."

"Good."

He hung up and said to Walsh, "It's safe. Now that the artist is dead you may want to keep it."

"You want to know what you can do with that painting, Captain?"

"When I do I won't ask you."

Cy called from St Petersburg to say that Karen Jaeger refused to talk to him without her lawyer present. Her lawyer, she insisted, was in Chicago. Phil obtained a warrant and found a .22 pistol in Karen's North Shore apartment. A quick check indicated that it was the weapon that had been used to kill

Norman Shield. Phil arranged for the St. Petersburg police to arrest her.

"Tell her we have the murder weapon."

"She won't talk to me."

"You talk to her when they bring her in."

7

Wives and girlfriends and a host of other claimants descended on the mortuary where Shield had been readied for burial. When Father Dowling began the rosary, they fidgeted uneasily but once he was launched into the first decade several voices joined in, one of them familiar. It was Amos Cadbury, and he came up to Father Dowling when the prayer was finished.

"It is consoling that you knew him, Father Dowling."

"I gather you did too."

Amos leaned toward the priest and whispered, "I am his lawyer." His eyes moved toward the people milling around in the viewing room. "The eagles gather."

"Do they have a claim?"

"The law often yields where common sense would not."

"Is there much?"

Amos's eyes lifted as if in prayer, but it was Mammon rather than God that induced his awe.

"He was a genius at portraits, Father Dowling, So of course he loathed doing them. He produced huge canvases with one or two geometrical objects floating in empty space. A child could have done them. The galleries thought the same. But his portraits made him wealthy because he kept raising his fee to discourage clients."

"He was doing a portrait of a woman at the parish center gratis."

"As a penance?" An alteration in the line of Amos Cadbury's mouth indicated that he had told a joke.

"Karen Jaeger has been arrested."

Amos shut his eyes for a moment. "I cannot discuss it, Father Dowling."

"Another client?"

Amos bowed but said nothing. The venerable lawyer had a keen sense of a client's right to expect total discretion of his legal representative. Nonetheless his reaction was eloquent. No doubt he knew that his client had been arrested because the murder weapon had been registered to her and was found in her apartment. Of course anyone who knew of her earlier unsuccessful attack on Norman Shield might assume that the gun was still in her possession. Her innocence might be very difficult to defend, given the unscheduled flight to Florida and invocation of her rights when Cy wanted to talk with her. She had to talk to him later, when a Florida lawyer was there to safeguard her rights. But he advised her to refuse to answer the questions of the police. Phil could surely be forgiven for seeing in this proof of guilt. The prosecutor was convinced that there was sufficient cause and sought and got an indictment from the grand jury. The lurid episode of Shield's previous gunshot wound, courtesy of Karen, was subjected to minute reexamination in the press. The inference was clear. The first time she had failed in her intent; this time she made sure the shot was fatal.

Amos Cadbury remained a veritable sphinx throughout this negative publicity for his client, not even satisfying the press with a "no comment." He moved through the crowd of importunate reporters as if they were not there.

"Bishop Berkeley," Roger Dowling said.

"Who's he?" Phil Keegan asked.

"He was a philosopher known for the claim that *esse est percipi.*"

"Yeah?"

"A thing does not exist unless it is noticed."

"How did he get to be a bishop?"

"He was an Anglican."

"Oh well."

When attention turned to the unfinished portrait of Gloria Walsh, Matthew went ballistic. He came to the rectory and demanded to know who had told the press of the portrait? Marie left him standing in the front parlor and detoured by the kitchen, where she had a leisurely cup of tea before telling Father Dowling he had a visitor. But the parlor was empty when the pastor went to talk to Matthew Walsh.

"He must have left," Marie said.

At the window, Father Dowling looked at the walkway which led to the school. Had Matt gone over there to castigate Edna? He opened the door and turned to Marie.

"I'll be right back."

"Where are you going?"

"You might check and make sure that Matt isn't lurking about the house."

He closed the door on the housekeeper's alarmed expression.

Matt Walsh had not been to Edna's office, Madeline Young assured him. Edna herself was not behind her desk.

"Is the portrait still in that closet?"

"The police took it. They had a subpoena."

"How did they hear of it?"

"It's in all the papers."

"How did the papers hear of it?"

"It wasn't exactly a secret, Father."

In the *Tribune*, a series began on the portraits Norman Shield had painted over the years. The theme of the series was that there were platoons of aggrieved females or their husbands who would have had ample motive to shoot Norman Shield in the forehead.

"She's innocent, Father," Amos Cadbury said, and the remark did not seem to be that of a lawyer defending his client.

"It's her gun," Phil Keegan growled. "She already took one shot at him."

Father Dowling split the difference between his two friends. Whoever killed Norman Shields had used Karen Jaeger's .22 pistol. She said she had not even thought of it since going off on her world cruise. Had she seen the artist since her return? Amos advised his client to say no more.

As the trial approached, the *Tribune* continued its series on the connection between those who had sat for their portrait by Norman Shield and the lurid life of the artist. So it was that, out of the distant past, his first great love, for Madeline Hart, had been resurrected. Edna's account of the reunion of the two artists in her office was touched with romance, and tragedy.

"After all those years! And it was to be their last meeting."

Madeline herself avoided reporters and questions as to what had gone wrong between her and Norman Shields so many years ago, but the artist's first wife was not so reticent. Suddenly Madeline Hart Young seemed to have motive and opportunity. Edna could not forgive herself for being such a chatterbox.

"Father, I even blamed her for leaving him, just because . . ."

But the first Mrs. Shield had been graphic as to what the cause of the breakup between the artist and Madeline had been.

"It's a long time to carry a grudge," Marie Murkin said, but her tone suggested that it was possible.

"Maybe you could testify for Amos Cadbury, Marie," the pastor suggested.

"Testify! I don't know anything."

"Would you say that under oath?"

Marie glared at the pastor but spoke neither oath nor under oath.

Father Dowling talked with Madeline. "If I was going to kill him, Father, it would have been when he betrayed me."

The priest believed that she was innocent. And he trusted Amos Cadbury's judgment about Karen Jaeger. Madeline wondered about Matthew Walsh's tireless pursuit of the matter.

"Is Gloria's portrait still here?" he asked Edna.

Edna opened the closet to reveal a canvas.

"What's on it?"

Edna turned it around. The smeared paint was reminiscent of Norman Shield's face when he was found dead in his studio.

"Who did that?"

"Jim McGrade."

Edna smiled. "When Norman saw it, he just turned it to the wall, and suggested that Jim take up drawing."

"Did he?"

Jim McGrade had been an infrequent presence at the school since Norman Shield's negative judgment on his artistic talent. When he left the parish center Father Dowling started back to the rectory, but after a moment stopped. When he began to walk again, it was to the garage. He backed his car out and drove to Jim McGrade's house.

No one answered the bell. Father Dowling went around the house and knocked on the back door. Still no answer. He peered through the window and saw a man lying on the kitchen floor. He was about to break the window of the door when he tried the knob and found the door was unlocked. Inside the kitchen, he was assailed by the smell of alcohol.

It was half an hour before he restored Jim McGrade to something like consciousness.

"Tell me about it, Jim."

"About what?"

"Norman Shield."

McGrade stared at the priest. After a moment, tears welled

up in his bloodshot eyes. He began to sob then, covering his face with his hands. Father Dowling got Phil Keegan on the phone and asked him to come.

"What for?"

"To hear a confession."

"I thought that was your job."

"Oh, I've already done mine, Phil."

"I can't give absolution."

"He's already had that."

After mercy came justice. The watercolors and oils found in McGrade's house showed no more talent than the canvas Shield had turned to the wall. But in doing that, the artist had touched a raw nerve. Jim McGrade had nursed the belief that he was an artist and had been awaiting retirement to give his talents free rein. Norman Shield's dismissive gesture, all but unnoticed by others, had been a public humiliation. He had used his police identification to gain access to Karen's apartment and took her .22, returning it when it had served its purpose.

The fact that Norman Shield had wanted to paint her portrait became part of Marie Murkin's standard repertoire in the months that followed. Father Dowling offered to drive the housekeeper to Joliet where she could sit for Jim McGrade.

"Jim McGrade! I know the seat I'd like sit him in, Father Dowling."

In the end, Madeline painted Marie's portrait. The pastor hung it in the front parlor. It was missing the following day, stashed in a closet.

"It's awful!"

"It looks just like you, Marie."

A little cry escaped her, she gave him an unforgiving look, and then retreated to the kitchen.

A FALLING STAR

1

When Marie Murkin opened the front door of the St. Hilary rectory there was no one there. That was funny. Not that she was laughing. She had heard the bell and come as quickly as she could. She had been stacking dishes in the washer and wanted to start the machine before hurrying down the hall, and now here she was standing in the open doorway looking at nothing.

"Who was it?" Father Dowling called when she passed his study.

"Did you hear that bell?"

She looked in, making a face and waving her hand in front of her eyes, but the truth was she liked the smell of pipe smoke. It was a good thing. The only smoke-free environment the pastor of St. Hilary's wanted was in the next world. Answering his question with a question was an effort to shift responsibility from her shoulders to his. Not that she wanted Father Dowling answering the door. That was her job and she was very jealous of her functions in the house.

"Was it Willie?" He looked at her over the bowl of his pipe.

"It was nobody."

Father Dowling's question was reasonable. The little maintenance man had been making a real pest of himself. Marie had threatened to send Willie packing back to the parish center where he allegedly worked if he kept stopping by the house

31

wasting the pastor's time. Father Dowling said that he would be the judge of when his time was being wasted. Honestly, the man was impossible. Of course Marie understood that a priest ought to be patient and suffer fools gladly, even deadbeats like Willie and all the rest, but there was no need to go overboard. If anyone was to go overboard, she would volunteer Willie. She might even give him a hand over the railing.

The front doorbell rang again.

Marie turned on her heel, glad to get away from the pastor when she was so vulnerable to his mild scolding. She looked out the window before opening the door again, and there unmistakably stood Willie. She pulled the door open and the little man jumped.

"You stay right there this time," she warned.

He tucked in his chin and made his eyes bulge. "What are you talking about?"

"Did you just ring this doorbell?"

"You came to the door, didn't you?"

"I mean before."

"Before what?"

If she ever got to heaven it would be because of moments like this. Behind her the pastor called out, asking who was there.

"Just me, Father," Willie piped. "If you're busy just say so."

Father Dowling came down the hall to the front door. "I don't want to interrupt," he said.

"Interrupt!" Marie cried.

But he ignored her. "Are you here to see *me*, Willie?"

Willie glanced at Marie, half smiled, stopped, didn't know what to do next. Marie could have brained the pastor, but she knew what canon law said about hitting priests or religious. Taking a swipe at Willie had its attractions. The idea! Suggesting that such a man should come calling on her.

"I've been wondering about falling stars, Father Dowling.

The theology of them."

Positioned between the pastor and Willie like the moon between earth and sun, Marie made an inarticulate noise that the parish center maintenance man found easy to interpret.

"Oh, I don't blame you, Marie. You're perfectly right. What business has an old reprobate like myself holding a job in St. Hilary's, let alone pestering the pastor."

"We only hire reprobates," Father Dowling assured him. "It's kind of a 'negative action' policy. I'm not sure there is a theology of falling stars, though. An astronomy, of course, but not a theology."

"I was thinking of Galileo, I guess."

"Were you now? Then you'd better come in and sit down. A rotating earth affects one's balance, you know."

Willie looked at Marie, unsure whether she would move aside for him. Marie looked at Father Dowling as mothers look at wayward sons, as Aunt Polly looked at Tom Sawyer, and as housekeepers look at pastors.

"We can talk in my study."

Father Dowling turned and went back down the hall. Behind him there was a scuffling, an impatient sound from Marie, and then Willie's muted whistling as he followed the pastor into the study.

"Let me just drink it in, Father."

Willie had stopped just inside the door and spread his hands as if in prayer; his eyes were closed and he inhaled deeply.

"Why did I ever quit smoking, Father?" He sank into a chair and inhaled deeply again.

"You used to smoke?"

"Like a chimney! Three packs a day. Now I chew that many packs of gum to keep away from tobacco."

"Well, I won't tempt you." He lifted his voice. "We won't be needing anything, Marie. Unless Willie wants . . ."

The sound of the kitchen door closing cut him off. Marie liked to keep au courant on parish affairs and was not above keeping an ear open when someone came to see the pastor.

"I'll get right to the point, Father."

"Good."

"You wouldn't expect someone like me to be suffering temptations to the faith of this sort, would you?"

"What sort?"

"The falling star sort."

"I should think falling stars would awake your wonder rather than threaten your faith."

"It's the uselessness of them! But that's only part of it. I've been reading up on the subject."

"Ah."

"There is an encyclopedia in Mrs. Hosper's office."

"And what does it say about falling stars?"

"Not much. Which is why I went to the library and consulted with Stokes. He's an atheist, Father, brazen as they come. An intemperate atheist with whom I had many conversations in the Place and a number of beers since, on my day off, probing his mind, you understand, looking for a point of entry where I might touch his heart with the Good News. Instead, I have come away with terrible doubts. They keep me awake nights." Willie hunched forward. "They're not falling when they're falling. They fell a zillion years ago before the earth was even formed, before there was anyone to see them, only they wouldn't have been visible then, not from here, and now that they are, they aren't, if you see what I mean."

"I do."

"Well then," Willie threw himself back in his chair. "How can I trust my eyes? How can I see something that isn't there and yet that something is, as you say, a matter of science if not theology, and science is supposed to be about the way things are, and . . ." Willie clapped his forehead. "It's driving me crazy."

"How does Stokes take it?"

"He thinks it's funny."

"That you should be having doubts about science?"

"About science?"

"That it develops theories about nonexistent things like falling stars."

"But Stokes . . ."

"What does Stokes say?"

"Well, we were talking about the Gospels and miracles and what people say."

"Aha. And he says they saw the miracles the way you see falling stars?"

"Something like."

"You must bring him around."

"Would you talk with him, Father?"

"Will he talk with me?"

"He is eager to."

"Then bring him around."

"I have, I have. He is over in the school, in my room."

Father Dowling rose. "Let's go see him."

They went down the hallway and as he was closing the front door, Father Dowling looked back. The kitchen door was pulled closed as he watched. Outside, he asked Willie if he trusted his ears.

"It runs in the family, Father. I'm afraid they'll only get worse."

"Is something wrong with your ears?"

"I have no trouble hearing you. Or Marie Murkin or Edna Hospers."

"And have you ever had the experience Huckleberry Finn had when from shore he watched a raft far out on the Mississippi? On it, a man was chopping wood, and Huck would see the hatchet descend and hit the wood and the pieces fly, and it seemed a whole minute went by before he heard the sound."

"Oh sure. But with me it was a man hammering nails . . ." Willie stopped and stared at the priest. "Like falling stars."

"In a way."

"Oh why didn't I think of that!"

At this time of day the school building which all day long buzzed with the sounds of senior citizens was silent. They went down the wide stairway and along a corridor to the apartment Willie occupied as maintenance man. Willie gave a little tap before opening the door and stepping in. Immediately he danced back into the hall. Father Dowling looked past Willie into the room. The body lay just inside the door, face down, motionless.

2

In a moment, Father Dowling was kneeling beside the body and lifting his hand in absolution.

"He didn't believe in God, Father."

"He does now."

The lack of expression that Willie had brought out of his years of confinement had given way to one of tragic sadness. His old friend and fellow alumnus of Joliet had met his end in Willie's room, there as a guest and gadfly. Stokes had tipped over his glass of beer as he fell. On the floor next to the low-slung easy chair where Willie must have sat stood a can of Coke.

"Dial nine one one."

"The police!"

Even in these circumstances it went against Willie's grain to enlist the help of the police. "Hand me the phone."

Willie punched out the three numbers before handing the phone to Father Dowling, who had gotten to his feet. The priest looked down at the body as he told the 911 operator that a man had been stricken at St. Hilary's. "I am almost certain he is dead."

There was a stain where blood had oozed from the body but now had apparently stopped. Willie had crossed the room to close the closet door. Father Dowling asked the operator to put him through to Captain Keegan and Willie swung around, leaning against the now-closed closet door.

"Keegan!" Willie whispered as Caesar had whispered to Brutus.

Phil Keeghan had been the arresting officer in the offense that had sent Willie to Joliet the last time. The priest pointed at the blood. Willie took a step toward the fallen Stokes, bent to see more clearly, then stood erect, his eyes pressed shut.

3

Chet Stokes had been librarian at Joliet, carrying on the profession he had practiced in Aurora, where he had been convicted of sweet-talking a widowed patron out of a good portion of her savings on the promise of wedding bells. But she had spotted him with his wife, made inquiries, and preferred charges. Mrs. Stokes had apparently made off with the money, and the susceptible widow changed her mind during the trial about Stokes's intentions, but by then it was in the hands of the prosecutor and Stokes was convicted. Soon he was behind the checkout counter of the prison library of which Willie was an avid patron. Almost from the beginning they had been engaged in an endless but amicable argument. Stokes, once a staunch Presbyterian, blamed his loss of faith on his misfortunes. Like all the other prisoners at Joliet he was of course innocent.

"Are you becoming cynical, George?" Father Dowling asked the Rev. George Irwin, the prison chaplain.

"Just representing the views of my flock." His tone altered. "Chet Stokes was a good fellow. I am really sorry to hear this."

"Any idea who might have done it?"

"Not you too, Roger."

Cy Horvath, a lieutenant under Keegan, had already been to Joliet to inquire into any difficulties the librarian might have had there that might explain his death. George Irwin assured Father Dowling that Stokes had been universally liked. He had introduced videos to the prison library and lobbied for VCRs in the cells and had earned the gratitude of his fellow inmates.

"Cy got the same story," Phil Keegan said, settling down at the table in the rectory dining room. It was a week since the death of Chet Stokes in Willie's apartment. Willie had been taken downtown for questioning the day before. Five minutes into it he had called the rectory.

"I need a lawyer."

"Surely they don't think you harmed your friend Stokes."

"Father, they're cops."

Roger Dowling called Tuttle and asked him to represent Willie. The case did not seem to require a highly skilled lawyer.

"For you, Father, I work pro bono."

"You'll be working for Willie. But send me the bill. He's an employee here."

"Is this a fringe benefit?"

Phil laughed when Father Dowling repeated Tuttle's question. "Given the number of crooks and thieves you've hired, I wouldn't be surprised." He turned and called toward the kitchen. "Housekeepers excepted of course."

"What is the case against Willie?"

"Everywhere we turn it gets worse. I don't know how many people say they heard the two of them quarreling whenever he and Stokes got together."

"It was an ongoing debate. And friendly."

Marie slipped into the room, pulled out a chair, and joined them. Eavesdropping from the kitchen was an imperfect science, and the housekeeper felt guilty about Willie.

"I was so uncharitable to him, Father."

"I didn't treat him very well myself."

"You were the soul of patience."

"Was I? Would you want to be the target of someone's patience?"

Reluctantly, senior parishioner after senior parishioner acknowledged that they had heard the two men quarreling nonstop whenever Stokes visited, including the day of the murder. When Father Dowling told Phil Keegan he thought Willie had been trying to convert Stokes, Marie went back to the kitchen. There were limits to her remorse, and the notion of Willie as missionary marked its boundary line.

"It seems as if the only one at the prison anyone could think of who didn't like Stokes was Willie."

"But they were friends. They got together several times a week." *Like us,* he wanted to add, but there was no need to overdo. He and Phil didn't argue, but deferred to one another. Phil was the police detective and Roger Dowling was the priest and if they sometimes trespassed on the other's territory, it had never led to a falling out. Roger could see that Phil considered his loyalty to Willie only a priest's mushy-headed unwillingness to admit that some apples are bad.

"People get killed by friends and relatives, Roger."

"You might just as well accuse Marie."

The startled face of the housekeeper looked around the half-opened kitchen door. The pastor did not look at her.

"She can't stand Willie and she can't stand his friends. It was bad enough having one ex-con around the parish but to have him filling his apartment with others, well . . ."

"Father Dowling!" Marie half stumbled into the dining room, her expression that of one betrayed.

"Of course Marie wouldn't harm a fly. No more than Willie

would." He smiled at Marie. "I was looking for a preposterous analogy."

"And you thought of Marie," Phil said.

Marie's hands twisted in her apron as she looked with exasperation at the two smiling men. Harsh words seemed to tremble on her lips, but she turned on her Cuban heel and banged through into the kitchen from which unnecessary noises continued to come for minutes. The two men adjourned to the pastor's study.

"You don't really think Willie did it, do you, Phil?"

All signs of merriment were gone from Phil Keegan. "It's not just stories of arguing, Roger. I got the lab reports just before coming here for the noon Mass."

Stokes had been killed by a single .22 bullet that had struck him in the middle of the chest, making it likely that he was dead before his body hit the floor. The target pistol from which the shot had been fired had been found in Willie's closet, on the floor, slid behind a rack on which he kept his shoes. There were no fingerprints on the gun. Father Dowling had the unwelcome memory of Willie closing the closet door when he himself turned and noticed the blood that had come from Stokes's body and stained the carpet in Willie's room. That had been the first indication that the librarian's death was due to violence.

"A twenty-two pistol?"

"Did you know about it?"

"Phil, I bought it for him. It's registered in my name."

"I know."

"Then you should be arresting me."

"For hiding the gun in Willie's closet? Why did he need a gun?"

The question pointed to possibilities the pastor of St. Hilary's wished he had thought of earlier.

"He wanted protection. He was afraid."

"Of what?"

"I didn't press him on it, Phil. I thought he was being theatrical at first, but it became evident to me that his fear was real enough. I bought the gun so he would stop talking about it. I didn't want Marie and Edna getting nervous. Neither one of them is particularly happy having someone with Willie's background here.

"Edna?"

Edna's husband was serving a sentence at Joliet, which is why she had been hired to manage the parish center, an idea that had come to Father Dowling as much to help her out as to provide a haven for bored senior parishioners. Although her husband had committed a more serious crime than Willie ever had, she did not want to think of Earl as a criminal. His had been a single terrible deed prompted by weakness and confusion, whereas Willie, and Stokes too, had been deliberate and dispassionate scofflaws.

"I wonder who he was afraid of?"

"It's worth looking into, isn't it?"

"Why?"

"Because Willie didn't kill Stokes. He was over at the rectory pestering Marie and me while the murder was committed."

"Possibly. But not for certain."

But Father Dowling thought he knew enough about human nature to have detected if Willie had come to the parish house directly from killing his old friend, as he would have had to do on the basis of the coroner's report. Blood had just stopped flowing when he and Willie had arrived at the school to engage Stokes in argument about the origin of the universe.

"Isn't it kind of odd that he would have left him there and come for you?"

It was. And odder still that Willie had seemed in no hurry and had not even mentioned Stokes for some time, bringing the man up as if as a sudden inspiration. Maybe Willie's conduct *was* compatible with that of a man who had just killed.

4

Tuttle came by the rectory to talk about his client.

"My client, your employee."

"Making you his employee."

"In a manner of speaking, yes indeed. I am trying to get to the bottom of this. Of course the killing was vengeance, the settling of an old score. We will probably find that Stokes had a falling out with members of his gang."

"He was a librarian, Tuttle."

"A brilliant cover, Father Dowling, Brilliant. He was obviously an ingenious man. He even had a degree in library science."

Tuttle made this seem an almost sinister accomplishment, the long years of study undertaken simply as a disguise for Stokes's planned unlawful activities.

"I think his only offense was bilking a widow out of her savings."

"Which were never recovered."

"That's right."

But Tuttle did not go on to speak of the wife who had debouched with the ill-gotten gains. No need to tell Tuttle of her; the little lawyer who never removed his Irish tweed cap except in recognition of a point made by himself or the priest, employing it as a biretta of sorts, had an elephant-in-a-china-shop modus operandi and remembering the wife seemed too important a fact to entrust to Tuttle. Or to Phil Keegan, at least for the moment. Roger Dowling drove down to Joliet and made a mandatory tour with Irwin before they settled down with mugs of coffee in the refectory.

"Did Stokes have visitors?"

Irwin smiled. "During his last year, yes."

"How long was he here?"

"Seven, I believe. He was a model prisoner and he was writ-ten up in the Naperville paper and of course received quite a number of letters. Father Dowling, there are a lot of lonely women in the world. Prisoners are constantly importuned by them. That write-up was the beginning of Stokes's great ro-mance."

"Who was the woman?"

"Priscilla." Irwin pronounced the name with obvious pleasure. "The name did not fit her at all. She was a stocky woman with a raspy voice who had a weakness for exuberant wigs."

"Priscilla what?"

Irwin thought for a time, then shook his head. "I was always stopped by her first name. I don't seem to remember her last."

"Don't visitors register?"

"Of course. Would you like me to check?"

The visits of Priscilla Barrett had begun eleven months before Stokes's release, and by the time he left she was coming to see him once a week, circumventing the rule for visitors by volunteering to work in the library. She had filled out a special form as a volunteer.

"It's not the same address," the priest murmured, then wished he hadn't when it became clear that Irwin hadn't noticed.

"I suppose she moved."

"No doubt."

"She must have moved again."

"Why?"

"They married. I performed the ceremony myself, just a civil ceremony. Stokes hadn't much wanted a clergyman presiding but she insisted."

Father Dowling did not comment on this. Irwin was a

dedicated chaplain whose whole life was caught up with that of the inmates of the prison. He only saw them afterward if they came back to visit. It was really no surprise that he did not know that no Mrs. Stokes had put in an appearance when Stokes was killed.

On the drive back to Fox River, Father Dowling stopped in at the Naperville public library. A woman whose hair was cut so close to her head that the enormous earrings seemed necessary to establish her gender was glad to be of help.

"That's why we're here."

"This is more or less confidential."

She pulled her chair closer to her desk. "Of course."

"The woman I am trying to locate might have been a librarian."

"Where?"

"In Naperville."

"Then I will know her. I've worked here eighteen years."

"That's hard to believe."

She beamed. The badge she wore bore only the legend Researcher. "Librarians don't grow old. They just turn to dust."

"It must be a pleasant job."

"It is. Except for two things. The homeless who use the reading room as a shelter and kids."

"Kids."

"Saturdays." Her eyes rolled upward. "This is my last year working Saturdays. I feel like a soul about to be released from purgatory."

"You're Catholic?"

"Are only Catholics confined to purgatory? Actually, I'm nothing. But I took a course in Dante one summer school and never got over it."

"*Lasciate ogni speranza . . .*" he began.

She pushed back from her desk, mouth open. "You know Italian!"

"So does everyone in Italy."

"I bought tapes but I didn't stay with them. All I wanted to be able to do was speak it. Pronounce it. Read Dante's own language. I can always look at a translation to find out what it means. It must be the most musical language in the world."

"Priscilla," Father Dowling interrupted, getting back to the subject.

"Yes?"

"The woman I'm looking for."

The researcher nodded.

"Her name is Priscilla."

"But that's my name."

It was Father Dowling's turn to be surprised. "Did you know a man named Stokes?"

"Of course."

"You did?"

"A friend of mine married a man named Stokes." Priscilla leaned forward. "He was a convict. They became pen pals and then they met and bingo."

"They got married?"

Priscilla nodded, smiling faintly. It was a nice romantic story. "What was your friend's name?"

"Frankie. Frances. She hated it either way."

"Not as nice as Priscilla."

"But I hate Priscilla. I won't have it on my badge."

"I noticed that. Have you kept in touch with Franky?"

"She went out that door to meet him the day they were going to be married. She said she would never be back and she hasn't been."

"I wonder where she went."

"With Stokes of course."

"Of course."

5

Willie came into the visiting room with a kind of shuffle, but when he saw Father Dowling he brightened and hurried to greet him.

"I thought it was Tuttle wanting to see me."

"I hope they didn't say I was a lawyer."

"They didn't say anything. Since it wasn't the visiting area, I figured it had to be Tuttle."

Lawyers and priests could see prisoners in a somewhat less forbidding setting. Father Dowling gathered that Willie wasn't impressed with Tuttle.

"He reminds me of the lawyer I had the last time I was convicted."

"You didn't tell me Stokes was married."

"Was he?"

"Reverend Irwin said he performed the ceremony."

Willie lit up. "Irwin! Chet got married by a minister?" His smile slowly faded. "And now he's gone and I can't rub it in."

"You didn't know about it?"

"I don't believe it. Are you sure?"

He told Willie about his conversation with the prison chaplain and with Priscilla at Naperville. Willie said he knew Priscilla all right, but he shook his head when Father Dowling described the librarian he had talked to in Naperville.

"That's not her. She wasn't at all like that."

Willie's description matched Priscilla's description of Frankie. Father Dowling got Stokes's address from the obituary that had appeared and drove to an apartment house in Elgin. There was an old man clipping bushes who didn't straighten up when the priest addressed him. Father Dowling felt he should bow too, out of fairness, but it was arthritis not an exaggerated respect for the clergy that explained the man's posture.

"Parini, Father. Look at these bushes." He shook his head in disappointment. The bushes looked all right to Father Dowling.

"Did you know Chet Stokes?"

"Not likely. Moved in and a month later he's killed."

"He only lived here a month?"

"Maybe a month and a half."

"Do you know where he moved from?"

"He didn't tell me." But Parini kept his eye on Father Dowling. "I found out by accident."

Parini had hesitated about throwing out the junk mail that continued to arrive after Stokes was killed. But he had found in the apartment a letter with an address in Aurora, and he forwarded the mail there. Father Dowling jotted down the address.

"Was he a parishioner of yours, Father?"

"He died in my parish."

That more than anything seemed to justify his pursuit of the trail of the elusive Stokes. Even if none of this proved to be of help to poor Willie, he felt it was worth finding out about the librarian. One thing was clear. Stokes had been unlucky in his wives. The first had absconded with Stokes's stolen money and the second . . . what had happened to the second Mrs. Stokes, Frances? Tomorrow he would drive to Aurora and see if she was to be found at Stokes's penultimate address.

Meanwhile Tuttle was exploring the possibility that Stokes had been done away with by someone he had met in prison and, unlike everyone else, had come to hate the librarian. Phil Keegan was not happy with the case against Willie; it was all circumstantial, but the prosecutor was certain it was sufficient to send Willie back to prison for life.

6

"Are you Father Dowling?" a voice called when he pulled into his driveway at St. Hilary's. A woman leaned out of the window of a car parked at the curb. Father Dowling walked over to it.

"Yes," he said, looking down at the woman. "I am Father Dowling. And you are Mrs. Stokes, aren't you?"

"Priscilla said you'd been asking about me."

"Won't you come inside?"

"I was about to ask you the same thing." Her hand came into view then. She was holding a gun and it was aimed at Father Dowling. Almost immediately she drew it out of sight.

"Father Dowling," Marie Murkin called from the house. "Captain Keegan is on the line."

"Good. Would you tell him to come out? Tell him Mrs. Stokes is here."

In her effort to get her car started, the woman put the gun on the seat beside her. Father Dowling opened the door and took her forcibly by the wrist.

"Won't you come inside?"

The next few hours were filled with excitement. The gun Frankie had when she was arrested was not a .22 but the weapon suggested that she was fully capable of making use of Willie's weapon to do away with her husband.

"He told me he was rich," she wept. "He said that when he got out there were hundreds of thousands of dollars he had hidden away. And I believed him. I could quit the library and we would travel and . . ." Her voice trailed off as if the memory of all those golden goals had paled or she was no longer sure they would have been so wonderful.

"So you killed him."

"Killed him?"

She claimed she hadn't even known that he was dead. Oh,

48

they had quarreled when it became clear that his story of hidden treasure was only that, a story, but then he had disappeared and she had assumed he had deserted her. When she heard of Father Dowling's visit to the library, she had come to see if she could find Chester.

"I wanted to kill him. I did. I bought this gun to do it with."

7

Willie was released and Frankie indicted and, sad as it was to think of Frankie's future, the fact of Stokes's deception established that Frankie could have come to St. Hilary's and killed her husband; she had no alibi. And she had come meaning to kill him, weeks after he was dead. And then a thought teased the pastor's mind and he wandered over to the parish center.

"Willie, remember when I bought that gun for you?"

"How I wish you hadn't, Father."

"You wanted it for protection."

"If I had known . . ."

"Willie, of whom were you frightened? Why did you think you needed a gun?"

Willie looked at him for a moment. "You know how it is."

"How what is?"

"The modern world. A man isn't safe anywhere. Look at poor Stokes."

"Whoever killed Stokes was after you, Willie."

"No, that's not true."

"Were you worried about Thorndike?"

"How do you know about Thorndike?"

"I looked up reports of your last arrest. Thorndike was your partner, wasn't he?"

"Never heard of him."

"Don't, Willie. Please. Thorndike is worse off than you'll ever be, Willie. He's in a federal prison in Kansas."

"No!"

Father Dowling handed the photocopied story to Willie. The little man's eyes flew over the page. Relief gave way to another reaction.

"Oh my God."

"What is it, Willie?"

"I killed him, Father. I killed Stokes."

"But you were with me at the time."

"That doesn't matter. Do you remember what we talked about, what Stokes had said about falling stars?"

"I don't understand."

"Stokes was killed by a falling star."

"You're going to have to explain that to me Willie."

Willie explained it to Father Dowling. He explained it to Phil Keegan. The prosecutor contended that what Willie said didn't really change anything. He wasn't going to arrest him again. But finally the prosecutor was persuaded to drop the charges against Frankie and she was released. With some pride, Willie showed Father Dowling and Phil Keegan how he had arranged a greeting for Thorndike.

"He told me he'd get me when I least expected. Just wait. A man can't live with a threat like that over him, Father."

"You should have told me."

"Would you have taken it seriously?"

"Maybe you have a point."

Willie took it seriously. Unbeknownst to him, Thorndike was already under arrest in Kansas when he persuaded Father Dowling to buy the .22. And Willie arranged the ambush.

"I never slept there, Father. At night, when I was alone in the school, I'd go upstairs and sleep on a couch in the room next to Edna's. Sleep! I spent half the night listening for Thorndike. I figured he would find out where I was and come for me. And a sneak like that would come at night."

Willie worked out a device that would trigger the .22 if someone opened the refrigerator. "There isn't an ex-con alive who can resist a refrigerator."

He could deactivate the gun by means of a contact that came through the ice-maker. "Good Lord, Willie. What if you forgot to deactivate it?"

"That's what happened, Father! I did forget."

And poor Stokes, an ex-con who could not resist a refrigerator, had pulled open the door and been shot through the heart.

"Sort of like seeing a falling star when it's no longer there," Willie said in dreamy philosophical tones.

"Sort of," Father Dowling said, not in agreement, but because the thought seemed to provide Willie with mordant satisfaction.

The Dunne Deal

1

The necklace that had been slipped into the poor box had to be artificial pearls.

"How can you tell?" Phil Keegan asked Marie Murkin, who had just returned from the church with the contents of the poor box.

Marie adopted a patient expression. "Who would put real pearls in a poor box?"

"Who would put fake pearls in a poor box?"

Father Dowling intervened. The three were seated at the kitchen table enjoying some of Marie's pineapple upside down cake. "Maybe someone thought it was lost and found."

Marie accepted that, since it left the genuineness of the pearls an open question. She drafted a little notice for insertion in the parish bulletin, stating that the owner of a missing necklace could claim it at the rectory.

"You didn't mention that it was a pearl necklace," Father Dowling observed. "Whether artificial or genuine," he added.

"They're fake," Phil said.

"We don't know that," Marie said.

The notice appeared. No one claimed the necklace, but two weeks later Marie came and stood in the pastor's study door, waiting to be noticed.

"What is it Marie?"

"How much is a hundred thousand lire worth?"

"Lire?"

She took a colorful bill from the pocket of her apron and tried to read the legend on it but gave up. "I can read the numbers anyway. One hundred thousand lire."

"Was it in the collection?"

Marie shook her head. And waited. Either he asked her or she would wait until spring before saying more.

"Where did you find it?"

"It wasn't lost. It was in the poor box."

"Hmmm. Better check with the bank."

"Don't you think it's real?"

"I meant, find out what it's worth."

Marie made the call in the kitchen and returned to say the bill was worth between seventy and eighty dollars. She was clearly disappointed.

"That's a very generous contribution, Marie."

It was also unprecedented. The poor box was seldom the recipient of large amounts. People dropped in dollar bills or a few coins on the way out of church on Sunday, but there was such a press that few of the departing congregation got near enough to the poor box to have the chance even if they had the intention.

"I'll put it with the necklace."

The pastor had to think before he remembered the pearl necklace that had been dropped through the slot of the poor box some weeks before.

"Put eighty dollars into the poor box account."

"What for?"

"I thought you wanted to keep the Italian money."

"Father Dowling, do you think for a moment that was meant for the poor? It's some kind of joke."

"Well, it will certainly bring a smile to some unfortunate person."

It was nearly a month later that the Krugerrand was put in the poor box. Marie just laid it beside the pastor's plate and waited for him to notice and ask about it. But it was Phil Keegan, who had attended the noon Mass and been invited to lunch, whose eye fell immediately on the shiny rectangular object. He picked it up and whistled.

"What is it, some kind of jewelry?" he asked.

"It's pure gold," Marie said.

"Come on."

Marie, having served the soup, took a chair at the table. "What do you think it's worth?"

"Was that in the poor box, Marie?"

"It was, Father. And I'm glad Captain Keegan is here. He will remember the necklace."

But Phil needed reminding. "Oh, those fake pearls."

"Is that fake gold? Was the Italian money fake?"

"What Italian money?"

It would not require Marie Murkin to seek a connection between the necklace, the lire, and the Krugerrand, even if the only thing that linked them was the fact that they had been found in the poor box at the back of St. Hilary's church. The two men finished their soup and she brought in the pasta and salad, then stood at attention beside the table.

"Join us, Marie."

"I've eaten."

"When?"

"What are we going to do about the poor box?" She put the question to Phil Keegan, appealing to his professional curiosity. As captain of detectives in the Fox River Police Department he could be expected to have his suspicions aroused by the odd contributions recently made to the parish poor box. But not while he was enjoying Marie's pasta. When he had finished and was having coffee, he seemed to have forgotten Marie's question. She conquered her annoyance and repeated the question.

"Put it in the bulletin."

"Put what in the bulletin?"

"Marie has already mentioned the pearl necklace."

"That proves they're fake. If they were genuine, someone would have claimed them."

"The question is, what are you going to do about it, Captain Keegan. I am reporting these facts to you."

"You say you found these items in the poor box?"

"I've said that."

"Were there any witnesses?"

"Witnesses to what?"

"To the alleged fact that you found them in the poor box?"

"Do you think I made this up!"

"Are those pearls you're wearing?"

Marie's hand flew to her throat and she emitted a little yelp. "I just tried them on. I forgot I was wearing them."

"No reason why you shouldn't," Phil said magnanimously, and Marie withdrew in confusion. But the field became level again some hours later.

"They're genuine."

Father Dowling, at his desk with Dante open before him, looked up. He had heard Marie speak but had not understood the remark.

"These pearls are genuine." She put them carefully on the pastor's desk. "Montrose the jeweler says they are real and perfectly matched."

"Well, well."

"He gave me an estimate of their value. Now, if we add up the value of the gold and the Italian lire . . ."

"It makes a very handsome contribution to the poor."

"No one would put that much in the poor box just to give something to the poor."

"Oh, I don't know."

In a burst of thanksgiving or contrition people were capable of unusual acts of generosity. It did seem hard to believe that different individuals had put these items in the poor box, however, and the variety and manner of giving were more than odd. Still, the pastor told Marie, he was prepared to live with a measure of oddness.

"Well, I'm not."

"Are you giving notice?"

"Don't you wish?"

"No I don't. However, if you think you can better yourself . . ."

"I have been here longer than you have."

"And now you're bored."

Marie waived away this red herring. "I think you should make a formal complaint to Captain Keegan."

"Complain that someone has been helping the poor?"

"Ask him to find out who it is."

"Would that be fair?"

"Don't you think he could do it?"

"I was thinking of the donor."

"Will you ask him?"

"I don't like to promise."

The matter became moot when Phil Keegan telephoned to say that he thought he knew from whom the items in the poor box had been stolen.

"Stolen!"

"Someone has filed a complaint of theft. Among the missing items were a large Italian bill, a Krugerrand, and a pearl necklace."

"Other things were missing as well?"

"One other thing. A Purple Heart."

"A Purple Heart!"

"The medal awarded to those wounded in action."

"I wonder if it's in the poor box."

"Wait until I get there."

2

Phil Keegan had lost his wife but only after the girls were raised, thank God, and his life ever since had been lonely. He was, Father Dowling had told him, a naturally uxorious man and if that meant he didn't care to live alone, Phil agreed. If it hadn't been the renewal of his old friendship with Roger Dowling, he didn't know what he would have done. Visits to the St. Hilary rectory were frequent and long, and he knew he was welcome there, even by the crusty housekeeper Marie Murkin. Nonetheless, he did work far longer hours than needed, involving himself in various investigations if only to cut down on those blank hours when he had little to do but watch television. His eye was caught by the theft report for two reasons. One, the complainant, Mrs. Dorothea Dunne, was the prominent widow of Fergus Dunne, who had made a fortune, married late, and died early, leaving Dorothea with the earthly goods he had accumulated. She had been in her thirties when they married and not twenty years had passed since that happy day, but ever afterward she had been the phenomenally attractive and eminently eligible Widow Dunne, not that anyone would presume to call her such a thing to her face.

"We were in school together," Lieutenant Cy Horvath said. Keegan had been bent over the counter, reading the report, but at this remark he straightened and turned to face Cy.

"You were in school with Dorothea Dunne?"

"She was just Dorothy then. Dotty Elmore."

"Where was this?"

"St. Casimir's."

"The grade school."

"She was no beauty then. Pig tails, a little fat . . ."

"Did you take the call when she reported this theft?"

"No, but I thought I'd follow up on it."

"For old time's sake?"

"She didn't come to the reunion."

"I'll tag along with you."

"I wonder where she went to high school?" Cy said when they were in the car.

"You can ask her."

"Good idea."

You never knew with Cy. He had only the one expression and nothing had ever been able to change it. He'd had his ups and downs, among them a thwarted football career. Injuring his knee during the first game of his sophomore year at Champaign had been the end of a dream. Not having any kids was another. These and other slings and arrows of outrageous fortune Cy had borne without a facial flicker. It was unlikely that his expression now would reveal whether or not he was joking. Phil decided to read the report again, aloud and carefully.

Mrs. Dorothea Dunne had registered a complaint and asked her lawyer Amos Cadbury to prod the police into action. Several items were missing from her home overlooking the Fox River. She was unsure when they had been taken; she was certain only that they were missing and she had no idea where they had gone. The thought that she had been robbed had eventually suggested itself. She wished the police to conduct a quiet and discrete investigation.

"Why didn't she hire a private detective?"

"I asked Cadbury that. She wants investigators who can arrest if they find the guilty party."

"Sounds like she has someone in mind."

Cy said nothing. The list of missing items was as follows: one matched pearl necklace; one large Italian bill, a memento of her honeymoon; one Krugerrand, suitable for wearing, if one were given to that sort of ostentation . . .

"Are these her comments, Cy?"

"Apparently she insisted that they be written down."

The fourth item was the Purple Heart her husband had won in Korea.

Given the size of the mansion and the imposing look of the main entrance it was something of a surprise to have the door opened by the lady of the house. Her eyes fixed on Cy.

"Police, ma'am."

"I know you."

"Cyril Horvath."

Her heavily mascared eyes narrowed. Her chin lifted higher. The great mass of her silver hair, freed from her shoulders by this movement of her head, cascaded down her rigid back. She tossed her head. If she was waiting for Cy to say more she had a long wait coming.

"St. Casimir's?" she asked.

Cy nodded. "Nineteen—" he began, but her hand flew out, grasped his wrist, and pulled him inside before he could complete the date. Feeling superfluous, Phil Keegan followed.

Phil's wife used to subscribe to magazines that featured homes like this one. They moved through the vestibule, on through a large living room with a great fireplace and into the sunporch where a tropical garden flourished despite the winter outside. She waved Cy to a chair but he remained standing.

"Captain Keegan and I are here to investigate a theft."

"I hope I'm not being an alarmist, Cyril, but some of the missing items are of great sentimental value."

"The Purple Heart?"

She turned her lovely head and looked at Cy from the corner of her eye. She hoped she didn't have to explain to him the significance of such a medal. Cy said he understood. Phil Keegan also had earned one. A wintry little smile was directed briefly at Phil but it was clear that Cy commanded her complete attention.

"Are you alone in the house, Mrs. Dunne?" Phil asked.

"How do you mean?"

"Do you live alone?" Cy said.

"Of course I live alone."

"No one else in the house?"

"There is old Mrs. Dunne, Fergus's mother. Her apartment is over the garages. And there's Thelma."

"Who is Thelma?"

"She takes care of things."

"Housekeeper?"

"You could call her that."

"What would you call her?"

"Companion wouldn't be right. She has worked here since before I married Mr. Dunne. There has never been any question of her not staying."

"What Captain Keegan is after is, who might have stolen the things."

"Well, certainly not Thelma. It was she who made me aware that the things were gone."

"Ah."

"She insisted I call Mr. Cadbury."

Phil left Cy with his old classmate and went to talk to Thelma. She might have been a twin, or at least a cousin, of Marie Murkin. She sat in a rocking chair in the kitchen, listening to music. Phil told her who he was.

"Good. Maybe now we'll get to the bottom of this."

"Mrs. Dunne said you discovered that things were missing."

Thelma looked as if she might want to amend the remark. "I urged her to call Mr. Cadbury."

"What would you say the value of the missing items is?"

"Their monetary value? I have no idea."

"Do you have any idea what happened to them?"

She inhaled deeply. "At first I thought Mrs. Dunne had simply been careless. If only one or two things had been missing, it would not perhaps have seemed so important. But the Purple Heart?"

"Mr. Dunne must have been proud of that."

"It was, he said, his tainted nature's solitary boast. Wordsworth."

"Wordsworth?"

"The poet. The phrase is his. He used it in another connection."

"Was there any sign of a break-in?"

"None. Casey was quite definite."

"Who is Casey?"

"He drives and looks after the yard."

Phil nodded. "Would there be any point in speaking with the older Mrs. Dunne?"

"It is an experience you should not deny yourself."

That could have meant anything. Thelma led Phil through a breezeway to where a stairway outfitted with an invalid's elevator rose to the area over the garage. Upstairs, Thelma just opened the door and went in. The apartment, unlike the main house, was a study in modernity. Clean lines, walls forming right angles with the ceiling, no molding, pastels, silver frames on the pictures, and, in the living room where they found the old lady, a picture window that gave a wonderful view of the back lawn. When Thelma announced him a fragile hand lifted from a wingback chair and its occupant sat forward. Keegan shook her hand but he had the impression she had expected him to kiss it.

"I can't hear a thing," the elder Mrs. Dunne said, although

Phil hadn't said anything yet.

"She won't wear her hearing aid," Thelma remarked.

"They don't work."

"You heard that," Phil said.

Thelma said, "She reads lips."

Thelma's help was indispensable in the interview that followed. The old lady grew animated as they discussed the theft. "Were those my pearls?"

"You gave them to Dorothea, dear."

"Did I say I didn't? Are those the ones that were stolen?"

"Fergus's Purple Heart was taken, too."

"Officer, get those things back."

"That's our job."

"Fergus was a great admirer of that black archbishop with the ballet name."

"In Chicago?"

"No, in Africa."

"Tutu," Thelma explained.

Hence the Krugerrand? Phil was becoming confused. Everyone in this house seemed sane enough but he couldn't make head or tail of what they said. He took Mrs. Dunne's pad and wrote, "Thank you" on it.

"For what?"

He left Thelma to explain and went in search of Casey in the garage below. There was the faintest odor of grease and oil, but the floor of the garage looked as if you could eat off it. Four cars were parked in a row, all of sober color except the white sports car. There was a door with a glazed window at the far end of the garage. On it was painted in Gothic script F. X. Casey. Keegan knocked.

"It's open."

Phil stepped inside. The man's back was to the door; he had

his feet on the desk and was buffing his nails. "They gone?" he asked.

"No, they're still here."

The man turned his head and looked at Phil. Then he uncrossed his legs and took his feet from the desktop one at a time. Finally he turned in his chair.

"I'm Frank Casey."

"I know. I read your door. Now I recognize you. I wondered where you ended up."

"That was a long time ago."

"Years ago."

Casey had spent a checkered youth and as a man been convicted of dealing drugs. Keegan figured Casey had been a free man for perhaps half a dozen years. The fact that he had kept out of the way of the police was a recommendation.

"How long you been here?"

"Since I got out."

"You know why we're here?"

"I know what Thelma told me."

"Theft wasn't in your repertoire, was it?"

"No way."

"What do you think happened?"

"For too many years I lived only with men. I didn't understand many of them. Here there are only women. I don't understand any of them. They are very different from men."

"Can I quote you on that?"

"These three are playing three-way tag and I'm never sure who's it."

"You drive them all?"

"When they let me. Mainly I take Thelma to the mall. To shop."

"The young Mrs. Dunne has reported missing items. She

wanted us to investigate so an arrest could be made if we find a suspect."

"She never liked me."

"Neither did I." But Phil smiled when he said it. "For the record, did you steal those items?"

"No. What were they anyway?"

"Odds and ends. A necklace, an Italian bank note, a South African gold piece. A Purple Heart."

Casey shook his head at the list.

"If it's an inside job and you're out, who did it?"

Casey displayed his palms. "Hey, I'm no fink."

"So you have a suspicion?"

"No! I didn't say that. And I don't. Why would any of these ladies steal? They have everything they want."

"Maybe you're a bad influence."

3

Father Dowling waited until Phil came before he let Marie open the poor box. There among the coins was a military ribbon, the distinctive Purple Heart.

"So nothing's missing after all."

"Did you tell Mrs. Dunne that some of her things had shown up in our poor box?"

Phil shook his head. "Not yet. Could any of them have put these items in the poor box? And don't ask me why they would. They are all unusual people."

"So what was the upshot?"

"Cy took Casey downtown for further questioning."

"Is he a suspect?"

"Of what? Putting things in the poor box? No. But Cy thought he would be a good source to find out about the others."

"I should think you would ask Amos Cadbury."

"I was hoping you would do that."

Father Dowling agreed to talk with his parishioner and friend about the supposed theft from the Dunne house. He offered to come downtown to Amos's office but the lawyer would not hear of inconveniencing the pastor of St. Hilary's. Father Dowling had learned not to quarrel with Amos's exaggerated respect for the cloth. It was quite impersonal. It was the priesthood Amos honored. But Father Dowling liked to think that they were friends as well.

"Now if Mrs. Murkin would make some of her tea . . ." Amos said after insisting that he would come to the rectory.

Father Dowling promised that tea would be made. Marie was delighted at the prospect of Amos Cadbury's visit. He was deferential to the gentle sex, as he continued to call women, and had flattered Marie Murkin's culinary capacities to such a degree that Father Dowling sometimes feared that Amos might lure Marie away. If the lawyer was not so patently sincere, Father Dowling would think him a flatterer. Another of his enthusiasms was the paragraphs the pastor wrote each Sunday for the parish bulletin. "I have kept them all, Father. At the end of the year, I have them bound."

Amos arrived in homburg and black overcoat with a fur collar. The pleats of his trousers were razor sharp, the shoes that emerged from his galoshes were shiny, his suit jacket was open to reveal the buttoned vest across which a chain stretched. It held the Phi Beta Kappa key he had earned at Notre Dame. Marie took the lawyer's coat as if she were an acolyte and Amos a celebrant. Father Dowling had come to the door as well and now led Amos to his study.

"Tea will be ready in a minute," Marie chirped.

"Deo gratias!" said Amos.

There would have been no way to avoid the ensuing ceremony even if Father Dowling had been inclined to. They moved into the dining room at Marie's call and the lawyer tasted with closed eyes and then having opened them praised the result of Marie's brewing. He also oohed and aahed appropriately over the sandwiches and fruitcake she served. For half an hour it would have seemed that the purpose of Amos Cadbury's visit was to take tea with Marie. But eventually the pastor and his guest withdrew to the study and to the topic of the theft from the Dunne house.

"I warned against hiring that man," Amos murmured. "I speak, Father Dowling, strictly *entre nous*. Dorothea Dunne would not be the first person to pay for a misguided compassion. Note that I speak quite generically. I do not know this man. Casey is his name. But it is a sad rule of human nature that one who has fallen once may fall again. But I need not explain such things to you."

"Do you think Mrs. Dunne suspects the man?"

"The elder Mrs. Dunne?"

The question seemed to be a species of answer. In any case, Amos wanted to speak of Fergus Dunne, whom he described as an equivocal fellow.

"How so?"

"How to put it? He was his own greatest admirer. But there was so much to admire. He was a very gifted man, a very generous man, a very driven man. He started from nothing and amassed a fortune."

"What exactly did he do?"

"What didn't he do? Business, sports entrepreneur, pilot."

"Pilot?"

"He was in the Air National Guard reserve. He was inordinately proud of it."

"And he won a Purple Heart?"

"He was not reluctant to say so."

"There is something I want to tell you, Amos. All those missing items turned up in the poor box at the back of the church. Including the Purple Heart."

"You don't say."

"First, there was the necklace, and then the other items, one by one at intervals. If they were stolen, the thief did not keep them."

"If?"

"It seems a way to draw attention, doesn't it?"

"To the theft?"

"Or to the fact that it wasn't a theft."

"Are they in your parish, the Dunnes?"

"Yes."

"This is quite mysterious, Father Dowling."

"Any ideas?"

"I am speechless."

4

Things that might have seemed insignificant before took on significance now, and Marie Murkin always kept a sharp eye out. She must have noticed that the two Mrs. Dunnes were driven to Mass each Sunday in a very noticeable car. The driver did not wear a uniform, but he did everything but tug at his forelock when he opened the back door for the ladies. He saw them safely into church and then sauntered back to the car where he spent the next hour smoking and reading the paper. Ten minutes before Mass ended, he aired out the car and had a final cigarette standing in the entrance of the school, a recessed area that afforded him some protection from the winter winds.

"They must come to Mass weekdays too," Edna Hospers said.

"I've never seen them there," Marie said.

"The car you describe has been parked in the lot on weekdays too."

"Are you sure?"

"They are not many Jaguars of that style cluttering up the parking lot."

"Is that the kind of car it is?"

"I checked with my son Carl."

Marie was certain she had seen neither of the Mrs. Dunnes at daily Mass. She took it as one of the duties of her job to notice such things. That must mean that the driver had come alone. His background and his apparent presence on the parish grounds pointed inevitably to a conclusion. He would not be coming for Mass, since he skipped that on Sunday when he had an obligation to attend. She drew her conclusion explicitly for the pastor.

"Have you told Phil Keegan?"

"Do you think I should?"

"He may be a little less grateful to you for doing his job for him than I am."

Marie refused to be gotten off on a tangent by his teasing. "I don't like to be the cause of another's trouble, Father."

"It's not your role to grant clemency, Marie."

"Are you saying I have an obligation?"

"I have every confidence you will do the right thing."

Try as she would, Marie could not get Father Dowling to tell her in so many words that she should tell Phil Keegan what she had learned about F. X. Casey, the Dunne driver. When that pest Tuttle the lawyer came by and actually said he had an appointment with the pastor, Marie was about to tell a little white lie but Father Dowling looked out of his study.

"Ah, Mr. Tuttle. I thought I heard your voice. Come in."

The door closed on them and Marie, without exactly pressing her ear to the door, still could not discover what they were talking of. The door was still shut an hour and a half later. Her curiosity overwhelmed her and, armed with a plate of cookies, she knocked on the study door.

"Come in."

She breezed across the room and put the cookies on the desk, then looked around.

"Where is he?"

"Where is who?"

"Tuttle!"

"He left hours ago."

Marie was so astounded, she dropped into a chair. How could that man get out of the house without her hearing him? But there was a more important question.

"Why was he here?"

"Are you sure you want to know?"

She hesitated at so easy a victory. "If you think I should."

"I hope I didn't do the wrong thing."

Marie waited, silently counting, dying to know.

"He asked if you ever thought of marrying again. His is a modest practice but his eye has been on you for some time . . ."

She leapt to her feet and was so miffed she took the cookies with her when she left. Honestly, she didn't know why she put herself in the way of such teasing.

Phil Keegan came by that evening, and Marie did not have to be the one to turn his professional attention to F. X. Casey.

"What put you on to him, Phil?"

"Edna Hospers has a pair of sharp eyes, Roger. She has seen one of the Dunne cars here. Probably when he came to drop things in the poor box."

"I was the one who saw that car!" Marie cried.

"You can corroborate Edna's testimony?"

It had been a dreadful day, and Marie was glad to creep away to her apartment over the back part of the house. Her thunder had been stolen.

And she still did not know why the pastor had wanted to talk to Tuttle. It was one of those moments when she really knew that God was her only refuge.

5

When Marie Murkin came to tell Father Dowling that a woman named Thelma Spooner was in the front parlor, she wore a quizzical look, as if she had just seen a ghost, or a lost cousin. Father Dowling went into the parlor where the woman sat slumped in a chair. She looked up but did not stand when the pastor entered.

"I work for the Dunnes."

"Ah."

"Amos Cadbury has been to see you."

"Yes, he has."

"Frank Casey is still in jail."

She seemed a treasury of items he already knew.

He said, "I understand he refuses to talk."

"They have bound him over to the grand jury!"

"I think that is the usual procedure."

"He did nothing wrong."

"Let us hope that will become clearer than it is. One of the Dunne cars was seen here at about the time that items were left in the church."

"That was me."

"You?"

She nodded. She sat forward and looked at the door. "Is that woman still out there?"

Father Dowling got up to close the parlor door, cutting off the sound of Marie's departure down the hallway.

"Tell me all about it."

She was embarrassed to tell the tale. Three women living together, none much caring for the others. The elder Mrs. Dunne had not hired Thelma, her husband had.

"She'd throw me out in a minute but she's afraid he would come and haunt her."

The two Mrs. Dunnes barely tolerated one another. The bond was the memory of Fergus Dunne.

"A complete blowhard, Father, but they worship his memory."

"Why would you have left those things in the church?"

"Spite. The pearls were the older woman's. Dorothea had convinced her that she had made a present of them to her."

A drama of petty vindictiveness emerged from the story. Thelma had resented her employers for years but the only retaliation she had thought of was petty theft.

"I am surprised that Frank Casey has kept quiet."

Thelma seemed to be about to explain that, but then her mouth formed a straight line and she rocked back and forth for a moment.

"I suppose they'll arrest me now."

Father Dowling's solution was to call Phil Keegan and Amos Cadbury and ask them to come to the rectory. They had no sooner arrived and got settled in the parlor, when Marie appeared, wearing a look of annoyance.

"Tuttle," she said to the pastor.

"Put him in the study."

Rebellion sparked in her eyes, but she went off to do as she was asked.

"Thelma, why don't you tell Captain Keegan and Mr. Cadbury what you have told me."

He excused himself for a moment and went into the study to talk with Tuttle. When he returned to the parlor Thelma was just finishing her account to a sympathetic Amos Cadbury and a skeptical Phil Keegan.

"It doesn't make any sense," Phil said.

"You have to imagine yourself living in that house," Amos suggested.

"Why the Purple Heart?"

Father Dowling intervened. "Should I tell them, Thelma?"

She studied the pastor's face. "Do you know?"

"I have just learned."

"Learned what?" Phil said, exasperated.

"Fergus Dunne never earned a Purple Heart. He never saw action and he never shed blood for his country, that being the *sine qua non* of the Purple Heart. As I needn't tell you, Phil."

A cloud formed on Phil Keegan's face but the face of Thelma was a mask of relief and almost joy.

"He was a phony," she said. "From the time he was a boy. Doing what he did was never enough, he had to claim to do more."

"How did you find this out, Father Dowling?" Amos asked.

"Tuttle found it out for me."

At the mention of Fox River's least distinguished member of the bar, Amos Cadbury winced.

"I'm not going to charge you for misplacing a few items," Phil Keegan said to Thelma.

"Then why did you arrest Frank Casey?"

"He has a record."

"That's not fair."

"Frank has been telling me the same thing."

"Will you let him go now?"

"Why don't you release him to Thelma's custody, Phil?"

Thelma actually threw up her hands in surprise. But she agreed. Phil took her with him when he left but Amos stayed on, seduced by the offer of a cup of Marie Murkin's tea.

"Spooner is her married name," Father Dowling said, when tea had been poured. Amos Cadbury's patrician brows lifted and he glanced at the pastor.

"You found that out too?"

"And that her maiden name was Casey. I assume she is

Frank's sister."

"Aunt."

"Ah."

Amos sipped his tea. "Dorothea never let Casey forget his criminal past. That, coupled with her almost oriental devotion to the memory of her heroic husband, eventually weighed Thelma down. She knew the Purple Heart had not been earned."

"She wanted to discredit the memory of Fergus Dunne?"

"Let us say she wanted revenge on his widow."

Silence fell over the parlor as the two men pondered the antics that take place on the stage of life.

"The means were ignoble, but her intention was not."

Father Dowling said, "She didn't put those things in the poor box."

Amos rattled his cup into its saucer. "Why do you say that?"

"I think you know, Amos."

Another silence set in. "What told you?"

"You expressed surprise about the necklace, but there had been a notice in the parish bulletin."

Amos opened his mouth, then closed it. He had no wish to deny that he was a close reader and collector of the bulletin. Father Dowling tried to imagine the stately lawyer slipping those items into the poor box.

"It was Fergus's claim to be a hero that explains my deed. To become involved in the quarrels of a nest of women—that I would never have done. But Thelma's cause seemed just to me." His eyes darted to the priest's, then fell. "I suggested the other things, to lead up to la pièce de résistance."

"No crime has been committed."

"Just sins? I am worse than those women. Father, I want you to say some Masses for the repose of the soul of Fergus Dunne.

I sincerely hope he has achieved the only reward that really matters."

6

"What about the Jaguar?" Phil asked some days later during a lull in the Bulls game. "The weekday visits."

"That was Dorothea."

"What was she up to?"

"Why do people come to church?"

Marie humphed. "To put things in the poor box."

"Exactly. We have been so distracted by those items that we failed to notice that some large bills were stuffed into the box during those weeks. American bills. And she also lit a candle for her husband."

"The hero," Marie said but her heart was not in it.

"Do you know how some people got their Purple Hearts?" Phil asked.

But Marie did not want to know. The thought of Dorothea Dunne as a grieving widow had softened her. As for Phil, he hunched forward when play resumed. Tomorrow Father Dowling would say the first of a series of Masses for Fergus Dunne, with a commemoration of other sinners, present company included.

The Cube Root of Ice

1

When old Sam Wilson died and his heir decided to sell the two-story building in downtown Fox River that had once been Wilson's Restaurant, interest in the property was intense. The building was sold at auction and when the dust settled and Dirk Simmons found himself the new owner he was a bit abashed at what he had paid for the building.

"Will you raze it?" he was asked by Harold Wilson, a grandson of the deceased.

"That depends." At the moment, he felt like selling it to an unsuccessful bidder and recouping his money.

"It's silly, I guess," Harold murmured, brushing upward on his chin with the palm of his hand. "But seeing our name on that building was always a source of pride. It reminded me of how much my family did for this town."

Not a subject to pursue, of course, since the Wilson building had been unoccupied for years. Unoccupied by people, that is. The empty restaurant, so far as one could see, peering through the windows, was unchanged, and there were citizens who felt a little catch in their throats when they looked at a scene that carried them back to the 1970s. Lydia Wilson had disappeared in 1979 and the restaurant closed soon after, but Sam Wilson would not sell. Twenty-five years ago it would have brought three times the sum Dirk Simmons had paid for it.

"Do you ever go inside?" Dirk asked.

Harold seemed surprised by the question. "I never realized before that I owned it. Mr. Cadbury has had the key all these years."

Amos Cadbury had been Sam Wilson's lawyer and had attended the auction in that capacity. He assured Dirk that the transfer of the property would present no problems.

"Could you be at my office tomorrow at ten?"

"I'll be there."

Meanwhile, he wanted to get away from the excitement of the auction. The hall now had the look of a pari-mutuel track after the running of the eighth race. Those remaining were mainly losers; Dirk hoped he would feel more like a winner the following morning at Amos Cadbury's office. He drove past the Wilson building on his way home and felt a little surge of ownership. The building looked spanking new and in excellent shape.

"I think he thought of it as some kind of memorial to Lydia," Amos Cadbury said the following morning.

"A mausoleum?"

But Amos was not inclined to pursue the simile.

"Was he really accused of doing away with her, Amos?"

A pained expression crossed the lawyer's face, and he glanced at young Harold Wilson who was there for the occasion.

"I never knew my grandmother," Harold said after an awkward moment.

"But you knew your grandfather." Amos's voice was mildly reproving.

"The way you know a hermit," Harold said.

If there was resentment in his voice, it was perhaps pardonable. Harold's father had fallen in Vietnam at about the age Harold now was. He and his mother had moved in with old Sam Wilson and Harold must have known a lugubrious childhood, raised in a house where two departed members were being perpetually mourned by old Sam, his wife, and now his son as well. Wilma, Harold's mother, became eccentric and frequented séances with the intention of making contact with her dead husband.

"Silly business," her father-in-law grumbled, as if his grief were more genuine for being without hope.

"Aren't you curious about the next world?"

"I'm not even curious about this one."

Wilma nodded. "It's only a stage."

"I wish you wouldn't go to those things."

He meant the séances. Wilma urged him to come along.

"That alarmed him," Harold said later in Feeney's, where the former and present proprietors of the Wilson building had gone for a drink. "I think he feared my mother would succeed." He drank thoughtfully of his beer. "I guess she did, when she died. And now he has, too."

"What will you do?"

"Go back to Indianapolis."

Young Harold had joined a firm there and for some years had put his Fox River origins behind him. Called back by the death of his grandfather as the only heir, he would return to his law firm considerably more affluent than he had left it.

"Would you like to take a tour of the Wilson building before you leave?"

Harold thought about it for a moment, then shook his head. "There hasn't been a Wilson inside that building for over thirty years. I think I'll leave it that way."

It was two days later that Dirk Simmons inspected his new property. Amos Cadbury came along, bringing with him Alison Larson, a young member of his firm. They were met at the door by Jack Fergus, who had been in charge of maintaining the building during the years of its disuse. As Fergus took them around he talked incessantly, hitching up his pants at thirty-second intervals, describing the furniture, the appointments, the vintage fixtures in the bar. Dirk had the feeling that Fergus had formed the habit of talking to himself in his lonely job, giving imaginary tours of the premises, and they were eavesdropping on his soliloquy. On the second floor were offices.

"Why didn't he rent these out?" Dirk asked.

Amos shrugged. "Why didn't he rent the restaurant? Why didn't he sell the building?"

The answer was twofold: Lydia and old Sam's consuming grief at the loss of his wife.

Dirk hesitated about going down into the basement.

"What's there?"

Fergus closed his eyes as he spoke. "The furnace. The air-conditioning. Hot water heater." His eyes popped open. "Everything's in mint condition."

"I suppose I ought to see everything."

After some hesitation, Amos Cadbury decided to come along. "I have never been down there," he said.

Overhead fluorescent lighting revealed that the basement and its contents were in every bit as good condition as the upstairs. After a tour of the area, as they were about to ascend, Dirk noticed a door beneath the staircase.

"What's that?"

Fergus hitched up his pants. "A freezer."

"Does it work?"

"Everything works."

Dirk found that he was annoyed by the increasing smugness with which Fergus showed off what he clearly regarded as his domain.

"I'd like to see it."

"I don't have a key."

"Where do you keep it?"

"I don't have one anywhere."

Dirk decided to make a fuss about it. Was he working off some of his own uneasiness at having bought this building? He had no idea what he would do with it.

"Open it up."

"But I don't have a key."

"Do you have an axe?"

Amos intervened. "I have some of Sam Wilson's effects at the office, Dirk. I think there are keys among them." He turned a questioning expression to Alison.

"I'll go see," she said, then scampered up the stairs.

While they waited for her to return, Dirk felt like a tyrant, pointlessly exerting his will. Did he have to prove to old Fergus that he was now the owner of the building? Ten minutes went by. Amos kept a silence that had an accusing aspect to it. Fergus had grabbed a broom and was touching up the polish of the concrete floor. Did he wax it? Dirk was about to call the thing off when Alison came back.

She had brought keys.

One of them fit the freezer.

Fergus had to find a bulb to replace the one that had burned out, perhaps a quarter of a century ago. But the freezer was indeed cold, intensely cold. Fergus held back when Dirk stepped into the freezer. Amos was at his side. There was a locker within the locker, but the door to it was not locked. Dirk pulled it open and then jumped back. Amos gasped.

"Lydia!" he cried. "Lydia Wilson!"

He might have been addressing rather than identifying the frozen figure who stared sightlessly back at them.

2

The burial of a woman who had been dead for twenty-five years was more morbid than sorrowful. McDivitt the undertaker could not keep quiet about how well preserved the body was.

"After I thawed her out I half expected her to sit up."

Marie Murkin listened with fascinated dread. Harold Wilson returned from Indianapolis. A week before he had buried his grandfather. Now he would bury his grandmother.

"Can it be just a private ceremony?"

Phil Keegan and Amos Cadbury explained to the young man that the discovery of Lydia Wilson's frozen body in the freezer in the basement of her husband's building had understandably excited a good deal of curiosity.

"There are no signs of violence," Amos said gently. "Isn't that right, Captain Keegan?"

But it was McDivitt who answered. "The body was in perfect condition," he enthused.

Father Dowling and Amos had a long philosophical conversation about what had transpired.

"Her husband must have known she was in the freezer, Amos."

The lawyer nodded.

"Phil Keegan thinks that the suitcase found with her suggests she was going on a trip."

"The pyramids," Amos murmured, and stepped back as if to distance himself from the fanciful simile. "Clothes. Provisions. There was food in the locker too."

Canned food. Frozen meats. Even if she had been disposed to eat in that improvised tomb, before the air gave out or the cold took over, she would have been unable to.

"Would the light have stayed on when the door was closed?"

Amos gave the priest a look of reproof. But levity seemed invited when the deceased had been dead a quarter of a century.

"No signs of violence," McDivitt repeated emphatically.

"Locking her in was violence enough," Father Dowling said.

Later, in his study at the St. Hilary rectory, Father Dowling found it difficult to concentrate on saying his office. It was Phil

Keegan's conviction that Sam Wilson had locked his wife in that food locker, closed his restaurant, and spent the rest of his life riddled with guilt at what he had done. Not selling a perfectly good building that he was not using invited curiosity and the old man must have wondered when his deed would be discovered. Is that what had happened?

Father Dowling had not known Sam Wilson well and he had not known Lydia at all. But he had attended Sam during his last days. Once the old man had beckoned him close, removed the oxygen mouthpiece, and whispered, "Say a mass for Lydia."

Father Dowling had nodded.

"My wife."

There were tears in the old man's eyes. He put the mouthpiece in again and breathed in the oxygen that kept death at bay. Was it possible that Sam was thinking of Lydia locked in the freezer in the basement of the restaurant?

"When did she die, Sam?"

The question was out before he thought. Of course Lydia's story had faded from most memories. Sam removed the mouthpiece.

"She could be still alive."

If Sam had been deceiving himself and Fox River for all these years, he could of course carry on the ruse on his deathbed. But why? If he had done it, he must have known that soon after he was gone, the truth would come out. Father Dowling had been a priest long enough to realize that human beings are capable of the most surprising behavior, good and bad, saintly and evil. With time, anything becomes ordinary and Sam could have adjusted long since to the realization that his wife sat frozen in the meat locker in the basement of his closed restaurant and that he had locked her into it.

But Father Dowling had another cause for wonder. He had heard Sam's last confession, helping him examine his conscience, and had been struck by the routineness of the old man's sins. Not that lukewarmness is a commendation, but if there was anything weighing on Sam Wilson's conscience he gave no sign of it. And, in the circumstances, there would have been no risk whatsoever in making a clean breast of it. What he said then was between him and Father Dowling or, more strictly, between him and God.

Of course Father Dowling could not tell Phil Keegan why he did not share the captain of detective's conviction that Sam Wilson had murdered his wife and managed to conceal it and avoid punishment all these years.

Several evenings later, Amos Cadbury came to the rectory for dinner. He fussed quite sincerely over Marie Murkin's cooking and the housekeeper gleamed with gratitude.

"Cooking for Father Dowling is like cooking for a Trappist," she cried. "He eats anything put before him."

"He is simply used to perfection," the lawyer said. "It requires a contrast to see what a culinary wizard you are."

Are the angels amused when they watch weak humans respond to flattery? Father Dowling shook the thought away. Who does not give the angels, good and bad, occasion for wonder? How galling it must be to the devils to think that the Son of God had chosen to take on the flesh of such a species. A word, a smile, a touch, so easily conquer the soul.

"Didn't I have this last night, Marie?"

"You did not!"

Amos cried, "I would be content to have such a dish every night."

"I do not serve leftovers when there is company."

Marie's chin lifted and she walked with dignified step from the dining room. The kitchen door swung to and fro for a moment after she disappeared.

"What was Lydia Wilson like, Amos?"

The lawyer thought a moment. "You saw her in death, Father Dowling. She was beautiful even then. She was a remarkably striking woman."

"A local girl?"

"Oh yes. She and Sam had known one another since childhood."

"Childhood sweethearts?"

"Yesss."

"That sounds like no."

"Oh there was a time, the summer after Lydia's freshman year at Rosary College, when they decided they had seen one another too exclusively. I myself had the privilege of dating Lydia a time or two then." Amos's voice became reflective and there was a far-off look in his eye. But then he reddened, and busied himself with his dinner.

"But they got back together?"

"And Sam forgave me."

"Were there other beaus besides yourself?"

"Oh I was never that. Does the phrase 'target of opportunity' mean anything to you, Father Dowling? I knew I was merely a poor substitute for Sam."

Father Dowling would have supposed that the regal and patrician Amos Cadbury would have been formidable competition for the shortish Sam Wilson. But of course in such matters, the outside observer is almost always puzzled by the conjunctions brought about by the attraction between the sexes.

3

When Oscar Gardner came to the rectory it seemed that it was Marie he had come to see. Father Dowling heard the bell ring and was aware of Marie going to the door, but then the cries of greeting, the laughter, and ten or fifteen minutes of more-or-less muted conversation in the front parlor convinced him that he would not be needed and he immersed himself in his book. He was rereading *David Copperfield* after enjoying intensely Chesterton's little book on the novelist.

"Dickens?" Marie had said, lifting her eyebrows.

"That's right."

"A novel?"

"David Copperfield."

"Oh."

"Have you read it, Marie?"

"I suppose," the housekeeper admitted. "When I was a girl."

Obviously Marie regarded the reading of fiction as one of those childish occupations that were to be put aside or grown out of. Father Dowling understood this heresy. After all, Jane Austen had once said that what she was at work on was "only a novel." Father Dowling was now reading the chapter in which Aunt Betsy deals with the Murdstones, brother and sister, and was filled with the satisfaction that comes from seeing justice done at last.

"Father?"

He looked up. Marie stood in the door of the study, and there was a tall man behind her with a large shock of white hair, a ruddy complexion, and a luxuriant mustache.

"This is Oscar Gardner, Father."

She stepped aside and the man came into the study, stooping as he thrust out his hand to the priest.

"Do you have a minute, Father?"

"Of course." He closed his book, and Marie quickly covered it with a copy of the diocesan newspaper.

"I'll leave you then," Marie said, reluctance in her voice. The two men watched as she withdrew, closing the door after her.

"You know Mrs. Murkin?"

"Apparently we met before, yes." This seemed a churlish

comment, after the extended and affable exchange in the front parlor. But Gardner was looking about him, obviously impressed by a room whose four walls were lined with books. "A good room. A man's room." He inhaled deeply. "Pipe tobacco," he said, as if identifying a rare perfume.

"Do you smoke?"

"Oh, I had my share, Father. But like most pleasures, it is now a fading memory."

Gardner looked to be in his mid-seventies. The white suit he wore was unusual but seemed exactly right for him. And he did have the look of a reformed roué, an old man left with only memories of misbehavior. Not that the pastor of St. Hilary's thought smoking misbehavior. Had Gardner been jollying Marie simply to take the rust off old skills? He looked at the priest from under his thick white brows.

"I have to talk to someone, Father."

"Good."

"I'm not a Catholic."

"What are you?"

"Not much, I guess. I tried to remember what we were when I was a kid, but we just didn't go to church, I guess. When I was in the army I identified myself as a Protestant, but that was just a way of saying I wasn't Jewish or Catholic."

"But now you're giving the matter some thought?"

He seemed surprised. "No. Not really. Well, maybe. I don't know. There is something I have to get off my mind."

Father Dowling waited. Oscar Gardner had come to talk and he would talk in his own way.

"It's about Lydia Wilson."

"You knew her?"

Gardner nodded. There was no bravura in it, no macho claim, but the meaning of his answer seemed immediately clear.

"My life has been lived far from here, Father, and I did not keep in touch after I left. Leaving here the way I did has always seemed to me one of the truly good things I have done in my misspent lifetime. But now that has been taken away from me."

He spoke at his own pace, as if he were himself searching for the meaning of what he said. He had come to Fox River as a journalist and had worked on the *Journal,* a long-defunct paper.

"I was in my twenties, single, just out of the service, the world was my oyster. I interviewed Lydia for a piece I was doing on the restaurant. That's how it began."

Again, his tone was simply matter of fact, not boastful. "I fell in love with her. She was shocked when I expressed my feelings and refused to see me again. But I was smitten and could not let it go. I wore her down."

"She responded?"

He nodded. "She agreed to go off with me. We would simply leave town."

"Did anyone suspect?"

"I don't know. By that time, neither of us really cared. We would clear out and who cared what we left behind us?"

"What happened?"

"I said this was one of the few things I have been proud of. The very day we were to leave, it suddenly occurred to me what I was doing. Lydia was a good woman, a good wife. A good Catholic. I had broken down her defenses and she had agreed to go off with me. But what kind of a future could I offer her? I told myself I should be content to have gained her love, however fleeting it might be. I determined to quit while I was ahead. I left without her."

"How did she take it?"

"I didn't tell her! I didn't trust myself. If I saw her again I knew I would weaken and want to go through with it. I didn't send to her, didn't call. Nothing. I just left town myself. Alone."

"The day she expected you to take her along?"

"Yes." He sat forward in his chair. "But what happened that day? All these years, I have taken solace from the thought that she was here, a wife and mother, respected. And all along she was dead."

"How did you learn?"

"It was in papers from coast to coast."

"Did you know Sam?"

"If he were still alive, I'd kill him."

4

Twenty-four hours had not gone by before Oscar Gardner's story was public knowledge. All the suburban and city papers carried extensive accounts; the local television, news as well as talk shows, hummed with the account of the man who had thought better of running off with another man's wife only to learn a quarter of a century later that she had been cruelly killed by the husband.

"If you had gone through with it, she might have been alive today," an interviewer suggested.

Gardner nodded, his expression wondrous. "How could I have known?"

"Sam Wilson must have found out about you and his wife."

"Yes. We weren't all that discreet, not toward the end."

In Indianapolis, Harold Wilson said that he wanted to just forget the whole thing. It was all water over the dam. What was gained by throwing mud at his grandfather and grandmother? The reporter seemed surprised at the reference to Lydia Wilson. But of course on Gardner's story, she had been ready to desert husband and family and run away with the dashing young journalist.

"I suppose even someone like Lydia Wilson was susceptible to his charms," Marie Murkin said.

"What kind of woman was she?"

"Promise you won't laugh."

"Laugh?"

"Father Dowling, she was a good woman. To all appearances she was a model wife and mother. And she was a pillar of this parish. It makes you think, doesn't it?"

"Daughters of Eve."

Marie's eyes narrowed. "And sons of Adam."

"Original sin is everywhere."

"But imagine, all packed and ready to run off and she is left in the lurch. I am sure that when Sam confronted her, she had no spirit left."

What had happened when husband confronted wife? And had that taken place in the restaurant? Gardner answered the last question.

"We were to leave from there. Sam was at home. She was in charge of the restaurant that evening. I would pull into the delivery zone in back, she would slip out, and we would be on our way. It would be hours before we were missed."

"But you didn't show up?"

"Oh, I drove to the restaurant. I circled the block. That was when my conscience struck and I just kept going."

Father Dowling said Mass for Lydia and Sam. There seemed no way to avoid thinking that the old man had deceived him on his deathbed or, worse, deceived God. Had he thought that going to confession would give him an advantage over Lydia? These were deep waters, appropriate to a French Catholic novel, far deeper than one would expect in Fox River, Illinois. Perhaps. As he had often done before, the pastor of St. Hilary's marveled at the mystery of human existence.

Dirk Simmons came by the sacristy after Father Dowling had finished saying the noon Mass.

"Got a minute, Father?"

"I'll take you to lunch."

"Let me take you."

"I mean in the rectory. People tell me that Marie is a good cook."

Marie served cold pasta and iced tea, because of the temperature, and sank into a chair at the dining room table.

"He won't turn on the air-conditioning," she said to Dirk.

"I don't like the house all closed up. Besides, when it's on, I need a sweater to keep warm."

"I've come into possession of Lydia Wilson's suitcase," Dirk said.

"You! Why?"

"It was part of the building I bought. The bid was for the structure and everything in it."

"But that would include Lydia."

"McDivitt sent me the funeral bill."

"I don't believe it."

"Neither did young Wilson fortunately. He insisted on paying it."

"Did you tell him about the suitcase?" Father Dowling asked.

Dirk shook his head. "I was afraid that would be ghoulish."

"Have you opened it?"

"The police examined it. It's nothing but clothes. Would you like them, Marie?"

Marie hesitated but then she shook her head, shivering. "Give them to St. Vincent de Paul."

"What have you done with the suitcase?"

"I left it with Amos Cadbury. He'll know what to do with it."

That night Dirk Simmons's house was burgled. A patio door was forced and the first floor of the house was a shambles. It looked to be the work of vandals rather than burglars. Nothing seemed to be missing. Throughout the morning, Father Dowling tried to drive the event from his mind as he busied himself with various pastoral responsibilities, but finally he went over to the church and knelt at the prie-dieu in the sanctuary. There was more than an hour before he would say his Mass and he did not pretend that the thinking he was engaged in was meditation. Still, it was not concentrated thinking. He let ideas roam about the edges of his mind without focusing on them. Two hours later, over lunch, they all seemed to come together.

He telephoned Amos Cadbury and asked if he could drop by his office.

"Any time, Father. You needn't have called. I am always here."

Father Dowling did not ask about the suitcase. Long shots are best played on the spot.

There was something solemn, almost sepulchral, about Amos's office. It had the air of a place where definitive solutions were reached. What client could fail to think he was in good hands as he looked around the paneled room, at the high windows whose drapes fell in elegant folds, providing a framed sight of the far horizon?

"I have been reading about the break-in at Dirk Simmons's," Amos said. He picked up an object from his desk and examined it before putting it down again. "Sam Wilson gave me that."

It was a cube of solid glass, four inches to the edge, with a W embedded in it. A paperweight.

"Dirk says that nothing was taken."

A small smile formed on the thin lips of the lawyer, and Father Dowling was certain that they had come to the same realization.

"The suitcase was not there."

"Is it still here?"

Amos rose and walked slowly to a door. It opened into a closet. He bent and picked up the suitcase that had spent over three decades in freezing temperatures with Lydia Wilson. Amos put it on his desk and then opened a drawer of his desk. A moment later he was fitting a key into the lock of the suitcase.

"Dirk Simmons said it contains nothing but clothes."

"That's surmise. It has not been opened."

"Didn't the police open it?"

"They ran it through a scanner and satisfied themselves it contained no clues to what had happened to Lydia."

"I wonder if it does."

The key turned and there was the pop of a released lock. Amos slowly lifted the lid. The expression on his face drew Father Dowling to the desk.

"Clothes," Amos said. Lifting items and then returning them. "Men's clothes."

"Sam's?"

Amos had just brought out a pair of trousers and held them by the waist let them hang. They would have been too long even for the lawyer, who was a tall man.

"They're mine," a voice said, and they turned to face Oscar Gardner.

He had pushed Miss Wise into the office before him and now flourished a gun.

"I'll take that suitcase," he said in an almost jocular tone. "And what's in it."

"Of course," Father Dowling said. "After all, it's your property."

Miss Wise was trying to say something, but fear prevented any sound from emerging. Father Dowling walked toward Oscar, his hand out.

"Why don't you give me that, Oscar. Surely you don't mean to kill us."

Oscar brushed past him and slammed the suitcase shut. He grasped its handle and turned from the desk, the gun raised menacingly. That was when Amos brought down in a clean arcing motion the glass cube paperweight he had been given by Sam Wilson. Oscar's knees buckled and his eyes, bright with surprise for a moment, dulled as he slumped to the floor. Miss Wise found her voice at last and emitted a piercing scream. The gun had slipped from Oscar's hand and Father Dowling kicked it across the room. Amos was on the phone and it was only minutes later that the police arrived.

5

"There is a passage in Aristotle's *Poetics* I have always liked," Father Dowling said to his guests. Amos and Dirk Simmons and Phil Keegan were in the pastor's study, having gone there from the dining room, where Marie had surpassed herself with a celebratory dinner. She stood now in the doorway, not willing to be left out of any explanation of recent events.

"I never read it," Phil said complacently.

"Aristotle speaks of a plot involving a man who is killed when the statue of a man he had murdered falls on him."

Dirk Simmons looked up from lighting his cigar, waiting. Phil Keegan shrugged.

Amos said, "Sam Wilson's glass cube paperweight."

"Poetic irony."

Phil said, "It didn't seem heavy enough to knock him out."

"Thank God I didn't injure him," Amos said.

"I'd like to hear his account of what happened that night," Phil said. He did not have to specify what night he meant. Father Dowling had had several conversations with Oscar, visiting him in the county jail, but he had to regard them as confidential. Accordingly, he was relieved to hear Amos say that Oscar had explained it all to him.

"What happened?" Marie cried, almost in a squeal.

"This is all his story, mind," Amos said. "I tell you only what he told me."

"What did he tell you!" Dirk was as impatient as Marie.

The story Oscar had told Amos was the same one he had told Father Dowling. Both the priest and the lawyer had had some intimation of what occurred on that long-ago evening, but without Oscar's account, it would have remained obscure.

"The suitcase was his," Amos said. "It was filled with his clothes."

"Clothes," Phil emphasized. That is what the scanner had revealed, clothes and nothing else. But it had not told the police that the clothes were a man's, not a woman's.

It was Lydia who had suffered a change of heart, if she had ever really agreed to run away with Oscar. He had concocted the elaborate plan and had assumed she was in agreement. He had shown up at the restaurant and carried his suitcase down into the basement. Lydia was waiting for him there.

"She told him she couldn't go through with it."

Oscar had bet everything on the venture. He had resigned his job. He had rented a car in which to take Lydia away. He had expected to find an eager woman as anxious as he to get going. They talked. He grew more and more angry. He drew her under the stairs, threatening her now. She had to go with him. He loved her. He would do anything for her. She shook her head.

Infuriated, Oscar pulled open the door of the freezer, thinking it was another room, a place where they could talk above a whisper. The blast of cold air told him that it was a freezer. He pushed Lydia inside and followed her. Behind him, the door began to close. He dropped his suitcase and dashed for it, stumbling through and falling. The door swung closed.

"He left her in there?" Marie said in horrified tones.

"He tried to open the door, but apparently he had engaged the lock when he scrambled out and now the door resisted all efforts.

"Why didn't he go for help?"

There were many things that Oscar Gardner might have done on that long-ago evening. He had had decades to think of them all. But at the time, he panicked. All he could think of was to get away. He ran outside and got into the rented car and drove out of Fox River.

He expected to be pursued. He expected to be arrested. In far-off cities he bought Chicago papers, looking for some explanation of the silence. It was months later that he learned that Sam had reported his wife missing.

"Just missing," Amos said. "Sam never drew attention to the fact that Oscar Gardner had disappeared at the same time."

"That's why Sam never searched for her?"

Sam had closed the restaurant, locked up the building, and mourned his lost wife, apparently unaware that she was in the basement freezer all along.

In the doorway, Marie shivered. "How awful."

"The prosecutor doesn't think we have a case," Phil said. "Gardner will be released in a day or two."

"Released!" Marie squealed. "After he's confessed?"

Phil explained to her the difficulties the prosecution would face if Oscar Gardner were brought to trial for a death that had occurred so many years before. Dirk was almost as indignant.

"He ought to be punished."

Punished. It could be argued that Oscar had been punished ever since that dreadful night. There was nothing he could do that would bring Lydia back. His dreams were often interrupted by the sound of a freezer door clicking shut, imprisoning all his hopes. He would remember himself, scratching ineffectually at that door, trying to open it and imagining Lydia on the other side, more desperate than he. He longed to be punished now, but the state would not add to what he had already gone through. He had come home in the expectation of paying at last for his misdeeds. The suitcase should have pointed to him, and he was furious when it looked as if he would go undetected still. He had intended to open the suitcase for the police and explain what its contents signified.

"I suppose he'll get religion now," Marie said with disgust. "That's what they all do."

She was more right than she knew, but Father Dowling did not want to subject Oscar Gardner's interest in the church to Marie's skeptical scrutiny.

"Remember the good thief, Marie."

"I remember the bad one, Father. Don't forget there were two."

Hic Jacet

1

Tom Higgins walked in the cemetery every morning, to prolong his life. From his front door to the cemetery entrance and then following the looping road out beyond the far section where his parents were buried came to three miles. He had clocked it in the car, getting the mileage just right. He wasn't just guessing when he said he had walked three hundred miles since he had the operation.

"Triple bypass. It makes me sound like the interstate."

"Not at your speed," Molly said.

"You should walk with me."

"You're the one who has to fight cholesterol, not me."

"Do you mean I don't have to fight you, only cholesterol?"

She let a dismissive noise suffice for an answer. After forty some years of marriage their communication was curt and coded, but affectionate withal.

"Withal?" Molly said over her shoulder when he expressed the thought aloud.

"Shakespeare."

She shook her head. "Thou shalt love the Lord thy God with all thy heart, with all thy soul, and with all thy might." Molly had volunteered to teach catechism to the parish kids who attended public school. "They're as innocent of the faith as Hottentots, Tom."

This pointed to a vast subject on which they had learned not to encourage one another: the language of the liturgy, sermons, the uneasiness in church that the priest might extemporize in any direction, the army of Eucharistic ministers that doubled the time it took to receive communion . . . Only rarely were they both really irked at the same time, thank God. It was better when Tom could get Molly's mind on other things, or Molly, Tom's. A more satisfying solution had been simpler than they had imagined. They began to attend Mass in the parish where they had grown up, St. Hilary's, and where Father Roger Dowling was now pastor.

The first occasion had been so wonderful they couldn't believe it. The years during which the Church seemed to be engaged in an endless series of somersaults seemed swept away. The church was packed, the congregation reverent, the priest devout, and the sermon was ten structured minutes of commentary on the readings that made old wine seem new and the applications obvious. It was not until the following Wednesday that they dared talk about it.

"I suppose he was just a visitor."

"No, that was Father Dowling, the pastor. I asked Lionel."

"Choo Choo Kelly?"

Tom laughed. It seemed right that Lionel should be remembered by the nickname he bore on the St. Hilary playground years before. The unmarried Kelly had never moved from the family house on Washburn.

"We hit him on a good day," Tom said warningly.

"He's too good to be true."

But they went back the following Sunday and it was every bit as good. So they made a habit of it, although Molly went on teaching catechism to the Hottentots in their parish of record. When the angiograph showed the blocked artery and Tom went in for surgery, it was Father Dowling Molly called to come visit him before the operation.

"We've been attending Mass at St. Hilary's," Molly explained when Father Dowling arrived.

"And came down ill?"

He was as delightful off the altar as he was edifying on it. He came by intensive care several times after the operation. When Tom was sufficiently recovered they again went together to Mass at St. Hilary's. Molly had been going all along, alone. It was during his morning walk in the cemetery that it dawned on Tom what they had to do. He got home in record time and sat puffing at the breakfast table.

"We have to register at St. Hilary's, Molly. We have to become regular parishioners."

"We don't live in the parish."

"I've thought about that."

"Well."

"We'll move back into the old neighborhood."

He had expected opposition, a rehearsal of the obvious arguments against such a move at their age, but Molly fell silent. She came back half an hour later and asked if he was thinking of buying his parents' house.

"Who told you?"

"Told me what?"

"That it's on the market."

Well, it had been. But when they drove to the old neighborhood they were dismayed to find that the house had been sold. A bright prospect for their remaining years seemed to have been snatched from them.

"Do you know what I've been thinking, Molly?"

"What?"

"Of being buried from the Taco Bell." This was their name for their parish of registration.

"Walking in the cemetery is getting to you."

"It concentrates the mind."

Choo Choo Kelly was sitting on his front porch and he leaned forward to see who was in the car that had gone slowly past his place twice. Tom rolled down the window and Molly waved. Choo Choo's mouth dropped open and he staggered to his feet, waving them over to the curb. Tom parked and they went up the stairs to the Kelly house. The climb seemed effortless, as if the remembered setting made them young again. Choo Choo brought them glasses of iced tea. He himself was drinking beer. "I've only got a few left," he explained.

"My folks' house has just been sold again."

"What do you care?"

"Maybe we would have bought it."

"Yeah?"

"You ever been sorry you stayed in this neighborhood?"

Choo Choo looked at Molly as if he had never even considered the question. "You could buy the Prentiss place."

"I don't remember it."

They still didn't remember it after several attempts on Choo Choo's part to evoke its image from their memories. He gave them the address. He had warmed to the subject. Such eagerness in a realtor would have been a professional flaw. They drove past the house on the way home, twice. After a couple of blocks, Molly made a U-turn and they went back yet again. It was what used to be called a bungalow, an almost mansard roof, solid brick, and not too much of a lawn.

"No stairs to climb," Molly observed.

The master bedroom was on the first floor, they discovered when Mrs. Lang the realtor took them through. They made much of that, as if that was the reason for their interest in the house. That night they sat up late explaining to one another how complicated it would be to leave their house and move to another. Mrs. Lang said she could get a buyer for theirs.

"A piece of cake," she emphasized.

They made an offer on the bungalow, far below the asking price. There followed a pro forma effort to lift them to the amount the Prentisses wanted, but Tom and Millie held fast, wondering if they would be saved from the disruptive move by a low bid. But the deal went through. Their house sold a week later. The die was cast.

Tom went through the Prentiss place with the inspector, a young man named Karl with a surprised expression, an indecisive moustache, and a thoroughness that was wearying. He was an engineer and could be relied on to find any structural flaws.

"This room was added on," he said when they were in the sunporch that looked out over the miniature but highly cultivated backyard.

"You think so?"

"No doubt about it."

"It looks as well built as the rest of the house."

"No doubt of that either."

"I wonder when it was done."

Karl thought about it. He shut one eye and looked at the ceiling. "Thirty, thirty-five years ago."

After they had closed on the house and were preparing their things for moving, they went one day, at Lionel Kelly's insistent urging, to the St. Hilary school, which had been turned into a center for senior citizens. Choo Choo informed a little old lady that they had bought the Prentiss place but she shook her head. Assuming she was deaf and hadn't heard, Molly repeated it. And the address.

"But that's the Farrell house," the old woman said in a querulous voice.

Molly and Tom looked at one another. The Farrell house! My God, she was right. But not even Choo Choo seemed to realize that they had bought the house in which Irene Farrell was murdered nearly forty years ago. "Maybe she's right," was the most he would say.

2

In the front parlor of the St. Hilary rectory was a map of the parish with the homes of parishioners marked with a star. In the parish ledgers were recorded names and addresses as well as the passage of good souls through this vale of tears, from baptism through First Communion and Confirmation, on to marriage and more baptisms and then the marriage of children until finally a funeral, seeing a person off to the next world. Marie Murkin did not disdain such visual aids and records, but after all these years she carried the parish around in her head. Not much had gone on during her long tenure as parish housekeeper that she did not know.

"The Farrells?" Marie replied to Father Dowling's question. The pastor had just returned from the school and doubtless there was a connection between that visit and his question. "Father Dowling, that was before my time."

"That long ago?"

Marie did not rise to the bait of his teasing. "How long ago do you think it was?"

"I'm not even sure what 'it' is?"

Marie waved him to a chair at the kitchen table. She refused to complain about her legs but she was intent on giving them less reason to complain about her.

"There was a murder. A daughter in her teens was brutally murdered."

"At home?"

"The body was found in old Asbury Park, which was where the interstate is now."

"Who did it?"

"Well, her boyfriend was never seen again. They searched the country for him, but he had disappeared from the face of the earth. Some thought he had joined the army and gone off to Vietnam to fight."

"Where did you learn all these things?"

It was not a question Marie could easily answer. Her sources had been many, most of them dead. But not all. "Lionel Kelly, for one."

"I don't know him."

"Small wonder. He hasn't been to church for years."

"Have you noticed the elderly couple that has been coming to Mass over the last few months, the Higgins?"

"Their families lived in the parish."

"They've bought the Farrell house."

"Glory be to God."

"Amen," Father Dowling said, and was willing to let the matter go. After all, Marie's information, however exhaustive and detailed, was secondhand. Nor did he need to know more about the house, of which it was said, according to Marie, that it was haunted. He was not at all inclined to encourage her credulity along those lines.

The Higgins moved into the house and asked Father Dowling to bless their newly acquired bungalow, which he dutifully did. It was the couple's plan to go through the house a room at a time and redecorate, so it looked as if they would be more than occupied by their new home. But first they wanted to extend the sunroom.

"The daughter of the family who lived here was murdered," Molly Higgins said. She had the air of a woman who would not hesitate to look a problem in the eye.

"Did you know her?"

"We knew the parents, the way younger people would. Not well."

"I understand it happened in a park that no longer exists."

"Who told you that?" Tom Higgins asked eagerly.

"Marie Murkin, my housekeeper."

Tom sat back. "This was before her time."

"You left the parish before Marie became housekeeper?"

They had. "Our memories of the parish are antediluvian," Tom Higgins said, and Father Dowling laughed.

"I'm being literal, Father. The Fox River flooded, water rose several feet above our first floor. Have you ever seen the marks on buildings in Florence that record the flood heights of the Arno?"

"What did you do before you retired?" Father Dowling asked.

"Retired? I'm not retired. I'm self-employed."

"That's like having a fool for a client," Molly said.

"What does that make my partner?"

"Don't get me started."

They were a caustic comfortable couple and Father Dowling liked them. Tom Higgins was a writer of nonfiction books for younger readers.

"I become an instant expert in whatever my agent wants and write it up as a book for kids."

He pointed at the shelves where the colorful jackets of his work filled shelf after shelf of a sizeable bookcase.

Before leaving, Father Dowling had persuaded Tom to give a talk to the people who came to the parish center.

"We'll do it together," Tom said. "Molly really is my partner. I still do everything in longhand."

"Even his book on computers."

It was a week later that the two of them came to the rectory to tell the pastor of St. Hilary's what they had discovered in the yard just outside the sunroom.

"The rock garden has to be moved."

"He shouldn't be lifting," Molly said to Father Dowling.

"There's more rolling than lifting."

The rock garden contained a basin into which water ran and then was recycled in a way Tom seemed eager to explain. Molly put a hand on her husband's arm. "You can give him your book on fountains. Tell him what you found."

Tom got squared in his chair. "There is a body buried beneath the rock garden."

"A body."

"Bones. Human bones. I know." Another book?

"Have you told the police?"

"It's a skeleton, Father. Not a corpse. Our question is, should we report it at all?"

Father Dowling thought about it. "You should talk to Amos Cadbury."

"Who is he?"

"A lawyer."

"Our concern was more religious, Father. To take those bones further out in the yard and rebury them, well, that doesn't sound right."

"We wondered if . . ."

His blessing of the house had suggested the idea to them, apparently. Might he not come out and conduct a private burial ceremony for the skeleton they had found beneath the rock garden behind their new house?

"Let me think about it. I'd like your permission to talk to some others about this. In confidence, of course."

"Cadbury?"

"And another friend of mine. Phil Keegan. He's captain of detectives downtown."

Tom and Molly exchanged a look. "I suppose it was foolish to think we could just cover this up."

"Or bury it?"

The two old people looked at him with appreciation.

3

Marie Murkin followed with foreboding the decision of the Higgenses to buy the cottage in which the Prentiss family had lived. It had been the Prentiss house for only half a dozen years and before that a series of families had come and gone in the house that Tom and Molly Higgins called the Farrell place. That was what the oldsters at the parish center called it too, as if none of the intervening families had laid sufficient claim to it. Only Lionel Kelly had called it the Prentiss house.

Marie was surprised to find Choo Choo among the others at the center. Oh, he was old enough, she supposed, although she did not like to think about what the qualifying age for senior citizenship was. Any number would be an average anyway, applicable to others, but not to her. Retirement was as far from Marie's mind as going into the real estate business.

"It's an unlucky house," someone said in an odd voice.

"Haunted."

"No one stays in the house long enough to . . ."

But the voices fell silent at the approach of Molly Higgins. Marie took comfort from Molly's cool, no-nonsense manner. This was not a woman to wonder whether there were ghosts prowling about the premises.

"Where's Lionel Kelly," she asked.

"Choo Choo? He never comes here."

"He promised to meet us here."

"He is here! There. He's playing shuffleboard."

And so he was, his great bulk looking oddly graceful as he pushed the puck across the sanded floor. A great "Oh!" went up. He had managed to knock his opponent off the board and advance his own position. He looked around with surprised delight at the applauding onlookers. Molly took his arm and led him away. Marie kept within earshot.

"Choo Choo, why didn't you tell us that it was the Farrell house?"

"What difference does that make?"

"None. Not to Tom and me, but it might to others. Besides, we had never heard of the Prentisses."

"Molly, you saw the house, you both did. You liked it. You bought it. What difference does it make what I called it?"

"I already told you. None. But I am curious about whatever happened there. Tom is making a little research project of it."

Choo Choo frowned. "It was all in the papers."

"Of course he'll start there. What was the name of the murderer?"

"The guy who ran away? Aaron. Aaron Watkins."

"Did you know him?"

"I knew who he was. We were classmates right here. He became a mechanic."

"What was he like?"

When Choo Choo tipped back his head, his eyes fell on Marie Murkin. Marie followed instinct and marched up to Choo Choo and Molly.

"Father Dowling tells me that your husband has agreed to give a talk here."

"It would have been hard to refuse."

Marie smiled up at Choo Choo. "And you must come, Lionel." A little pause. "It wouldn't be like coming to church."

She left the flustered Choo Choo and the somewhat puzzled Molly Higgins and set off for the rectory. Let the fallen-away Lionel Kelly explain to Molly why he had stopped coming to church.

"Stopped?" Father Dowling said, when she recounted the episode in the center to him. "I don't remember ever seeing him in church."

"He must have gone at one time."

"You're sure he's Catholic?"

"You could look him up in your ledger."

Lionel Kelly showed up several times in the parish records. Baptism, First Communion, Confirmation. And he had been an altar boy. A yellowing bulletin indicated that he had served Mass along with Aaron Watkins.

"They were in the same class," Marie said.

"Guessing?"

"No."

"How did you learn that?"

But she smiled enigmatically and drifted back to the kitchen. A magician does not reveal his secrets.

4

"How long ago?" Phil Keegan asked in disbelief.

A cooperative reporter at the Fox River *Tribune* had sent Father Dowling printouts of the relevant issues from the paper's microfilm archives. Irene Farrell's body had been found in Asbury Park and soon the search was on for Aaron Watkins, the young man she had been seeing against her parents' wishes. Watkins had repaired the young woman's car, and love had bloomed among the grease guns and racks of Foley's Ford. Irene was a college girl of great promise, president of her class at River Forest. The Farrells felt their daughter should be interested in young men with interests and talents closer to her own. Aaron had not returned to his rooming house on the night of the murder and the theory was that, in guilt or panic or both, he had run. The story went on for weeks and then faded and was gone.

"What's this got to do with the body under the rock garden?"

"Cy tells me that Dr. Pippen is looking into the matter unofficially. The owners of the house hope the matter can be kept from the media."

"Pippen," Phil repeated with misgiving in his voice.

"You probably have the same thought I do."

"What's that?"

"That the skeleton is that of Aaron Watkins."

"Did you suggest that to Pippen?"

"Oh, it was her first reaction."

"Roger, what's your point? You want two murders instead of one, but where are the murderers? Gone to where the victims went long ago. The chance of getting any presentable evidence after all these years . . ." Phil waved his hand, as if to chase these thoughts away. "I am not going to devote the resources of my department to a maybe murder of thirty years ago."

"I was hoping you would say that. So were the Higginses."

"The who?"

"Molly and Tom Higgins, the new owners of the house. They found the skeleton."

"Why didn't they just keep quiet?"

"They think there should be a Christian burial if it is Aaron Watkins. Apparently he was an altar boy at St. Hilary's before he became a mechanic at Foley Ford."

"And they want you to do it?"

"The body was found in my parish."

The body was indeed that of Aaron Watkins, as his dental records proved. But Dr. Pippen wore a little frown as she said it. "It's more difficult to determine time of death. There are some broken bones and the skull was worked over with something sharp and heavy."

"That sounds like a lot."

"Well, it's something. But don't you wonder how a body could have been buried that shallowly near a house and not attract notice? I mean, death means corruption and corruption means . . ."

But the rock garden had running water and there were plants

and all the outside olfactory competition. Dr. Pippen conceded the point with reluctance.

Amos Cadbury brought the tips of his fingers together and worked his mouth a moment before he began to speak. What he had to say emerged from a long lifetime of experience in the practice of the law during which he had attained that wisdom which, expecting little by way of heroism of himself or his fellow man, often laid him open to surprise at what men and women might do in moments of stress.

"I knew Jamison Farrell, Father Dowling. He was a lawyer in this city. He survived his daughter by three years and I was the executor of his estate. Among his effects was a long letter in which he told of the devastating effect on him of his daughter's murder. It was a blow from which he never recovered."

"How did he himself die?"

"He committed suicide."

"God rest his soul."

"Indeed, indeed. I have had Masses offered for him to that end over the years. Did I mention that he was a member of this firm? The manner of his going caused us no end of trouble, as you can imagine. Jamison's clients particularly had to be reassured. Many feared that he had been a speculator and their fortunes were at risk. The fate of his poor daughter occurred to very few of them. Odd, isn't it, that the one thing that obsessed Jamison had faded from the memories of others."

"Was there any great revelation in his letter to you?"

"Such as?"

"Did he offer any clue as to how Aaron Watkins's body ended up beneath the rock garden in his yard."

"Yes, he did."

Father Dowling waited. A rictus of pain had momentarily twisted the normally implacable countenance of the lawyer. He looked at Father Dowling from the far end of decades of experience of human folly.

"He identified the young man's murderer."

"Himself?"

The lawyer shook his head. "Oh, no. No, that wasn't it at all. He had become convinced that his wife had killed the young man."

No wonder Cadbury spoke in such sepulchral tones of that long-ago day. His erstwhile partner was dead, a suicide; still grief stricken at his daughter's death three years earlier, but he had gone to his death in the conviction that his wife had killed Aaron Watkins. Cadbury picked up the pages that had lain before him on his desk and handed them to the priest. Father Dowling looked at the firmly written lines, the ink periodically darkening, then fading, until the nib was once more dipped in ink. This was not the nervous scrawl of a hysteric about to take his own life. Somewhere among Jamison Farrell's effects there must have been a certificate attesting to his mastery of the Palmer Method of Penmanship.

On the night Irene was murdered but before we received the terrible news, Aaron Watkins came to our door. I refused to speak to him. I ordered him from my house. Mrs. Farrell laid a restraining hand on my arm, as well she might have. I was about to smite this insolent pup who persisted in pursuing my daughter. Irene refused to see him for what he was. She had driven away the young man she had hitherto favored. And for this ruffian! "I will speak to him," Josephine said. Could she accomplish by sweetness what I had failed to bring about by threats? I went out to my car and drove aimlessly for an hour. When I returned there was a police car at the curb and the worst experience of my life was about to begin.

There followed a graphic description of being taken to the

scene of the murder to identify his daughter, the endless questioning by police, the newspaper and radio reporters, the nationwide search for the absconded Watkins. And then, after making a firm line across two-thirds of the page, Farrell began again.

Amos, I now know why the young man was never found. That night, while I was out driving, he too was killed and in my own house. All these years he has been lying in unconsecrated soil in my backyard, beneath the rock garden put up in memory of Irene. A strange odor that I had noticed for some time was no longer a mystery. It was while I was moving rocks to get at the garden's water supply that my pick unearthed a human hand. I proceeded more carefully but I think I knew from the beginning whose body it was I had discovered. The realization came to me like a flash of light. Josephine had been more opposed to Irene's interest in Aaron Watkins than I had been. Somehow she had managed to kill him and drag his body into the yard. Hysterical mothers can lift the vehicles that pin their child. But Josephine would have done calmly what she felt had to be done. I have said nothing. I covered up the dreadful thing but I cannot confront her with my discovery. I cannot live with this terrible knowledge either. Amos, I entrust the disposition of the matter to you. You will know the wise and prudent thing to do.

Father Dowling returned the pages to the desktop. "What was the wise and prudent thing to do?"

"Nothing."

"Ah."

"Jamison's death made Josephine almost autistic with grief. Her hair turned white, or perhaps she simply stopped dyeing it. In any case, overnight she became an old woman. I asked myself what earthly good could be accomplished by acting on her husband's guess."

"Guess?"

"What else was it, after all?"

"You have some other explanation of the young man's body ending up beneath the rock garden in the Farrell backyard?"

"I treated that as hearsay."

"But now the Higgenses have discovered the body."

"There are so many things I cannot explain."

"Did you ever speak to Mrs. Farrell about it?"

"Not to this day."

"This day? Is she still alive?"

"At St. Paul's Nursing Home."

5

Father Dowling drove slowly up the drive to St. Paul's Nursing Home. He was not a stranger to this last station on life's way. But he had never visited Mrs. Farrell. Of course he would have, if someone had told him she had lived in St. Hilary's. But she had been here for so long, perhaps no one remembered where she had come from. Her large wary eyes met his when he stood in the doorway of her room.

"Mrs. Farrell?"

She said nothing. He crossed the room to the chair she sat in, her eyes following his progress. He sat beside her.

"I am Father Dowling. From St. Hilary's. I am pastor there."

His visit was a long monologue. But that was considered to be the most one could do for one in her condition. Talk reassuringly, give news of the outside world, say nothing to upset her.

"Does she ever speak?"

The nurse had the harried look of someone who dared not sit for fear of being summoned. "Not really."

"But she can?"

The nurse's name was Lobkowicz. She seemed unsure. But

her job was to care for the patients, not to analyze them. In any case, she would not have had time to sit and chat with any patient, let alone one as mute as Josephine Farrell.

"I have offered Mass for you," he said on the second visit.

The great eyes registered no reaction.

"And for Irene and Jamison too." He had decided that such remarks could not disturb her if she did not understand them. But her reaction indicated that she did understand. Her eyes moistened and tears began to form in their corners.

"And now I shall pray for the man whose body was found buried behind your house."

The old woman gasped and her skeletal hands gripped the arms of her chair.

"Aaron Watkins," Father Dowling said.

"Oh, my God."

"You knew he was buried there, didn't you?"

The reticence of years trembled in the balance and then she began to nod vigorously. "Yes, yes, yes, of course I knew."

The floodgates opened then. The nurse came into the room and looked with astonishment at the old woman, animated by grief. Father Dowling took her hand and hers tightened on his. It might have been a bony hand emerging from the soil, clinging to him, begging to be pulled back into the light. He nodded to the nurse and she went squeakily away.

"God is merciful, Josephine."

"I know, I know. But there are some sins . . ."

"All sins can be forgiven."

"I want to think that. I believe it. But . . ."

"How long has it been since your last confession?"

The question puzzled her.

"This conversation can be your confession, Josephine. Put yourself in God's hands. God is mercy."

"But can I confess for him?"

113

It was Father Dowling's turn to be surprised. He sat there for a minute without speaking, wondering what she had meant. Perhaps he had been wrong to think she had emerged so easily into clarity of mind after so many years of elected silence.

"Tell me what happened, Josephine."

Her account did not have the clarity and straightforwardness of her husband's, but then he had been composing a narrative for his partner Amos Cadbury to read. Josephine just let the words come. What she had to say was significantly different from what Father Dowling had read in Amos Cadbury's office.

As in Jamison Farrell's letter to Cadbury, Aaron had come to the house. Her husband threatened to throw the mechanic out on his ear, but Josephine had calmed him. She would appeal to him as a mother. He must see that her daughter's promising future would come to nothing if she succumbed to Aaron.

"He said he loved her, of course. He thought that was enough."

Father Dowling listened to her jumbled account of the conversation she had had with Aaron Watkins. He agreed he was not good enough for Irene. But Irene insisted. She had told Lionel. She must have told him.

"Lionel?"

"The worst of it was that he was right. If it had been a play or a story, the sympathy of the audience would have been with him. I was the stupid old mother, standing in the way of true love. I think that infuriated me more than anything else, knowing we were wrong to oppose this."

"How did he die?"

"The sirens sounded then, coming closer. I think I already sensed they were bringing horrible news. When they stopped in front of the house, Aaron started to go out to them, but I pulled him back and told him to leave."

"And he did?"

"He went back through the house and out the back door."

Father Dowling looked closely at the old lady, but her expression was that of someone trying to remember exactly. That long ago evening seemed to be playing like a film in her head. He could hear the sirens. With her he opened the door to the police. How much time had passed before they made clear to her what had happened? But they had begun with questions about Irene. When had she last seen her?

"Last seen her! And I had seen her for the last time without realizing it. And we had quarreled."

"About Aaron."

"Yes."

"What happened to Aaron?"

"Amos Cadbury knows. Jamison wrote him a letter before killing himself."

"I have read it."

She opened her hands. "Then you know."

"Jamison said that you had killed Aaron."

She shook her head, the mildly corrective movement of a schoolteacher. "No, no. I found the body in the yard. Can you imagine, he had left it lying where it fell. I saw in a moment what had happened. Of course I couldn't leave the body there."

"So you buried it."

"Yes."

"And Jamison helped you?"

"When he saw what I was doing, he helped me, yes. Neither of us said a word about how the body of that boy had come to be there. But Jamison's manner told me all I needed to know."

"You think he killed Aaron."

"Father, dreadful as that was, it was forgivable. But to kill himself . . ."

And so the visit ended with him consoling the widow who thought her husband had been a murderer as well as a suicide.

And the husband had written solemnly that he believed his wife had killed their daughter's unwelcome suitor. They could not both be right. But could they both be wrong?

6

Father Dowling sat with the Higgenses on their front porch after the reburial ceremony, sipping the hot chocolate that Molly had made.

"The backyard has lost some of its charm for us."

"I used to walk in the cemetery every morning," Tom said.

His wife made a face. "Now you won't even have to leave home."

It was early evening but darkness had fallen. The little ceremony in the backyard had been conducted in the gloaming. Amos Cadbury's response to Father Dowling's formal question as to the legality of what he proposed to do had been uncharacteristic. He covered his eyes, then his ears, then his mouth. That was his answer.

Phil Keegan had laughed mirthlessly when asked if he intended to try to resolve the conflicting stories of Josephine and Jamison Farrell as to what had happened to Aaron Watkins in their backyard the night their daughter Irene was found murdered in Asbury Park.

"Do you want me to send Cy Horvath out to St. Paul's nursing home and have him grill the old lady?"

"If she said anything it would be that she thinks her husband did it."

"And he said that she did."

"But they buried the body together."

"In a flowerbed below the windows of the sunroom."

"Not a smart way to get rid of a guy they couldn't stand."

"Kill him?"

"Bury him under their noses."

Cy Horvath, acting unofficially, had helped collect the bones beneath the rock garden, placing them in a wooden crate. Thus were the bones of St. Anthony kept in the cathedral at Padua, worn smooth with veneration and carefully stored away. Father Dowling had seen a photograph of a recent opening of the repository. Mitered prelates seemed to be elbowing one another to get a glimpse of the contents of the casket. But their predecessors had sorted and stacked the bones.

Tom and Cy lowered the crate into the hole that had been dug at the end of the yard, and it was there that Father Dowling called down the mercy of God on the remains of Aaron Watkins. It was distracting to wonder about the circumstances of the young man's death at that moment. Cy shoveled the dirt back into the hole, covering the crate, and Tom eased a stone onto the tamped-down dirt.

"Maybe I'll take Choo Choo up on his offer to relocate the rock garden here."

They crossed the yard to where the rock garden now was. Water sputtered from a vertical pipe, trickling into the concrete basin. The overflow was carried around behind the basin and eventually would emerge once more from the pipe.

"You'd have to run water out there," Cy said.

"There's a sprinkling system. Maybe we could tap into that."

"Does Choo Choo know how to build a rock garden?"

"Anyone can build a rock garden," Tom said.

"You've written about them, not built one," Molly said.

At the edge of the concrete basis there was an inscription. Father Dowling leaned over to read it. "LK 1973."

"Choo Choo," Tom explained. "He built it as a memorial to Irene Farrell."

"That was thoughtful."

"I think he had a crush on her," Molly said.

Cy couldn't stay for chocolate, so the three of them adjourned to the front porch.

"Do you regret moving back into your old neighborhood?" Father Dowling asked.

"As long as there are no more grisly surprises."

"It's good to be in St. Hilary's," Molly said.

Her tone suggested that she would like to go on. Father Dowling had heard something of their grievances with the parish from which they had come. He had no reason to doubt what they said. Nor was he able to explain why such aberrations went on. But that wasn't his job. His job was to be pastor of St. Hilary's and he must do it as best he could. That is what he would be held accountable for, not the general state of the church in North America.

7

The turnout when Tom and Molly spoke at the parish center was historic. Husband and wife bantered with one another and it was as much a comic routine as an informative presentation. Molly had the foresight to bring a supply of books, and afterward Tom sat signing them for those who wished to present them to their grandchildren. Tom might write books for young adults but there had been nothing condescending in the way he had spoken to his audience. Marie Murkin led a somewhat embarrassed Lionel Kelly up to Father Dowling.

"The lost sheep has been found," she announced triumphantly.

"I just came for the talk," Lionel protested.

Father Dowling led him away. "Marie has a missionary impulse but she means well."

The lights along the walk that led to the rectory were on. Father Dowling pointed to a bench and they sat down. Choo Choo eased his considerable bulk down with a puffing effort. He looked around and nodded.

"It's the same, only different. These lights are new, aren't they?"

"And the bench."

"That's a good use for the school. I wish it was still a school, but this is better than shutting it down."

"You went to school here, didn't you?"

"Yes."

"And served as an altar boy."

"We still had to memorize the Latin then."

"Introibo ad altare Dei."

"Ad deum qui laetificat iuventutem meam." Choo Choo's mouth fell open. "Now how did I remember that?"

"Why do they call you Choo Choo?"

"Did you ever have a train when you were a kid?"

Of course. "Lionel Trains."

"That was Irene's nickname for me."

"Irene Farrell."

"We were classmates here."

"Along with Aaron Watkins."

Choo Choo lowered his chin to his chest. He might have been commemorating his dead classmates. Father Dowling let the silence prolong itself and then said, "I wonder where we might put a rock garden here."

Choo Choo looked at him.

"You made a rock garden for the Farrells, didn't you?"

"How did you know that?"

"I noticed your initials."

"It was a kind of memorial."

"For Aaron."

Choo Choo frowned. "For Irene."

"Tell me what happened."

"What do you mean, what happened?"

"Have you ever visited Mrs. Farrell. She's at St. Paul's Home.

All these years she has been convinced that her husband killed Aaron."

Choo Choo shook his head. "Why would she think that?"

"He thought she did it."

He told the huge man of the letter Jamison Farrell had written for his lawyer to read.

"Why are you telling me this?"

"I think you know."

"Yeah?"

"Both Mr. and Mrs. Farrell can't be right. They buried the body together."

"I know. I found it when I put up the rock garden."

"And said nothing."

"What was there to say?"

"If neither of the Farrells killed the boy they buried, someone else did. Someone who was as upset as they were about Irene's going with Aaron. Did you kill Irene too?"

The huge man pushed at the priest and then tried to heave to his feet. He teetered forward but couldn't raise himself to a standing position. He plumped down on the bench again and it rocked backward. Father Dowling managed to get off before it toppled backward, rendering Lionel Kelly as helpless as a turtle.

Back along the walk the lighted school was visible and the sound of voices drifted on the night air. Father Dowling knelt beside Lionel.

"I can't get up by myself."

"None of us can, Lionel. But the help we need is always there for the asking. Tell me what you did, tell me as a priest."

"Confession?"

"God wants you back, Lionel. He wants you more than anyone."

The lost sheep Marie had called him, speaking more truly than she knew. Lionel had stalked his rival after killing Irene in

Asbury Park, tracking him to the Farrells. When Aaron emerged, Lionel fell upon him and killed him. He looked at Father Dowling with an awed look in his eyes.

"I seemed to be someone else. These things seem something someone else did."

Father Dowling did not encourage this effort to attribute the dreadful deeds to some mysterious other. That other is ourselves, and Lionel knew it. He had darted into the shadows when Mrs. Farrell came outside, perhaps to see if Aaron had gone. She let out a cry when she discovered the body.

"But right away she started to dig. Then he came along and they buried the body in the flowerbed beneath the windows."

"Where you built the rock garden?"

"I kept thinking of someone finding the body."

Lionel was not in the most dignified position to confess his sins and receive the pardon of the Lord, but that is what happened. He had finished when Cy Horvath came along the walkway.

"Hey what happened?"

"Give me a hand with Lionel, will you, Cy. This bench fell over."

Cy had Lionel on his feet with one great tug. He was lifting the bench when the penitent looked the priest in the eye. "Should I tell him?"

What could human justice add to the divine mercy? At most there would be a flurry in the media, a prurient recalling of a long-ago murder in a park that no longer existed. Choo Choo could shout his guilt at the top of his lungs and nothing would come of it. The police would not devote their finite resources to investigating a slaying that had long since passed into the record books. Whether or not there was a statute of limitations on murder, evidence disappeared, witnesses died, nothing could be known with certainty.

Father Dowling once more took Lionel's elbow and steered him toward the rectory. Over his shoulder he thanked Cy for his help. To Choo Choo, he said, "I don't think it will be necessary to mention this to anyone else, Lionel."

PAST TIMES

1

Mrs. Spenlow sat in the sun-filled plant room of the home in which she had lived her long life, raised her family, and now awaited, as she supposed, final extinction. The future, if any, was not a matter to which she devoted much thought. Her aim as she sat in the beam of light which, as Catherine might explain, had traveled an unimaginable distance through total darkness to be finally filtered through the earth's atmosphere to become light and heat, lay warmly on Mrs. Spenlow in her sunporch. She was surrounded by her plants, Maurice her canary twittered in his cage, all was a mindless peace, the state for which the old woman strove as she sat mornings in the sun.

There was the sound of Catherine in the kitchen. "Where is the cream?"

"In the fridge," Mrs. Spenlow called patiently.

"That's *real* cream."

Catherine, her granddaughter, just starting off in life, was staying with Mrs. Spenlow until she was ready to take an apartment in town. The drive from Fox River to the Loop that Catherine took on weekdays was one that Mrs. Spenlow preferred not to think about. Once intrepid pioneers had faced less physical danger crossing the continent than the average commuting suburbanite confronted daily.

"*Your* cream is there too. Behind the juice."

Catherine was a fierce advocate of the simple life, of return-

123

ing to nature and sealing herself off from the modern world. In practice this meant that she was much given to chemically prepared substitutes for allegedly lethal packaged foods. Dairy products were particularly perilous and she substituted a creamer.

"Remember Thoreau on vegetarianism," Mrs. Spenlow advised.

"Thoreau?"

Dear God, was the author unknown to Catherine? She could not get used to her granddaughter's illiteracy. Admonished that he could not live without meat, Thoreau had pointed to a cow. But Catherine could scarcely invoke the cow in her war against milk and cream. She was a graduate of a college that ranked among the top ten in the nation yet she seemed as innocent of history and literature as any member of the tribes of natives that had roamed this region centuries before. Catherine came barefoot onto the sunporch now, holding a bowl filled with some preparation she bought in health stores. She bent over her grandmother and planted a wet kiss on her forehead.

Catherine in her youth and naiveté was a reminder of mortality, of how many years it had been since Margaret Spenlow had brimmed with energy and looked with boundless curiosity about the world. Catherine wiped some artificial cream from the corner of her mouth, then rubbed at Mrs. Spenlow's forehead, apparently to remove a similar blemish. When she sat, she studied her grandmother for a moment, chewing methodically.

"Can we talk about the family tree now?"

Mrs. Spenlow sighed. It mystified her that a young girl should have such an obsession with the past of the family. Such curiosity was new, at least among the Spenlows. Harry had often warned about what polecats might be found in the branches of the family tree.

"I quote my father," he had said.

Margaret Spenlow had never met her husband's father. His mother had been a wispy presence at the wedding and then gone off to California to live with Harry's sister. Or not to live. Within months word came of her death. In those days, it would have been difficult to go that far for a funeral, but it turned out that it had already taken place. Just like that, Harry's past seemed to have evanesced. It was what they both had wanted, it seemed. Margaret Spenlow had been an only child, orphaned early and raised by strangers. Meeting Harry Spenlow had been a fairy-tale rescue from the bleak prospects of her life.

All that was so many years ago. Catherine was the daughter of Hugh Spenlow, Margaret's only child, who lived in Houston but whose head, as a NASA scientist, was in the stars. Catherine had developed a deep curiosity about her roots and spent hours at her computer tapping genealogical databases, trying to discover a connection between the British Spenlows and the stock from which she sprang.

"If we were Irish, there would be help available."

Apparently the Irish government catered to the atavistic curiosity of those who were generations removed from the Old Sod and nostalgically sought to connect with the country their ancestors had fled.

"Tell me about my great grandfather."

"I have told you, Catherine. I never met him."

"But what did Grandpa tell you about him?"

"Harry was a source of aphorisms, not family information."

"Where did Grandpa grow up?"

"He was raised right here in Fox River."

"Do you have his birth certificate?"

Margaret sighed. "It must be somewhere."

"In the attic? May I look?"

There was no birth certificate for Harry Spenlow in the attic. "I did find a marriage license, though."

"Good Lord."

"It says my great-grandparents were married at St. Hilary's. Isn't that a Catholic church?"

2

Young Gerry Krause, Captain Phil Keegan's nephew, was visiting Fox River and was often in the rectory, talking with the pastor of his intention of pursuing graduate work in theology. Father Dowling did not actively discourage the idea, but then he thought that Gerry might have a vocation to the priesthood and that this explained his interest in theology.

"Most theologians are laypeople now, Father."

"Are they really?"

"It's just another academic discipline."

Marie Murkin could tell that it cost the pastor much not to express his dismay at this fallen condition of a once-great discipline. Marie had no opinion about theology but she was certain Gerry was not meant to be a priest. Accordingly, when Catherine Spenlow showed up at the rectory, Marie regarded her visit as providential, a sign that Gerry was not meant for the altar, at least not in the sense Father Dowling imagined.

Marie was returning from the parish center when she saw the young woman get out of her car and then look hesitatingly around. Marie left the walk and headed across the lawn.

"I'm not sure where to go," the young woman said when Marie approached her.

"Well, there's the church and there's the parish center, but you're not old enough for that, it's for seniors. And there's the rectory."

"I want to ask about a wedding."

Marie felt a twinge of disappointment. The thought that she might deflect Gerry from clerical dreams by introducing him to this lovely young person went.

"Is your fiancé with you?"

The young woman's laughter rivaled birdsong in joyousness. Marie found herself laughing too.

"I want to check up on my great-grandparents' wedding."

"Come along."

Marie took the girl's arm and started toward the rectory. "I am Marie Murkin."

"Catherine Spenlow. Are you the parish secretary?"

Marie could not decide whether this would be a promotion or the opposite. "You'll want to talk to Father Dowling."

And then, as if in proof that there is a God and his eye is on the sparrow, Gerry burst from the rectory and came running toward them. Marie stopped, to give Catherine a good look at Gerry.

"Marie, Father Dowling wants you."

"What is it?" Marie asked soothingly. She liked the suggestion that panic ensued when she stepped outside for a moment.

"The oven's buzzing and he doesn't know what to do."

Good grief! She had a cake in and had forgotten all about it. She cut across the lawn toward the rectory, calling over her shoulder.

"Gerry, her name is Catherine."

3

There were two kinds of boy, those who didn't notice her and those who did. Unfortunately the ones who did were the ones she wished didn't and vice versa. This made Gerry an unusual case. His smile was warm and receptive; he was tall and trim and roughly good-looking. The only way she could retain her two categories was to imagine that if she had a girlfriend with her Gerry's interest would have passed her by.

"She's kind of nuts."

"Marie?"

"She's the housekeeper."

"She was going to help me."

"I think she delegated me."

"I came to ask about a wedding." She waited and sure enough there was a little flicker of disappointment in his eyes. "My great-grandparents." His full interest returned. "I found their wedding certificate and they were married here and I wondered if I could find out more about them."

"Come on."

He didn't take her arm as Marie had, but they headed for the rectory. The aroma of over-baked cake came toward them as they neared the house. Marie had placed the blackened result of her oversight on the back porch, where it gave off a kind of charred sweetness. She looked shamefacedly at them.

"I haven't done a thing like this in twenty years."

"Can't you scrape it?" Gerry asked, but she just gave him a look.

"Father is in his study. I told him you were coming."

Catherine followed Gerry through the kitchen. Had she ever met a priest before? She was sure she hadn't. Her only experience of them had been on the screen or in books and she had no idea what they were like in the flesh. The man behind the desk in the study was no Tom Bosley. Of course he was scarcely visible through the cloud of pipe smoke. She liked it that he didn't apologize for smoking when he rose and extended his hand. After all, this was his house.

"My great-grandparents were married here. My hope is that you have records that will tell me a little more about them."

"Thanks to Gerry, that'll be less trouble than it once would have been."

Apparently the records had been turned into a computer database by Gerry.

"Were they Spenlows?"

"Yes."

"Gerry, why don't you show off your handiwork?"

But Father Dowling came with them down the hall to a smaller room, where the computer was. Within minutes, by a magic of which they themselves could not have dreamed, the names of Sarah Harrison and Jason Spenlow formed on the screen.

"Where's Morley?" Gerry asked, when it emerged that the groom gave his home as Morley.

"North of here. On the river."

"Have you every been there?"

"I had the sad task of closing the church there."

With modern transportation, the shortage of priests, and the meagerness of the Catholic population in Morley, the archdiocese had decided that it was an unaffordable luxury to keep St. Jude's open.

"St. Jude's," Marie Murkin said, in a keening voice.

"Patron of lost causes."

"All causes are lost causes."

"Only in the short term, Marie," Father Dowling said, but he seemed almost pleased by the housekeeper's melancholy.

"Don't you remember the group that tried to save the church at Morley?"

"A loyal remnant."

"Hmph. I don't see many of them coming here for Mass."

It was true that, feeling abandoned by the Church that was closing their parish, some Morley Catholics had done some abandoning of their own. Father Dowling had tried in vain to reconcile them to the closing of St. Jude's, but without complete success. The truth was that he sympathized with their anger. Why was there a shortage of priests? If he had an assistant, they could have taken turns and driven over to say Mass each Sunday at Morley, even if there wasn't a priest in residence there. But the Church had a long way to go before it came out of the prolonged slump She had been in for over a quarter of a century. Decades of dissent and discontent had taken their toll on the faithful. If Catholicism was something you could construct to your own specifications, adhesion to it weakened and faith thinned down to a minimum that did not offer sustenance.

"I wonder if there's any point in my going to Morley?" Catherine asked.

"I could take you there," Gerry offered.

She was obviously grateful but a pained look appeared. "I couldn't go until Saturday."

"So we'll go Saturday."

Gerry walked her out to her car and Marie came in and out of Father Dowling's study, humming. It sounded like "Those Wedding Bells Are Breaking Up That Old Gang of Mine," but Marie's unsure sense of pitch made it difficult to tell.

Left alone, pipe relit, Father Dowling found it difficult to shake off thoughts of Morley and St. Jude's. The Hoovers, Will and Madge, had organized the protesting group that had behaved civilly at first, sending a petition to the chancery laying out the history of the parish, pledging increased financial support. But the decision had been made and that was that. It was then that the Hoovers, Oliver Foster, and several other couples got really angry. Father Dowling failed in his attempt to stop them from protesting publicly. Will and Madge got hold of the cardinal's schedule and followed him from place to place, raising angry placards.

"It's not right, Father," Madge said, stamping her foot.

Will nodded fiercely. "Why should people be loyal to a Church that treats them like this?"

This was the way little schisms started, parishes breaking away, claiming to be "real" Catholics. If their priest went with them, the schism might last as long as he did, but there were cases where the schismatic priest ordained someone, often his son, and the thing went on for a generation or two. But there was no way the Hoovers could continue St. Jude's without a priest. The other protestors eventually saw that, just or unjust, they had to accept the decision. One couldn't be a Catholic without a bishop.

From time to time, Father Dowling visited Morley and he always stopped by Hoover's Hardware. The store had been moved to a mall from its original location on Main Street in historic Morley. Will's disposition improved after he sold the store and decided to become the historian of Morley. He spent much of his time in the courthouse and library, piecing together the history of the little town that had formed on the west bank of the Fox River in the mid-nineteenth century. He had collected papers and diaries from the older families, promising them immortality in the work he was writing. There were daguerreotypes and photographs everywhere in the room above his garage, in which Will worked. The workroom was reached by a stairway inside the garage.

"The laying of the cornerstone of St. Jude." Will passed a yellowing newspaper to Father Dowling. There was a sketch of the proposed new house of worship.

"The editorial urges readers to tolerate our superstitions."

"Ah, civilization."

"This was wild country around here, Father. You wouldn't believe some of the things."

It was on one such visit that Father Dowling reconciled the Hoovers to the Church. Their anger had subsided, the shadows lengthened and Will's absorption in the past of the town had made their resentment seem less cosmic in proportions. And of course they missed the Mass that had been part of their lives since childhood. Who were they punishing by staying away—God?

"We'll come to your parish in Fox River," Madge promised.

Father Dowling was about to mention the parish center and the old folks who gathered there, but somehow the Hoovers did not seem ready for that.

"How about Oliver Foster?"

But Will and Madge just shook their heads.

4

Gerry deflected Mrs. Murkin's barrage of comments and questions about Catherine Spenlow, but the fact was he found her very attractive.

"Of course she's not Catholic," Marie said.

That puzzled Gerry, given the fact that her great-grandparents had been married in St. Hilary's church. That would not have been the present building, of course. Something of Catherine's interest in the past rubbed off on him and he went to the offices of the newspaper and looked up early accounts of the parish.

It was now Friday. It would be nice to have information to give Catherine when they met tomorrow to go to Morley. The thought struck him that he could do some preliminary spadework, see if there was anything of interest, and that would give them time for other things on Saturday.

"Keep an eye on the left rear tire," Father Dowling said when Gerry asked to borrow his car. "I think there's a slow leak."

He spoke as if this were the only flaw in the historic car he insisted would last as long as he did. Maybe it would. Fortunately, on Saturday, they could go in Catherine's car.

Morley lay on the west bank of the Fox River, a remnant of a nineteenth-century village forming the nucleus of a later town that had flourished in the decades before the Second World War and had been in slow decline ever since. Both shores were highly prized sites for vacation homes and their seasonal residents supported the mall. The river was now a waterway for the pointless traffic of recreational craft of all kinds. Speedboats churned up the current, sedate pontoon boats covered with bright awnings went upriver and down, sailboats that indolently relied on the movement of air and water were blown about—all these presented obstacles for the paddle wheeler that took passengers north to the Wisconsin border and back again. Gerry thought that he and Catherine could take that round trip on the paddle wheeler. That was more than motive enough to gather as much information for her as he could.

The courthouse seemed missing its wings, as if the architect had run out of ideas or the county out of money. It was a narrow building rising three flights to a dull dome that stood out against a cloudbank to the west. There was a Civil War cannon on the lawn as well as a howitzer from World War II and a generally uncared-for look to the place. The windowed entrance doors were dusty and when he pushed his way through, the musty smell almost drove him back. He felt that he had entered a time capsule that had been sealed a century before.

From beneath the dome one could look up at the railings marking the different floors. One weak light was trained on the inner dome, eliciting some response from the fading stars scattered across its firmament. A sign directed him below to Records.

The woman behind the counter rose for combat. He noticed the name before she turned her nameplate around. Florence Linster. He seemed to provide her an opportunity to be unhelpful. She repeated every question as if to overcome her incredulity.

"Spenlow?"

"Jason Spenlow."

"Jason Spenlow?"

"He married Sarah Harrison."

"Harrison?"

"Sarah."

She did not repeat the name and Gerry felt they had passed a barrier. He mentioned the date of the wedding in Fox River and said anything she might have would date before then. She stepped back from the counter.

"There's nothing here."

"Nothing?" It seemed to be habit-forming.

"Will Hoover has most of the old records. I let him take them home."

With some reluctance she told him where he could find Will Hoover. Belatedly she became curious about his curiosity, but he was at the door.

"Thank you, Florence. Good morning."

"Morning?"

She was right. A tinny bell was chiming noon when he went out to Father Dowling's ancient car.

5

Will Hoover did not tie his stroke of luck to getting back on track with the Church, but the fact was that he had come upon the old newspaper story the Monday morning after they had attended their first Mass at St. Hilary. The initial story sent him in search of earlier accounts and before the day was out he had pieced it all together. It read like an old western novel.

The gang that had robbed a train bringing gold from the West had been tracked down and brought to trial in Morley. Only two incriminating gold bars had been found on the men, and they refused to say where they had stashed the rest. Clearly they saw that information as their means of cheating the hangman. The local sheriff, on the other hand, was confident that he could discover the hidden gold without the help of the thieves and the trial went forward. The four thieves were convicted and sentenced to hang. Then occurred the event that had first caught Will Hoover's eye. When the sheriff went to lead the condemned to the gallows, one of them was missing. Bart Meadows.

The other three had been hung and apparently neither Bart Meadows nor the missing gold had ever been discovered. That meant that somewhere in the vicinity of Morley the stolen gold still awaited discovery. Wallowing in the past has its satisfactions, but to have a purpose in the present is better. Will Hoover made up his mind that he would find out where that gold was hidden.

Three months of reading had brought the conviction that the money would be found in some cave along the Fox River. Recently, an article had appeared which told of the way frontier outlaw gangs had used such caves as meeting points and hideouts. He read the account of sporadic explorations with his heart in his throat. But the theory about outlaws was based on artifacts and graffiti on the cave walls. Thus began Will Hoover's systematic search of caves along the Fox River.

"If someone already found it, they probably didn't make an announcement, Will."

Madge might be right. If he himself found the gold, he meant to keep it and he sure wouldn't want to tell the world of his good luck. But how could you keep that much gold a secret unless you just kept it hidden? In any case, Will had made up his mind to give ten percent of his findings to Father Dowling and St. Hilary parish in Fox River. Oliver Foster thought he was nuts.

"After what the Church did to us?" Foster still seemed as angry as he had been years before when they closed St. Jude. "And don't forget that Dowling was the hatchet man."

Of course Foster also thought Will was nuts for wasting his

days dreaming of buried treasure. Sometimes Will thought Oliver's steady anger had more to do with his shiftless son than anything else.

"How's Hank?"

"Don't ask."

On the day he found the treasure, Will didn't know what to do. To leave the cave and hurry back and tell Madge meant the treasure would be unguarded. But he couldn't spend the rest of his life here. How he wished he had brought the cellular phone from his car! The only thing to do was to get back to the car and call Madge and . . . Well, he didn't know what next. Have her come out. Maybe bring Foster. He didn't know.

Excited as could be, he took one gold bar and scrambled up the bank and reached the high ground where his car was parked when he saw the man looking over his car. He had parked behind Will, an old crate of some kind. Will approached him with the wariness of a man who has just discovered a fortune lost for over a century.

"I'm Gerry Krause. Your wife said I might find you out here."

6

Catherine's genealogical search enabled her to trace Spenlows as far west as St. Joseph, Missouri, but then they petered out. There seemed no way in which her great-grandfather could be linked to the Spenlows of whom there were records. Perhaps such mysteries are part of the pursuit of the past, but Catherine was disappointed. The trip to Morley on Saturday looked less promising, except that she looked forward to being with Gerry Krause.

"Why aren't we Catholics?" she asked her grandmother.

"I never was."

"But Sarah and Jason were married at St. Hilary right here in Fox River."

"Does that make them Catholics?"

Only gradually did her grandmother admit that Grandfather Spenlow had been raised Catholic. "It was more his mother than his father," she said this dismissively, then fell silent. After all, she herself had played a role in her husband's falling away from the faith in which he had been born.

"It's odd to think I might have been a Catholic."

Her grandmother smiled. The old woman seemed to have reached a point where few things engaged her mind or interest. She was drifting toward death as comfortably as she could. Maurice, her canary, chirped away as if he were her protection against noxious gases. When he went, she went. Margaret Spenlow intended to go gentle into the dark night awaiting her and did not want to be disturbed by questions of religion.

Catherine found an old ledger in the attic in which her grandfather had kept accounts and also a kind of sporadic diary. And there were slips of paper that had been kept pressed between its pages. One was a clipping from the Morley *Picayune,* a story commemorating the fiftieth anniversary of a famous hanging. The name of the thief who had cheated the hangman was underlined in the clipping that also had a frontier artist's depiction of the fugitive.

"Who was Bart Meadows?" she asked her grandmother.

"I haven't any idea."

The clipping was intriguing enough to be kept for its own sake, Catherine supposed.

On Saturday she drove to Morley with Gerry, and when he suggested they take the paddle-wheel trip, she was at first reluctant.

"Three hours!"

"We can have lunch on board. We'd have to have lunch anyway."

"That doesn't leave much time to search records."

"I think I've found a shortcut."

"What do you mean?"

"Later."

The sight of the boat tied up to the dock, painted white, flags flying, the great paddle wheel ready to churn, was irresistible. It was not a crowded cruise and they went to the top deck and watched the shore slip past. There were cottages from time to time visible along the banks, but it was possible, as Gerry said, to see the banks of the Fox River as they had looked a century before.

"See those caves."

On the west bank, obscured by brush, were small apertures that Gerry said led to caves.

"How do you know all this?"

"A local historian. We'll see him later."

Then he told her of his visit two days before. She was miffed until she realized that he had taken a real interest in her research.

"I should have been a Catholic," she said.

"Everyone should be. I am quoting Father Dowling."

"My grandfather just stopped being one. I think it was my grandmother's influence."

"What is she?"

"Nothing."

"Nothing?" He laughed.

"What's so funny?"

And he told her about Florence Linster at the Morley courthouse.

"I wish I'd been with you."

"If there was nothing I wanted to spare you the disappointment."

And of course such offices would not be open on Saturday. The paddle wheel turned over and over and the wake of the boat slipped away. They had lunch. They talked about themselves. They sat in silence. He was nice to be with.

"What's it like to be Catholic?"

"What's it like not to be?"

At the moment she felt shut out of something that had once included her relatives. Grandmother Spenlow seemed to have no reason other than indolence and indifference. Why had her grandfather been so easily influenced? She thought of his ledger and that old clipping with the name Bart Meadows came to her.

When the boat returned to Morley and they came ashore, there was a little woman standing there with a uniformed sheriff at her side. She pointed at Gerry.

"That's him. That's the man who killed my husband."

7

Phil Keegan came to the parish house to tell Father Dowling that his nephew had been arrested in Morley. The phone call from Catherine had come moments before. Almost immediately they were headed north, seen on their way by Marie Murkin, who stood in the rectory door for five minutes after the car disappeared, twisting her apron in her anxiety.

"Murder?" Father Dowling asked.

Phil shook his head, but he could not shake away the seriousness of what had happened. Sheriff Ozzie Burger had not telephoned Phil. Maybe he did not yet realize that the young man he had arrested for the murder of Will Hoover was the nephew of the Fox River captain of detectives. But he called in the news media to make the announcement.

"The wife made the accusation."

"Madge?"

"Do you know her?"

"They came to Mass at St. Hilary."

"Now I'm twice as glad I came by to get you."

Phil himself had not been to Morley since he was a boy, but the town had a familiar look to it. Neither he nor Phil was prepared for the excitement that awaited them.

A deputy had checked out Madge Hoover's jumbled account, and a fortune in gold had been discovered in a cave just below where Will Hoover's body had been found, lying beside his parked car. Ozzie Burger was beaming with pride when they got to his office.

"This is the biggest thing since the hanging," he was telling a gaggle of reporters.

"What hanging is that?"

Ozzie clasped his hands behind his head and tilted back in this chair. Then he saw Phil Keegan, tipped forward again, and got to his feet. While the two lawmen shook hands, Father Dowling slipped away. He had half hoped Catherine would be in evidence. But he wanted to talk to Madge Hoover first.

Madge's behavior suggested that it had never crossed her mind that she might end up a widow, but doubtless the suddenness and violence with which Will had departed this life had something to do with the near hysteria of her grief. At the sight of Father Dowling, she flew to him, grasped both his hands and began to wail, with the tears running down her cheeks.

"Thank God he was right with the Church, Father."

He led her to a couch and got her seated. Neighbor women who had approved of Madge's inconsolable grief seemed less pleased when she became subdued. But someone brought Madge a cup of tea and she sipped it slowly, her eyes traveling around her living room as if she wondered how all these people had gotten into it. The woman who had brought the tea sensed that Madge would like to be alone with her priest and coaxed the others into the kitchen.

"Tell me about it, Madge."

Real-life narratives do not begin at the beginning and move

logically toward the end. Father Dowling heard a jumble of elements—a long-ago train robbery, a fugitive who cheated the hangman, buried gold and then Will's pursuit of it. The young man had come asking about things and Madge had told him where he might find Will.

"What a fool I was."

Father Dowling went to see Gerry, certain that by now Phil Keegan would have had a chance to speak with his nephew.

"The coroner thinks he was killed with one of the gold bars."

"Wasn't the gold still in the cave?"

"There was gold in the cave, yes."

"Have you talked to Gerry?"

"He doesn't understand what all this is about."

Gerry certainly didn't look worried when Father Dowling was taken into the room where Catherine Spenlow was talking with him.

"They think I killed that man, Father." He said it as if he considered it a joke.

"Had you ever met him?"

"Sure. He showed me what he said was a bar of gold. I thought he was kidding. I tried to talk to him about Spenlows but he was jumping up and down with excitement. I got out of there when the other guy arrived."

"What other guy?"

"I don't know."

"What did he look like?"

The image of Oliver Foster did not match the description that Gerry gave. Father Dowling was almost disappointed.

There was a commotion in the outer room and Tuttle the lawyer burst in.

"Don't say anything," he cried and then recognized Father Dowling. "I'm going to represent this boy, pro bono, as a favor to Captain Keegan."

"Have you told him?"

"It'll be a surprise."

Tuttle might not be the lawyer Phil would have picked for Gerry, but then the little lawyer fitted into the general implausibility of events. As it turned out, he was a whirlwind of activity and soon Gerry was standing before the local magistrate while Tuttle argued for his client's release.

"Item. There is no murder weapon. Item. There is no proof that the accused was at the murder scene. Item. There is no motive. If the accused intended to steal the gold, he would have done so. Item. His carefree return to Morley argues his innocence."

The magistrate was a young woman in her late twenties, recently elected to her position. She asked the county prosecutor what he had to say.

"Wilma, I haven't even had a chance to speak to Ozzie yet."

A Solomonian frown appeared on Wilma's brow. And then she made her decision.

"I remand the accused into the custody of Father Dowling."

Gerry took Catherine off for the tour of the town they had been prevented from making earlier. Father Dowling drove to the edge of town and walked slowly up to a small frame house and knocked on the door. It was some minutes before it was answered.

"What you doing here?" Oliver Foster asked fiercely.

"Have you heard about Will Hoover?"

"If Will Hoover wants to drive to Fox River and make his peace with the Church that's his business. Will always was a little nuts—

"Oliver, Will is dead."

Foster just sat down on the floor inside his doorway and stared up at Father Dowling with his mouth open. Father Dowling opened the door and stepped inside. He helped Oliver to his feet. They went outside together and sat on wicker chairs on the porch.

"His heart?"

"His head. Someone struck and killed him."

"My God."

Oliver stared out at his anemic lawn. Then he turned to Father Dowling.

"You going to bury him from your church?"

"Yes."

"Who will bury me?" Oliver asked desolately.

"We can talk about that later. Can you cast any light on what happened to Will?"

"Can you imagine a man his age all excited about lost gold?"

"He told you about it?"

"Of course he did. We were best friends."

"Would he have told anyone else?"

"Besides Madge?" Oliver shook his head.

"Did you?"

A look of indignation was gone as quickly as it formed. There were sounds in the house behind them. Oliver swung around and looked at the figure in the doorway as if in continuation of the conversation with Father Dowling. The priest rose and identified himself, but the man in the doorway just stared at him.

"That's Hank."

"Hello Hank. We were just talking about you."

"Yeah?" The screen door flew outward and Hank lumbered onto the porch.

Father Dowling turned to Oliver. "Did you tell Hank about the treasure Will Hoover was after?"

It is difficult to say what might have happened if Oliver Foster had not jumped to his feet and interposed himself between his son and the priest. He grabbed the arm that Hank swung at the priest and the momentum sent the old man spinning across the porch. At that moment, a car roared up the street, siren screaming, and came to a cloudy halt in front of the house. Tuttle jumped out and ran toward the house, holding on to his tweed hat. Hank, flustered by this arrival, looked beyond the lawyer at Peanuts Pianone. The Fox River officer had come around the car and then gone into a stance that owed more to television than to training at the police firing range. He held his weapon with both hands, pointing it at Hank. By the time, Father Dowling had helped Oliver to his feet, Peanuts had handcuffed Hank and was leading him out to his patrol car. Tuttle looked indecisively after the prisoner, as if he would like to propose his services.

"How did you know?" Father Dowling asked.

"Mrs. Hoover mentioned that Mr. Foster had known of the gold."

Unable to resist further, Tuttle hurried after Peanuts and his potential client. Clearly Gerry Krause would have no further need of his professional attention.

8

The gold bar found in Hank's room proved to be the murder weapon, making the surly son's confession redundant. Hank's impaired mental abilities made it unlikely that he would be brought to trial, but his days of freedom were at an end. Oliver was almost relieved.

"He was always too much for me, Father."

Oliver was a pallbearer at the funeral and seemed to find being back inside a church less repellant than he had expected.

The friendship between Gerry and Catherine continued, the strange events in Morley lending zest to their relationship. Gerry no longer talked of graduate school, unless the quest of an MBA could be called a variation on a career in theology.

"God did not become man in order that man might become a theologian," Father Dowling said. "I quote Saint Ambrose."

"I hadn't made up my mind," Gerry said.

Margaret Spenlow came downstairs one morning to find Maurice dead in his cage. She reacted to the passing of her canary with superstitious fright and was suddenly forthcoming about her husband's loss of faith.

"He became interested in his forebears too, Catherine. His father had told him nothing of his origins."

Catherine and Gerry exchanged a look. She had shown him the clipping from her grandfather's ledger and the underlined name of the fugitive, Bart Meadows. A comparison of the newspaper drawing and a daguerreotype of Great-grandfather Spenlow made it clear that he and Bart Meadows were the same man.

"He was told there might be horse thieves in his background," Margaret Spenlow said. "People he wouldn't want to know about."

"That's hard to believe," Catherine said.

Alone together, Gerry and Catherine talked about what they had discovered. There seemed no reason to tell anyone else about it.

"That means we really aren't Spenlows at all."

Catherine looked at him, as if her life was some radical imposture.

"Imagine changing your name like that," she said.

"I want to talk to you about that."

When she grasped his meaning, she came easily into his arms.

The Coveted
Correspondence

1

Father Dowling thought that there were two major motives for
an interest in genealogy: A person either wanted to contrast his
current eminence with humble forebears or to wallow in the
lost past grandeur of the family.

"Where does that leave Sally Murphy?" Marie Murkin asked.

"The Irish are different."

Marie humphed. "Don't tell me about the Irish. I married
one."

Silence fell. Marie looked as if she regretted alluding to the
long-since-departed Mr. Murkin, gone not into that bourne
from which no traveler returns—at least word of his demise had
never reached her—but simply disappeared, here one day and
gone the next. It had turned Marie into a grass widow,
prompted the beginning of her long career as housekeeper in
St. Hilary's rectory, a post that justified, if only in her own eyes,
a freewheeling curiosity about the people of the parish. Sally
Murphy had been reluctant to avail herself of the opportunities
of the parish center where seniors gathered every day under the
capable direction of Edna Hospers. Not that it was a regimented
day. Edna simply created an atmosphere in which the elderly
men and women could enjoy themselves. Sally had finally succumbed to Marie's urging, become a regular at the parish
center, and apparently was soon boring others to death with
stories of her Uncle Anthony.

"Edna hasn't mentioned it," Father Dowling said carefully. He was not yet sure what Marie was up to.

"Oh, she wouldn't." Marie spoke with great conviction and then added in an altered voice, "If she is even aware of it."

There was an ancient enmity between the housekeeper and Edna Hospers, nothing seriously disruptive, but an endless flow of ambiguous criticism from Marie and of impatience from Edna when Marie tried to make inroads into her fiefdom in what had once been the parish school.

"Someone has complained to you, Marie?"

"I am a victim myself."

"Tell me about it," the pastor said, closing his book. It was clear that Marie had some point that she would eventually make and there was no use in his kicking against the goad.

Sally Murphy was not a woman who, on the face of it, one would expect to draw attention to her family, either present or previous generations. Her brothers, after tumultuous teenage years, had joined the navy after a kind of either/or was presented to them by the judge and had kept in sporadic touch with Sally over the years, postcards arriving from brigs and jails around the world. After dishonorable discharge from the navy they had joined the merchant marine and continued their adventures. Meanwhile, Sally's parents, proprietors of a tavern that changed from being a respectable neighborhood watering hole to a somewhat unsavory dive, enjoyed their wares as much as they sold them, and ended up in perilous health that had taken them to fairly early deaths. Not, all in all, a background one would be inclined to celebrate. But Sally's claim to fame was oblique, her Uncle Anthony on her mother's side.

"She insists that he was a famous writer."

"What was Mrs. Murphy's maiden name?"

"Fogarty. But he wrote under a pseudonym."

"Did she say what it was?"

Marie sighed. "I hesitated to prod her into more lying, but I did ask."

"Well?"

Marie closed her eyes, in search of the name. They snapped open. "F. Connor Tracy."

The pastor sat back, his eyebrows lifting.

"Have you heard of him, Father?"

"Oh yes."

Marie looked crestfallen, but then she brightened up. "Of course she would pick a real writer to brag about. That doesn't make him her uncle."

The reputation of F. Connor Tracy had known the usual literary ups and downs. As a young writer, his short stories had captivated readers of the *New Yorker,* the *Atlantic,* and the *Partisan Review.* Only a Catholic could have written them, but their interest far transcended his coreligionists. Indeed, Catholics came to them later than the general reader. No Catholic college could claim him because no college could. When he came out of the service in 1945, discharged at Great Lakes, he had spent a few weeks with his parents in Aurora, sitting on the porch and looking at the Fox River move slowly southward. Acclimated once more to peace he decided to set about doing what he had pondered while a marine. He wanted to be a writer. The GI Bill would have supported him at the college of his choice, but his ideal of the writer was a man of the people, who lived and worked as others did, and wrote besides. And so had he. He moved to Wisconsin and took a job with a county highway department and at night, in the room he rented in Baraboo, wrote. Eventually he sent manuscripts to New York and they were invariably accepted. Later he would admit that since this is what he had aimed for, he had not been as surprised as he should have been. With much critical and some monetary success, he quit the highway crew and moved to Ireland, where he could live cheaply and devote himself entirely to his writing. Alas, there his craft found the formidable rival of the local pub. The two decades left him were spent producing the fiction that would offset the tragedy of his life.

"He received the Last Sacraments," Sally said to Father Dowling when, having determined that her story about being related to the great writer was possibly true, he sought her out to talk about it.

"Thank God. How do you know?"

"The priest wrote to my mother."

"Ah."

"She put that letter with those she had received from him."

"From Tracy?"

"From Tony, she would say. That was his name."

"Where did the pseudonym come from?"

"F was for Fogarty. The others are family names as well."

"He has always been a favorite of mine."

Sally beamed in a proprietary way. "I must confess I've not read much of him myself, Father."

"What happened to the letters your mother received from him?"

"Oh, they came to me."

"You should be careful of them."

"Of course."

She mentioned them as well to the journalist who interviewed her, alerted by those who were moved by Father Dowling's acceptance of Sally's story. Katheryn Reynolds, a local writer, was with Sally when she was interviewed.

"I know every story by heart," Katheryn said.

She also knew a good deal more about the writer than Sally did, and her remarks formed the staple of the story in the Fox River *Tribune,* the enigmatic headline of which was "Niece of

Famous Writer Fox River Native." Sally's mention of the letters nearly derailed the interview. Katheryn begged to be allowed to read them, to see them. "Just let me touch one," she said, breathlessly. The adverb was the journalist's but anyone who knew Katheryn would have found it accurate.

"Did you see the story in the *Tribune*?" Father Dowling asked Marie Murkin.

"The three-car accident?"

"The interview with Sally Murphy."

"You'd think she'd written those stories."

"She has a right to be proud, Marie."

"And what is Katheryn Reynolds's excuse?"

It seemed best to drop the subject. Marie obviously thought that Sally's sudden prominence diminished the housekeeper of St. Hilary's. But he couldn't resist a little dig.

"They might want to do a story on your letters, Marie."

"What letters?"

"You must have kept those of your many suitors."

"I had one suitor and I married him and lived to regret it."

2

The story prompted Father Dowling to take a volume of Tracy's off his shelf. The novel, remembered as good, proved even better than his memory suggested, and for the next week and a half the pastor of St. Hilary's worked through the slim oeuvre of F. Connor Tracy. He read slowly, wanting to prolong the pleasure, if pleasure was the word. Tracy had a melancholy imagination which in the bogs and pubs of Ireland exuded a keening music that gripped the soul and made the heart heavy with an all-but-unbearable sorrow at the follies and failures of men. Phil Keegan on a visit to the rectory picked up a volume, frowned at the jacket, opened it and read a line or two, then shut it and returned it to the table. Father Dowling introduced the inexhaustible topic of the Cubs to forestall any negative remark from Phil. It was not necessary for salvation to enjoy the fiction of Tracy but to denigrate it could not be considered morally neutral.

"Funny you should be reading him," Phil said, not rising to the bait of the Cubs.

"Rereading," Father Dowling said and then, because that sounded smug, added, "He was always a favorite."

"I hope his letters are worth something."

"His letters."

"His niece had a collection of them he had written to her mother. They're missing."

"Tell me about it."

Sally Murphy had been enjoying the quasi-celebrity the story about her uncle's letters had conferred upon her. She continued to annoy others at the parish center because of the frequency with which she brought up the connection. There was nearly a fight when old Agnes Grady suggested that the writer had lost his faith and wrote about degenerates.

"He writes about the Irish," Sally had protested.

Agnes née Schwartzkopf just lifted an eyebrow in QED. Sally demanded to know if Agnes had read anything of Tracy.

"I don't read that sort of thing."

"You don't read any sort of thing," Sally said hotly.

It was Katheryn who soothed the troubled waters. "No one could read the letters he wrote Sally's mother without being transported."

She spoke with a calm authority that carried the day.

Katheryn had attached herself to Sally, having received permission to read the letters in the Murphy home. Her suggestion that Sally keep them in a safe deposit box at her bank had not been taken up. Katheryn had embarked on a campaign to be named editor of the letters, something she offered to do gratis.

"It would be a privilege, Sally."

"But they're private letters."

Katheryn explained to Sally that nothing was more common than to publish the letters of the great, particularly those of great writers. Sally did not think that many breaches of decorum constituted a new moral code. Her lips became a line and she shook her head firmly at the renewed suggestion; finally Katheryn had let it drop.

"It is selfish to want to keep such a treasure to oneself," Katheryn told Edna Hospers, needing some outlet for her frustration and finding it in the sympathetic director of the parish center.

"Would there really be such interest?"

"Edna, any publisher would snap it up. As for the originals . . ."

"What do you mean?"

"Someone recently paid ten thousand dollars for an old pipe that had belonged to Tracy."

If a mere object elicited such a covetous reaction from collectors, what would dozens of letters written over an extended period of time and in the very hand of the great writer bring?

"Sally would never let them go."

"I don't think she should! But she has no idea of their value."

When he was told of the exchange the pastor had been reminded of the chiding tone of guidebooks that lamented the way the natives failed to keep up the artifacts and buildings that brought tourists from afar. Why didn't the Italians restore all the churches in Rome? Since there was at least one church in every block this would have proved a vast enterprise. So Katheryn chided Sally for thinking of her uncle's letters to her mother as letters to her mother rather than as messages to the world at large.

When the letters were missing, there was no need to speculate on what had happened. Sally said it outright.

"Katheryn has them, of course. I want them back. I don't care if you have to arrest her."

"How long have they been missing?"

On this Sally was vague. The last time she had definitely laid eyes on the correspondence had been a week before.

Katheryn was not at home. She did not answer her phone and there seemed little point in leaving more messages on her answering machine. The police made inquiries but Katheryn had left no trail. It was Edna's guess that Katheryn had simply lost patience with Sally's intransigence and acted on her own.

"Taken them to a publisher?"

Edna nodded. "You had to hear the fervor with which she spoke."

Calling all possible publishers of literary correspondence would have been a formidable task, but Phil Keegan was prepared to undertake it. In order to give it focus, he got a court order to enter Katheryn's house, hoping to find some indication of what she might have done with the letters. So it was that the body of Katheryn Reynolds was found.

3

Perhaps if she had been found earlier, Katheryn would have been thought to be asleep or unconscious. The blow that freed her from this Vale of Tears had left no visible mark and only a close examination by the coroner revealed the lesion on her head. She had been struck from behind and fallen forward onto a sofa, this breaking her fall, and then apparently rolled gently to the floor. Her still-open but unseeing eyes prompted Edna, who had accompanied Cy Horvath, to speak to Katheryn as if she could hear. And then the stillness and strangeness brought a gasp from Edna. Cy had already seen the body and its condition and was on the phone to Dr. Pippen.

Given the reason for the court order, Cy, unable to do anything for Katheryn and Edna having been taken away, began the search for the letters. Letters he found, but only of the kind that any household would contain—bills, junk mail—until he came upon half a dozen replies from publishers in response to the inquiry Katheryn had indeed presumed to make. All but one of the publishers was interested; on Katheryn's answering machine, furthermore, were several voice messages from publishers who had not wanted to trust to what was now somewhat disdainfully referred to as snail mail.

"Did you find a copy of the letter she sent, Cy?" Phil Keegan wanted to know.

"No."

"I suppose we can ask one of these publishers for a copy."

"Why?"

"It should tell us whether she had the letters in her possession."

Cy had an impassive Hungarian countenance and it would have been difficult to know what his reaction was. Agnes Lamb, who had returned from guiding Sally to solace and sanctuary, wrinkled her nose as Keegan spoke.

"Those answers tell the story, don't they? That and the fact that she is dead."

"Maybe."

Maybe not, however. The search for the letters suggested that someone else had been searching the house, perhaps in quest of the letters.

"They must have found them," Agnes said.

"Maybe."

"That would explain their not being here," Agnes explained patiently.

"If they were here in the first place."

Agnes started to laugh and then stopped, not wanting to be amused all by herself. Neither Phil Keegan nor Cy Horvath seemed to think the captain's agnosticism was misplaced.

"We are going to proceed on the assumption that she was killed for some letters she didn't have?"

"We are not going to proceed on the assumption that she had the letters."

"That's the same thing."

The silence suggested that she had been guilty of a fallacy.

When Phil stopped by that night he brought Father Dowling up to speed on the investigation. This did not take long, since all the results were negative. It was not certain that the one who had murdered Katheryn had got what he had come for, if he had indeed come for the letters.

"Was anything else missing?"

"Nothing obvious. But we don't have an inventory so it is difficult to say. He was a very neat thief, and murderer."

"He?"

"Inclusive. We don't really know that either."

Several publishers had been contacted and one had faxed a copy of the letter received from Katheryn. It was an enigmatic epistle.

I am writing to ask if you would be interested in publishing a collection of some 47 letters, many of them lengthy, written by F. Connor Tracy to his sister over a span of some twenty years, all of them after he had settled in Ireland. My preliminary study of the letters suggests that they have great importance, both biographical and literary. In some of the letters, he begins sober and ends drunk, something deducible not only from the handwriting but also from the repetitiveness, but all in all they have an elegiac quality that admirers of his work will recognize

as his peculiar voice. On the other hand, some of his reminis-
cences of childhood strike a whimsical even nostalgic note not
normally associated with his outlook.

"What do you think, Roger?"

"That she was presumptuous. I gather that Sally had not authorized such an inquiry."

"Does the letter suggest to you that she had taken the letters?"

In one sense, it emerged, she had. A school notebook was found in her bedroom in which were transcribed more than a dozen of the letters. Apparently Katheryn had taken advantage of the time Sally had allowed her with the correspondence to copy them.

"She asked if she could take notes," Sally said. "I didn't dream she would copy them out word for word."

It was clear that Sally was not yet fully convinced of the intrinsic value of her uncle's letters. She had accepted the publicity and exploited it, but apparently expecting that at any moment someone would question the importance of her uncle's letters.

"Katheryn was right about publishers being interested in the letters."

"What good does that do me now, Father?"

"You're sure the letters are missing?"

"Of course I'm sure."

Father Dowling looked at Edna but she avoided his eyes. This was a delicate matter, but he had promised Phil Keegan he would try.

"It occurs to me, Sally, that if Katheryn put the letters away in a different place . . ."

"She did that all right. In her own house." But Sally's expression softened. "God rest her soul. Imagine getting killed over some old letters."

"That's my point, Sally," Father Dowling said.

Sally looked at him blankly.

"Sally, if I can imagine the letters are still here, someone else can too. Perhaps the same person who killed Katheryn."

"But he has the letters now."

"But what if Katheryn never took them? What if they are still here, in this house, and the killer comes to the same conclusion . . . ?"

Sally's hand went to her throat and she moved closer to Edna on the couch.

"Why don't you and Edna conduct a thorough search?"

Sally's reluctance was gone; indeed she was now eager to turn the house inside out to see if the letters were there, even while professing that she didn't believe for a minute that they were.

If they were, they were not found by Edna and Sally after a search of hours.

"It was a long shot," Phil said, shrugging. "Chances are the killer got the letters."

"You sound surer now."

"Well, if Edna Hospers couldn't find them I doubt they are in Sally's house."

"I don't suppose a thief would be stupid enough to try to sell them immediately."

"How would he go about selling items like that?"

Roger put Phil Keegan onto Casper Barth, the rare book dealer. Meanwhile there was Katheryn's funeral to preside over.

McDivitt pulled Father Dowling into his office when the priest arrived at the funeral home for the rosary that night at seven o'clock.

"Am I early?"

"There are only half a dozen people here," McDivitt said in hushed tones. "I could understand it if the weather was bad."

"We'll start fifteen minutes late."

This calmed the funeral director. He offered Father Dowling a little something, knowing it would be refused, but poured a dollop for himself and tossed it off. When he put the bottle back into a drawer of his desk he chuckled. He drew out a card and held it up for the priest to see. *Let McDivitt replace your last divot.*

"I hope you don't plan to use that."

"Good Lord, no. I was given it at our last convention. Undertakers have a strange sense of humor, Father Dowling."

"I wasn't aware they had any at all."

"You'd be surprised."

"I am."

At seven-fifteen they went into the viewing room. There were a dozen people there now, all wearing the expression one saves for wakes and funerals. Most of those there were regulars at the parish center. Sally's absence seemed conspicuous, and Father Dowling thought less of her for it. Whatever Katheryn may or may not have done, she was dead now, cruelly murdered. Sally might have chosen to be flattered by Katheryn's interest in her famous uncle, but she seemed to resent it. Father Dowling nodded to the mourners and then took his position on the prie-dieu set up beside the open casket and began the rosary.

Repetitive prayer is conducive either to meditation or distraction and Father Dowling found his mind straying. What was it Hamlet's uncle had said? "My words fly up, my thoughts remain below, words without thoughts never to heaven go." Of course it was a distraction to remember that. He put his mind to concentrating on the mystery being commemorated by the decade they were reciting. When he finished he felt that he had been engaged in physical labor. It occurred to him that Katheryn looked serene and peaceful lying there. He might have mentioned this to McDivitt but it would have seemed lugubrious.

Others had come in while the rosary was said and Father Dowling was delighted to see that Sally was one of them. She was speaking with a man Father Dowling did not know. Phil Keegan had brought Marie Murkin with him.

"Katheryn's beau," Marie said of the unknown man.

"I hope you locked the rectory doors, Marie."

She narrowed her eyes. "The answering service is on."

This was a device that Marie abominated, particularly when she was on the receiving end of someone's recorded message. Those who reached the rectory heard only "St. Hilary's," a beep and silence. It was Marie's theory that everyone now knew enough to speak after the beep. "If they haven't hung up, that is."

Hanging up was what Marie did when after enduring many rings she was answered by a taped message made God knows how long ago.

That remark seemed oddly apropos when Phil Keegan asked Father Dowling to listen to the tape that had been taken from Katheryn's answering machine. Her cheerful message, addressed to the world at large, brightly inviting the caller to leave a message long or short after the beep, was a voice from beyond the grave. The microcassette was all but filled with messages going back nearly a year.

"Who is Hughes, Roger?"

There were several messages from him, usually saying that he would arrive at such and such a time at O'Hare. Hughes was the name of the man Marie had called Katheryn's beau. It had been the pastor's understanding, and, he learned, that of Edna as well, that Katheryn was single and seemed to have no inclination to change her marital status at her age. She had been forty-seven when she died. The messages from Hughes had begun two months before. Hughes had been at the funeral but Father Dowling did not have an opportunity to speak to him.

"I did," Marie said when he lamented this.

"Ah."

Silence. She wanted him to ask what she had learned. He knew she was incapable of not telling him. All he had to do was wait. But Marie's willpower had strengthened in the hard school of the rectory under Father Dowling's teasing regime, and it was more than an hour later that she came into the study and began to talk before she had taken a chair.

"He is from Indianapolis. He was almost the exact age of Katheryn. Her little book on Tracy came to his attention and he got in contact with her."

"And visited her?"

"Who knows what might not have happened if Katheryn had lived." Marie's sigh seemed freighted with the mystery of things.

"Did he go back to Indianapolis?"

"He has to work."

"At what?"

"The main thing is whatever he felt for Katheryn has been cruelly crushed."

"Didn't you ask him what kind of work he does?"

"What difference does it make?"

"Probably none."

"Probably."

4

The wild-haired young man from the Emerald Isle, who wore a corduroy jacket and turtleneck sweater, chose not to waste his sweetness on the desert air of Fox River. Instead he poured out his story to a reporter from the *Chicago Tribune* who, once she had acquainted herself with recent events in Fox River and received assurance from the book review editor that F. Connor

Tracy was indeed a major writer, pulled all the stops. The natural son of the famous writer had come to the area to visit the ancestral spots of his deceased father. There were anecdotes about F. Connor Tracy, vignettes of his own childhood, and a vow to make good his claim to be the heir of the literary property of his father.

His putative cousin was shocked. "My uncle never married and never had any children. Period."

This was the sole quotation from Sally Murphy in the story but she had no sooner put down the phone than she called Tuttle the lawyer, demanding that he put a stop to this desecration of the memory of her uncle. Tuttle assured her that he would go about it with the same vigor he would treat an attack on his dear departed father.

"It's those letters that are causing all this," Sally said when she went to Tuttle's office.

"The letters." Tuttle scratched the tip of his nose with the wrong end of a ballpoint pen, creating what looked like blue veins.

"You must have read about them."

"I want it in your own words."

There was the distinct sound of snoring from the lawyer's inner office. Tuttle rose, kicked the door, and shouted, "Peanuts!"

Sally half expected a vendor to appear and supply Tuttle with a package of peanuts. But the snoring stopped.

"My associate," Tuttle murmured. "Go on."

He paid close attention to her narrative but his spirits sank as he did so. Letters from a drunken brother in Ireland? She called him a writer but he was certainly nobody famous like Elmore Leonard or Louis L'Amour. But Tuttle perked up when she unfolded the story from the *Chicago Tribune*. He hadn't read a paragraph before he tipped back his hat and said, "Libel. We'll sue for libel."

"He's just a boy. He has nothing."

"I mean the paper."

"Oh."

Here was an opportunity Tuttle could warm to. He would be David, the *Tribune* would be Goliath, the outcome had a biblical inevitability.

"I want the letters back, too."

"Your cousin take those, do you suppose?"

"Don't call him that."

"Did he?"

"I don't think he was even in the country when they were taken. I gather he just got off the boat."

"Boat?"

"Just arrived."

Tuttle's loyalties wavered as he imagined a young man newly arrived from a foreign land being pounced upon by a huge metropolitan newspaper and then by relatives he had never before seen. If only Sean had come to him before Sally Murphy had . . . But Sally's connecting the death of Katheryn Reynolds with what she was saying brought home to Tuttle that the job being offered him might have all sorts of possibilities.

"You think she was killed for the letters?"

"I'm lucky I wasn't."

"They must be pretty valuable."

"Or life is held pretty cheap."

"That too."

After she left, Tuttle roused Peanuts Pianone and over shrimp-fried rice at the Great Wall pumped his old friend about the status of the police investigation.

"I'm not assigned to that."

"What have you heard about it?"

Peanuts dipped his head, now the to right, now to the left. raising his eyebrows and rolling out his lower lip as he did. But that was it. Tuttle doubted that Peanuts had even heard of Katheryn's murder. His career as a policeman consisted in putting in time until he was eligible for a pension. His family connections gave him tenure and the department preferred that he remain uninvolved in police work.

"Why do you want to retire?" Tuttle asked. Millions would kill to get Peanuts's situation; it was far better than retirement.

"Stress."

Tuttle went around to St. Hilary's to have a chat with Father Dowling. The pastor was thick as thieves with Phil Keegan. Marie Murkin told him the pastor was busy. "This will only take a minute," Tuttle said, brushing past her and heading for the study. The housekeeper was clinging to his arm when he stopped in the open doorway.

"You make an impressive couple," the pastor said, and Tuttle felt the grip on his arm loosen. There was a young man seated in an easy chair, holding a bottle of beer, grinning at the new arrivals.

"Sean, this is Tuttle the lawyer."

"I've already met Marie," the young man said, half rising and extending a very large hand.

"The writer's boy," Tuttle said, recognizing the young man from the *Tribune* article. The boy beamed.

"How do you know that?"

"You're famous. I am your Cousin Sally's lawyer."

"She denies the connection."

"There wasn't much about your mother in the article."

Father Dowling broke in. "Tuttle, I can see that you have much to talk about with my young visitor. Sean, come back tomorrow for lunch. It's just after the noon Mass. Come for that if you like."

A noncommittal nod.

"You sure you don't want to spend the night here?"

"The *Tribune* is footing my bill at the hotel."

Tuttle was on his feet. "We will leave you to your devotions, Father Dowling. Young Sean and I will go somewhere for a beer."

"This stuff is like water," Sean observed, then apologized to his host.

"It is not Guinness, I grant you."

"You want Guinness, we'll have Guinness," Tuttle promised.

The pastor showed them out, the housekeeper seemingly having disappeared. Tuttle got Sean into the passenger seat and then set off for the hotel with all deliberate speed. There they could charge everything to the boy's room and be in effect the guests of the *Tribune*.

The luxury of the modest hotel seemed sybaritic to Sean, and Tuttle himself was far from immune to its charms, the chief of which was watching the young Irishman scrawl his name on the bills as they came.

"It's a lot better than where I stayed at first."

"First?"

"Before I called the reporter."

"And where did you stay?"

But Sean waved the topic away. Some minutes later, Peanuts arrived. Tuttle did not think it seemly to keep Peanuts from this bonanza.

"If only they served Chinese food."

"You'll complain in heaven," Tuttle chided.

"Not if there's fried rice."

The human mind is a wondrous thing. That night Tuttle awakened from a just and well-fed sleep to find that of all the badinage of the evening what had stuck in his mind was young Sean's mention of a period prior to calling the reporter. The newspaper story had the reporter meeting Sean as he flew in on Aer Lingus. It was the kind of detail that would interest the police. And they were bound to learn it. Tuttle was not surprised when he learned, later that day, that Keegan and Horvath had taken young Sean downtown for questioning.

5

Marie Murkin greeted Phil Keegan coldly and let him find his own way to the study. Nor did she offer him refreshments.

"What's wrong with her, Roger?"

"Sean."

"Ah."

The newspaper accounts of the arrest were decidedly unfriendly to the police. The suggestion was that in desperation they had decided to frame a young immigrant. The fact that neighbors of Katheryn's would testify that they saw the young claimant in the neighborhood prior to the killing did little to right the balance. Nor had Sally's belated statement that Sean had come to her door and she had turned him away as soon as she saw what he was up to.

"Besmirching my uncle's reputation," she scoffed. "I was having none of that."

The fact that Sean did not have the missing letters was regarded by the prosecutor if not the fourth estate as an exonerating factor. Perhaps he would not have resorted to violence if he had come into possession of the letters themselves. So went the theory, but the theory was soon exploded by Tuttle's discovery.

The little lawyer came to Father Dowling in a moral quandary. He had come upon information injurious to his client but as an officer of the court he could not withhold evidence.

"Evidence of what?"

"Father, he had the letters. The missing letters. He had checked a bag with the porter of his hotel and he asked me to pick it up and keep it for him."

"And the letters were in the bag."

Tuttle nodded. "They'll hang him, Father."

Even if he could have told Tuttle to conceal the letters, he knew the lawyer would not believe him.

"Let me talk to Sean first."

The young fellow sauntered into the visiting room and plopped into a chair across from Father Dowling.

"Well I must be a goner if they're sending me a priest."

"Would you like to talk as penitent to priest?"

"I didn't kill that woman, Father."

"But you had the letters."

He slapped his forehead. "Has he told the police?"

"He won't be able to keep them a secret from the police, Sean."

"You know, Father, I never got the chance to sit down and read them. That's all I wanted, to see what my father had written when I was this age or that. Had he never so much as alluded to my existence in writing to his sister? It's in a parish record out in Sligo. I've seen it myself. Maureen Shanahan, son; father, Anthony Fogarty. That's his real name."

"You have some claim to the letters then."

"I don't want them. Not now. I wanted Tuttle to give them back to Sally Murphy."

"So you took the letters from Katheryn?"

"I went there, yes, The door was open and I called and went in, the way we do in Ireland, and there she was, lying on the floor. I thought she was asleep. Truth is, I thought she might be drunk. I knelt down next to her. That's how I discovered the letters. She had hidden them under the couch. I took them— borrowed them really. I never meant to keep them."

It was all too easy to imagine what Phil Keegan and Cy Horvath and the others would make of this alibi. The letters would effectively hang him, as Tuttle had said, but of course there was no death penalty in Illinois.

"That boy wouldn't hurt a fly," Marie Murkin declared, filling the pastor's coffee cup. Sun illumined the dining room curtains and became polychrome in the prismed edge of the mirror over the sideboard.

"Perhaps he thought he wasn't. It was an unlucky blow."

"I believe his story."

"It's too bad you won't be on the jury."

Sean's story that he had entered the house of a woman just murdered and taken the letters he happened to discover when he knelt beside her to see if she was asleep was not a logical impossibility, but it did not rank high on the scale of plausibility. Of course his story explained why he had been seen in the neighborhood, and why he was in possession of the letters, for that matter, but his instructions to Tuttle suggested someone with much to hide.

"I have a professional obligation to believe him," Tuttle said, not a ringing endorsement.

"What can I say?" Sally Murphy said. "It all comes from his telling that preposterous story."

But it was not a preposterous story. Monsignor Hogan in the chancery had connections in Sligo, and he obtained for Father Dowling a photocopy of the parish record in which the name of Anthony Fogarty, American, was given as father of the child Sean. The mother had gone to God due to complications in a later out-of-wedlock pregnancy. Sally held the photocopy at arm's length, wrinkling her nose as she studied it.

"What's to prevent any man's name being used on such an occasion?"

"I doubt that the priest would be party to something like that, Sally."

If Sally did not share his doubt she would not of course say so, not to his face, but Father Dowling could see that she was indeed convinced. Whatever Sally's distaste, the young man from Ireland was her uncle's son and thus her cousin. But even her distaste had lessened. A shocking claim, repeated, loses its shock value, and the fact of the matter was that few others seemed to react as Sally had. Of course the godless newspapers took it as gospel; they knew a Catholic country like Ireland must be rife with hypocrisy. If only Ireland would join the modern world Sean's mother could have gotten an abortion and that would have been the end of it. Not that they said that, of course. Sally did not expect consistency from the devil's disciples.

"I almost wish I could believe his story, Father."

Such sympathy, and it was widespread, would not keep Sean from being tried for the murder of Katheryn Reynolds. Even if he had not meant to kill her, he had entered her house as a thief and presumably had struck her down when she confronted him.

"Of course if his story is true, someone else must have killed Katheryn."

6

Later, eyes closed, tipped back in his chair, drawing on an aromatic pipeful of tobacco, it occurred to Father Dowling that in one sense there were many possible suspects. There were the publishers to whom Katheryn had written, any one of whom would have seen the value of her literary trove. But they were far away and it would have taken a dark view of publishers to imagine them flying to Fox River to burgle and kill even for some very valuable letters. Acquired in that way, the letters could only be possessed; they could bring nothing further unless the owner revealed that he had stolen property. The unlikelihood of this did not stop Father Dowling from asking to see that correspondence with the publishers that Katheryn had inaugurated.

Tuttle's request that Father Dowling sit at the defendant's table, gently refused at first, became a week later less off-putting. Marie was appalled.

"It puts you on his side."

"A murderer's side?"

"That's the whole point of the trial."

"What kind of a world would it be if priests avoided murderers?"

Marie was certain there was a logical flaw involved here but she did not have time to point it out. Of course she was right. Sitting at the defense table would be a public act, suggesting he was less concerned with mercy for the wrongdoer than that he be found innocent of a crime. But a series of phone calls to Indianapolis had so clouded things that Father Dowling told Tuttle he was prepared to accept the invitation.

"Better late than never."

"Things are going bad?"

Tuttle drew a finger across his neck while emitting a chilling sound.

From his vantage point at the front of the courtroom, Father Dowling had a good view of the little balcony from which a dozen spectators looked down over a large clock at the proceedings. Brendan Hughes was a most attentive observer in the front row, his arms on the railing, his chin on his folded arms. The note Tuttle passed him while a neighbor of Katheryn's was on the stand, identifying Sean as the man she had seen lurking in the neighborhood the day the murder occurred, had an address on it. An airport hotel. Hughes was waiting for him in the lobby.

"I think you're expecting me," he said, as Hughes rose eagerly at mention of his name.

"He said you'd be wearing a collar. I saw you in court."

"I understand you teach English."

"Celtic literature. F. Connor Tracy is a favorite of mine."

"Could you identify his handwriting?"

"Yes."

Father Dowling withdrew from his pocket one of the letters that had been recovered from Sean. Hughes's eyes brightened at the sight of the envelope.

"This is an authentic letter from the writer." He took another envelope from his pocket. "But I want you to look at this one first."

Hughes took the second envelope impatiently. It was not sealed and he soon had the single sheet of paper in his hands. His eyes glided over it and then he looked at Father Dowling. "This is a fake."

"And this one."

Hughes's reaction to the second letter was completely different. He nodded, he smiled, he held the pages as if they were a sacred document. "That is one of the letters. No doubt about it."

"I wish I could say that you have been a great help to the guilty party."

"What will they do with him?"

"I'm not a lawyer."

"You really do look like a priest."

Hughes in turn really looked like a professor. He was a learned man, and a delightful conversationalist. But Father Dowling did not discover this on that first occasion. The fingerprints on the bogus letter matched those found in Katheryn's house, a fact determined within an hour after Father Dowling turned it over to Phil Keegan. Much later that night, Phil came by the rectory.

"He admitted it, Roger. Cool as could be. I had to stop him and tell him to get a lawyer."

Katheryn had shown Hughes some of the letters on a previous occasion; she had shown him her transcriptions of others. His desire to have them became overpowering. The combination of the letters and Hughes's amorous attentions were more than Katheryn could resist. She agreed to take the letters.

"In fairness, Father, she had no idea I meant to steal them. She thought we were merely cutting a corner for the good of literature. Those letters belonged in the public domain. When she realized what I intended, she objected. She snatched at the letter she had shown me and I pushed her away. I had no intention to harm her. Or to let that young man go to prison. I was agonizing over what to do if he were found guilty."

"You are lucky to have Amos Cadbury as your lawyer, Brendan."

"What will happen to the letters?"

Sean and his Aunt Sally entered into an agreement with a publisher to bring out an edition of the letters. The obvious editor would have been Brendan Hughes, but that of course was out of the question.

"And the originals?" Father Dowling asked the cousins.

Sean beamed. "They will go to the Notre Dame library, Father."

"That's very generous of you, Sally."

"Oh, they'll pay for them."

And there were other mementos and papers that the two of them could make available to the world of letters with adequate compensation to themselves. Tuttle in turn would actually collect a fee for his successful defense of his client.

"Peanuts wants a leave as a reward for tracking down where Hughes was staying." Phil said this in a neutral voice.

"Will he get it?"

"Roger, he's been on leave ever since he joined the department."

DEATH WISH

Roger Dowling pushed back the curtain ringing the bed before he gave old Mrs. McGrath the Last Sacraments. It was bad enough dying in a double room; there was no need to make a secret of this Christian farewell. Besides, apart from Marge, the unmarried McGrath daughter, there was only Leonard, who had married too often, breaking his old mother's heart if not those of his three wives. What Roger had hoped was the smell of aftershave lotion on Leonard had now established itself unmistakably as bourbon. Chalk it up to grief. What protocol specified that a man of Irish extraction must show up at his mother's deathbed sober?

Leonard stared solemnly as the priest anointed the dying woman. Marge sniffled in a plastic chair, shaking her head as if disapproval could alter the course of events.

"Should we say the rosary now?" Roger Dowling asked.

Marge had beads in her purse but Leonard counted off the prayers on his fingers, keeping his voice low, taking his cue from Marge. How long had it been since he'd said his prayers? Marge's voice grew louder and more plangent as the rosary progressed, the children of the deceased alternating the Hail Marys and Our Fathers with Roger Dowling. The other patient in the room had been in a coma for months and was unlikely to be disturbed by their storming of heaven. His wife, seated on the far side of the other bed, looked on with wide, curious eyes.

Mrs. McGrath passed away during the fourth decade of the

rosary, but Roger Dowling finished before ringing for the nurse, knowing the commotion that would follow on the old woman's death. An hour later, the body was gone and Roger Dowling was sitting with Marge and Leonard in a room down the hall.

"I suppose McDivitt," Marge said when the matter of an undertaker came up.

"They do a good job."

Leonard made a noise. "What a way to earn a living! Profiting from the grief of others."

"Do you want to bury her yourself?" Marge snapped, then burst into tears. Leonard went to her and patted her shoulder.

"I'll call McDivitt."

"I don't care if you do or not."

Leonard made a face at Father Dowling: women. Well, Leonard was a better judge on that score than the pastor of St. Hilary's.

"What do we do now?" Marge asked, looking at Father Dowling with tear-filled eyes.

"There's nothing more to do here."

Leonard said, "Will you say the funeral Mass, Father?"

"Of course he will!" Marge struggled to her feet. "Thank you for coming, Father Dowling. Mom must have known the end was near. She asked me to call you."

A premonition? Perhaps. But then Mrs. McGrath had been told by her doctor that she had only days to live. Roger Dowling said goodbye to Marge and Leonard and went off down the hospital corridor.

"Father? Excuse me, could I speak with you?"

He recognized her as the woman who had sat wide-eyed on the other side of the room while he administered the Last Sacraments to Mrs. McGrath, keeping her own vigil beside her comatose husband. He hesitated, not wanting to return to the lounge where he had left Marge and Leonard.

"We're not Catholics," the woman said, as if addressing his indecision.

They went back to where her husband lay, in full possession of the room now. "Father, I need advice."

Her name was Sheila Thomas. She had a narrow face which looked thinner because of the great helmet of wavy hair. Large liquid eyes fixed on him.

"They want to pull the plug on Paul."

"Your husband."

A nod. She bit her lower lip and her eyes filled with tears. "He has been in a coma for weeks. Three weeks. They say he will never come out of it and even if he does he'll never be the same."

"What plug do they want to pull?"

"It's an expression. They're feeding him intravenously."

"And they want to stop feeding him?"

Apparently he had said the right thing. She blinked away her tears. "It would be like starving him, wouldn't it?"

"Is that how the doctor describes it?"

"No. He just gives me my options."

"So it's up to you."

"And then there's Dr. Rand. He's not a medical doctor. He's an ethicist."

"I see."

"He went through it very carefully with me, the pros and cons. The decision is mine, of course, but his advice is to accept the fact that Paul has in effect already died."

Roger Dowling looked at the man on the bed. An IV tube was inserted in his arm, his color was not good, but the steady sough of his breathing was audible in the suddenly quiet room.

"Is that what the medical doctor says?"

"He told me to discuss the matter with Dr. Rand and decide however I want to. I know what they all want me to do."

"Pull the plug?"

She nodded. "He could be here for years, that's one of the possibilities, years and years of being a vegetable, and then he'll die and what will have been the point of it all? Is that my future, visiting *that* for years?" Her voice took on an edge and she cast an angry glance at her husband.

"It sounds as if you've made up your mind."

"To starve him?"

"That sounds as if you haven't decided."

"I don't know what to do."

"Are you asking my advice?"

She looked at him almost warily, as if she dreaded what he might say. Her nod was almost invisible.

"You said you're not a Catholic. What are you?"

"Nothing. Neither is Paul. We weren't even married in a church."

"Do you believe in God?"

"I thought I did. I never really paid much attention."

"What do you suppose God would want you to do?"

"I thought you'd say that." But there was no triumph in her voice at having anticipated it. Rather she looked depressed.

"You don't *have* to decide against feeding him."

"Ha. You don't know Dr. Rand."

"I'm sure no one would force you to make such a decision. My guess is that they think they're giving you a chance to get out of this."

"Oh, they want out of it, too."

"What do you think you'll do?"

"I'm asking your advice."

The most important thing about the conversation was not that she was speaking to him, but that she clearly did not want to accept the advice of Dr. Rand. Maybe if she had religious beliefs, she would understand the reason for her hesitation. Not that he thought faith was needed to sense the obligation to cherish human life even in the extremity to which her husband had fallen.

"I think you know what you ought to do."

At the moment that seemed the right thing to say. Of course she was disappointed. She wanted the decision made by someone else. But would she have taken his advice if he had been explicit? Having just attended to Mrs. McGrath, he might seem to her a figure of authority, hieratic, one easily capable of monitoring the border between the quick and the dead. She was not Catholic, she did not even know if she believed in God, no doubt she was disposed to regard her comatose husband as a burden and would be easily persuaded that the compassionate thing to do would be to withhold food and liquid and let him die. Let him starve to death. She had put it that way herself.

Medical ethics was a forest into which Roger Dowling had little desire to enter. The problems now posed by medicine were wholly unlike those of only a few years ago. In the natural rhythm of nature, as it had seemed, sixty-five had once marked the end of a person's active life. A few years of retirement and then the fatal attack or the more lingering exit of cancer. But today the retirement homes of the nation were packed to the seams with octogenarians, nonagenarians. Living to a hundred was no longer a rarity. And at the other end of the scale, there was an insufficiency of young people to bear the financial, to say nothing of the emotional, burden of all the elderly. From the point of view of convenience, let alone selfishness, the thought was bound to occur that there should be a legal way to terminate these apparently useless lives. There was a religious answer to that, of course. Sometimes it seemed that the only obstacle to such a grisly policy was religious belief. But even without it, in the nature of things, it should be clear that a human life is not something to be disposed of so casually.

Not that Paul Thomas fell into the category of those who exceeded their biblical three score and ten. He was still relatively young. He was, his coma apart, physically healthy. There was the prospect that he could be kept alive as he now was for years. For decades. Oh, it was a difficult prospect, no doubt of that. Father Dowling wished that he had been of more help to Mrs. Thomas.

"Well?" Marie Murkin said when he arrived back at the rectory. The housekeeper had come to the door of his study as if awaiting his report. But of course she and Mrs. McGrath had been old friends.

"She's dead, Marie."

"God have mercy on her soul. You gave her the Last Sacraments?"

"Yes."

"She'll go straight to heaven."

He said nothing. On such next-world matters, Marie was as much an authority as he was.

"Was it an easy death?"

One Christmas he had given Marie the poems of Emily Dickinson, thinking she would find a kindred soul in the Maid of Amherst, who seemed forever to be sitting beside a deathbed, but if Marie had read them she never gave any indication of it.

"Was Marge there?"

"And Leonard."

"Leonard!"

"Her son."

Marie gave him a look. "I know who he is, Father Dowling. I am surprised that he had the gall to face his mother at such a moment."

Marie's remark suggested that Mrs. McGrath had died in the sitting position, raking the room with her last glance before rattling out of the world. Her valedictory eyes would have fallen on the miscreant son with his three wives and their judgment would seem to come from the next world. Of course it hadn't been like that at all.

"They want McDivitt to do the funeral."

"I should think so."

McDivitt provided the parish calendars, each month featuring a picture of the kind called devotional, the hours of daily and Sunday Masses and other parish lore, with the saints of the day and days of obligation clearly marked. In return for this, McDivitt expected the pastor to steer the parish funeral business his way. Roger Dowling tried to keep free of the notion that McDivitt and St. Hilary's were one concern, but Marie's regard for what she called tradition made this difficult. Besides, it was a tradition. Most parishioners turned to McDivitt when the grim need arose.

"Was it an easy death?" Marie's eyes had widened as she asked the question and a moment later a little cry escaped her. She got her hankie out of the pocket of her apron and fled to the kitchen.

An easy death. It was not an absurd idea. Certainly Mrs. McGrath's death had been a lot easier than Paul Thomas's would be. But for whom would it be hard? Slipping out of this life from a coma might seem an attractive exit, but Roger Dowling decided he would prefer some minutes of lucidity before he met his maker. A little late for prayer, perhaps, but not too late. And of course he would want the enormous boon of the Last Sacraments. The dying woman had known when he began those prayers, it wasn't something simply done to her, but Paul Thomas was an object already disconnected from the world. His death would be difficult for his wife, Sheila, more difficult in the prolonged waiting than in the event itself. In a sense, she had already lost her husband. And she would be under pressure from doctors and the man with the grandiose title of medical ethicist to ease him on his way.

She knew it was wrong. However she would phrase it to herself, she knew she was being urged to do something that was wrong. Would she want the same thing done to her in similar circumstances? But it wasn't a matter of giving permission to another if what was being done was murder. And how else could you describe withholding food and drink from a still-living human being? It would be necessary to deny that Paul Thomas was still a human being. What was he, then? He wasn't dead. Whatever he was, he was alive. And Sheila Thomas was not inclined to give the go-ahead to those who wished to cut him off. But how long would she be able to withstand the pressures?

The day after the funeral of Mrs. McGrath, Marie was still discussing the behavior of Leonard at the funeral. Not only had he brought the seven children he had sired on his three wives, his current spouse sat beside him in a front pew, and the two former wives sat with their children just behind. Marge sat loyally with her brother.

"She should have refused to sit with him," Marie said.

"What would that prove?"

"Prove! It would prove that Catholics still take marriage seriously. The nerve of that man, bringing his whole harem to his mother's funeral."

Marie was often technically correct, from the standpoint of canon law, and she did not like being told that there was more to being Catholic than abiding by canon law.

"That still is part of it, though, isn't it?"

"It's still a part."

"That's my point."

"Leonard's mistakes don't give us a license to stop being Christian."

"What's that supposed to mean?"

"Love your neighbor."

"It's because I love him that I want him to straighten his life out."

That, alas, was not as simple as Marie made it sound. In fact, it was impossible. There was no way Leonard could deny the children he had fathered. His mistakes had had consequences in the real world and nothing could undo them.

"I suppose we could drown the children he had with the second and third wife."

"Drown them?"

"Pursuant to canon law. With all those bastards out of the way, as well as the two women, Leonard could be restored to the bosom of his first and true wife."

"Why are you pretending you don't agree with me?"

"Let's agree to feel sorry for Leonard. And pray for him."

Marie controlled herself with difficulty. Finally she said, "On one condition."

"What is it?"

"That we feel twice as sorry for his wife."

When Roger Dowling had been a member of the archdiocesan marriage tribunal he had confronted cases like Leonard's again and again. There was no canonical solution to them, the Church could not pretend that what had happened had not happened. People got themselves into messes from which there was no exit. Nor are they the only ones in need of mercy and forgiveness. But he had no desire to preach to Marie. Even if he had, he would have been saved by the bell. Marie answered the phone.

"Shei-lah Tho-mas," she pronounced silently, her hand over the phone.

He remembered the name immediately. Since it meant nothing to Marie, she was prepared to protect him from the caller. He took the phone and said hello.

"Father Dowling? We met at the hospital."

"I remember." Marie remained in the study, pretending to tidy up, wanting to get a clue as to the identity of the caller.

"About my husband."

"Yes. How is he doing?"

"No change. He's the same. The reason I'm calling is your asking whether we were Catholics? I said no."

"Yes."

"It's true I'm not, but I think Paul is."

"How so?"

"His baptismal certificate was among his papers. It's from a Catholic church in Minneapolis. Wouldn't that make him a Catholic?"

"Why don't you bring it over?"

"Now?"

"Are you free?"

"I'll be right there."

Half a minute went by after he hung up before Marie asked him who the woman was.

"You don't know her."

"That's why I'm asking."

"Sheila Thomas. She just discovered she's married to a Catholic. She's on her way over."

Roger Dowling lit a pipe and settled down with Dante, reading Canto XIII of the *Inferno* in the translation of Dorothy Sayers.

"I wonder where she is?" Marie asked, looking in at him. Father Dowling glanced at his watch. It had been forty-five minutes since Sheila Thomas called.

"She said she'd be right over."

"Where was she calling from?"

"She didn't say."

Marie's expression was not flattering, nor was her lengthy inhalation of air. Clearly she thought Father Dowling was responsible for Mrs. Thomas's tardiness.

Only she wasn't just tardy. Two hours passed and still she had not come. Maybe she had gotten cold feet at the thought of actually entering a Catholic rectory. It was one thing to talk to a priest on the phone or in a hospital, but in his parish house? He could imagine her shiver with dread.

Marie served dinner with an aggrieved air and Father Dowling was glad when Captain Phil Keegan called and asked if he could stop by.

"Is there a game on?"

"I just want to talk."

When Phil arrived, he settled into a chair, took the beer Marie offered him, then watched her leave. "What's wrong with her?"

"Someone failed to show up this afternoon."

"Sheila Thomas?"

"How did you know that?"

Phil sipped his beer. "Because your name and phone number were in her purse."

"Her purse?"

"She was found dead at five o'clock."

There was a gasp in the hallway and then Marie came into the study, her face a mask of guilty surprise. "I knew it," she cried. "I knew something was wrong."

What was wrong was that Sheila Thomas was dead and her death had been caused by a blow on the head, struck, presumably, when she was setting out for St. Hilary's. She was found in her garage, lying beside her car, the driver's door of which was open. The doors of the garage were shut.

"The remote control unit wasn't in the car," Phil added.

"Have you any idea who did it?"

"A thief, apparently. Her purse had been rifled pretty thoroughly and there was no money in it."

Phil's preliminary guess was that Sheila had been robbed by a stranger who was desperate for money in order to buy drugs.

"How did you know her, Roger?"

"I met her at the hospital. Her husband has been in a coma for weeks."

How ironic to think that she had talked to him about the rights and wrongs of ending his life, little knowing that soon her own would be violently taken.

"We haven't located any relatives yet. Any idea where we might look?"

"I hardly knew her, Phil. One short conversation. Pressure was being put on her to agree to stop feeding her husband."

"Was she going to do it?"

"Well, she hadn't."

Days passed and little more was learned about Sheila Thomas. Father Dowling told Phil that she had indicated her husband was originally from Minneapolis and the police there were contacted but without result—until the very day that Father Dowling was to officiate at her funeral. A call from Minneapolis indicated that James Cross, a cousin of Paul Thomas, was on his way. The funeral was postponed until he arrived.

It had been a week since Sheila Thomas was found dead that Jimmy Cross showed up. He was a tall man with sun-streaked hair, deeply tanned skin, and eyes that squinted. He was a professional golfer who made a living on the lesser tours. He was surprised that Sheila was still unburied.

"We postponed it for you," Father Dowling said.

"I hardly knew her."

"Paul is your cousin?"

"I haven't seen him for ten years."

"He's in a coma."

"Was he attacked too?"

Father Dowling read the Twenty-third Psalm at the gravesite and then took Jimmy Cross to lunch.

"I thought that prayer was Protestant."

He meant the Twenty-third Psalm. They talked about Paul then, whom Jimmy had now discussed with his cousin's doctors.

"Did they suggest that he be taken off intravenous feeding?"

Jimmy's eyes widened.

"Sheila felt she was under pressure to do that."

"Wouldn't he die then?"

"That's the idea."

"You mean he isn't going to wake up?"

"No one knows for sure."

Jimmy seemed more resistant to the idea of removing life support from the comatose Paul Thomas than Sheila had been. He said he was going to stay around and look after his cousin.

"Don't you have to get back to the tour?"

"Some things are more important than golf."

Father Dowling was cheered by his attitude and felt that Paul Thomas was in good hands. It came as a surprise, accordingly, when two days later he learned that Paul Thomas was dead. Phil Keegan told him the news.

"They pulled the plug. They had permission of the next of kin and they just stopped feeding the guy. The prosecutor won't go near it." Phil shook his head. "Why the hell that isn't murder beats me."

The following day, Marie announced with a look in her eye that a Mr. James Cross had come to see the pastor of St. Hilary's. Father Dowling touched a match to his pipe, not liking the prospect ahead. Would Jimmy expect to be told that he had done the right thing?

"Paul's dead, Father Dowling."

"I heard."

He rubbed his leathery face with a leathery hand. "They cut off his food."

Father Dowling waited. Cross looked at him confusedly. "What should I do?"

"About what?"

"They killed Paul. They starved him to death. Is that legal? Can they get away with that?"

"You didn't give the go-ahead?"

"To kill Paul? No!"

This was a matter better put to Phil Keegan, so Roger Dowling called him. Roger had by that time heard the story but he listened while Jimmy told it to Phil. Doctor Jepson claimed Jimmy had given permission for life support to be withdrawn, but the golfer insisted he had done no such thing.

"You want to accuse him of killing your cousin?"

"He did, didn't he?"

The dispute was not about that, however, but about whether Jepson had done so with the permission of Jimmy Cross as next of kin. The doctor assured Phil that the cousin had given permission.

"He told you to stop feeding his cousin?" Phil asked.

Jepson was nervous with Father Dowling looking on, but the priest wanted to know what exactly had happened.

"No. He told Dr. Rand, the ethicist."

Rand had a large inner office near the main entrance of the hospital. He looked out before the secretary let him know they were there, a little man with raised eyebrows and a wispy goatee. He seemed to see a colleague in Father Dowling, but when Phil said he was a policeman the little man's brows lifted higher.

"Come in, come in."

"There seems to be some confusion about Paul Thomas's

death," Phil said.

"Confusion?" His eyes darted to Father Dowling, then away. "He was finally allowed to die."

"Dr. Jepson says you told him James Cross gave permission to have the tubes removed."

"Yes, he did." The brows lowered then went up again. "Is something wrong?"

"James Cross denies giving permission."

Rand was astounded. "But that's not true. He told me he saw no point in prolonging it and to go ahead." He thought. " 'Go ahead.' That's just what he said."

Confronted with this, Jimmy Cross thought about it. "I told him to go, to get the hell out, not to kill my cousin."

If nothing else, Rand had made a massive mistake in not having Jimmy Cross sign a release form. After the extended effort to settle the matter, he had told Jepson immediately, figuring the form could be taken care of later. When he returned to his office, James Cross was no longer there. He seemed to have left the hospital. Even then, Rand had not been concerned. Now, confronted with Cross's denial, his brows settled slowly into normal position while in his eyes there dawned the realization that he had put the hospital in a vulnerable position.

"They can't get away with this, Father Dowling," Jimmy Cross said after telling him of his conversations with Tuttle the lawyer. "I am inclined to accept Tuttle's advice and bring suit against the hospital."

Father Dowling would have preferred to have someone like Amos Cadbury advising Jimmy Cross. Tuttle was a bit of an ambulance chaser. That a cousin who had not been at all close to the deceased should seek to profit from Paul Thomas's death was unseemly. Particularly when he seemed to be the sole heir as well, now that Sheila too was dead. Two days before, he had talked with Phil Keegan about Sheila.

"Has there been any progress in the investigation of Sheila Thomas's death?"

Phil made a face. "Random killings are the hardest, Roger. Whoever killed her wanted her money, that's all. It was utterly impersonal."

"Didn't you say the garage doors were down when the body was found?"

Phil nodded. "She would have opened them with the remote control that was in the car."

"She went from the kitchen into the garage, opened the car door and had not yet opened the garage door. So her assailant was already inside the garage. That sounds premeditated rather than random."

The garage door could be opened from the kitchen as well, and this suggested another scenario. She had opened the doors before entering the garage and then, about to get into her car, had been bludgeoned from behind.

"By someone who was just passing by?"

"What are you getting at?"

Father Dowling wasn't sure. Either supposition—that Sheila had opened the doors or had not before going into the garage—made it difficult to think that some stray passerby had just taken it into his head to assault and rob her. If she hadn't opened the doors, the assailant must have been lurking in the garage. If she had opened the doors, the assailant had to be lurking in the neighborhood, looking for an opportunity to rob someone, anyone, and Sheila just happened to be it. How much money could she have had in her purse to justify such violence? Wouldn't a determined thief, having killed her, gone into the house to see what valuables might be there? But the house had not been entered.

Now, with Jimmy Cross seated in the rectory study, telling Father Dowling of his plans to seek damages in the death of his cousin, the priest asked what the golfer intended to do with the house.

"What do you mean?"

"Everything comes to you, doesn't it?"

"I guess it does."

"Why do you suppose Dr. Rand would have lied about your giving permission to remove Paul's life support?"

"You'll have to ask him."

"I did talk to him. I got the impression he was telling the truth."

Jimmy Cross bristled. "Then you're saying that I'm lying."

"That makes more sense."

"What do you mean?"

"People lie, or kill, for a reason. Rand had no motive. You on the other hand did. I suppose at first it was just the money the Thomases already had. Now there is the added chance of getting a judgment against the hospital."

Jimmy Cross's great tanned hands gripped his kneecaps and he leaned toward Father Dowling. "I hope you haven't talked such nonsense to anyone else."

"Your big mistake was in closing the garage door."

Cross rocked back in his chair, his eyes narrowing.

"Fingerprints, Jimmy. When you pressed that button . . ."

Jimmy got to his feet, a smile on his face. "I'm not going to listen to any more of this, Father. I will say this. If you keep up this kind of talk I'll bring a suit for slander." He shook his head sadly. "And you're a priest."

The big man left the study and stomped down the hall to the front door, which he pulled noisily shut after him.

For nearly an hour, Father Dowling tried to read, tried to distract himself, tried to get his mind on something other than Jimmy Cross. Finally, he went over to the church, but he wasn't any more successful there in driving it from his mind. When he headed back to the rectory, Marie came hurrying toward him.

"Phil Keegan called. He said to tell you 'bingo.' "

"Thank God!"

"Father Dowling, you're not starting bingo at St. Hilary's, are you?"

"I think I'll quit while I'm ahead."

Phil came by later with the full story. Jimmy Cross had been followed when he left the rectory and led the police to a county road where he had parked. The police waited until he searched the field and found the remote control before taking him into custody.

"Did he confess?"

"It doesn't matter. There were letters in the house he had written to Sheila Thomas, thanking her for telling him about his ailing cousin. He had been making only peanuts for years and must have seen the prospect of at least a small inheritance."

"If there was no widow when Paul Thomas died."

Phil shook his head at the perversity of men. "He had been off the golf tour for weeks and he wasn't in Minneapolis. Chances are we'll find he was right here in Fox River."

"Was he much of a golfer?"

"Cy tells me Cross was good. But not under pressure. He had a record for losing in playoffs."

"Sudden death?"

Phil looked at Father Dowling. "This time he'll really lose."

"I'll go see him."

THE GIVEAWAY

1

The sunlight streaming through the west window of the front parlor of St. Hilary's rectory was alive with dust, no matter the fastidious housekeeping of Marie Murkin. The woman seated across from Father Dowling was the housekeeper's age, more or less, although it was difficult to imagine Marie as elegantly attired as this caller. Her name was Amity Doremus. "Mrs. Amity Doremus." She sat erectly, her shoulders not touching the back of the chair, her face a mask waiting an expression.

"And how can I help you?"

"I murdered my husband."

Her voice was calm. The only indication of feeling was in the large eyes, their effect heightened by mascara.

"Literally?"

"I am quite serious."

"Are you making a confession?"

"I'm not a Catholic."

"Tell me about it."

"I have the impression that you don't believe me."

"Why are you telling me this?"

This surprised her. "But you're a priest."

"And you're not a Catholic. If you were a Catholic, you would be here to confess your sins and ask God's pardon."

"I don't believe in God."

"All the more reason that I should be surprised."

"My husband was a Catholic."

"I see." After a moment, he said, "Tell me about the murder."

She hesitated, unsure whether he was patronizing her. She must after all realize he would think her mad. Father Dowling did not know what to make of her extraordinary remark. Mrs. Doremus gave the impression of a woman who never lost control. It was difficult to imagine her murdering her husband in a fit of anger.

"I wanted to be rid of him. I thought I loved another and Andre would not let me go." She lifted the gloves she held, then let them fall back on her lap. "He said he was Catholic and could not divorce me. He said this almost gleefully. He himself had no need of divorce."

"I don't understand."

"He led a very active love life."

"Who was your accomplice?"

"Does it matter?"

"He seems essential to your story."

"His name was George."

He let it go at that. "You make it sound as if this happened long ago."

"It did."

"How long ago."

"Nearly ten years. It will be ten years in April."

Father Dowling sat back. "Ten years ago?"

"Yes. And it was all to no avail. The man who said he was in love with me lost interest once I was free of Andre and had become an eligible widow. Of course the circumstances had something to do with that."

"Circumstances."

"The body was never found."

"Andre Doremus! I remember now. But he drowned in the Fox River. There was a flood." The memory came vividly back.

"His riverside cottage was swept away by the flood . . ."

Her Arctic smile confirmed the accuracy of his memory. "Yes. That was the story."

The Fox River periodically overflowed its banks during a spring thaw after a winter of heavy snow, sweeping trees and boats and even houses before it. Father Dowling had often marveled at the way people would rebuild in the vulnerable spot, as if counting on disaster not striking twice in the same place. The name of Andre Doremus stood out in memories of a long-ago flood. The man had tried valiantly to save his cottage and was swept away with it when his efforts failed. Father Dowling looked across the table at his visitor.

"There was a search."

"A prolonged search. At my urging. I offered a reward."

"So how could you have murdered him?"

"He was bound and unconscious in the cottage when it was swept down river."

"You offered a reward for the recovery of his body?"

"Yes."

"Did you have to pay it?"

"The body was never found."

"I thought not. Perhaps he survived."

She shook her head. "He would have let that be known, believe me." But she was done with that topic. "I have come to make a contribution to your church."

"Why?"

"In memory of Andre."

"He was not a member of this parish."

"Nor of any other. I have indicated the kind of Catholic he was. He never went to church. Mass, isn't it? He lived like a pagan but insisted he was a Catholic."

"Do you think money can make up for what you have done?"

"I would like you to say prayers for him. He always said that in the end he would straighten his accounts with God. He wore a medal. He said it was miraculous."

Had the poor fellow thought a miraculous medal was a license to sin boldly?

"You seem more concerned for his soul than he was."

"The money. It is an embarrassment to me. I wanted to be rid of Andre, not become a rich widow." She took a check from her purse and placed it on the table. Father Dowling glanced at it. A series of zeroes followed a digit. She turned it toward him: $100,000.

"Good Lord!"

"Not even Andre knew he would come into so much money."

An ancient aunt had squirreled away stock that she had bought when the computer revolution was a mere twinkle in the eyes of youthful visionaries. In making Andre the principal beneficiary of her estate, Aunt Rhoda had thought the riverside cottage was the main bequest. The dimensions of her fortune became known when the IRS gained access to her all-but-forgotten safety deposit box. Her electronic shares had not been discovered until long after the flood that had carried off the beneficiary.

"I cannot accept this," Father Dowling said, pushing the check toward her.

"But you must!"

"You are wrong if you think that could be recompense for what you have done. You must tell your story to the police."

She stiffened in her chair. "You can't tell anyone what I told you. This conversation is confidential."

"You must confess."

"To you?"

"You are not a Catholic, you do not even acknowledge the existence of God. What would be the point?"

"It would bind you to secrecy."

People who knew nothing else about the church knew of the seal of the confessional, but then it had figured in so many bad stories and films.

"I will keep in confidence what you have said. But you must go to the police."

"Only if you accept this check."

The money lent credence to her otherwise improbable story. The check also seemed a way to motivate her to go to the police. Two minutes later, he watched her walk out to her parked car and get in. What does a woman who has murdered her husband look like? The answer seemed to be: like any other woman.

2

Marie Murkin could not believe her ears. She had monitored the conversation in the front parlor to the degree that she could without calling attention to herself. Of course it would not have done simply to stand in the hallway and cock an ear at the parlor door. It was essential to her image of herself that Marie not engage in such obviously censurable conduct. If she overheard things it had to be in the line of duty. So she had tiptoed from the dining room to the study and back again; she had advanced down the hallway to see if there might be someone standing at the door who was unable to bring himself to ring the bell, she went back to the study and stood in the doorway thinking what she would do to that room if the pastor had not put it outside the bounds of her housekeeping responsibilities. All in all, she managed to catch the gist of what went on in the front parlor.

"You must get it into the bank, Father, a check that size."

"It's the same size as any other check."

She was the soul of patience; it was her only defense against his teasing. "I mean the amount."

"What is the amount?"

"Let me see it."

"I think you're right. I'll put it in a safe place. In my study."

"It won't earn interest there."

"Oh, I don't plan to keep it."

Marie was aghast. A parish is of course a nonprofit operation, but Father Dowling's indifference to finances forever threatened that St. Hilary's would plunge into debt. Marie had a horror of debt. During the reign of the mad friars before Father Dowling was assigned as pastor, the mendicants had diverted large sums to their order, entering the sums as salary, of course, but Marie had been appalled. They had all taken the vow of poverty yet they dunned the parish for everything, taking their brothers in religion out to dinner and recovering the money from parish funds. There was nothing exactly dishonest about any of this, but Marie had been shocked. The parish might go bankrupt but their order would flourish financially.

Father Dowling took nothing for himself; his salary was one that would have caused rebellion in an assistant, and he seemed more embarrassed than delighted when donations came his way. Now here he was treating a large and unlooked for gift as if it were a bill to be paid rather than needed replenishment of parish funds.

"Of course God will look after us," Marie said.

"He always does."

"So it isn't presumption to count on it?"

"Do we need money, Marie?"

"Money? What for? We can eat at the center for the homeless. Or I could beg from door to door. Perhaps you could rent out a room or two."

"Things aren't that bad."

"Would you like to go over my accounts?"

For answer he opened his desk and took out the check. "Take it."

Marie staggered backward when she saw the amount. Her outside guess had been ten thousand dollars. Would the pastor have been reluctant to take a check for several hundred dollars? Or a thousand? His reaction required a large amount. But one hundred thousand dollars! And he was telling her to put it into her household account.

"This would last me forever."

"That's the idea. You'll never be able to complain about money again."

But Marie was looking at the signature. "Amity Doremus."

"The widow of Andre. Do you remember him?"

She had distinctly heard Father Dowling tell the woman that her husband had not been a member of St. Hilary's parish. "Why should I remember him?"

Listening to his account of the flood and the damage and the man missing along with his cottage did not trigger any memories in Marie Murkin.

"It is good of her to commemorate him in this way, Father."

"It is a holy and wholesome thought to pray for the dead."

"Who said that?"

"He's dead now."

Marie took the check with her into the kitchen where she inspected it as if it were a relic of some especially important saint. She had never before held so much money in her hand before, and she felt that the check should look different because it was worth so much. But it could have been made out for ten dollars rather than the breathtaking amount that Amity Doremus had written it for.

Doremus. Doremus. Marie repeated the name, feeling that she were practicing her scales. And then the scales dropped from her eyes, or at least from her memory. This was the wayward nephew of old Rhoda Farley, who had been a daily communicant and had often enlisted Marie's cooperation in novenas for the coming back of her nephew Andre. Yes, that had been his name. Andre. Marie had never met the man but she had developed a definite image of him from his long-suffering aunt's lamentations.

"His aunt was Rhoda Farley," she said to Father Dowling, having marched right into the study to tell him.

He looked at her blankly.

"Andre Doremus, the man whose widow gave us all that money."

"But Rhoda Farley was poor as a church mouse. I remember the funeral. McDivitt cut costs to the bone."

"She was frugal," Marie said.

"Did you know she had money?"

"Money?"

"That check comes indirectly from her."

Marie sat. Was it possible that Rhoda Farley had been a wealthy woman? But this question was edged out by the memory that was forming of the church on the day Rhoda was buried. It was a small group of mourners, mainly other women who like Rhoda had frequented the church for Mass and other devotions. But a front pew had been reserved for relatives, and there had been a woman in it. And the woman was Amity Doremus! But for all her efforts, Marie could not recall ever having seen Rhoda's nephew. God rest his soul. Her hand went to the apron pocket in which she had put the check.

3

Captain Phil Keegan had neither the resources nor the desire to investigate ten-year-old deaths, and Mrs. Doremus's statement that she had been responsible for her husband's death during the famous flood only annoyed him.

"You hurried right down to turn yourself in?"

She closed her eyes. "I am here and I have told you why."

"You killed your husband?"

"I did."

"By leaving him tied and unconscious in a cabin that the flood conveniently swept away?"

"That was my intention."

"I remember that at the time you insisted on a protracted search for the body."

"That was a calculated risk."

"What would you have said if he had been found with his hands and feet tied?"

"Nothing."

"I wish you had kept it that way."

"Am I under arrest?"

"No."

"No?"

"You've told me a story without corroboration or witnesses. And without a *corpus delicti*. It is best to have a body when you make a murder charge. Even with a body there is need of evidence."

"But I am confessing."

"To having killed a man whose absence is explained by being in his riverside cottage when it was washed away in a flood."

She seemed reluctant to be given her freedom but at the same time Phil Keegan had the sense that he was playing a role in a script she had written. That evening he stopped by the St. Hilary rectory to chat with Roger Dowling. In the course of the evening he told him of Amity Doremus's visit to headquarters.

"Where is she now?"

"At home, I suppose."

"You let her go?"

He told Roger what he had told Mrs. Doremus. "There might not be a statute of limitations on murder, Roger, but waiting this long to mention it has the same effect. If she is telling the truth."

"Why would she lie about a thing like that?"

"People are nuts."

"She gave me a check for one hundred thousand dollars."

Marie was in the doorway of the study with a beer for Phil Keegan. She looked at him expectantly to see what his reaction would be to their good news.

"Have you tried to cash it?"

Marie nearly dropped the tray she was holding. It had never occurred to her that the check might not be good. The fact that the woman had gone downtown with a story about murdering her husband made anything possible. Marie wished she had gotten a better look at their presumed benefactor. The pastor had answered the door and the two were ensconced in the front parlor before Marie knew there was anyone in the house. Then she had to have recourse to a number of subterfuges to keep herself *au point* on parish business.

"Marie?"

She put down the tray and drew the check from the pocket of her apron. Suddenly it had the look of monopoly money. She handed it to Phil in a careless gesture, lest he think she was easily taken in by mad widows distributing large rubber checks on their way to confess to long-ago murders.

"It looks all right," Phil said.

Marie harrumphed. Neither the pastor nor Phil Keegan could have told from her stoic exterior that she was crying on the inside. For some hours the large benefaction in her apron pocket had made her buoyant.

"Marie will put it in the bank in the morning."

"I am not going to let them think I think it is any good."

"I'm sure it's good," Father Dowling said. "Remember Rhoda Farley."

Marie left them alone, and Phil and Roger Dowling talked of the flood and the extended search for the body of Andre Doremus.

"It was never found."

"Only a section of the roof of the cottage was certainly identified. It had taken a real beating. If Doremus was in there, even conscious and unbound, it is doubtful he would have survived."

"Wouldn't his body rise?"

It seemed a theological question. "That depends."

He suggested a number of ways in which a submerged body might not come to the surface, but Roger stopped him.

"Well, it may have taken her ten years but she did try to confess."

"And she gave you a hundred thousand dollars."

"She gave the parish a hundred thousand dollars."

"If the check is good."

But the next day Roger Dowling called Phil to tell him that the bank had indeed accepted the check.

4

It was with some satisfaction that Amity Doremus called Charles to tell him that everything had gone off as planned. But the grateful congratulations she had expected were not forthcoming. He was merely matter-of-fact.

"Will he publicize the gift?"

"He was reluctant to accept it. As we suspected."

"*You* suspected. No preacher turns down money."

"He is a priest."

"What's the difference?"

Amity did not know any preachers but she was sure Father Dowling was different. It had been difficult to take satisfaction in enacting the little scene that Charles had dreamt up because of the priest's unsettling way of avoiding the role assigned him.

From his initial skepticism to his reluctance to take the check, she had to keep tight control of herself in order to bring off the scene. What sustained her was the thought of Charles's approval and how they would celebrate their little victory afterward. Yet he seemed distracted while she told him of her visit to police headquarters.

"Are you listening, Charles?"

"To every word." His voice became vibrant as she regained his full attention. That was how he was. To observe Charles, to watch him with others, was not to be under his spell, but when she was the focus of his attention she felt that she had become the center of the universe. She was forty-two years old, a widow, and often before unlucky in love, yet she felt like a schoolgirl with Charles. When he was attending to her. The thought suddenly came home to her that she had given away one hundred thousand dollars of her own money simply because Charles had asked her to.

"As a precaution."

He explained to her that they would have more than enough money, millions, but that he would find it difficult to explain how he had come into such wealth. He had managed several pension funds and over time had sequestered a goodly sum that was safe in a Swiss bank account.

"It must appear that we are living on your money, my love. And that you have it in abundance."

She had explained to him that he was the first one to whom she had given any idea of the amount of money that had come her way from Andre's Aunt Rhoda. Nor had she lived as a woman of wealth. If she could have thought of an unobtrusive way to do it, she would have given it all away long ago. She was ashamed of it. Not because she had inherited it from a husband whose death she had contrived, but because her partner and supposed lover had deserted her before Aunt Rhoda's safety deposit box was open, enriching Amity as a result of killing Andre. Would George have left her if he had learned of the money first? She knew the answer to that and was plunged into gloom. She should have felt remorse for killing Andre. What she did was finance a long, much-publicized and hopeless search for the body, wanting to make George uneasy. What if the body were discovered, what if the wrists and ankles were still bound with the rope that George had purchased and could likely be traced to him? She indulged herself in fantasies of his apprehension, and her own denial of any knowledge of what he had done to her beloved husband.

But the body was not found, she never saw George again, and she had sought substitutes for him on cruises, European travel, always elsewhere, until her heart felt sodden as a dishcloth. For six years she had lived like a nun, but then Charles came into her life.

Her first thought was that he was a scoundrel and her second that she did not care. He seemed the belated reward for what she had done to Andre and what she had suffered from George. He told her of his embezzling without blinking an eye and she listened to him without surprise.

"You should not tell me such things."

"Oh, it's untraceable. At least to me."

He had transferred money to a trustee of the fund, unbeknownst, and waited. More than enough time went by for the man to discover the sum. He said nothing. Thus the trustee had colluded in his own fate if the auditors began to wonder where even larger sums had gone. Charles laundered his own assessments, as he called them, through the trustee's account, but in a way undetectable by his unwitting collaborator.

"How lucky that you have money of your own," he said to her.

She fought the suspicion that he had known this from the

beginning, that he had selected her for that reason. He wanted a wife with whom he could enjoy the fruit of his embezzling while creating the impression that it was her money that enabled them to live in the style he envisioned.

"The police sent you home?" He chuckled.

"Despite my pleas."

She basked in the approval his tone conveyed. He was in Minneapolis; he would be flying back to Chicago in the morning.

"I'll pick you up."

"That's not necessary."

"I didn't imagine that it was. What airline will you be on?"

She detected his reluctance but he gave her the name of the airline. Once more, it seemed, she had a purpose in life. She wanted to hold him on the phone, keep the line open throughout the night, even if he were not talking to her. It was an umbilical cord that connected her to the source of her existence. Of course they hung up. And of course she sat there in the darkening room and cried, not knowing the source of her tears, somehow certain that they were not temporary. Charles was a rogue, an opportunist, a thief. And she didn't care.

Giving money to a Catholic priest had been her idea, and he had regarded it as inspired, particularly when she explained that Andre had been a Catholic of sorts. "The aunt who left him the money was very pious. Her parish was St. Hilary."

"Maybe you should give the money in memory of her."

But she had insisted that it had to be for Andre. Her affair with Charles was meant to round out once and for all what had begun with Andre—or rather with George. Charles wanted to marry her, he wanted the respectability he thought she represented. When she told him how she had watched George tie up her unconscious husband as the cottage was beginning to lift with the rising waters, he looked at her with a new respect.

"You're a girl after my own heart."

A girl of forty-two. But the gift to Father Dowling established that she could write out a check for that amount without batting an eye. The truth was that it was a significant fraction of her money. But that was its appeal. She was casting the dice insouciantly, betting on her future with Charles. Confessing to the murder of Andre was more complicated. Of course she knew that it could not be proved. She herself could not prove that she had done it. The only witness was George and he could only implicate her by implicating himself. But then she did not even know where George now was.

She slept on the couch, sitting up, not wanting to leave the spot where she had talked with Charles.

The next day she was apprehensive when he came into view among the deplaning passengers, but he greeted her with a smile and took her in his arms. All the way back to Fox River he outlined for her the donations she would be making.

"Charles, that will use up everything I have."

He laughed and squeezed her hand. "It doesn't matter. Then you will be completely dependent on me."

The prospect, if somewhat unsettling, was in the main pleasing. A woman wants to be dependent on her man.

5

Two days later Father Dowling could not find the morning paper anywhere. It was not in the clip beneath the mailbox, it was not on the stoop or in the flanking shrubbery. Not to have one's morning paper is a small thing, but large enough to generate annoyance.

"It's not outside?" Marie asked, not turning from the sink.

"No."

"It's outside every morning."

"And every morning you bring it in. Did you look for it?"

There was silence. Marie had stiffened.

"Marie, where is it?"

She hunched a shoulder toward a cupboard. He opened it and the paper cascaded out, section by section. But, as if fated to do so, the headline of the relevant section stared up at him. *Fox River Parish Receives Six-Figure Gift.* Marie had turned toward him and seemed to cringe, as if fearing a blow.

"How on earth did they hear of that?" He tried to keep accusation from his voice. There was something corrupting about having this much advantage over another human being. Marie was the picture of guilt. But she was also capable of recovery. And she grew bold when she saw that he had decided on a course of sweet reason.

"I should not have told anyone, Father. I see that now."

"How many did you tell?"

"I will take the blame." Her chin lifted and an expression of nobility formed on her face.

What taking the blame came to was difficult to say. Out of danger, Marie began to reap the fruits of her indiscretion. Father Dowling found her on the phone every time he picked it up, and her excited voice made it clear what the topic was. Finally he cleared his throat, silence fell, and the phone went dead. Ten minutes later Marie headed down the walkway toward the school and the parish center for senior citizens. She had dozens of oldsters there to bring up to date on the Doremus benefaction. That is why Marie was not there when the man came up on the back porch and ran his palm over the screen door as if it were a musical instrument. Father Dowling turned from the counter where he had been pouring himself a cup of coffee. The silhouetted figure raised an arm in dramatic greeting. "Peace."

"Peace."

Father Dowling stepped onto the porch and sat on the railing looking at his caller. What was visible of his face through the full beard was weatherworn and his pouched eyes seemed serene. "I'm Father Dowling, the pastor here."

The man nodded and his beard shaped itself into a smile.

"Could I offer you something to eat?"

"That would be very nice."

"Come in."

"Oh I can eat it out here."

"Nonsense. Come in."

Father Dowling made the man a sandwich and poured a glass of milk, then sat across the kitchen table from him.

"What brings you here."

"I'm a Catholic." He reached into his shirt and brought out a chain with a medal on it.

"Where do you live?"

He made an expansive gesture. "Wherever I am. I roam the world like Oedipus."

Father Dowling lifted his brow. "Oedipus?"

"I read, Father. Homer, the Greek dramatists, Virgil."

"You should read Dante."

"I have."

Matter-of-fact, no braggadocio about it. The myth of the wise and benign tramp had not survived Father Dowling's experience with gentlemen of the road. Rectories were an attractive target, and most wanderers claimed to be Catholic, though a question or two sufficed to show that the claim was merely instrumental. Marie had an aversion to visitors like this one and would run them off after giving them an apple or orange.

"Do you know how monks think of each guest?"

"Guest! That was a bum, Father Dowling."

"They treat guests as Christ in disguise. When I was hungry—"

"I give them an apple."

He did not however press the point. It was one thing for him to ask a hobo in but he did not want Marie doing it when he was not there.

"How long have you been traveling?"

Another smile. "That is a kind way of putting it. One of the advantages of the life I lead is that I no longer have to count time. Or bother with the news of the day. The war in the Gulf was over before I knew of it."

"You don't read newspapers?"

"Not as a habit."

"We have an interesting local paper."

"I've seen it."

"Ah."

The man accepted the offer of another sandwich, and Father Dowling enjoyed being there with him although it was unpleasant to be downwind of him.

"What's your name?"

"The name Ulysses gave to the Cyclops."

"No man?"

"Or nomad." He laughed at his own joke. His teeth seemed in remarkably good condition. He was still there when Marie returned.

She hurried into the kitchen, stopped, and stared at the bearded man sitting at her table. On any other occasion she would have played a dramatic scene with such materials. But not this time.

"Father, have you heard? He's dead. It was just on television."

"Who is dead?"

"Charles Blanding."

"Who is Charles Blanding?"

"They said he lived with Amity Doremus! He was found in her car in her garage. Gagged and bound with the motor running."

Father Dowling picked up the phone and put through a call

to Phil Keegan. While he waited, Marie continued to chatter. Phil wasn't available and Father Dowling left a message asking him to call. Then he realized that his visitor had left.

"Why did you let him in?" Marie asked.

"I think I knew his aunt."

6

His name, Phil Keegan told Father Dowling twenty-four hours later, was not Charles Blanding.

"At least not always. His fingerprints identified him as Ernest Whelan. He's been in prison off and on. Short stretches. He's a con man. That appears to be the motive."

Father Dowling said nothing. The police were proceeding on the assumption that Amity Doremus had done in her live-in lover. Or die-in, as it turned out. The bank on which she had drawn the check for one hundred thousand dollars had discreetly divulged without the need for a subpoena that the Doremus account had been all but drained in a matter of days.

"At Whelan's instigation?"

Phil nodded. He had put down his beer and was having the usual difficulty getting the cellophane off the cheap cigars he smoked.

"He persuaded her to give her money away?"

"All of it. There may be a few thousand left."

"What advantage was there in that for Whelan?"

Phil lit his cigar, taking his time. He smiled at Father Dowling through the smoke. "All the charities turned out to be Whelan."

"Isn't it amazing that she would give away everything?"

"People are nuts, Roger. Particularly women."

Well, it was a theory. The fact that Amity Doremus had confessed to the murder might be said to bear it out. Phil did not seem to find a conflict between his view that she had given away all her money and then killed the man at whose suggestion she had become a benefactress. Unless she had found out that he was the beneficiary. Except of course for the one hundred thousand Marie had put into the bank. There seemed more than pastoral reasons for going downtown and talking to Mrs. Doremus.

"I don't want to talk to you," she said, when she had seated herself in the visiting room. "But this is a change of scene at least."

"You could go home."

She looked at him. "They won't set bond for me."

"You could take back your confession."

She looked at him in silence. He waited for a full minute, but she said nothing.

"Did Andre get in touch with you?"

The question so surprised her that her controlled exterior shattered. "Andre! Andre's dead." Her eyes narrowed. "Is that part of your praying for him, that he appears to me?"

"That almost never happens. Never, in my experience. So you haven't seen him?"

She thought he was mad or a fanatic, and she could be right. In any case, he was not inclined to tell her his guess that the hobo who had come to the rectory was her long-lost husband. And who else had better reason to duplicate the attempted murder in a way that would incriminate Amity? If Amity had known her husband was alive and in the vicinity, she might have drawn the same conclusion. Her confession then could have been a belated opportunity to atone for the attempted murder, and why not, if the man she had loved was now dead?

From the courthouse, Father Dowling went to the center for the homeless, where he chatted with Madeline Carey, who ran the place.

"That could be a dozen persons here," she said, nodding toward the tables where dinner was being eaten.

And indeed every other man bending over his tray of food wore a luxuriant beard. He supposed there was little motive to be clean-shaven when one was living on the streets. Madeline nodded.

"In many cases, it's also a reaction to prison life. Some prisons are lenient, but most are not. Hair cuts, clean-shaven."

The remark prompted Father Dowling to drive off to Joliet the next day, having made arrangements for someone to say his noon Mass.

"Who?" Marie asked in apprehension.

"There are so many kinds of Franciscan—"

"Oh dear God, no!"

He was teasing her. Old Father Kelly lived retired in the parish with his sister. Although she was eighty-four, he referred to her as his "kid sister."

It was bumper-to-bumper to Joliet. The mushrooming of the western suburbs over the past decade had been phenomenal. Now fields and farmhouses had given way to housing development after development. Where fields remained, the crop was sod to cover all the new yards. He got to the prison just before noon, and concelebrated Mass with Joe Blatz, the chaplain. Afterward, they had lunch on a metal-covered table in the refectory.

"This reminds me of the center for the homeless."

"At least they have a roof over their heads here, Roger. And three squares a day."

"Do you remember Ernest Whelan?"

Blatz shook his head sorrowfully. "I had no doubt in the world he would go back to doing the one thing he did well, cheating other people. But to be murdered like that."

"When did he take on the name Charles Blanding?"

"After he left."

211

"Do you suppose a man could serve a sentence under a false name?"

"If he committed a crime under that name, maybe." Blatz looked as if he could tell Roger stories but he listened while Roger told him of the hobo who had visited the rectory and of his suspicion that he could be the missing husband of the woman who had confessed to the murder of Whelan.

"Because he wore a miraculous medal?"

Roger Dowling smiled. "It does seem far-fetched. I guess I hoped he would turn out to have been here while Whelan was and then when he . . ." But he let his voice trail off.

"It's the ones they share cells with they often get together with afterward."

"Who shared a cell with Whelan?"

"There were several, over time. The last man was George Drew."

7

Few murders involve mysteries, and long experience had taught Phil Keegan that the most likely killers are spouses or children of the victim. Amity Doremus's irregular relation to Whelan made him as good, or as bad, as a husband, so her confession had fitted into Phil's conception of the likely. Fitted almost too well. He hadn't liked her seeming eagerness to say she had done it. When she came down to headquarters to state that she had arranged the death of her husband ten years ago he had the sense that she was playing a part. He had felt it even more in the case of Whelan.

"The man with whom she planned her husband's death was George Drew."

"I made the connection, Roger."

"Are you going to talk to him?"

"As soon as we find him."

Roger had called Phil from Joliet to tell him what he had learned from Father Blatz. Phil had been skeptical. Whatever his uneasiness about Amity Doremus's confession, the prosecutor liked it. Nonetheless, Phil put out an APB on George Drew. His prints were on record, which was a plus. He also asked, informally, that those in patrol cars keep an eye out for bearded homeless men. If they found one named Andre, he wanted to see him.

"Any identifying marks?" Cy Horvath asked. "I mean, beside the miraculous medal."

"Rope burns on his ankles and wrists."

Cy looked at him and he looked at Cy. Phil won, if that's what it was. Cy left without commenting.

George Drew was picked up in Sarasota a day later. Fortunately he had neglected to tell his parole officer that he was leaving the state, but then he had probably not planned to return. He was sullen and still untanned when Cy brought him back after fetching him from his flight at O'Hare.

"What is this?" he demanded, with the indignation that only a bad conscience can produce.

"You violated parole, George."

"Is that a capital crime?"

George had a narrow face and weak but dimpled chin. Only a woman could find him attractive, and many had. People are nuts, especially women.

"We thought you'd want to be a pallbearer for Ernest Whelan."

"You didn't have to arrest me for that. Of course I'll be a pallbearer. What a rotten thing to happen to him."

"It reminded me of another case, years ago."

"Yeah?"

"One involving a man named Andre Doremus."

George gripped the arms of his chair. He was still wearing

clothes fit for Florida weather. He looked from Phil to Cy Horvath.

"I want a lawyer."

8

The discovery of George Drew's fingerprints on the door leading from Amity Doremus's house into the garage changed a possibility into a likelihood. That Drew had wanted a lawyer need only be the precaution of someone who had learned that an arrest can lead to an indictment and then to prison. But not even being represented by Tuttle the lawyer could offset the physical evidence that George Drew had been at the scene of the crime. The victim was someone he knew.

"We hatched it at Joliet, Father," Drew said. He had been chain-smoking ever since Roger Dowling had been admitted to his cell.

"Tell me about it."

"Is this confidential?"

"Is the pope German?"

The fact that the body of Andre Doremus had never been found cast a pall over what George thought he had accomplished. And he had soon found Amity overly possessive, as if their shared secret bound them together no matter what. The prospect of the inheritance had not prevented his going.

"The question was, would she even get the money, and if so, when? The husband had to be declared legally dead." He waved the thought away, as if it were more annoying than the acrid cigarette smoke. "I never did understand it. But there she was, expecting me to support her until she got the money. I began to doubt that she ever would. It was years later that I found out she had come into a fortune."

"Why didn't you go back to her?"

George tucked in his chin and stared at Father Dowling.

"You don't understand women, Father."

"That's true. Of course I don't understand men either."

George had enlisted Ernest Whelan's assistance in separating Amity from the money he felt belonged to him. Whelan had played his part, all too well. The checks he had persuaded Amity to make out were all to bogus entities of which he was the only non-fictitious officer, and he had opened the accounts into which Amity's checks went.

"He didn't put a nickel into the partnership we had formed."

"So you killed him?"

George thought about him. "No, the exhaust from her car killed him."

"Why did you tie his ankles and wrists?"

"That was a message."

"To whom?"

"Amity."

And one that apparently she understood. Confessing to the crime was her way of getting police protection from her former partner in crime. The confession she had made to Phil Keegan about conspiring to kill Andre kept her in custody. She seemed not to object.

"I've nothing to live for, Father."

"Because you have nothing you would die for."

"I may die for what I did ten years ago."

Her money had been recovered from the late Ernest Whelan, but, as Amos Cadbury explained, she could not benefit from an inheritance on the basis of a crime. "If she killed her husband and thereby became his heir, the money is not hers."

"If she killed her husband."

"She says that she did."

And so the matter seemed to rest. An indictment was brought against George Drew for the murder of Ernest Whelan. The grand jury still puzzled over Amity Doremus's claim to have murdered her husband. With improbable gallantry, George refused to give testimony against Amity.

"Ten years ago? I have trouble remembering what happened ten days ago."

"You were in Florida," Phil reminded him.

"Yeah."

One afternoon Father Dowling looked up from his book to see Marie in the doorway of his study. Her lips moved while her face formed exaggerated expressions.

"What is it, Marie? If you don't want to speak audibly, you can write it down."

She inhaled through her nose, mastering her annoyance. She leaned toward him. "He's back."

"Who?"

"Him. That tramp."

She had left him on the back porch. Father Dowling went out to him and suggested that they sit in lawn chairs, in the shade of an oak. The bearded man shuffled along beside him. When they were out of earshot of Marie, they sat.

"You're Andre Doremus."

"I heard about the trouble Amity is in."

"If you come forward, she'll be in less trouble."

"I can't have her being punished for killing me."

"She tried."

He nodded and his eyes drifted over the lawn. "It's a sobering realization, that someone wished you were dead. Enough to kill you."

He fell silent, and they sat there as if meditating on his words. Then he said, "I thought I had loved life before, Father, but I really didn't. When I got my hands and feet free and got out of that cottage before it disintegrated, it was like being born again. Just being alive was a miracle."

"You were being looked after."

Pouched eyes looked at the priest for a long moment, and then Andre Doremus nodded. "I believe that."

"What are you going to do?"

"Madeline Carey said to ask your advice."

The first thing was to get Amity out of jail. Twelve hours later man and wife confronted one another after a separation of ten years. Amity, despite her detention, was the picture of stylish elegance. Andre with his beard and tangled hair and faded clothing looked like the homeless wanderer he had been, but there was a hard-won wisdom about him that was almost palpable.

"The money of course is yours," Amos Cadbury said.

Andre smiled. "No, Amity had the right idea. Just give it away."

And he meant it. He gave the lawyer instructions and then signed the checks without hesitation.

"Will they get back together?" Marie Murkin wondered. "The Doremuses?"

For a decade Andre had felt his marriage had been dissolved by his wife's treachery. There seemed no way now that he could reenter the middle-class life he had been washed away from by the flooding Fox River.

"You're a romantic, Marie."

"He's Catholic, don't forget."

A lot more than he had ever been before. But it was Amity who dismissed any thought of a reunion. How could she live with a man she had tried to kill?

"You recognized me the first time I came to the rectory, didn't you?" Andre asked Father Dowling.

"I made a guess."

"What was the giveaway?"

"Your medal."

He fished it out as he had on his first visit. "A miraculous medal. And it is. It worked."

"What will you do?"

"Today? Just live."

"And tomorrow?"

"The same, if tomorrow comes."

Marie came up beside Father Dowling as he stood watching Andre walk slowly off into the eternal present in which he lived. He was like some holy eccentric from a Russian novel. Or a medieval mendicant. Franciscan.

"He should have been a Franciscan, Marie."

She let out a wail, threw up her hands and stomped off to her kitchen.

THE PRODIGAL SON

1

Father Dowling entered the school by the side door and stood in the hallway looking in at the seniors, who were diverting themselves in what once had been the gym. Someone came up beside him and touched his arm. He turned to the beatific smile of Genevieve Rush.

"Our Blessed Mother loves you very much, Father Dowling."

"I certainly hope so."

"Oh, she does, Father. She does."

Genevieve passed on into the room and took a chair at a card table. A minute later she was frowning over her bridge hand.

Father Dowling went off down the corridor to the erstwhile principal's office and looked in at Edna Hospers.

"What can I do for you, Father?" Edna asked.

"Nothing. Just being nosy."

"Come on in. There isn't anything much going on around here."

"You sound disappointed."

"Do I? I'm not."

"How's Genevieve Rush doing?"

Edna pushed back from her desk. "How did you know?"

Father Dowling took a chair opposite her. "Know what?"

"About her son, Harold."

"Tell me about her son, Harold."

"You honestly don't know?"

219

"Honestly."

Genevieve was in excellent physical health at the age of seventy-eight and faithfully frequented the Parish Senior Center where she could play bridge to her heart's content.

"She is the most cheerful person I know," Edna assured him.

"What about Harold?"

Harold was Genevieve's only son, although there was a daughter in Detroit. Edna's estimate of Harold's character was not flattering. He had been married twice but was childless and at the age of fifty-three had returned to Fox River and moved back in with his mother. By all appearances, Genevieve was happy as a lark to have his company.

"So what's the problem?"

"He wants to be declared her legal guardian."

The priest wrinkled his nose. "As her son, isn't he already responsible for her?"

"Father, he wants control of her property, of all her savings."

"Surely she can't have much."

"She has more than Harold and he wants it."

"How do you know this?"

"Genevieve told me. With a smile, as if it amused her, but I think I can read her moods and she is upset."

Father Dowling promised Edna that he would look into what was involved in such an effort as Harold Rush contemplated.

"She seems all right to you, doesn't she?"

"How do you mean?"

The priest hesitated. "Is her mind clear?"

"As a bell! Just watch her at cards. She seems to remember every hand she has ever played."

When Father Dowling returned to the rectory a message awaited him, and he was off immediately to the hospital, where old Fred Gissing was in a state of rapid decline. He had given Fred the last rites a few days before and now Fred had sunk into a coma which was complicated by pneumonia. The nurse gave Father Dowling a serious look when he came into the room in intensive care.

"Bad?"

"A few hours at most, Father."

Fred had outlived most of his friends and had no close relatives, so despite the constant medical attention he received he seemed abandoned. Father Dowling sat next to the bed, placed his hand on Fred's forehead and whispered a prayer. Then he opened his breviary and settled down. This was as good a place as any to say his office and if the end was near for Fred he wanted to be with him.

When he closed his book he looked around the room, a room like so many others in this building, nothing distinctive about it. The bed in which Fred lay was the standard one; the liquid trickling down the long plastic tube from the bottle hanging beside the bed brought whatever sustenance Fred could now take. The sounds from the hallway and from the nurses' station were almost soothing and the dark screen of the television mounted high in a corner did not compete with the monitor that kept the nurses informed of Fred's declining condition. He thought of the long journey Fred had taken over the years that would end in this room. Fred had already bade adieu to the conscious world and would slip from sleep into eternity.

Fred's condition was unchanged when Father Dowling left late in the afternoon, having been assured that the patient would make it into another day. He was no sooner seated behind the desk in his study when Marie stepped in and closed the door, her brows knit.

"Genevieve Rush is in the kitchen."

"Helping you get dinner?"

Marie just shut her eyes for a moment. "I have to tell you this."

"All right."

Marie leaned forward and whispered. "She says Our Blessed Mother smiles at her."

"I hope she does."

"In the church, Father Dowling. The statue of Mary."

"Ah."

"She says Mary speaks to her too."

"Why is she in the kitchen?"

"She has brought a message."

"What is it?"

"She wants to tell you." Indicating perhaps that Marie had been unsuccessful in prying the message from Genevieve.

"In that case, you had better ask her to come to the front parlor."

He pushed away from the desk as Marie hurried off. On the way to the front parlor, he found himself trying not to think of what Marie had said. Of course it connected with what Edna had told him earlier. If Genevieve claimed to be receiving messages from the statue of Mary in St. Hilary's church, it could prove to be very powerful ammunition for her son, Harold.

"Good afternoon, Father," Genevieve said brightly as she came into the parlor. "Or perhaps I should say good evening."

"Evening, I'm afraid. I suppose most people have gone home from the center."

Genevieve nodded vigorously, still smiling. "I was about to leave myself when I decided to make a visit. I like to say good-bye to the Blessed Mother before going home."

The priest nodded in approval.

"She asked me to tell you something."

"Our Lady asked you to tell me something?"

"She said not to worry about Fred. He'll be all right."

"Fred?"

"I assumed you would know. I didn't ask her which Fred."

It was of course no secret that Fred Gissing was ailing. News of ill health, particularly of mortal illness, spread quickly among the old people at the center. Doubtless Genevieve had heard of it. Perhaps Marie had told her the pastor had been at the hospital visiting Fred.

"Well, that is certainly good news."

Genevieve beamed. "She said it as if she knew you would think so."

It was all Father Dowling could do not to tell Genevieve to give his regards to the Blessed Mother. It was important not to patronize the old and of course he did not want to encourage her to think that she was getting messages from heaven.

"Thank you, Genevieve. That's very considerate."

And off she went, mission accomplished. Two minutes later Marie looked into the study. "Well?"

"Just fine. You?"

"I am referring to Genevieve."

"You're asking after her health?"

"Her mental health. Did she tell you she's having visions?"

"She just delivered a message."

Marie was stymied. She could hardly say that miraculous apparitions do not happen, but in her experience they did not happen to senior parishioners at St. Hilary's parish in Fox River, Illinois, but to peasant children in far-off countries you'd never heard of, countries that might as well be on the far side of the moon, the way they looked in the pictures, where anything might happen. On the other hand, she pardonably felt that if heaven had any special communications to make locally they could do worse than use the housekeeper of the St. Hilary rectory as spokesman.

"I hope you didn't encourage her."

"You doubt her word, Marie?"

"Of course I do."

He adopted a serious expression. "Marie, I have to tell you that judgments as to the veracity or non-veracity of such apparitions must be left to the Church."

"You think Our Lady is speaking to Genevieve Rush?"

"I don't want to anticipate the official judgment of the Church, Marie."

Exasperated, Marie stomped off to the kitchen where she would have burned the pastor's dinner if she could have brought herself to damage her own reputation as a cook.

In the meantime Father Dowling called up Amos Cadbury and asked the distinguished lawyer how a son would go about having himself declared the legal guardian of his aging mother.

"Is this about Genevieve Rush?"

"Has Harold been to see you?"

"I sent him packing. The idea of that ne'er-do-well returning after all these years and trying to take his mother's money and property away from her."

"So he can't do it?"

"Oh, he'll try. But I refused to be of any help in the matter. Some lawyer will take him as a client."

"What is the procedure?"

"Well, a judge would have to be shown that Genevieve is no longer capable of taking care of herself."

"That's nonsense."

"If you were to testify to that effect, that would influence the judge."

"Edna Hospers would say the same thing."

"All the better."

Marie served his dinner in silence, entering and leaving the room audibly but emitting only sounds of disapprobation and impatience. He was being punished. Actually, it was not unpleasant to have her give him the silent treatment. If they talked it would be about Genevieve and there was nothing more

to say on that score.

Phil Keegan was coming over later to watch the Bulls. Marie was making a maximum amount of noise in the kitchen, and Father Dowling was considering ways to mollify the housekeeper. It would not do to have this develop into a feud. But his thoughts drifted back to Genevieve and he hesitated. Fred will be all right, she had said, claiming to be passing on the message from the Blessed Mother. He reached for the phone and called the hospital.

"This is Father Dowling of St. Hilary's. Could you tell me the condition of Fred Gissing. He's in intensive care."

"I'll switch you there."

After a moment another voice came on the line. "Father Dowling calling. How is Fred Gissing?"

"Just a moment." He braced himself but the inevitable Muzak did not begin. Instead he heard as from a distance the sounds of intensive care. And then the nurse returned. "He's no longer here, Father."

"When did it happen?"

"Just an hour ago."

"God rest his soul."

"Oh, no, Father. He's better. He came out of the coma. He's been taken back to a room. His condition has been changed from critical to serious."

"He's gotten better?"

"Would you like to speak to a doctor?"

He told her no, that wasn't necessary. There had been an edge of resentment in her voice, as if she thought he didn't believe her. Well, it was welcome news, even if the circumstances made it particularly surprising. He went out to the kitchen.

"How about popcorn while Phil and I are watching the Bulls?"

"Yes, Father."

"He likes lots of butter."

"I know that, Father."

"Thank you."

They stood looking at one another in silence. It seemed an Olympic event. Who would give in first?

"I just called the hospital."

"Aren't you feeling well?"

"Fred Gissing's condition has improved. They moved him out of intensive care."

Her mouth dropped open and her eyes narrowed. She had been on the verge of relenting and here he was teasing her more.

"It's the truth, Marie. Call down there yourself."

"I will not."

But she did make popcorn, lots of it, and was very voluble once Phil arrived, pointedly addressing everything she said to him. She had a second beer in Phil's hand before he had finished the first.

"What's wrong with her?" Phil whispered.

"Has she changed?"

2

Tuttle of Tuttle & Tuttle was not apt to turn away a client, his practice being what it was, but in the case of Harold Rush the little lawyer's moral fiber was put to the test. The one virtue Tuttle would be granted by friend and foe alike was piety. His devotion to the departed father who had sustained him financially and morally during the twelve years it had taken his son to get through law school, and who had not wavered when Tuttle *fils* flunked the bar exams again and again, had been rewarded by Tuttle's undying gratitude. The father was the first Tuttle in the name of the firm, although he had been not been a lawyer nor was still in this vale of tears when his son finally put up his shingle and opened his office. That Harold Rush should

aspire to gain title to his mother's savings and the house in which she lived struck Tuttle as beneath contempt.

"She doesn't know up from down," Harold said. "God knows what she might do."

"Have there been any incidents?"

"I don't want any incidents, okay? She's pushing eighty."

"My father was eighty-two when he died."

"It's different with men."

"How so?"

"People aren't as likely to take advantage."

Tuttle pushed his tweed hat to the back of his head and looked beyond Harold. The man's unshaven beard was gray stubble on his dewlapped face; his nose had apparently been broken and set imperfectly. It seemed to be making a right turn when Harold was looking straight ahead.

"It is a complicated process."

"I'll be able to pay you. After it's done."

Tuttle took his feet off his desk and sat erect in his chair. "You want me to proceed on the assumption that you will pay me with money you get from your mother?"

"What's wrong with that?"

"From your point of view? Not much. From mine, everything."

"You're betting against yourself?"

Tuttle did not like the matter put in just that way, not least because it had a semblance of truth. "My contingency fee is of course considerably higher than a simple fee to represent you in such a matter."

"How much more?"

"Say you had an accident claim and I represented you. What percentage of any award do you think would be mine?"

"I don't know."

"Fifty percent."

Harold literally fell of his chair. He scrambled to his feet, his face flushed with anger. "You lousy crook. I'm going to report you to the bar association."

"Why don't you do that? They may censure me for suggesting so low a fee."

Uttering profanities, Harold stormed from the office. Tuttle was happy to see him go. To celebrate, he called up Peanuts Pianone and suggested that they meet at the Shanghai Wharf for a full-tilt Chinese dinner.

"You're on. What are we celebrating?"

"Integrity. Professional ethics. Hunger."

Peanuts was waiting for him when he got to the restaurant and they devoted an hour and a half to a massive intake of Chinese food. Afterward they were sleepy and repaired to Tuttle's office for forty winks. It was there, some time later, that Tuttle was rudely wakened by the voice of Harold Rush.

"Okay. I change my mind. You're my lawyer."

"Fifty percent."

Harold gritted his teeth and nodded. In the circumstances there was little else Tuttle could do. The only problem was that unless he really worked on the case he would make nothing, But then that is what he would have made if he had not taken it. It followed that he had nothing to lose by taking plenty of time to decide whether he would help Harold Rush's cause prosper. It went against the grain. He felt that he had been retained to help the Prodigal Son dispossess his unsuspecting father.

3

Edna had just set out new chalk for the pool tables, a commodity she had to ration because of the tendency of pool players to fancy themselves Minnesota Fats. Before each shot, they sent up clouds of chalk dust preparing the tip of their cue for what usually amounted to a mediocre result. Of course they played in the conviction that their every move was monitored by adoring women at their card tables. Once Genevieve, having watched the macho antics of the players, crossed the room, took a cue, spun it like a baton, got half her bottom on the table, leaned forward, and put the seven ball into the side pocket after banking it twice. She slid off the table, twirled the cue again, presenting it handle first to the astounded Waddick. Later Edna came back and lifted a cue out of the rack. Genevieve had handled it as if it were weightless but it was a heavy weapon.

When Genevieve looked into the room now her expression was so serious that for a moment Edna did not recognize her. Her characteristic smile lent such youthfulness to her face that now Genevieve seemed to have aged ten years. Her lips were moving, perhaps in prayer. Edna went over to her.

"Is something wrong, Gen?"

The lips kept moving and then Edna heard what Genevieve repeated over and over.

"Something has happened to Harold."

"Did he call you?"

Genevieve looked distractedly at Edna and then abruptly wheeled and hurried toward the outside door. Edna watched her hasten, bent-headed, toward the church. It was a worrisome performance, all the more reason Edna resolved to keep it quiet. How Harold would pounce on such erratic behavior. And now he had Tuttle on the case. The little lawyer dropped by minutes after she returned to her office.

"Long time no see," he said, sprawling on the settee in her office.

"I'm here every day."

"And it's a noble work you do, Edna Hospers. I admire you for it. I have seen the respect with which you treat your wards."

"Why thank you."

229

"How is Mrs. Rush?"

Warnings began to go off in Edna's head. "I didn't realize you knew her."

"The family generally."

"Including the son?"

"Harold," Tuttle said, frowning. "He came to see me."

"If you are representing him this conversation is at an end."

"We may be on the same side."

"Not if Harold Rush is your client."

"I have not accepted a retainer," Tuttle said carefully, leaning toward her as if he expected her to appreciate the significance of what he said.

"He is trying to become his mother's guardian. He has had enough trouble taking care of himself. All he wants is her money. He would probably squander it immediately and she would end up in the county home."

"Has he upset her?" The beginnings of anger were evident on Tuttle's face."

Remembering the distraught Genevieve who had just gone off to the church, Edna decided to tell Tuttle about it.

"Yes, the poor thing. She is trying to convince herself that something happened to Harold, that he's changed, I suppose. As if she can't believe he would do this after she took him in again."

Tuttle nodded and rose to his feet, inhaling, his chest expanding. He swept off the tweed hat he had kept on while they talked.

"Mrs. Hospers, you have my word. Harold Rush is no client of mine."

Edna did not see Genevieve again that day. But several times the old woman's refrain echoed in her mind. Something has happened to Harold. Something has happened to Harold.

The words took on another significance that night when, the kids having gone to bed, Edna settled down to watch the late news. It was the lead story. The body of Harold Rush had been found at his home that afternoon. Few details were available. The victim had been bludgeoned to death and there was speculation that he had surprised a burglar and paid the price.

4

Phil Keegan would have liked it better if Mrs. Rush didn't blame herself for what had happened to her son. "It's all my fault," she keened. "I did it. I should not have argued with him."

"Argued about what?"

"It doesn't matter now."

"It matters a great deal, Mrs. Rush."

But of course he already knew about Harold's plan to become his mother's guardian and come into control of her money. That could have been a widow's mite, but it turned out that Mrs. Rush had been left in a very healthy financial condition by her late husband. A combination of Social Security, a railroad pension, and stock holdings that had increased dramatically in value without Mrs. Rush even being aware of it. Harold, it seemed, had made himself knowledgeable in his mother affairs. The stock certificates were found in his room, along with financial pages with the values circled. It did not take a mathematical genius to see that those certificates represented a goodly sum. Harold had apparently not informed his mother of her wealth.

The mother had found the body and set off the alarm. When the first patrol car arrived, she stood beside the body, holding the baseball bat that turned out to have been the murder weapon. Mrs. Rush was surprised to find she was holding it.

"I must have picked it up."

Some hours later, Cy Horvath brought Keegan the news that the only prints on the bat belonged to Mrs. Rush. The next time Phil talked with Mrs. Rush, Amos Cadbury was at her side.

"You said you had an argument with your son?"

"You questioned my client without a lawyer present?"

"As a witness, Mr. Cadbury. She reported the crime and gave us what information we have about what happened."

"Let us have no more references to arguments. Mrs. Rush found her unfortunate son and immediately summoned help."

"She was holding a bat."

"I must have picked it up."

"Captain, I will ask you what the import of these questions is. Surely you are not suggesting that Mrs. Rush attacked her son."

"I did it," the old woman broke in. "I'm responsible. I should have just given him what he wanted. What difference does it make anyway, at my age?"

"Please don't say anything more, Mrs. Rush," Cadbury said.

"The Blessed Mother hasn't spoken to me in days."

This silenced both Cadbury and Phil Keegan. Phil said that was all for now and was happy to get away. He went almost immediately to the St. Hilary rectory, where Marie opened the door to him.

"Is he in?"

"He'll be back."

Phil sat at the kitchen table and nodded when Marie offered him coffee. She made a cup of tea for herself and sat across from him.

"What is it, Philip?"

"I've just come from Genevieve Rush."

"The poor woman. Imagine coming on her dead son like that. But I can't help wondering if it isn't a kind of punishment for pretending to have visions and the like."

"What do you mean?"

"I'm not sure I should talk about it." Marie sat back, her closed lips a line, the picture of the responsible rectory housekeeper.

"She said the Blessed Mother has stopped talking to her."

Released from whatever restraint she had felt, Marie sat forward and told him all about Genevieve's claim that the statue of Mary smiled at her and gave her messages.

"She came in the other night and said Mary had told her that Fred would get well."

"Fred Gissing?"

"Yes."

"He did get better, didn't he?"

"A pure coincidence."

Perhaps, but later Phil was told by Edna Hospers that the day Genevieve found her son she had been muttering that something had happened to him.

"But that would mean she didn't do it."

"If you think she's clairvoyant."

That was not a line of argument Phil cared to pursue with the prosecutor, who was of a mind that they ought to make a charge against the old lady. "Manslaughter. She can plead innocent. Maybe she can claim he was threatening her and it was self-defense."

"Clarence, she is a little old lady."

"It doesn't take much strength to swing a bat."

"Let's not rush into this. The newspapers will make mincemeat out of you if you charge a frail old lady with decking her middle-aged son with a baseball bat."

Clarence was impressed by that line of argument.

5

Vincent Barth, who covered the far western suburbs for the *Tribune*, preferred to do his writing in the pressroom in the Fox

River courthouse. Other reporters, sipping coffee, keeping their journalistic labor to a minimum, letting CNN run with the sound off, were more annoyed than impressed by Vince's diligence. When he wasn't banging away at his word processor he had his nose in a book. When someone finally asked what he was reading, he half turned away, pressing the open book to his bosom.

"Just a book."

"Is that what it is?" Trefoyle drawled. "I wondered what a book looked like."

Cantor noticed that it was covered with heavy paper in the way they had protected their textbooks in school. The noisy inference was made that Vince was polluting the pressroom by bringing in X-rated fiction. Trefoyle managed to wrest the book from Vince and it slid across the floor, open to the world. When they gathered to look down at it, there was a moment of embarrassed silence. Its title was *Writing the Blockbuster Novel*. Then the razzing began again. The title page of the novel Vince was writing attributed it to Randolph Bacon. More hoots.

"Haven't you every heard of pseudonyms?" Vince asked, trying to retain his dignity.

"It looks more like a pseudo novel to me, Vince."

"Vince, what's a blockbuster? Isn't it some kind of bomb?"

After that, Vince had been left alone. There was not a journalist in the room who did not intend some day to do what Vince was doing.

That afternoon just after Tuttle stopped by the pressroom for a free cup of coffee, which was about what it was worth, a call came from the *Tribune* telling Vince to contact a man in Naperville. Others, roused from their slumber, watched him as he dialed.

"Vincent Barth of the *Tribune* speaking. Yes, that's right. I wrote the story." He covered the phone and whispered, "It's about Harold Rush." He went back to the phone and while he listened a frown formed on his face.

"Of course it was Harold Rush. The body was identified by his mother."

Impatience grew as he listened, but then he broke in again. "No, it was not Raymond Pewter. It was Harold Rush."

He hung up. "What an idiot. He says the picture we ran in the paper was the picture of a Naperville man named Raymond Pewter."

"You could have told him it was a pseudonym," Trefoyle said, but the taunt was not taken up.

"You handled him well," Tuttle said to Vince. "You might have asked him why Pewter didn't complain."

"Pewter is missing. Hasn't been seen for months."

Eyes rolled, hands were lifted, sighs at the stupidity of the masses were heaved. Soon the pressroom resumed its drowsy afternoon tempo. The sound of Vincent's keyboard was counterpoint to the regular breathing of others who had sunk back into their restorative naps.

Tuttle went back to his office, sat behind his desk, put his feet on it and tipped his hat over his eyes, but he could not sleep. Something teased the edges of his mind. Every effort to court unconsciousness, to make of his mind a blank slate on which nothing was written, failed. Finally he gave up, got on the phone, and called police headquarters.

"Officer Pianone, please."

"I'll switch you to complaints."

"I want to talk with Peanuts. This is Tuttle."

"Don't get so huffy."

When Peanuts finally came on, Tuttle asked him if he could sign out an unmarked car.

"No dents?"

Tuttle paused. It was a condition of their friendship that he never alluded to the limitations of Peanuts's mental capacities. Only family and political connections explained Peanuts's membership on the Fox River police, where the demands made on him were minimal. Work for Peanuts meant getting through the years to retirement and he was prone to grouse about his sinecure. Now he said he would be by with a car in fifteen minutes.

"Where to?" he asked when Tuttle slipped into the passenger seat.

"Naperville."

6

Father Dowling could see that it was with obvious reluctance that Phil Keegan pursued his investigation into the death of Harold Rush. But despite the improbability of Genevieve as a suspect in her son's death, more and more things seemed to point to the old woman. That she might not have been able to wield a baseball bat in the requisite manner was put into question by stories of her prowess with a pool cue. A cue, it turned out, was not much lighter than the bat and considerably more difficult to handle, but the image of old Genevieve performing like a majorette with a pool cue was hard to credit. There was also her mysterious and repeated statement that something had happened to Harold. Genevieve had been repeating this like a mantra at a time after her son had been killed. But so far Amos Cadbury had managed to dampen the prosecutor's ardor to bring charges.

"Where did she get a baseball bat?" the patrician lawyer asked, his voice heavy with skepticism.

"What do you mean?"

"We know where she found the pool cue. But where did she lay hands on that bat? Obviously it was on the scene and she picked it up, as she said. Captain Keegan, I suggest that you

236

devote your energies to ascertaining the provenance of that bat."

Phil just stared at the lawyer.

"Find out where it came from," Father Dowling said helpfully.

"It's a standard kind of bat," Clarence the prosecutor said.

"They don't play baseball at the parish center, do they, Father Dowling?"

"No, Amos."

"My client never played baseball in her life, so the bat could not be a memento of more agile times. Besides, it seems quite new."

"Maybe she was just defending herself," Clarence suggested. "I mean, no one is talking Murder One. The son was by all accounts a worthless bounder."

"He was seeking to get control of his mother's property. He had the stock certificates in his room."

"He could have just disappeared with those."

"What is your point, Amos?"

"Why would he attack his mother, or frighten her to the point where she defended herself with excessive force? No, that avenue is as much a cul-de-sac as any other you have come up with."

Father Dowling managed to get Amos alone, walking with him along the path that led from the rectory to the school.

"How is Genevieve holding up under this?"

"I am surprised you ask. She says she is spending as much time here as before."

"I haven't seen her."

Amos paused, bringing back the long leg that had just entered into another stride, and stopping on the walk. His eyes rose to the steeple of the church.

"Mrs. Rush is a most unusual client."

"How so?"

"She told me that the Blessed Mother did not want me to waste any time on her case. She was in no danger." Amos fixed his eye on Father Dowling. "What do you make of that?"

"I hope she's right."

"That doesn't answer my question."

"I can scarcely comment on the message. How could I affirm or deny that it had been given to her?"

"Do you think it's possible?"

"Did you ever see the movie *The Song of Bernadette,* Amos?"

"Several times. And never without weeping. It brings back memories of the grotto at Notre Dame. But that happened long ago, and in France. And Bernadette was a child."

"I particularly liked Vincent Price in that picture. But then I suppose it is easier to play the skeptic."

They resumed walking then, uncomfortable in different ways. Before they parted, Amos said, "I dread an indictment, Father. She would invoke celestial messages and end up in an institution."

It seemed ironic that Harold's apparent aim for his mother could be realized in that way. Ruth, the sister from Detroit, had arrived for her brother's funeral. She was obese but as good-tempered as her mother. Her expression of sadness at what had happened to Harold seemed threatened by her irrepressible spirits, as if she might suddenly break into a smile.

"Mother can come home with me," she said, when Father Dowling told her of Amos Cadbury's fears. "Or I'll move here. There's nothing to keep me in Detroit."

"If only you had done that sooner."

"Oh, Mom wouldn't have me. I was surprised she gave Harold his old room back. Of course he's a son."

"What do you mean?"

"Mothers always prefer sons."

"Always?"

"Well, I have only daughters, but no matter what Harold did he was still Mom's little boy."

"She would never have hurt him?"

"Of course not. Maybe if she had spanked him when he was young . . ."

Father Dowling's homily at Harold's funeral mass was a model of equivocation. But his prayer that the deceased might rest in peace was all the more fervent. The sight of Fred Gissing in a pew was almost as big a surprise as Lazarus had been. Father Dowling found himself looking closely at the statue of Our Lady, but for him the smile was fixed and no message came.

Phil was an infrequent visitor of late. He might have been relieved that the prosecutor had not made a fool of himself over Genevieve, but the prospect of yet another unsolved murder did not warm his policeman's heart.

When Father Dowling returned from the cemetery after burying Harold Rush, he found Tuttle waiting to see him. The little lawyer held his tweed hat in both hands as he stood when the pastor entered the front parlor.

"Did Marie offer you anything?"

"I'm fine, Father. Just fine."

Father Dowling sat and looked receptive.

"An interesting thing, Father Dowling. Before returning home Harold Rush lived for years over in Naperville. Under another name. Pewter."

"He did! How did you learn that?"

Tuttle tapped his head. "A lawyer learns things. If he stays alert."

"And what did he do in Naperville?"

"He was co-owner of a sporting goods store."

7

Naperville is a town, a post office address, and a state of mind. Father Dowling's thought that he would find Off Base Sports in a storefront looking out onto the town square evaporated as he entered and began to maneuver through the immense sprawl that is Naperville. The store was located in a mini-mall that featured a Crown Bookstore, a theater where four films showed simultaneously but presumably to different audiences, a discount shoe store, a Chinese restaurant, and a Domino's Pizza. On the corner was a filling station with a car wash and convenience store. Father Dowling parked and went into the convenience store, where three clerks were taking money for gas and selling lottery tickets.

When his turn came, he put down a dollar for a lottery ticket, a little gift for Marie, and asked the clerk if she knew of a sports store called Off Base. Her answer was a stare and half-opened mouth. Off Base was twenty-five yards from where she stood, but the clerk had never heard of it.

"Good luck," she said, mechanically, when he took his ticket and turned to leave.

"What you want to know about Off Base?"

The man was almost as wide as he was tall and his arms seemed an advertisement for over-exercising. His nose had been broken and widened on his face, giving his lidded eyes a simian look.

"I'm looking for a man named Pewter."

The man stepped back as if to avoid a jab. "Yeah? So am I, Father. Where you from?"

"Fox River."

His name was Nolan and he and Pewter were partners in Off Base. He invited Father Dowling to come see the store and it said something of its present fortunes that he unlocked the front door to let himself back in.

"I let Seymour go. My clerk."

"This seems to be a good location."

"My problem is my partner. Partner!" He turned as if to spit, but thought better of it. "Fifty-fifty, that was the deal. Of net profits. He keeps the books."

"Where is he?"

Nolan snuffled and moved his feet. Then shrugged. "I think he took off. He's been gone . . ." He closed his eyes in thought. "Couple months?"

"You think he left town?"

"I wish I'd thought of it first." A sly smile. "Just kidding."

"Have you reported this?"

"Hey, I thought something had happened to him at first. Called the cops, it was in the papers. Big deal for a few days, then nothing."

"Have you any idea where Pewter might have gone?"

"What's your interest?"

"I'm doing a favor for his mother."

"Where's she?"

"Fox River."

That was twice he had mentioned Fox River and neither time was there any significant reaction from Nolan. Father Dowling went to a rack and took out a baseball bat, held it in one hand, then in two, cocked his wrists.

"That's top of the line."

It was identical to the bat that had killed Harold Rush.

The back door opened and someone entered and was heard shuffling around in the rear.

"That you Seymour?"

"No, it's O.J."

"Someone's here."

Silence and then a spare man in his early forties, his hair in a ponytail, a bandanna tied pirate-like across his forehead, appeared. "A customer!"

"He knows Pewter's mother."

"Yeah?"

"They're looking for him in Fox River too."

"Oh we know where he is," Father Dowling said.

"Where?" Nolan asked eagerly.

"He's undercover."

Nolan's eyes narrowed, but he did not pursue it. Perhaps he wanted his clerk to think he understood. Perhaps he did. The muscles in Nolan's arm rippled in unconscious flexing as he stood there. He was still holding the bat Father Dowling had returned to him.

The drive back is always shorter, and knowing his destination permitted Father Dowling's thoughts to wander from the road. If it came to a choice between Nolan and Genevieve, it was no contest. But it was not a choice for him to make. In any case, he had little doubt what Phil Keegan would do when he learned of Off Base Sports.

The priest became conscious of a white four-wheel drive that had taken up a position in the outside lane, just out of range of his rearview mirror. The side mirror showed only a grill that like most grills had the look of an idol about to speak. There was something irrational about being annoyed by the vehicle. Its driver had as much right to the road as he did. But why didn't he pass? Father Dowling slowed up, but the vehicle did too, retaining its distance. To blot out the annoyance, Father Dowling got out his beads and began the recitation of the rosary.

He was just beginning the Third Sorrowful Mystery when the bridge across the Fox River came into view and with it the realization that he was nearly home. In peripheral vision he noticed that the white vehicle was now even with him, apparently about to pass at last. But suddenly it veered toward him, and Father Dowling pulled at his wheel, getting a tire off the pavement and into a groove beside the road that wrested control of the car from him. As he fought to gain control, he left the road entirely and suddenly he had no choice. If he succeeded in pulling back onto the road, he ran the risk of running into the bridge. Gripping the wheel, Father Dowling began the steep descent toward the dark swirling waters of the Fox River.

8

It was one of Father Dowling's jokes that Marie Murkin was housekeeper with right of succession. "My coadjutor," he added to clerical friends. Sitting in the waiting room of St. Mary's Hospital, mulling over the enigmatic reports of the pastor's condition with Phil Keegan, Amos Cadbury, and Enid Hospers, Marie was numb with the thought that Father Dowling had all but drowned in the Fox River when his car went off the road.

The little band of friends had exhausted the hypotheses that occurred to them. A stroke, a heart attack, a fainting spell. Perhaps just loss of the skills a driver needed.

"His mind was on other things," Marie snapped, to stop this speculation. "He has never been sick a day in his life."

The others seemed more relieved than reproved by this, and silence fell. Two minutes later, Dr. Curran came in and looked around as if not sure whom to address.

"How is he?" Amos asked, rising like a barometer.

"Okay. Fine."

"What happened?"

Curran shrugged. "He drove into the river."

"But why?"

A crooked grin. "He missed the bridge."

And that was all Father Dowling said when they were allowed into his room. His bed was cranked up, and he looked fit as a fiddle, if a little sheepish to be the cause of their concern.

"What do you mean you missed the bridge?"

"My car got off the road and I couldn't get it back on. If I had, I probably would have smashed into the bridge. So I took the scenic route."

The relief was general, and Marie saw that she would have to take charge or these people would spend the rest of the night here, keeping Father Dowling awake.

"I won't be able to say the noon Mass tomorrow, Marie."

"I'll take care of it."

"Better get a priest."

Marie did not join in the laughter. He knew that that was what she meant to do, as long as someone other than a Franciscan was available. Now that they had all had their fun at her expense, she suggested that they leave the patient alone. This was reluctantly agreed to. But when Marie had everyone outside, he said, "Ask Phil to come back, will you, Marie?"

"You are supposed to get some rest."

"I'll rest better after I talk with Phil."

9

The arrest of Seymour Pane was made not on the basis of Father Dowling's identification of him as the driver of the vehicle that had forced him off the road, but because previously unidentified fingerprints at the scene of the crime turned out to be his. His prints were not on the bat itself, but careful investigation at the back of the house turned up tire prints that matched Seymour's vehicle, the one in which he had sought to prevent Father Dowling from carrying his suspicions back to Fox River. Nolan might not have understood some of the priest's remarks in Off Base Sports, but his clerk had.

"Did you suspect him?" Phil asked when he came by the rectory to bring the pastor up to speed on the investigation into the murder of Harold Rush.

"Seymour? I suspect everyone, Phil. Not of everything, but of something. Nolan might have been sent from central casting, he was so perfect for the role. But Seymour . . ."

"Was it the ponytail?"

"No."

"The ear ring?"

"Probably the bandanna."

"Are you serious?"

"Of course not. When can I talk to Seymour?"

"Not during batting practice."

Seymour and Harold had conspired to loot the business and leave Nolan holding the bag of bankruptcy, but a man who can betray a partner will not hesitate to betray a clerk. Stunned by his supposed ally's perfidy, Seymour devoted himself to revenge. He determined that Raymond Pewter was an assumed name, and a susceptible secretary in the Naperville police traced the fingerprints Seymour provided to a man named Harold Rush. A perusal of area phone books had turned up a raft of Rushes but Seymour went systematically down the list until he tracked his prey down in Fox River. He was willing to describe the relish with which he had performed his lethal task.

"That's a good bat," he concluded.

It was an endorsement unlikely to earn him any money.

Genevieve, reconciled to her son's death and with her widowed daughter under her roof, settled back into her routine. One day Marie came into the study to tell Father Dowling that Genevieve had come to see him. Her face was expressionless; she would not meet his eyes. He told Marie to bring Genevieve into the study.

"All these books!" Genevieve cried when she came in. Then she closed her eyes and breathed deeply. "I love the smell of pipe tobacco. Harold smoked cigars."

"God rest his soul."

"I told them they were dangerous to his health." She shook her head. "He is in purgatory now."

"All the more reason to pray for him."

"Our Lady said a little boy at Fatima would be in purgatory until the end of the world. A little boy!"

"That makes our prospects fairly sobering."

"The First Saturdays, Father. The First Fridays." She sat back. "But I should tell you."

He waited, but it was prelude to no revelation. They had a nice chat and afterward he took her back through the kitchen so she could go over to the church. Marie was busy at the sink and did not turn around. Father Dowling stood at the screen door watching Genevieve hurry toward the church. Just inside the side door was the altar of the Blessed Virgin. Whatever Genevieve had meant by her earlier remarks, it was good to remember that the faith was grounded in visions—angels had appeared to Mary, and to Joseph, the Holy Spirit had descended on the apostles. Throughout the ages, privileged souls had been the recipients of special revelations.

Father Dowling turned and went to the telephone, then punched the button on the answering machine. Marie wheeled.

"What are you doing?"

"Seeing if there are any messages."

The swoosh of the door as he pushed through to the dining room blended with the exasperated reaction of the housekeeper.

Imaginary Sins

1

In the weeks prior to the book sale that was intended to raise money for the center for seniors at St. Hilary parish, shopping bags and boxes filled with contributions were dropped off at the school. Eventually the books would be unpacked, classified, and readied for the tables that would be set up in the erstwhile gym of the school, which was now the main meeting place in the center.

The thought of all those books drew Father Dowling from the rectory and along the walkway to the school. Forsythia had bloomed. Could lilacs be far behind? But the scented air, however pleasant, did not distract Roger Dowling from the thought of all those books.

From time to time, he would stop at garage sales to see what books might be on offer. There was nothing systematic about this, but he had found a few treasures. The boxes and bags of books lined up along the lower corridor of the school suggested a garage sale par excellence. The pastor paused, peeking into shopping bags at their contents but his eye was drawn by a cardboard box with a fitted cover, the kind of box that was used in archives. The priest stooped and lifted the cover. Soon he was kneeling on the floor, examining a volume that had lain on top. He stood and headed for the stairway.

"Would it be unethical for me to buy this before the sale, Edna?"

"Father, all those books are gifts to the parish."

He managed not to cheer at this confirmation of his own thinking as he had come up the stairway.

"What did you find?"

"The *Conrad Argosy*! I read this collection when I was a boy. I've always hoped to find a copy."

Ten minutes later, seated in his rectory study, Father Dowling opened the book and felt the years drop away. He was once more fourteen years old, reading Joseph Conrad for the first time. He leafed through the volume. The woodcuts were so familiar he might have seen them only days instead of decades ago. And then he came upon the folded sheet of paper, yellowing with age. Here was a bonus of secondhand books. Previous owners often left intriguing mementos behind, forgotten bookmarks, keepsakes. He unfolded the paper. He read it twice, then lay it on the desk and stared across the room.

Last Will and Testament

May God have mercy on my soul. Tonight will be my last on earth and I leave this life with fear but also with hope. Am I wrong not to prevent what will be done to me? My darling will regard the crime as an act of mercy. Have mercy on us both. I cannot help feeling grateful. The thought of prolonged and hideous suffering frightens me more than death.

Father Dowling turned to the front of the book and found a firm and legible signature. George Williams. Was it he who had printed this will in block letters?

2

"Of course I know George Williams," Marie said when he asked her.

"How long ago did he die?"

"Die? He's as alive as I am."

"How old is he?"

Marie searched for a circumlocution. "My age, I would say."

"He's not a member of the parish?"

Marie's expression turned sad. "He lives in that Franciscan retirement home. Where they take all your money . . ."

Father Dowling smiled. Marie's understanding of the arrangement the elderly made with St. Claire House when they moved in was colored by her lingering distaste for Friars Minor.

"But you remember when he lived in the parish?"

Father Dowling had gone into the rectory kitchen to talk with Marie. Now she pulled out a chair and sat at the table and adjusted a place mat. She looked at the backs of her hands, then turned them over. He had never before found her reluctant to display her uncanny memory for parishioners.

"Amos Cadbury is the one you should talk to, Father."

"You make it sound very mysterious."

"Oh, it is. It is."

The books had been donated by a granddaughter of George Williams when she cleared the shelves of the ancestral home not three blocks from the parish. Of course Father Dowling knew Florence Gatler.

"They would have gone to St. Vincent de Paul, but then I remembered the parish book sale."

"That was very good of you."

Florence was wearing a baggy sweat shirt and jeans, and little Gatlers swarmed around her. "Father, they're just old books."

"Old books are the best."

Florence conveyed no sense of a mystery involving her grandfather, but Amos Cadbury sat suddenly upright at the mention of George Williams. Amos had attended Father Dowling's noon

Mass and then joined the pastor for lunch. Marie had not hovered over the table as was her custom when Amos Cadbury was there, and soon the two men adjourned to the study.

"You knew him, Amos?"

"We were close friends. I was his lawyer."

"Marie suggested there was some mystery connected with him."

"Mystery." Amos repeated the word, as if tasting its inadequacy. "I would call it a tragedy."

Amos got up and closed the door, but when he regained his seat he kept silent for a minute. "It was the low point of my professional career, Father Dowling."

"If you would rather not talk of it . . ."

But the lawyer shook his head. "Of course I confessed it. But I was never sure the priest understood the magnitude of what I had done. It has weighed on my mind ever since." Again he shook his head. "No, I flatter myself. The incident sank into forgetfulness, but whenever I did remember . . . Father, I concealed evidence of a crime."

And then Amos told the story.

"Margaret Williams was a lovely woman. She and Mrs. Cadbury were closer than George and myself. She was not yet forty when she was diagnosed with cancer. In those days, that was a death sentence."

"And she died?"

"She died. It was a sad occasion. The wake and funeral were crowded. She was the first of our generation to go and there were many mourners. George was inconsolable. I received the letter in the week after Margaret was buried."

"A letter!"

"A simple statement. In it George informed me that Margaret had not died a natural death." Amos looked at Father Dowling. "He had hastened her death in order to spare her the pain and suffering of her illness."

"Killed her?"

"While she was asleep, he came into the room and pressed a pillow to her face. When he was sure she was dead, he left the room."

"Why did he tell you?"

"It was a secret he felt he could not keep to himself."

"So he sent you a letter stating he had murdered his wife?"

"Thereby putting the burden on me. I made discreet inquiries. The doctor was not suspicious of her death. He regarded it as an unlooked-for blessing. Of course George wondered what I would do."

"What did you do?"

"Nothing. It was the end of our friendship, needless to say. He had made me a partner of his deed by putting his fate in my hands."

"I'm surprised no one noticed that the oxygen had been turned off."

"When the doctor came the next morning, the tap was on."

"What did you do with the letter?"

"I destroyed it. As if that could destroy what George had done."

Amos fell silent. He had been absolved of his sin, but by a priest who had shown little curiosity about what exactly Amos was confessing. At the time, something might have been done to right the wrong that had been done. After that unsatisfying confession, Amos destroyed the letter. Perhaps the statue of limitations never ran out on such deeds, but it was the weight of divine law that Amos still felt pressing on him. Father Dowling took a stole from the drawer of his desk and aided his old friend in finding pardon and peace at last.

3

St. Clare House was a pleasant place, an erstwhile Franciscan convent set among ancient trees and lush greenery. The few nuns who remained were patients themselves; the Franciscan fathers had taken over the management of what was now the terminal station on life's way for the old people who inhabited its narrow rooms.

Father Dowling, following directions given him at the reception desk, went down a long corridor at the end of which a frail figure in a wheelchair was silhouetted against large doors that gave a wonderful view of the grounds. At the sound of his name, the old man turned his chair toward Father Dowling before lifting his eyes.

"I'm Father Dowling. The pastor of St. Hilary's."

"Ah. That was our parish."

"So I understand."

"One of my granddaughters lives there now with her family."

"Florence Gatler."

"Of course you would know her. Sometimes she brings the children."

In getting to George Williams he had passed vacant-eyed old people, staring mutely at the floor, gripping the arms of their chairs, their minds focused on an incomprehensible present. But George Williams seemed alert.

"Are you allowed to go outside?"

"Yes."

"Would you like to now?"

His pale blue eyes sparkled. "Very much. But I need help, because of the front doors."

"I'll go outside with you."

So small a thing was an event in George Williams's day. When Father Dowling had pushed the old man through the front doors, a hand rose shakily. "I like to visit the rose arbor."

When he had pushed the old man's chair to the arbor, Father Dowling sat on a bench. George Williams closed his eyes and inhaled deeply. He had called it the rose arbor, but the perfume he smelled came from lilacs.

"My wife loved roses."

"I understand she's dead."

"Many years ago. Next week we would have been married for sixty years."

"What was the cause of her death?"

A pained look came over the old face. Father Dowling murmured a silent prayer. Perhaps, as Amos had in the study, George Williams would feel an urge to confess.

"Only a few years later, she could have been treated. They knew so much less then."

"Amos Cadbury mentioned that you two are old friends."

George Williams turned his chair so that he faced the priest. "Former friends, I'm afraid. Our friendship did not long survive the death of my wife."

"I should have thought that would affect your friendship with Mrs. Cadbury rather than with Amos."

"I came to see that life as a widower is very different from that of a husband with a lovely wife. One naturally is set aside."

Seated in such a fragrant setting, redolent of new life, stirring up the past seemed cruel. But Father Dowling wondered if George Williams, as he approached the end of his life, had acknowledged the sin he had confided to Amos Cadbury. The thought that he might relieve the old man's mind as he had the lawyer's emboldened him to go on.

"Your granddaughter donated some old books for a parish sale we are having. Many of them were yours, I gather."

"Reading was a habit I learned from Margaret. It was my great consolation when she was gone."

"You liked Joseph Conrad?"

"He was a favorite of mine."

Father Dowling took the folded paper from his pocket and handed it to George Williams.

The old man looked at it, and then at the priest, no recognition in his manner, but then he unfolded it and brought it close to his face. His lips moved as he read. His eyes were full of tears when they rose to meet Father Dowling's.

"I found that in *A Conrad Argosy.*"

"With the woodcuts?" He smiled at the memory.

"With the woodcuts."

How alive with muted noise the natural world is. Birds twittered, new leaves rustled in the slight breeze, there was the buzz of bees.

"You wrote that?"

"Yes." He folded the paper, as if to hand it back, but then kept it.

"And you told Amos Cadbury what you had done."

George Williams sat back, surprised.

"Amos?"

"I have talked with him about it. It has pressed on his mind all these years. Of course he did nothing with the information you had given him."

"Dear God."

"Keeping silent was very likely the one professional lapse in Amos's career."

"The poor man."

"Why did you tell him what you had done?"

George Williams turned his chair so that it was his profile Father Dowling saw. The old man looked like a confessor rather than a penitent.

"How this brings it all back."

"It must have weighed heavily on your mind all these years."

After a long silence, the old man shook his head. He turned

his chair to Father Dowling.

"I had forgotten all about it."

"Forgotten?"

"It is a long story."

"Would you like to tell it to me?"

What George Williams had to say was not the confession Father Dowling had expected. He spoke slowly, searching his memory and finding there aspects of his wife's death that had lain dormant all these years.

"When I left her that last night, she was near despair. She begged me to . . ." His eyes drifted away. "She wanted to die; she wanted relief from the dreadful pain."

"What did you do?"

"I was near despair myself. I would have given anything to take on her pain myself."

"You granted her request?"

"Oh no. No. I couldn't do that."

"What did you do?"

"We prayed. We said a rosary together. She grew peaceful then. Eventually I went off to my own bed."

"That's all?"

"In the morning, I found her twisted in the bedclothes, her face pressed into the pillow, dead." Again his eyes filled with tears. "I assumed that she had done what she wanted me to do."

A blue jay flew shrieking past. A bee burrowed into a flower in search of nectar.

"That was when I decided to take responsibility for her death."

Again he opened the slip of paper and looked at it. "I could not have given a convincing sample of her handwriting, so I printed it."

"And then wrote to Amos."

"Yes. As soon as I had written this. It was later, after the funeral, that I spoke to the doctor and told him what I had done." The old eyes searched Father Dowling's face. "He actually laughed."

"Laughed!"

"A kind of laugh. He assured me that Margaret's death had been natural. Though she was dying of cancer, death had been caused by a heart attack."

"You didn't tell Amos?"

"Imagine my relief that Margaret had not been responsible for her own death. I put this in the book where you found it. I was disgusted with myself for suspecting her of suicide and my noble attempt to divert suspicion seemed ridiculous. I suppose I wanted to erase it all from my mind. What I had written Amos Cadbury was irrelevant. If I thought of it, I must have thought that I could tell him when he came to me about the letter. He never did. Perhaps he had talked to the doctor himself. And all these years he has thought . . ."

"I'll talk to him."

"And tell him to come see me."

4

The book sale was a great success. While it went on, Father Dowling moved among the tables in the gym where the books were displayed. From time to time, he opened one and riffled its pages, as if any book might divulge some secret from the past. He bought nothing, but he kept *A Conrad Argosy.*

"I've visited George," Amos Cadbury told the pastor over a sumptuous tea Marie had prepared for his guest. They were in the front parlor, the windows raised on a world where spring was busy at its work of regeneration.

"I don't think he had any idea what telling you meant."

"Father Dowling, it is a relief to have that blot removed from

my escutcheon." Amos sipped his tea. "But I thought I was destroying evidence of a crime."

What a mystery the human person is. Sometimes horrible effects of our choices come that we in no way intend. Sometimes the difference between what we think we are doing and what we are actually doing is total. But it is the inner intention that then characterizes what we do or do not do. Father Dowling did not have to explain this to Amos Cadbury.

"More buttered toast," Marie cried, sweeping into the parlor.

"Marie," Amos said, "you could tempt the dead."

"That is not a flattering compliment, Amos Cadbury."

But Marie looked flattered nonetheless. Father Dowling of course was drinking coffee.

"Did you buy any books, Marie?"

Marie looked at the lawyer and made a face. "What would I want with old books."

"What indeed?"

The eyes of Amos Cadbury met Father Dowling's then drifted to the window, but his gaze was inward where time resides, its past tense present to memory, chock full of good and bad, real and imaginary.

A Life Sentence

1

The body was found when workmen were preparing the St. Hilary parking lot for resurfacing. Marie Murkin had been wandering around the rectory with her hands clapped over her ears, trying to drown out the sound of the machine that was loosening the old blacktop. Now, the housekeeper removed her hands tentatively, testing the silence, wondering if the lull in the noise meant the job was done. Her hands were still at the ready when Father Dowling came out of his study and saw her.

"Praying?"

"How can you stand that noise?"

"Noise?"

"It's stopped."

"When I start complaining about inaudible noises, call the cardinal."

"You must have heard it."

"Only when it was audible."

The front doorbell sounded then and Marie hurried down the hall and opened the door to a man wearing overalls and a hard hat.

"I gotta see the priest," he advised Mrs. Murkin.

"What on earth for?" She was looking at his shoes, not wanting him tracking that dirt on the rectory floor.

"We just uncovered something . . ." He looked at Marie and then back at Father Dowling. "Something strange."

"How strange?"

"It looks like a human body."

Marie fell back, pale, and steadied herself with the wall.

He took off his hard hat and made a face. "I was afraid of that."

His name was Griffin and Father Dowling had contracted with him to repair the parking lot, which was full of worn spots and potholes. He had accepted Griffin's judgment that a decent job required removing the old blacktop. Father Dowling asked Griffin to show him what he had found. Marie followed several paces behind as the pastor and Walt Griffin walked to where two other hard-hatted workmen leaned on shovels and took turns staring at the exposed dirt. The jackhammer used to loosen the blacktop, so it could be shoveled away, lay on its side, a casualty of the discovery.

Father Dowling looked to where Griffin pointed. What appeared to be a human hand, fleshless, the bones surprisingly white, was visible as if someone had been trying to emerge from the ground when the blacktop had been poured. Marie cried out at the sight.

"Call Phil Keegan, Marie."

Grateful for a reason to leave, Mrs. Murkin scampered back along the walk to the rectory.

The medical examiner's vehicle arrived minutes after Cy Horvath and Phil Keegan got to St. Hilary's. They would have driven right onto the parking lot if the pastor hadn't held up a hand. Griffin had been telling Father Dowling that his bid hadn't taken into consideration any delay. His workmen had withdrawn to the shade of a tree and wore the expression of beneficiaries of an act of God. They were being paid by the hour, no matter what.

Cy and Phil followed Griffin to the corner of the lot where

the old asphalt had been removed. The contractor pointed, leaning forward, as if he intended to touch the bony finger that emerged from the ground, Adam seeking his creator.

The medical examiners, operating like archeologists, began the painstaking task of uncovering what turned out to be the skeleton of an adult male. Yellow tape had been strung to keep back the seniors who had come out of the school that functioned as a parish center and pressed close to the scene. Father Dowling decided that he would give better example by returning to the rectory. It was now midmorning and he would say a noon Mass.

"You busy now, Roger?"

"Come along," the pastor said to Phil Keegan.

"Take the car," Keegan said to Cy Horvath.

"I think I'll stay around."

"Good idea."

2

All the records at police headquarters were now computerized; taped reports were scanned into a machine; the past was available at the click of a key. It was spic and span and efficient as sin. Watching the pastor of St. Hilary's search for any records of the original paving of the parking lot, Phil Keegan envied Roger Dowling this homey chaos. The file cabinet drawer he had pulled open seemed to overflow like a cornucopia, corners of papers sticking up every which way, the tabs on the dividers bent and broken.

"You'll never find it," Marie Murkin said from the doorway.

"Have you taken it?"

"Hmphh." She retreated to her kitchen.

"What are you looking under?" Phil Keegan was in no hurry—the body discovered in the parking lot had been there a long time—but Father Dowling looked as if he were embarked on an endless search.

"Miscellaneous."

"How about maintenance?"

"For heaven's sake, look at this." Standing at the file cabinet, Father Dowling was examining an old newspaper clipping. "I had no idea the parish had a monastic vocation."

"Are there records over at the school?"

Father Dowling continued to read the clipping. Then he put it back into a folder and lay the folder on his desk. "I really should make a systematic search of that cabinet some day."

"You ought to computerize."

Roger Dowling looked at him. "I suppose that is a recognized word now."

"Could there be records in Edna Hospers's office over in the school?"

"Give her a call, will you?"

Keegan called the old principal's office at the school, from which Edna Hospers directed the programs for seniors sponsored by the parish. The demographics of the area had lifted the average age level well above the retirement age, and turning the parish school into a center for seniors seemed preferable to simply closing it up. The center had been a huge success, thanks largely to Edna.

"Do you know what they found in the parking lot?" she asked when Phil Keegan identified himself.

"That's why I'm here. I'm at the rectory, with Father Dowling. We're trying to find out when the parking lot was first paved."

"Why?"

"It could give us an idea how long the body's been there."

"Of course."

"Father is searching the records here. Would you have any records over there? Since the parking lot is next to the school I thought . . ."

"I'll look."

Father Dowling turned when Phil hung up the phone.

"She'll call if she finds anything."

"Good. I'll wait until we hear from her." He sat at the desk and splayed his hand over the manila folder he had removed from the cabinet.

Meanwhile, Phil gave Roger an extended account of the advantages of getting all one's records onto a computer, but his heart wasn't in it. Once he had had such a file cabinet in his office, filled mainly with junk, but it was his junk. It had always been a tonic to open a drawer, see the mess, and shut it up again. He had found that it cleared the mind and what he was trying to remember often came to mind. A computer keyboard and pale screen did not have the same effect on him.

"It would be a waste of money, Phil."

"Maybe you're right."

The phone rang and it was Edna. Father Dowling jotted down what she told him, nodding as he listened. "How much was the bill for?"

He listened, laughed, and put down the phone. "The parking lot was done by Stormquist Contracting. For seven hundred dollars. Do you know what Griffin is charging me?"

"Stormquist went out of business years ago."

"Well, we know the date anyway."

"When was it?"

"Twenty years ago. Before my time."

3

It was always a pleasure to watch Dr. Pippen at work but it was a pleasure Cy tried, usually unsuccessfully, to deny himself. Her honey-blond hair hung in plaited glory to the small of her back, and her open lab coat swirled about her as she moved, creating the impression of a graceful dance. Cy had convinced himself that it was for the good of the investigation that he was hanging around the St. Hilary parking lot while Pippen supervised the excavation of the body, did a preliminary on-site examination, and then oversaw preparations for taking the body to the lab.

"He was a young man," she said to Cy.

"How'd he die?"

"His neck is broken."

"That would do it."

"His hands and feet were tied."

This was suggestive of a gangland killing. When Phil came from the rectory to say that the lot had been paved twenty years ago by Stormquist Contracting, the two men exchanged a silent glance. Stormquist had married into a family that had for a time contested the Pianones for control of the seamier side of Fox River. Eventually the Freddosos had cut their losses and moved to another city in the greater Chicago area, but they left a bloody mark before going. Several of the unsolved homicides on the department computer bore a link to the family but one that could never be made tight enough to convince the prosecutor that he had half a chance of a conviction.

To prove to himself that he had willpower, Cy left Dr. Pippen and walked to where Griffin and his two workmen were waiting in the shade.

"How much longer is it going to be?" Griffin asked.

"That's hard to say."

"I'm going to lose money on this job."

"I'm told the lot was first paved twenty years ago."

"I have to pay these two whether they work or not."

"Stormquist Contracting did it."

"Yeah? I used to work for him."

"They're out of business, aren't they?"

"Stormquist is retired down in Arizona. I got part of his business, not much. He had connections."

"That's what we always thought."

Griffin adopted an enigmatic expression. Whatever the legal limits, there was no statute of limitations on anyone who talked too much to the police about the wrong people.

"I did the patching on that corner."

"Patching?"

"That's why we started there. All they'd pay for was a thin coat over the broken surface. Someone had already done an amateur job on it. I'm talking about the man before Father Dowling, you understand. I told him it was a waste of money but he wanted it to look nice. It did, for a while."

"Tell me about it."

Griffin frowned. "Tell you what?"

"Let's walk."

The presence of the idle men whose hourly wage he was paying obviously made Griffin edgy. Cy started along the walk toward the rectory and Griffin fell in beside him. Cy explained to them that, given the fact that the parking lot was first paved twenty years ago, they would go back that far in search of the identity of the man buried beneath its surface.

"When did you do the patching?"

Griffin thought. "Seven, eight years ago."

"Had the surface just been worn away?"

"I told you, someone had applied a coat before I was brought in. The surface was broken up and a coat of tar wouldn't repair that. They might just as well have painted it black."

"What if I asked you if that body could have been buried there about the time you did that patch job?"

"Maybe. Maybe not."

4

Phil Keegan didn't like doubt cast on how long the body might have been buried under the St. Hilary's parking lot. Besides, the Stormquist connection had two attractions. Given the contractor's associations, it was no stretch of the imagination to think that he might have been asked to get rid of a body. Second and more important, that pretty well assured that they could stop further inquiries with impunity. The department had enough to do without stirring up memories of a time when Fox River had to deal with more than the Pianones. Any such effort would be quashed by the prosecutor, the chief, the mayor.

"There's no proof that the body hasn't been there twenty years?"

"There's no proof it's been there twenty years. Maybe it was buried there years before the lot was paved. Maybe it was buried just before Griffin did the patch job."

"There's no way of telling?"

"From the remains?"

"Yeah."

"I'll check."

Cy forbore whistling and took his time as he went across the street to Pippen's lab. This was strictly business. Maybe he would have to deal with Lubins the coroner and not his lovely assistant. But it was Pippen who turned and gave him a big smile when Cy entered the lab. If Cy had been a smiling man he would have smiled back.

"You finished with those bones from St. Hilary's?"

"You make them sound like relics."

"Are you Catholic?"

"On my mother's side."

Cy welcomed the information but didn't pursue it. He told himself he would now think of her as a sister. Not a nun, a sister. If she was even half Catholic he felt immunized against temptation but he would not have wanted to be asked to explain why.

"There are at least two possibilities on how long they could have been buried there."

"Not more than ten years." She hadn't hesitated.

"Seven or eight years?"

"To be exact I would have to run some complicated tests. Do you want me to?"

"Maybe. But not yet."

5

Two days later Father Dowling, having said the noon Mass and had a light lunch, was seated in his study reading his breviary. The daily reading of the priest, once called the *Breviarium Romanum,* was now called the *Liturgy of the Hours.* Father Dowling had tried saying it in English for a year and then turned with relief to the four-volume *Officium Divinum, Liturgia Horarum* that he had ordered from a bookseller on the Via della Conciliazione in Rome. He had followed the quarrels over the English translations of liturgical texts, he subscribed to *Adoremus,* but he did not himself want to enter the fray. He could bypass it by reading his office in Latin and offering Mass, the *novus ordo,* in Latin several times a week and once on Sunday, the indult happily granted by the cardinal.

He paused in the reading of Psalm 36 and his eyes lifted. *Junior fui, et senui.* I was young and now I am old. He did not of course read his office in search of autobiographical tidbits—the point was to pray the prayer of the Church—but from time to time a verse or phrase would leap out and capture the imagination. He felt now that he had come upon words that might serve as his motto. *I was young and now I am old.* It was not a melancholy thought.

He looked up to see Marie standing in the doorway.

"I didn't want to interrupt," she said in a whisper.

"I was daydreaming."

"Hmph. Someone wants to see you."

"I'll come into the parlor."

But a small elderly woman appeared at Marie's side and Father Dowling rose. "If the smell of pipe smoke bothers you . . ."

"No, no, of course not."

Marie handed the woman into a chair and withdrew to the doorway. Before closing the door, she said, "This is Mrs. Williams."

"Martha Williams, Father."

Marie shut the door. Father Dowling put his hands on the desk and waited.

"Father, I have had the strangest thought."

"Oh?"

"The body that was found here the other day, under the parking lot?"

"Yes."

"I wonder if it could be my nephew." She clapped a hand over her mouth after she said it. "I know that sounds ridiculous," she added through her fingers.

"Tell me about it."

Martha Williams had no children of her own and thus had always taken a special interest in her sister's son and daughter. Actually it was her nephew-in-law she had been prompted to think of when she heard of the discovery in the parish parking lot.

"He just disappeared, Father. Poof. Gone."

"What was his name?"

"Basil."

"That was his first name?"

"Of course. Basil Flannery."

"Have you told your niece?"

"She no longer lives here. I'm the only one left. I know it sounds crazy."

"I suppose there are ways to identify the body."

"If it's Basil, I want him to have a Christian burial. Imagine, being put into the ground like that."

Father Dowling made a call to Dr. Pippen, and while he had the assistant medical examiner on the line, he put her question to Mrs. Williams.

"Do you know who his dentist was?"

"His dentist!"

"Dental records are a way of identifying a body."

Father Dowling thanked Dr. Pippen and hung up. Mrs. Williams sat for a while in thought and then got to her feet. "I will see what I can find, Father. I would rather not call my niece. It would be dreadful to bring all this up again if that should not be Basil . . ."

6

When Mrs. Williams called in the information, Cy drove to the office of Llewelyn Evans DDS, which was located in the remodeled garage of his home. At Evans's age, the house was more used than the office.

"I only look after patients I've had for years," Evans said in slurred tones. Then he fished a denture from his pocket and popped it into his mouth. "Can't stand this thing. Made the impressions myself and that was a mistake. I'm not taking any new patients."

"I'm here on official business."

Evans looked at him with narrowed eyes. "What business would that be?"

"Fox River police."

"Let me see your identification."

He studied closely the ID Cy showed him. He nodded and handed it back.

"Can't be too careful."

"That's right."

"Some of my patients . . ." Evans shook his head and whistled.

"I don't understand."

"They weren't on your side of the law."

"You've kept all your records?"

"Of course."

"Do you remember a patient named Basil Flannery?"

"I'll have to look it up. If they did memory transplants, I'd sign up."

"You wouldn't get the same memory."

Evans turned and stared at Cy. Then he laughed, a barking noise that stopped abruptly. "Never thought of that. What was that name again?"

"Flannery. Basil."

"Last name Flannery?"

"That's right."

Evans's arthritic fingers moved painfully over the tabs in the drawer he pulled open. He kept repeating "Flannery" to himself as if he was afraid he'd forget it.

"Here we are! Basil?"

"Basil."

Evans turned and suddenly clutched the record to his chest. "Why do you want this?"

"For evidence in a malpractice suit."

A long stare and then again the barking laugh. He thrust the record at Cy.

"Go and be damned."

"I'll sign for it."

"No need for that. Look at the note after his name."

Cy looked at the record. "Flannery, Basil." And then in

pencil, "Dead."

"I hope he's the right dead man."

"If he isn't, come back. I have lots of others."

Cy had never before wondered how a doctor went out of business. But all he had to do was let his patients age out of any further need for his care. In the old joke the doctor buries his mistakes, but in the end he buries all his patients—if he lives as long as Llewelyn Evans DDS. In the car, Cy studied the record. Basil Flannery. He had played high school football with a guy named Basil Flannery.

7

Father Dowling drove to Mrs. Williams's house so that she would have the news of the identification of the body before it went out over the radio.

"Dear God in heaven," the old woman said when he told her that it had indeed been Basil Flannery who had been buried beneath the parish parking lot. "I have never put any stock in intuition, Father, but I had a feeling . . ."

"Tell me about him."

"Will you give him a decent funeral, Father?"

"In good time, yes."

"We all need prayers, of course, but Basil . . ."

Present passion can seem silly to an observer, but the story of past folly is in many ways sadder and more difficult to understand. Basil Flannery had lain dead beneath the asphalt of the parking lot for nearly nine years but Martha Williams told a tale of an unfaithful husband.

"It was my niece he cheated on. Oh, I know we should speak well of the dead, but I tell you these things so that you will especially remember him in your prayers. This needn't go beyond you, need it?"

"How did you happen to know of it?"

"Oh, everyone knew at the time. I mean, Louise, his wife knew. There were terrible arguments. Of course there could be no question of divorce."

"Was the other woman known too?"

"Father, I feel like such a terrible gossip."

"The police will probably want to talk with you about this."

"I almost wish I had kept my thoughts to myself when I heard of that body. How did he die, Father?"

"Violently."

"He was killed?"

"It looks that way."

"God have mercy on his soul."

"Your niece left town?"

"It was awful for her. Perhaps she suspected at the time what had happened. Basil had disappeared, there was a lot of talk. She felt abandoned. What will she think now when she learns that all this time Basil has been lying dead?"

"Are you in contact with her?"

"Less and less. Hardly more than a Christmas card anymore. I write her on her birthday as well. She has dropped her married name . . ." Mrs. Williams shook her head in disapproval. For better or worse was the phrase that must have occurred to her. Nor did she seem to think even death dissolved the marriage promises.

8

It was Thelma Horvath who remembered it all. Cy had played football with Basil but Thelma had known about Basil and Veronica.

"He should have married Veronica, Cy. They went together all through high school."

"What happened?"

"She got swept off her feet."

"What was Veronica's married name?"

"Freddoso. It still is."

"Veronica Freddoso?"

"They married other people but obviously they couldn't forget one another. People started seeing them together."

Cy sorted it out for Captain Keegan. Basil Flannery, whose body had been found under the parking lot at St. Hilary's, had been having an affair with a woman married to a Freddoso. The Freddosos had given organized crime a bad name during their bloody reign in Fox River.

"I was sad to see them shut down here and move elsewhere," Captain Keegan said. "They policed one another, them and the Pianones."

"Where did they go?"

"Many of them still live here. But they are doing business in Skokie."

Veronica had married Mario Freddoso. There was a Mario Freddoso in the Fox River directory.

"A broken neck, hands and feet tied, buried under an asphalt surface," Cy said.

"I see what you mean."

"You think I should look into it?"

Keegan hesitated. Inquiries into the death of Basil Flannery nine years after the fact were already hard to justify, but when they led to the doorstep of a family like the Freddosos, hesitation was advisable.

"See what you can learn without stirring up a hornets' nest."

Cy talked to Thelma. "How long has it been since you've seen Veronica?"

"Cy, I was in her wedding! But the last time I saw her was at our twentieth anniversary."

"Our twentieth anniversary?"

"Of graduation from Ignatius High."

"She was there?"

"All you did was talk with former teammates about games you'd played in."

"Freddoso wasn't there."

"Veronica was a cheerleader."

"He was on the football team. I don't think he played much."

"You want me to look up Veronica or something?"

"I don't suppose she would want to talk about Basil Flannery."

"I'll find out."

9

Mrs. Williams came to tell Father Dowling that her niece had no intention of returning to Fox River to attend the second burial of her long-gone husband.

"She says now she thought all along he was dead."

Marie Murkin was critical of the now-confirmed widow of Basil Flannery, but Father Dowling wondered what the housekeeper would say if such a widow showed up in deep mourning to weep over the remains of a husband who had vanished into thin air nine years before. Mrs. Williams was more understanding.

"It would only dredge up memories best left alone, Father. When I think of the dissension in the family then."

The old woman had not drawn any connection between the manner in which her nephew had died and the fact that he had been having an affair with the wife of a known racketeer. Phil was convinced that the Freddosos had exacted a rough justice and executed Basil Flannery.

"Why they buried him here, Roger, I couldn't begin to say."

"That's no mystery."

"Oh?"

"They were parishioners."

Father Dowling had checked the parish records and found several Freddosos on the books, among them Mario and Veronica Freddoso. They had since moved out of the parish, of course. While he was checking records, he looked up the name of the man whose file he had found a week before, the parishioner who had gone off to a Trappist monastery. George Mahan. The name seemed familiar. But of course it would. He had come across it in the manila folder from his file cabinet. A letter from a former pastor, assuring the abbot of New Mount Mellaray that George Mahan was a parishioner in good standing and fully eligible to pursue a monastic vocation.

10

Thelma returned from her lunch with Veronica with a story of a woman brokenhearted that the body of Basil had at last been found. It was the fate her husband had threatened would meet her lover. She had promised never to see Basil again.

" 'To save his life.' " Thelma looked at Cy with a strange expression. For a moment she found such abnegation in a woman caught in sin more noble than the fidelity of a lawful spouse. Cy had fleeting guilty memories of Dr. Pippin.

"Let's go out to dinner."

"I've already made goulash."

"Won't it keep?"

She stared at him and then a little smile formed on her lips. She laid her cheek on his chest.

"I'd love to go out to dinner."

"It was the Freddosos," Phil told Roger Dowling. "Maybe the husband himself. You don't fool around with a Freddoso woman and live to tell of it."

"A matter of honor?"

"Something like that."

A wronged husband would think he had a right to revenge whether or not he was a member of the underworld. Honor, that is, not to lose face with others, had to be restored.

"Of course that's the explanation," Marie Murkin agreed.

Mrs. Williams too found it only logical that her niece's husband had been executed gangland style by the gangster whose wife he had been sinning with.

"May God forgive him all his sins."

"And all ours as well. Your niece's maiden name was Mahan?"

"That's right."

"There was a nephew too?"

"Brother Joachim. He's become a monk. I have already written him about all that has happened."

It did not seem to be a tale that a contemplative monk would want to hear, at least not in the detail Mrs. Williams suggested she had gone into.

"He entered the monastery eight years ago?"

She looked at him. "Has it been that long?"

"I found something about it in the parish records."

"The pastor then wanted him to become a Franciscan. But George had not found that austere enough."

"That was after his sister was abandoned?"

"Things became so quiet after Basil was gone, almost peaceful. George might have thought he was already in a monastery."

11

New Mount Melleray is located just outside Dubuque. Father Dowling had not been there for years. Once, long ago, as a seminarian, he had made a retreat there and had felt the almost sensuous attraction of the austere life. He felt it again now as he settled into his room at the guest house. Once, absolute silence had been kept and the heads of the monks were shaved like those of marine recruits, except that this was a boot camp that lasted as long as life itself. It was said that the Trappist life was less demanding now, changes having been made in the wake of Vatican II, but after the romantic glow wore off it was still a life too difficult for anyone other than someone with a vocation for it.

Brother Joachim came to the guest house the evening of Father Dowling's second day in the monastery. He was a tall, lean man, with close-cropped hair gray over a face tanned from work in the fields. He was a lay brother.

"I am pastor of St. Hilary's parish, Brother."

The gray head nodded. How transparent his blue eyes were.

"Your Aunt Martha has written you about the discovery of your brother-in-law's body?"

The monk had remained standing after entering the parlor of the guesthouse. Now he sank into a chair. His body seemed to go on collapsing inside the voluminous habit after he sat.

"What should I do, Father?"

Roger Dowling felt that his mind had been read and the question that had brought him here to the Iowa countryside was answered without the need to frame it. Joachim's blue eyes bore into his and from them radiated the awful truth. Joachim had lost the art of dissembling. He lived his life under the eye of God, who can neither deceive nor be deceived. What would be the point of deceiving Father Dowling?

"I think you should do nothing."

"Nothing!"

"Except what you are doing already. Isn't that what brought you here?"

"It was the occasion. Must it be the occasion now for my leaving?"

"That would serve nothing."

"I have thought often of him lying there. I acted in such

haste and anger I knew that eventually it must come to light."

"He has received a proper burial now, Brother. At your aunt's request. Let us hope that he sleeps at last in peace."

"I will go on praying for him."

"Remember us all, Brother. Remember us all."

12

Some weeks later an item in the paper brought Marie Murkin grumbling into the study where Father Dowling and Phil Keegan were watching the post-Jackson Bulls.

"It makes me so mad, Father." She thrust the folded newspaper beneath the pastor's nose. Mario Freddoso smiled from the page, the recipient of some civic honor for service to the community in which his family now did business.

"He very likely deserves it, Marie."

"You know what he deserves and so do I."

"Who you talking about?" Phil asked the housekeeper.

"What do you think of a man who gets away with murder?"

Phil frowned. "Which one?"

The pastor's laughter did not seem directed at her but Marie took it as occasion to leave the men to their game. Which one indeed!

On Ice

1

The frozen steaks arrived packed in dry ice in a Styrofoam box. Marie signed for it and carried it down the hall to the pastor's study.

"Package for you."

Father Dowling waved away a cloud of pipe smoke. "What is it?"

Marie shook the box. "It's not heavy."

"Who's it from?"

"Fleischhaecker's Specialties. In Florida."

Father Dowling wondered who in Florida would be sending him a package. Marie, less patient with wonder, plunked the box down on the desk and opened it. She stepped back at the sight of the packet of dry ice atop the contents.

"Be careful," she warned.

The pastor reached in for the envelope he had spied and soon was reading the card it contained. "Future burnt offerings for the pastor of St. Hilary. Omar Johansen."

"Omar Johansen!" cried Marie Murkin and clamped the top of the box on again. "I'd send it right back to him."

"Of course it's really meant for you, Marie."

The housekeeper regarded him with a baleful eye. Omar Johansen had been a trial to Marie throughout the fall. Daily he came to the senior center situated in what had once been the parish school, but he came there only to sidle along the walk to the rectory and sneak up on Marie in the kitchen. He had actually tried to tickle her! When she brought this scandalous news to the pastor, she had not received the sympathy she had every right to expect from a man of the cloth and ex officio defender of the moral law. What was the world coming to when a parish housekeeper wasn't safe from amorous elderly men who surprised her in her own kitchen?

"I think he likes you, Marie."

"The man is nearly eighty."

"That means delay is not advisable."

"Delay?"

"Marie, I won't have you thinking your duties here should stand in the way of your happiness. If you and Omar . . ."

Speechless with anger, Marie had turned on her heel and then repeated the operation so that she once more faced the pastor. Now Marie watched as Father Dowling removed the contents of the Styrofoam box. The neatly wrapped packages were hard as a brick.

"Filet mignon," he noted. "Phil will like that."

"You know what it means, don't you?" Marie had tipped her head to one side and looked wisely at the pastor.

"Filet mignon?"

"The box, the frozen meat. Don't you remember?"

After a moment, Father Dowling smiled ruefully. "You may be right, Marie."

"Of course I'm right!" She paused. "Do you suppose he's gone ahead and done it?"

2

"It" was a possibility that Omar Johansen had come to discuss with Father Dowling. There was always something he wanted to discuss with Father Dowling, since that gave him an excuse to be in the rectory and thus closer to Marie. The seventy-year-old housekeeper was clearly a concupiscible object to his aging eye and when he wasn't engaged in discussing the state of his soul he asked about Marie.

"Is she married, Father?" he whispered.

"You should ask her such questions, Omar."

"Call her in here."

"I don't think that would be the most effective way."

"Advise me, Father. Tell me the way to her heart."

"I am the last person on earth to give you that kind of advice."

"Is it because I'm not Catholic, Father?"

Father Dowling was surprised. He had simply assumed that so regular a visitor to the parish center was a Catholic. Omar came to Mass on Sunday and sometimes during the week as well, but it occurred to the pastor that it was always when Marie Murkin was in the church.

"What are you, Omar?"

"I wish I knew. I believe in God, of course, and I know I'll be back."

"Back?"

"Sometimes I can almost remember previous lives. The memory is just around a corner of the mind but I can't sneak up on it."

"You believe in reincarnation?"

"I think we are born again and again, yes."

"Why?"

"Why many times?"

"Yes."

"Why once?"

Father Dowling mistakenly entered into this discussion, not yet seeing that such metaphysical overtures were merely ploys on Omar Johansen's part to remain in the rectory in the hope of seeing Marie Murkin. He had suggested that, if birth means the coming into being of someone who had not previously existed, then the cycle of births Omar spoke of simply made no sense.

"It turns the body into an overcoat you put on and take off, replacing it with another. Do you think you are simply a soul?"

Omar nodded in approval at this response and urged Father Dowling to go on. But the pastor felt foolish.

"I know I'm scared to death of dying." Omar said this quite seriously.

"Most of us are."

"Do you think death can be cured, Father Dowling?"

"Cured?"

"A way found to prevent it, some drug . . ." He waved his hand vaguely.

"I would not care to live forever in our present condition."

"It's the only one we're sure of."

"No."

"Oh well, you're a priest. And a Catholic. But I'm not so sure there is a next world. I'd rather keep my hold on this one."

"Not many men your age would say that."

"I felt older at sixty." As if in proof of his youthfulness, Omar turned at the sound of approaching footsteps. Marie came into the study and then stopped, clearly surprised to find Omar Johansen there. He rose to his feet in exaggerated gallantry, not the way to Marie's heart.

"How did you get in?"

"Why don't you come to the mall with us this afternoon, Mrs. Murkin?"

The suggestion that the housekeeper was the same vintage as the denizens of the senior center represented strike two in Omar's effort to worm his way into Marie's affections. He would have to go to the mall without Marie, riding out with the other oldsters in the parish minibus. It was a fateful excursion. That was the day Omar had come upon the cryogenics exhibit at the mall.

"It's the cure I dreamt of! Or the next thing to it. They freeze you and then revive you when science has found a cure for what ails you."

"What ails you is mortality, Omar."

"Exactly. When they find a cure for it, they can bring me back."

"I don't think they ever will."

"Then I won't know, will I?"

Suspended animation brought on by lowering the body temperature and storing the body in a locker for all the world like frozen meat seemed an ill-conceived science fiction story to Father Dowling. But Omar was hooked and prepared to make arrangements for his departure.

"First, though, I'm going to make a trip to Florida. That's where I'll live when I come back. You'd like it, Marie."

"I prefer Illinois."

"That's because you don't know Florida. I'd like to show it to you."

But this effort was only halfhearted. Omar's heart had now been given to the Achronic Cryogenics Society. His daughter was appalled by the idea and came to the rectory to discuss it with Father Dowling.

"Why would you put such thoughts into an old man's mind?" Mrs. Laila Landon was visibly uneasy in the presence of a priest but was sustained by her indignation.

"They got there without any help from me."

"I'm surprised Catholics believe in such nonsense."

"You're laboring under a misapprehension, Mrs. Landon. I have been trying to turn your father's thoughts along quite different lines."

"You mean turn him into a Catholic?"

"He told me only recently that he wasn't a Catholic. He was such a frequent presence in the parish center I just assumed that he was one of us. Not that he need be to come to the center. His visits to me have had at least a dual purpose."

"The woman?"

"What has he told you?"

"That he has met a woman he wants to make his wife. I don't know which is crazier, thinking of getting married at his age or thinking about being frozen."

"Are you his only child?"

"Child." She smiled. "I scarcely think of myself as a child. I am his only daughter. Who is this woman?"

"I could only guess."

"I would like to talk with her."

Father Dowling looked more closely at his visitor. "What would you say to her?"

"I don't want her taking advantage of my father. He seems clearheaded enough but he gets these antic ideas. As you probably know, he has a great deal of money."

"I didn't know."

"I'm sure the woman does."

What Mrs. Landon called her father's antic ideas concerned her not simply as a daughter, but as the sole immediate heir of that great deal of money. She had a son whose future was also linked to inheriting a sum when his grandfather died.

"He wouldn't be legally dead if he had himself frozen, would he?"

"I hadn't thought of that."

"I have. Are you saying that you've tried to talk sense to him on these matters?"

"On being frozen? Yes."

Mrs. Landon appreciated the implied distinction. "I am almost more concerned about the woman."

3

The son's name was Henry and he came by the rectory the following day. He was over six feet tall, his head was shaved, and his neck was very thick in a muscular way.

"I was a split end," he explained.

"What team did you play on?"

"Tampa Bay. Now I'm a bodybuilder." He meant that he was assistant manager of a health clinic where people came to exercise. He gave Father Dowling a card. *The Body Shoppe. Age Is a State of Mind.*

"It seems to run in the family."

He looked blank. "My grandfather has my mother worried."

"So she told me."

"I don't know why. He's in Florida now so the woman can't get him and he isn't likely to get frozen in Florida. People go there to avoid that."

"He doesn't want to die."

Henry thought about that. At his age, the fact of mortality had probably not really gained a hold on his mind. Or his body. He obviously spent a good deal of time keeping his own body in top condition as an advertisement of what he could do for clients of The Body Shoppe.

"Why are you in Fox River?"

"My mother sounded so upset I thought I'd better come up."

"It's your grandfather you should talk to."

"I wanted to talk to you first." He hesitated. "Can they really do that?"

"What."

"Freeze you and then bring you back later?"

"I don't know that it has ever been done."

"I can see why my grandfather would be interested."

"I'd try it on an animal first."

"Like steaks?" A grin crept over Henry's face like a desert sunrise.

Marie had been busy about something in the dining room during this visit and after Henry left, she came into the study.

"The whole family's crazy."

"I'm reminded of one of the prayers in the Mass for All Souls Day. In the old liturgy, that is. We prayed that the souls of the faithful departed might be given a *refrigerii sedem*. It sounds like a spot in a refrigerator. Away from the flames, in any case."

Marie looked at him reproachfully. That he might give any credence whatsoever to Omar Johansen's absurd desire to be locked away in a freezer shocked Marie.

"But I suppose you're thinking of Dante, Marie."

Marie shifted her weight and rearranged her crossed arms.

"The lowest depths of the Inferno where we are shown Satan frozen in ice? When he fell, he plunged halfway through the earth and is caught there in a frozen lake. Dante and Virgil have to skate around him—"

"Why doesn't that young man stop his grandfather?"

"Well, we agreed on one thing."

"What was that?"

"The only thing that could divert him would be the influence of a good woman."

That was enough for Marie. For half a day she gave the pastor the silent treatment, what on any other occasion he might have called the cold shoulder. Even when the chill lifted, she did not become her usual voluble self. But two weeks later she found her voice again when she heard the news on the radio. She fairly flew from the kitchen to the study.

"He's dead!"

"Who?"

"It was just on WBBM. Omar Johansen is dead."

"God rest his soul."

"Amen."

Surprisingly, the body had not been found in Florida, but in a motel across from Fox River's largest mall. The death was said to be under investigation. Father Dowling picked up the phone and called Phil Keegan.

"How do you know him?" Phil asked.

"He often came to the parish center."

"Do you know much about him?"

"Why don't you come for dinner?" He paused. "We'll have steak."

4

Philip Keegan, Fox River captain of detectives, was what the Irish call a spoiled priest. As a boy he had been a student at Quigley, the preparatory seminary for the archdiocese of Chicago, but he had found Latin intractable and in those days that was taken to be a sure sign that he had no vocation. He went into the service, did a tour as an MP, and joined the Fox River police department after his discharge. Widowed, lonely, sharing Quigley memories with the pastor of St. Hilary, Phil Keegan was a frequent presence at the rectory.

"What do you know about cryogenics, Roger?"

"Why do you ask?"

"Some society wants to claim the body. They produced a document showing that the deceased had authorized them to keep him on ice indefinitely."

"Will their claim be recognized?"

"It's unclear. We've never had a case like it. Meanwhile, the body is in the morgue, cold if not frozen."

Marie, in the kitchen doorway, shuddered. "The man was a pest, but you ought to speak of him with respect."

"What did I say?"

"Never mind."

"*You* called him a pest."

Marie looked warningly at the pastor. She did not want to be teased about the attention Omar Johansen had paid her.

"What did he die of, Phil?"

"Dr. Pippen is undecided." He said this with some impatience. The assistant medical examiner was a woman of imagination and was inclined toward complicated and *recherché* causes of death. "She did say there was evidence of frostbite."

"Frostbite!"

It was a beautiful Illinois autumn, with daytime temperatures in the seventies and the temperature seldom going below forty-five at night.

"I thought he was in Florida."

"He checked into his motel three days ago."

"He had an apartment here," Marie exclaimed. "He mentioned it," she added in a lower voice.

"His daughter refused to believe it was her father at first. She said he was in Florida. But it's the body of Omar Johansen all right."

Laila Landon wanted to cremate her father's remains but her wishes could not be carried out so long as the matter of Omar's agreement with the cryogenic society kept his body in the morgue.

"This is outrageous," she said to Father Dowling. Her son Henry was with her and the three were sitting in the front parlor of the rectory. Laila Landon's manner suggested that she held Father Dowling at least partially responsible for what was happening.

"They're disputing the death certificate," Henry said. He held one meaty hand in the other and seemed to be flexing one muscle or another as he sat there, the endless exercising of the professional bodybuilder.

"How so?"

Laila Landon cried out in frustration. "They say he is merely asleep. Death does not occur for several days."

Henry added, "They have to freeze him quick to keep him suspended." As an afterthought, he said, "They're crazy."

"That's not all," Laila said.

"Oh."

"He gave them money."

She had said that her father had a considerable amount of money. But his bank and broker informed Mrs. Landon when she made inquiries that her father had closed his accounts, withdrawn his money from the bank, and sold his portfolio.

"And given the money to the cryogenic society?"

"That's only a guess," Henry said.

It was a guess Laila Landon was prepared to act on. She accused the Achronic Cryogenics Society publicly. The society denied everything, but of course that is just what Laila expected them to do. It was clear to her that the society was simply a scam to separate such elderly people as her father from their money. To take money for something you could not possibly deliver was a racket if there ever was one. She grew ever more eloquent in her accusation. She promised to sue.

5

"They only care about the money," was Marie's verdict. "Is anyone mourning Omar Johansen?"

Father Dowling arranged a memorial service for Omar and most of those who had known him from the parish center came. He held it in the school, in what had been the gymnasium when the parish had had a sufficient number of families with children to have a school. He read several passages from scripture, having first noted that Omar had not been a Catholic. Perhaps not even a Christian, but that did not prevent their praying for the repose of his soul.

"When's the funeral?" someone asked.

"I don't think that's been decided."

"He's been dead almost a week!"

"That's why I thought we might get together like this."

"I would like to read something," said a woman whom Father Dowling did not know, rising dramatically as she spoke. "Something for Omar."

She was tall and wore a coat that reached almost to her ankles and she carried her head high, chin uptilted as she came forward with a book in her hand. When she stood next to Father Dowling, she said, "A poem."

"Ah."

He glanced at the book, fearful that it might be the Rubaiyat of Omar Khayyam. But it was something far more obscure and difficult.

"Perhaps you will know Edith Sitwell's 'The Song of the Cold,' " she began and then, at a quite audible whisper, "Who is she?" she introduced herself. "I am Cynthia Keller. Omar's friend. I had read this poem to him not two weeks ago. He found it very moving."

The audience in the gymnasium were perhaps less appreciative, despite Cynthia's assuming a bardlike voice for her recitation. She would read, she said, only the second part of the poem.

> *There were great oscillations*
> *Of temperature . . . You knew there had once been*
> *   warmth;*
> *But the Cold is the highest mathematical Idea—the*
> *   Cold is Zero—*
> *The Nothing from which arose*
> *All Being and all variation . . .*

On and on she declaimed, while the elderly listeners stirred in their chairs and glanced at Father Dowling, who had gotten them into this. When Cynthia Keller finished there was the frenzied applause of a relieved audience as chairs were pushed back.

"I don't know that poem," Father Dowling said to Cynthia. She had seemed of indeterminate age when she first came forward, but it was clear she too was elderly.

"Edith Sitwell is my favorite poet."

There was some resemblance too, Father Dowling thought, between the poetess and the fan, which might have provided a basis for the liking. "You said you read the poem to Omar?"

"In Florida. We met there. He was a fascinating man. Very spiritual."

"How well did you know him?"

"We agreed that we had met before. In another life."

"Ah."

"I introduced him to Edith Sitwell. He told me about cryogenics."

"It was an obsession with him."

She seemed to disapprove of this description. "His wishes must be respected!"

"His daughter intends to have him cremated."

"How cruel!"

6

Marie did not think the memorial service had been a good idea and Father Dowling was inclined to agree. Edith did not sit well with the parish seniors. But it did seem a shame that there was no one to mourn for Omar Johansen. His daughter and grandson resented him and treated his death as some senile folly. Cynthia seemed unwilling to think of him as dead. For her the body was in a kind of limbo between life and death and only cryogenics could preserve it so Omar could come back as Omar Johansen. But if his remains were cremated, he would come back anyway, but as someone else. Those, for Cynthia, were the terms of the debate. Father Dowling had more sympathy with the cryogenic option; at least it had the appeal of a degenerate form of resurrection.

"Like Lazarus, if you need a scriptural precedent."

The speaker was Basil Laramie, who sat on the edge of the chair across from Father Dowling's desk looking relentlessly sincere. When Marie answered the door he had identified himself as president of the Achronic Cryogenics Society and asked to see the pastor. He admitted that he was the man who had persuaded Omar to have his body frozen and, in response to Father Dowling's reaction, cited Lazarus.

"When Lazarus came back to life, he was the same man who had died, wasn't he, Father?"

"Are you a Christian?"

"I accept all the world's great religions. I cite Lazarus because of your faith."

"That was a miracle."

"One time's miracle is a later time's science."

"How many members does your society have?"

"A modest number. Slightly more than the twelve with which Christianity began."

"Have there been any successful resuscitations of frozen bodies?"

Basil tipped his head back as if to get a better view of the ceiling. "If we waited until everything is certain we would do nothing. But those who are frozen will be in a condition to be brought back when technology has solved the problem."

"So it's a gamble?"

Basil lowered his gaze and smiled across the desk. "Isn't faith

291

always a gamble?"

"Did Omar leave his money to the society?"

Basil's expression grew sad. "Then you have heard that accusation?"

"It's not true?"

"No. I had no idea he had any money but I would have been delighted if he had chosen to back up his trust in the society with an amount of money. Alas, he did not do so." His face clouded. "Unless his wishes in this respect are being thwarted too."

7

Amos Cadbury, the attorney, stepped into the sacristy after Father Dowling's noon Mass on Wednesday and asked if he could have a word with the pastor.

"Can you join me for lunch?"

"A Mrs. Murkin meal? I'd be delighted!"

There was little mystery about the esteem in which Marie held Mr. Cadbury. The lawyer's manner as he consumed the pasta salad Marie had prepared was eloquent, but he put his appreciation into words as well. The housekeeper beamed, at once dismissing his praise and relishing it. When Marie had brought in tea for the attorney and withdrew, the point of Amos Cadbury's visit became clear.

"I speak in confidence, of course, Father."

"Of course."

"I believe you knew Omar Johansen."

"Yes."

"A week and a half ago he came to me with a large amount of money that he carried in a plastic shopping bag. He entrusted it to my care under terms that were, to say the least, extraordinary. He wanted me to ensure that his money would be waiting for him when he returned from the dead."

Cadbury paused. He was almost as old as his client in this case, and to accept the assignment smacked of presumption.

"How long did he expect to be dead?"

"I realize this sounds bizarre."

"It sounds familiar. I talked with Omar about this."

"Did he tell you what he wanted done with his money?"

"No."

"He wants it frozen with him."

"Frozen assets?"

"Of course his daughter will make a claim on the money as soon as she learns that I have it. Here is my dilemma. As the late Omar Johansen's attorney, I feel obliged to honor his wishes. But of course it is madness to think he himself will have any further use for that money. In opposing Mrs. Landon's inevitable claim, I will be fighting against common sense. I shall be a laughingstock."

"Oh, I doubt that, Amos."

"There is more."

"Oh."

"He instructed me to give you fifty thousand dollars." Cadbury brought his briefcase from beside his chair and released the clasps with a snap.

"Fifty thousand dollars!"

"For the parish center. He spoke quite movingly of the time he had spent there. There is another small amount as well."

Father Dowling might have guessed it before the lawyer spoke. Omar had left five thousand dollars to Marie Murkin.

"With a message."

"Can you tell me what it is?"

"Wait for me."

8

Dr. Pippen's definitive verdict on the cause of Omar Johansen's death was pneumonia. The strange burns on his body that she had originally diagnosed as frostbite were the result, she felt, of dry ice being applied to the body. This, she opined, was the proximate cause of death.

"Cy Horvath turned up some strange things at the motel where Johansen died. Johansen and his girl friend kept hauling buckets of ice to his room. The maid said they filled the bathtub with ice cubes."

"By girl friend you mean Cynthia Keller?"

"The same. We arrested her."

"What for?"

Phil paused. "Manslaughter. Freezing a man to death. Crispin, the prosecutor, wanted to charge assisted suicide, but we would never get a conviction on that."

"Do you think you'll get a manslaughter conviction?"

"Nowadays, who knows?"

What the police were to call Cynthia's confession was called a declaration by the media who attended the press conference that Tuttle her lawyer called.

"Death is an illusion," she said grandly in answer to the charges. "How can I be charged with bringing about a condition that cannot exist?"

Was she saying that Omar Johansen was still alive?

"As alive as you or I."

"He still exists," Tuttle said helpfully, moving his tweed hat around on the table top before him. "He's in the morgue so he must exist, right?"

Cynthia was dramatic in her assertion that her role in preparing Omar for the ultimate ministrations of the Achronic

Cryogenic Society was only what any friend might do for another.

"Was he naked in the tub full of ice?"

Cynthia cast a cold eye on the questioner. "Your prurience ill becomes you, young man."

"How much money did he leave you?"

"I don't know what you're talking about."

"He gave another woman five thousand dollars."

This clearly came as news to Cynthia. She had a whispered conference with her lawyer, after which Tuttle said that was all and hurried to catch up with his client as she headed for the door.

The question had been based on knowledge of a petition Amos Cadbury had filed a few hours before. In it he detailed the wishes of his client and asked for ratification in order that he might proceed. The bequest to Marie Murkin was thus there to be discovered by anyone with patience enough to read.

9

The testimony of motel employees along with Cynthia Keller's declaration seemed to remove all mystery from the cause of Omar Johansen's death. Much as his grandson Henry prepared his clients for the rigors of life with demanding exercise, so Omar and Cynthia had sought to accustom his body to a dramatic lowering of temperature. This would make the transition to suspended animation in a frozen state easier for his body. But the news that Omar had left money to Marie Murkin transformed Cynthia Keller.

"He was an animal," she confided to a reporter from one of Chicago's largest daily newspapers.

"At eighty?"

"A man is a man."

"For a' that?"

"Burns," Cynthia said, and went on. "I had thought him spiritual. Now I realize he was carnal. It is best that his soul be released from the foul body of Omar Johansen and come back as somebody better."

So Cynthia became an ally of Laila Landon and her son Henry in an effort to prevent Amos Cadbury from doing what he was disinclined to do in any case.

"Imagine stashing all that money in a coffin or whatever they use." Phil's words materialized with the cigar smoke that issued from his mouth.

"People are buried with their jewelry, aren't they?"

"Remember Huckleberry Finn?" Phil said suddenly, a grin breaking out on his face. "It's kind of like that, isn't it?"

"What will happen to Cynthia?"

"Crispin doesn't think the case will get past a preliminary hearing. So she'll get away with it."

"With what?"

"Killing Omar Johansen."

"If she did it."

Phil, fearing metaphysical speculation, turned the talk to the Bulls. But Father Dowling's mind was not on the game that he and Phil watched on television that night, and when he had gone upstairs to his room and had turned off the light, he sat in a chair and looked across the parish lawn at the silhouette of the school that had become the St. Hilary Parish Center.

10

"Do you intend to accept it?" Mrs. Landon asked the following day when he called on her and told her of the surprising bequest her father had made.

"I wish I had an excuse not to."

"He was demented when he gave that lawyer those instructions. Fortunately, we seem most likely to prevent the rest of the money from being buried with him. Not that I believe for a minute that Basil Laramie would not avail himself of it."

"Rob the grave?"

"Isn't that the point of his whole silly society?"

"Where is Henry?"

She glanced at her watch. "He should be here now."

Henry arrived in a jogging costume, a sweatband around his head, the glow of health upon his meaty features. He wrapped himself in a massive towel and sat at the dining room table with a glass of juice before him.

"Your grandfather once sent me a package of frozen steaks."

"From Fleischhaecker's?" Henry said.

"You know the place?"

"I put him on to it. Fleischhaecker is a client."

"Are you a client of his?"

"How do you mean?"

"I was thinking of how the meat was kept frozen in transit."

"Dry ice."

"Yes."

Henry looked at Father Dowling expressionlessly. Mrs. Landon stirred and cleared her throat. Neither said anything.

"The burns on your grandfather's body were made with dry ice."

Mother and son kept silent.

"At the motel there was ice, regular ice, cubes. But it was dry ice that killed him."

For ten minutes he remained there with the silent heirs of Omar Johansen. Then he rose and left. In his car, he sat and considered the difficulties Phil Keegan would face if he accepted this surmise. But for Father Dowling it had become a certainty. That Henry had visited his grandfather at the motel could be established by asking the day clerk, as Father Dowling had done before calling on Mrs. Landon. Henry had not mentioned this, but what could be made of it in any case? Of course that was not the main problem.

If dry ice from one of Fleschhaecker's packages had been the means of bringing on Omar Johansen's death, it was now wherever dry ice goes when it evaporates. Doing Omar in with dry ice was like stabbing someone with an icicle, the weapon dying with the victim.

11

Eventually, Mrs. Landon got possession of her father's wealth. Amos Cadbury said only that it had been over a half-million dollars.

"She has decided not to sue you for the money her father left the parish."

"I wish she had."

"She might have won."

"She is happy with what she has?"

Amos Cadbury seemed in search of a delicate way to put it. "She said she wanted nothing more to do with you in any way whatsoever."

Father Dowling brightened at this. "Henry agreed?"

"He did."

That was even better. The bothered consciences of mother and son might be their salvation yet.

"Don't bet on it, Roger."

But faith is not a gamble, despite what Basil Laramie believed. Omar's money was a welcome contribution to the expenses of the parish center and a fitting memorial to him.

"Air-conditioning?" Phil asked.

"When the school was built air-conditioning was a luxury. It will make the center more tolerable in the summer."

Marie was mum about her five thousand dollars and did not respond when Phil asked if she had sent it to the missions. What she had decided to do did not become clear until an indignant Cynthia Keller showed up at the rectory and threw an envelope on Father Dowling's desk.

"I want none of his money. I remember now who he was before."

There was no need to prompt her with questions.

"A thousand years ago in Cairo, he was my husband. A beast of a man. It is well that he did not escape from the cycle of rebirth. Imagine wanting to go on being Omar Johansen."

"It sounds as if he owes you money."

A cry escaped her and her eyes sparked in anger. "I never expected such an insult from a minister of the gospel!"

Her departure was dramatic, and definitive. She slammed the front door resoundingly, bringing Marie into the study.

"She brought back the money, Marie."

"I don't want it."

"I have an idea."

She looked at him warily. "What?"

"How old is your refrigerator?"

Marie's departure could not rival that of Cynthia Keller, but it made up in vigor what it lacked in panache.

THE BALD-HEADED
HUSBAND

1

On the first Wednesday of every month, Father Dowling said a Mass for the deceased members of the parish. It was a popular event, almost doubling the usual attendance at the noon liturgy, and always prominent in the front row was Mrs. Wortman. The elderly widow dressed for the occasion, wearing black, a hat with veil, and snow-white gloves that somehow negated the solemnity of her attire, giving the suggestion of a minstrel player. This was a thought Father Dowling always drove from his mind but it unfailingly returned each first Wednesday when, having emerged from the sacristy and proceeded to the center of the sanctuary to kiss the altar, he looked up to see the familiar figure of Mrs. Wortman. But then in October he looked out at the congregation, prepared to discard distracting and irreverent thoughts brought on by the sight of white gloves, and there were no white gloves in evidence. Mrs. Wortman was absent from her usual place in the front pew.

"Mrs. Wortman wasn't there," he said to Mrs. Murkin when he returned to the rectory for lunch.

"I'll check on it," Marie Murkin said.

Had he counted on Marie's doing that? He found he was disinclined to tell her to let it go. After all, Mrs. Wortman had no obligation to attend the memorial Mass. The soul of her husband was only one of the many the Mass was offered for that day. But Mrs. Wortman had always insisted on giving him a

300

stipend for saying that Mass.

"Would you like me to say a special Mass for your husband?" he had asked her.

The old woman thought about it, then shook her head. "I like it better this way. He has company."

No doubt everyone has his personal little theological twists, not quite orthodox, perhaps, but innocent enough. If Mrs. Wortman imagined that her late husband was somehow less lonely in the beyond for being prayed for along with all the other departed of the parish, so be it. But it made him hesitant to ask her just what she thought the next world was like.

"How would she know?" Marie Murkin asked indignantly when he mentioned Mrs. Wortman's remark about her husband's otherworldly company to the housekeeper.

"I wasn't referring to personal experience."

"How else could she find out?"

Father Dowling let it go. The prospect of a doctrinal dialogue with the housekeeper was daunting. Marie had all the theological skills except sound doctrine, and was unlikely to give way or concede defeat in any exchange. Father Dowling had the suspicion that Marie regarded him as her backup in pastoral work and would not think it appropriate to defer to him on the matter, particularly since her indignation had been aroused by the implication that the Widow Wortman might know something the housekeeper did not.

An hour later, he was nodding over a novel in his study when Marie looked in. "She's in the hospital."

The pastor looked thoughtfully at the housekeeper. He had forgotten the earlier conversation and was trying to connect Marie's words with something that would make them intelligible.

"St. Mary's Hospital," she added.

"Ah."

"I told the nurse to let her know you'd be down to see her."

"Good."

Marie remained in the doorway, frowning into the middle distance. "They didn't really get along, you know."

"How would I know that?"

"Of course you wouldn't. Andy Wortman died before you came here." Marie had assumed the expression of a veteran reminiscing to a recruit. But at least he now knew what she was talking about.

"Of course I'll go see her."

"That's what I said."

2

Visiting the sick is incumbent on everyone but it is peculiarly the task of the pastor. At St. Mary's, Father Dowling looked into the open door of the chaplain's office, and the smiling countenance of Jimmy Dolan, looking flush beneath his helmet of silver hair, peered out at him.

"Roger!" He leapt from his chair and bounded to the doorway. Once he had Roger Dowling's hand in his, he pulled him into the office, shutting the door by a deft conga line movement of his hip. It was difficult to imagine a hospital chaplain as lonely, but Jimmy obviously needed company. "The halt and the lame, Roger. The going and gone. And their mourners. It is a grim life. You look in the pink."

"You look pinker."

"It's not high blood pressure!" The suggestion that he had an ailment himself filled Jimmy with indignant terror. No doubt he was privy to the many perils of health delivery in his post.

"Have you checked on our Mrs. Wortman?"

Jimmy frowned. "Is she in St. Hilary's parish?"

"Didn't she say so?"

"She's in a coma, Roger."

"Is there much point in looking in on her?"

"I'll call and ask when you want to go up there." Jimmy glanced at the door, as if contemplating locking it. It was going to be difficult to break away from the lonely chaplain in order to look in on Iris Wortman.

"Roger, what do you think of the cardinal?"

Of course Jimmy wanted to tell Roger what he himself thought of the new man. Apparently His Eminence had already made the rounds of the hospitals. "Rumor has it that he intends to just pop into places, catch people unawares."

"I'll warn Mrs. Murkin."

"It won't do any good."

"Do you know Marie?"

"Is she the one who telephoned?" Jimmy looked cross-eyed. "At least I don't have to keep a housekeeper in line down here."

Jimmy might have roomed in a nearby parish, but he preferred to live in the suite the hospital provided its chaplain. "At least I can smoke here."

"In the hospital?"

"I have a smoke eater."

"You could smoke in my rectory."

"It's too far away."

Roger Dowling spent fifteen minutes trading clerical gossip with Jimmy and then, when the chaplain had been lulled into complacency, rose quickly, got to the door, and opened it in a single swift movement.

"Where you going?"

"To visit my parishioner."

"I was going to call to check on her condition."

"Thank you."

Jimmy picked up the phone with a somewhat petulant expression. Roger's felt a pang of sympathy. A priest needs other priests to talk to; no layperson can quite substitute for another who has been through the mill, born the heat of the day, run the race, fought the good fight—and all the other verses clerics were likely to apply to themselves in moods of self-reflection. Jimmy turned from the phone.

"Iris Wortman has come out of it." He seemed surprised. But he added, "No saying how long it will last."

Roger Dowling waved and started for the elevators. "Look in before you leave," Jimmy called after him.

3

Iris Wortman looked diminished, lying hatless in a hospital bed, her rather large veined hands crossed ungloved over her breast. Her eyes seemed to have been waiting for him to appear in her doorway. She let out a small gasp and seemed to shrink into herself. In the circumstances, the arrival of a priest must seem to have terminal implications. Father Dowling dragged a chair beside the bed and said, "I understand you've been out." He added, "Unconscious."

"Was I?"

"So I'm told."

"They didn't even tell me where I was. I don't remember getting here. What hospital is this?"

"St. Mary's."

"Oh good."

Had her late husband departed this vale of tears from St. Mary's hospital? Not a question he was likely to ask. He did say that he had missed her that morning at the memorial Mass. She nodded and looked at him with large unblinking eyes.

"You never knew Andrew."

"No."

She lay in silence, drawing her lower lip between her teeth. She looked at him and then looked away. Her voice was scarcely audible. "I have something terrible to confess, Father."

He nodded. "God is merciful."

"It was a great sacrilege, but at the time I didn't care."

He waited. All remaining obstacles to speaking seemed to be falling before the relief she felt at having said as much as she had. She inhaled deeply. "Andrew didn't die."

"I don't understand."

"Whoever it was we buried that day it wasn't my husband."

"Tell me all about it."

The story came out as if she had rehearsed it and so no doubt she had, over the years, those long-ago events impossible to eradicate from memory. She stared at the ceiling while she told him the story as if it were being projected there from her memory.

As a girl she had been pursued by both Andrew Wortman and Bill McDivitt, and she had been unable to make up her mind which of the two men she really loved or loved the most or wished to marry. It had been very confusing and she might never have decided if Bill McDivitt had not been drafted and gone off to the army.

"Andy was so jealous. He tried to enlist but they wouldn't have him. He was certain that Bill had acquired the status of a hero for me and he would be eclipsed. Actually all Bill did was waste a year of his life in a camp in the state of Washington. He was in no more danger in uniform than Andy was right here in Fox River. But Andy did have the advantage of nearness. I accepted his proposal and by the time Bill returned we were man and wife. As soon as I saw Bill again I knew I had made a terrible mistake."

Whatever her feelings, Bill McDivitt had remained a perfect gentleman and she did her best never to let her husband know that in her heart she longed to be the bride of his old rival. And for some time, she kept her secret from Bill as well, but eventually, in a moment of weakness and with fatal consequences, she succumbed. The admission robbed them both of all good sense and they fell into one another's arms. It was thus that Andrew found them. He stared at them in awful silence, then turned and walked away. In that moment, her marriage died. Communication between husband and wife all but ceased. Her efforts to explain to Andrew what had happened, to ask his forgiveness, were disdainfully dismissed. Bill, on his side, was devastated by his own disloyalty to his old friend. The realization that Iris loved him was bittersweet. He felt condemned to eternal bachelorhood.

Andrew apparently believed that there was an ongoing affair between his wife and his onetime friend rather than a single moment of weakness he had been unfortunate enough to witness. But what might not the sequel of that moment have been if they had not been discovered? Such agonizing questions came to define Iris's life. Her husband refused to talk to her, and of course there was no exchange of affection between them. Bill McDivitt held equally aloof. The three erstwhile friends had become disconnected points that could not make a couple, let alone a triangle.

The second chapter in the drama occurred when Iris's mother died and was buried from McDivitt's Funeral Home. In making arrangements, Iris was alone with Bill in his office, but the somber reason for the appointment seemed protection against their feelings. Who would imagine a funeral parlor as aphrodisiac? But so it proved to be for the star-crossed couple. Behind the closed door of Bill's office, they poured out their hearts, straining toward one another across the intervening desk, able after years at last to speak. If they had not been Catholics, they would have plotted her divorce from Andy and their eventual union, but of course that was out of the question. Iris may have made a mistake, but it was one she must live with until death relieved her of it. Nor could Bill and Iris repeat the moment that seemed to have destroyed their lives. Theirs fingers intertwined on the desktop and then withdrew. It was then that Iris began to wear gloves. They would not have been human if they had not imagined themselves in that very office discussing arrangements for the funeral of Andrew Wortman.

And then one day, Andrew failed to return home from his office. Iris waited supper while the shadows lengthened. The one way they could still communicate was by telephone; he could scarcely refuse to take her call when she phoned his office. But that evening his office telephone rang and rang. Of course the office would be empty now and if Andrew was still there he did not answer the phone. Iris sat in the gloaming, staring at the telephone, then watched her hand reach out and pick up the instrument again. Her finger punched numbers she had not consciously remembered and moments later the voice of Bill McDivitt spoke in her ear.

"Andrew is missing," she whispered.

"What do you mean?"

"He hasn't come home and he isn't at his office."

"When did you last see him?"

"This morning."

He might have laughed, but he didn't. His questions made clear that Bill understood that she wanted Andrew to be missing, longed for the millstone of her marriage to be somehow magically removed. The fact that her first impulse had been to telephone Bill McDivitt made amply clear what future she dreamed of.

"Have you eaten?"

"I was waiting for Andy."

"Have dinner with me."

She managed to refuse, but the phone call established the thought between them that they were waiting for Andrew to stop being an obstacle to their love.

Andrew did not come home all night and the following day he did not appear at his office. Bill offered to pursue the matter for her.

"In case something has happened . . ."

He said he would check the morgue. Iris looked out the window where clouds were scudding across a slate gray sky. She fought the impulse to pray that Bill would call back to say she was a widow. But the body of Andrew Wortman was not in the morgue, not that day, nor in the days that followed. Nor did he show up at work or at home.

After she reported him missing, as Bill urged her to do, the police came and talked to her. She knew they found her manner puzzling. She could not pretend that she was brokenhearted. When one of the detectives assured her they would find Andrew, it was all she could do not to protest.

"Had he ever threatened to leave?"

"In an argument? Yes."

"You had arguments?"

"Don't most couples?" But she was certain that she and Bill would never argue.

"Have you checked your bank accounts?"

"My husband took care of those."

They wanted information about savings and investments and Iris referred them to Alex Sciacca. Andy had sung the praises of their financial advisor. But Sciacca had been vacationing in Sicily for some weeks, and when he returned he telephoned the police after some preliminary inquiries into his client's affairs.

"I would have opposed it. He would never have expected me to do it."

An assistant in Sciacca's office had acquiesced when Andrew sold off his portfolio.

"The taxes!" Sciacca said, and seemed about to curl into a fetal position. "He sold off things that had tripled in value since he bought them."

Iris understood none of this. All she knew was that her husband had disappeared and gone with him were all their common assets and savings. Clearly he was a missing person and, whether in Fox River or Timbuktu, he remained an obstacle between her and Bill McDivitt. If he had met with an accident, if his body had shown up in the morgue, she would have been a widow and after a decent interval of time, she and Bill . . .

4

Seated beside the hospital bed, listening to this, hearing the words that seemed to be squeezed from the old woman's very soul, Father Dowling's memory was stirred.

"Did you apply for an annulment?"

"I received no encouragement at all."

And then the memory came! Roger Dowling had been a member of the archdiocesan tribunal that had reviewed her petition. In the absence of the husband, it was impossible to test her claims that their marriage was invalid. The suggestion that his abandonment of her told in favor of her claim did not prevail.

Her words lifting ghostlike from her hospital bed had brought back that one case out of thousands, plucked it from the filing cabinet of memory in which were stored all the heartbreaking cases that had characterized Father Dowling's time on the marriage court. Subsequently, annulments became easier to get, too easy perhaps, and Iris Wortman might have received a quite different judgment. But in the time of Father Dowling's service, annulments were rare and granted only after prolonged waiting.

A nurse with J. Cashman in white letters on her blue nameplate had come into the room while the old woman talked and stood frowning at the exertion it cost her to speak.

"Is this necessary, Father?" The nurse looked sternly at the priest.

"Leave us alone!" Mrs. Wortman said imperiously. "I am speaking to a priest."

The nurse bristled at such insubordination but after glaring at Father Dowling left the room. Mrs. Wortman seemed to sink into her pillow, breathing in short gasps, her eyes fixed on Father Dowling.

"Would you like me to give you absolution?"

"I haven't finished."

"Are you sorry for all the sins you have committed because they are an offense against almighty God?"

She nodded, still breathing rapidly. Father Dowling said the formula of absolution and made the sign of cross over Mrs. Wortman. A minute later, her breathing stopped and Father Dowling rang for help. J. Cashman bounded into the room as if she had been waiting to be summoned. She was followed by others and Father Dowling withdrew to the hallway. J. Cashman came out to him.

"Is there anything else you have to do?"

"How is she?"

"Dead." She looked coldly at him, as if he were responsible.

So he had been wise to interrupt her tale and give her absolution. Or was it J. Cashman who deserved the credit for that? Father Dowling went into the room and looked down at the still body of the old woman. Now he would never hear the rest of her story. What had she meant when she said that it was not Andrew Wortman who lay in the grave?

5

The funeral mass and burial of Andrew Wortman had been recorded in the parish records two years before Roger Dowling was named pastor of St. Hilary parish in Fox River, Illinois.

Father Dowling opened the old ledger on his desk and stared at the noncommittal entry. It looked to be a burial like any other, but if Iris had been telling the truth . . . Why in such circumstances would she tell anything but the truth? Frail and feeble as she had seemed lying in the hospital bed, her mind was clear and the words had come fluently from her dry lips. The nub of the story, so far as the entry in the parish ledger was concerned, lay in her claim that it had not been the body of Andrew Wortman for whom a funeral Mass had been said and who had been consigned to the earth on that long-ago day. But Iris had insisted on making a generous offering to the parish to ensure that Andrew would be remembered in the monthly Mass said for all deceased parishioners.

"Do you remember the Andrew Wortman funeral?" he asked Marie Murkin.

"Of course."

"I see that McDivitt's took care of things."

"You noticed that, did you?"

"Noticed what?"

"That was the first time McDivitt's did a St. Hilary funeral. He was a friend of the deceased so Father Placidus allowed it. Grudgingly. It was so much better than Father Placidus's cousin had done that from then on it was always McDivitt we suggested."

"His cousin."

" 'Twice removed' he used to say. Not far enough I say."

Father Placidus had been pastor when the parish was still in the hands of the friars Marie had never liked. There were always two in residence and they never let her in on parish gossip. Not that Marie framed her charge in that way.

"They didn't have the pastoral touch, Father."

"Ah."

"You know what I mean."

"I'm afraid I do."

Marie decided against pursuing that line of conversation. Father Dowling pushed away from the table. McDivitt's had suggested that the wake be held at the parish, in the auditorium of the parish center, formerly the school.

"That way the old people won't have so far to go."

McDivitt's Funeral Parlor was now flanked by roaring ribbons of concrete and access to the parking lot required some of the skills of a Formula One driver. Willis McDivitt was the last of a long line and Marie opined that the family business would die out with him.

"Death of a funeral parlor."

"They would have to move to the suburbs to survive."

"Are there more dead people in the suburbs?"

"There's more parking anyway."

There was a great turnout for the wake and after the rosary the old people lingered on, darting glances at the open coffin, all too conscious that soon they would be the central attraction at such a gathering. McDivitt wanted a cigarette and thought it would be bad example to light up in front of so many potential customers, so Father Dowling went outside with him.

"She outlived her husband by nearly a quarter of a century."

"The ladies survive us, Father. It's the will of God."

"Do you remember her husband's funeral?"

Willis blew smoke at the cloudless sky. "Did you really mean a quarter century ago?"

"Yes."

"I was still selling insurance. To tell you the truth, I only reluctantly joined the family business. Bill would have been in charge then."

"Is he still alive?"

"If he were I would have gone on selling insurance. No, he died almost twenty-five years ago. An accident. Hit-and-run.

That's when I gave up insurance and decided to put my undertaking experience to use."

One question Father Dowling would have liked to ask Iris was answered by Willis McDivitt's remark. Iris had lost her husband and her old flame at almost the same time. He found Phil Keegan in the rectory when he returned and they settled in the study.

"What did you find?"

"The man had been missing for almost a year and then one day his body showed up in the morgue. John Doe, but he was identified and the body released for burial."

"What if it really wasn't Andrew Wortman's body?"

Phil moved his cigar from one corner of his mouth to the other. "What are you getting at?"

"Who identified the body as Wortman's?"

"Roger, the widow would have recognized her own husband."

"Did she identify him?"

"I suppose." He dug papers from his pocket and glared at them. Then he looked up triumphantly. "William McDivitt identified him. A boyhood friend."

"Phil, I have a somewhat ghoulish request to make."

Phil listened with a blank expression, then shook his head. "That's crazy."

"Will you do it?"

Phil agreed. Actually, it did not pose a great many obstacles. Many had commented on Iris's wish to be buried in the same grave as her husband. That made examination of the coffin that had been interred all these years much easier. After the funeral Mass the following day, a small band accompanied the body to the cemetery and after the graveside ceremony all withdrew.

Father Dowling, Phil Keegan, and Willis McDivitt waited and then followed the sexton to the shed where the coffin removed from the grave of Andrew Wortman had been taken. Now that the moment arrived, Father Dowling regretted having made the request. What good could come of stirring up old mysteries? With the death of Iris the books could be closed on that long-ago melodrama. But the sexton was already loosening the lid, a little whistling sound issuing from his pursed lips as he worked. He had waved aside the offer of a mask but the rest of the party ringing the coffin looked like a macabre team of surgeons. Phil's eyes met Roger's over his mask and the priest could see that his old friend regretted having acquiesced to this.

The sexton stepped back as he pushed the lid up and open, its hinges complaining at the movement. All flesh is grass, as the psalmist says. The masked group stood looking at the all-too-mortal remains of the occupant of the casket exposed to the air of the living after decades beneath the ground. It was the red hair that caught the eye, providing the one accent of color in that grisly scene.

"Was Wortman a redhead?"

No one there knew the answer to the question, but did anyone sense that something was wrong? Father Dowling had not of course mentioned the deathbed confidence of Iris Wortman that it was not her husband's body that lay in that grave.

"You want this left open?" the sexton asked. He seemed to have been holding his breath.

"That's it," Phil barked, stripping off the mask. Outside the shed, he said to Roger, "What was that all about?"

Roger busied himself with his pipe. There seemed little reason not to explain it to Phil. "Mrs. Wortman expressed doubt that her husband's body had been buried in that grave."

Phil stepped back and stared at his old friend. "And you took her seriously? How old was she?"

"Old enough to die."

6

Phil's interpretation was attractive, no doubt about it. An addled elderly woman mumbling nonsense on her deathbed. But Father Dowling had heard the long and complicated story of Andrew and Bill and Iris. Mrs. Wortman had reached the point in her story when she would have explained her opening remark that her husband did not lie in the grave marked with his name. He could not stifle his curiosity. He told himself he owed it to the old woman to pursue the matter. But how? She was dead, her husband had doubtless died somewhere by this time. Bill Mc-Divitt was dead. Perhaps if it had not been for the red hair, the mystery would have remained.

Father Dowling found a picture of the deceased in the issue of the local newspaper that announced the death of Andrew Wortman. He was bald as an egg. Father Dowling did nothing with this information. He now knew that Iris Wortman had told the truth when she said it was not her husband's body in that grave. Had she wanted her coffin atop the one already there, to seal her secret even more securely? But what harm could revelation do now? The only other person Iris had mentioned was Alex Sciacca, the Wortman financial advisor.

"He sent flowers," Marie said when he asked if she knew the name.

"He must be quite old."

"The flowers came from Tanglewood."

This was a posh retirement village in which inmates declined from more-or-less autonomous apartment living through stages of increased nursing and medical care until they came to the end of their road. Alex Sciacca was in what he called the "penultimate stage" in the system.

"The next step, I go ga-ga and get strapped into a bed and fed through a tube."

"This seems a pleasant enough place."

"As Dante said of Hell."

The remark was not idle. Sciacca had developed a fierce pride in his lineage and knew Italian literature as only a dedicated amateur could. "Manzoni?" He shook his head. "He's too much of a northerner. Give me Dante. Give me *The Leopard*. My favorite was born not fifty kilometers from my grandfather's village."

"Who's that?"

"Pirandello."

"You were a financial advisor."

Sciacca seemed irked to be diverted from his literary interests. A few wisps of still-black hair lay flat on his domed skull and his teeth seemed far too large for his wizened face. "The best."

"I just buried Iris Wortman."

Sciacca nodded solemnly. "A tragic case."

"She told me something about it before she died."

"Her husband abandoned her. Ran off with their considerable savings. I would have opposed selling those stocks with my life but I was in Italy on a vacation."

"He just disappeared?"

Sciacca nodded and left his chin on his chest. "He came back, Father. They all do. God knows what he'd been up to. One fine day his body showed up in the morgue. John Doe."

"There was no doubt it was him?"

Sciacca shook his head. "Not a doubt in the world, Father. I identified him."

"I thought Bill McDivitt did that."

Almond-colored eyes lifted over Sciacca's glasses and stared at the priest. "We both did."

"Why?"

"What do you mean?"

"Why did you identify a redheaded derelict as Andrew Wortman? Andrew Wortman was bald."

There was an almost audible whirr as the financial advisor processed this information. He exposed his teeth in a smile. "Did he pick the redhead?" Sciacca's eyes were merry and his chin had lifted from his chest. A plosive noise and a shaking of his body suggested laughter.

"So you knew it wasn't Andrew Wortman who was buried in that grave."

"I knew the man in the morgue was not Wortman. It was McDivitt who buried him."

"Tell me about it."

Sciacca grew animated as he spoke and the years seemed to fall from his frail body. He sat erect in his motorized chair, his gestures became expansive, his artificial teeth glistened as he smilingly told the tale.

"She married the wrong man. McDivitt went into the army and she married Wortman and it was a mistake. Wortman found out that she was sporting around with McDivitt and probably started plotting getting out from that moment. He cashed in and vamoosed."

"How much money would there have been?"

"After taxes? Not a million dollars. Of course money was worth more back then."

Sciacca gave Father Dowling a brief lecture in his investment philosophy. Buy stocks and bonds and hang on to them. Never sell. The historic direction of the market is up. It seemed a miser's message and Sciacca wore a crafty, half-mad look as he spoke. "Never sell," he repeated.

"Did you learn that from Dante?"

Sciacca laughed his odd laugh. "I never mix literature and business."

His story was that Bill McDivitt had buried a John Doe as Andrew Wortman to clear the way for him to marry Iris.

"But if you knew what he was doing . . ."

Sciacca waved away the implicit accusation. Well, at his age he probably thought the statute of limitations had run out on all the delinquencies of his active life. Not that he had put his lifelong interests away. He had a massive computer installed in his room and spent much of the day trading in the various financial markets of the world.

"What were some of the stocks Wortman sold?"

The question seemed to surprise Sciacca. "That was a long time ago, Father."

"I wondered what they would be worth today."

"Millions!" Sciacca cried. "Never sell."

7

It was that motto that prompted Father Dowling to continue to pursue the spoor of his curiosity. Sciacca Investments still operated although the eponymous broker had sold the firm to others.

"Is there anyone here who worked for Sciacca?"

"Jill?"

Jill was almost as old as her former boss and like Sciacca was unable to turn her back on the ups and downs of the markets.

"I only work mornings now," she said. She might have been confessing a sin.

"Do you remember Andrew Wortman?"

There was a long pause. Jill took a meditative sip of coffee.

"I see that his widow died."

"Alex Sciacca has still not forgiven Wortman for selling all those stocks."

"Selling?" The idea was offensive to her as well. "What stocks?"

"Before he disappeared."

"Did Alex say that?"

"I thought he said that Andrew Wortman unloaded a great

many valuable stocks."

"Not through this firm."

"Apparently Sciacca was in Italy at the time."

"Italy? He wouldn't go to Iowa."

"Who else worked here then?"

"There was just Alex and I."

"And Wortman didn't cash in his investments before disappearing?"

"You must have misunderstood Alex."

The present is full of mysteries, but the past is more so. If Wortman had not taken his wealth with him, he must have left town empty-handed. Had freedom from Iris come to mean that much to him? But why would Sciacca have insisted that Wortman had done the unforgivable, selling stocks of proven fecundity?

It was while pondering this that Father Dowling picked up the phone and called Phil Keegan. "Don't think me a pest, Phil. Could you find the records on the death of William McDivitt?"

"I'll bring them tonight. We are watching the game, aren't we?"

"Of course."

Will McDivitt had been struck down by a hit-and-run driver in the parking lot of the funeral home.

"The parking lot!"

"That is puzzling. That's where they found the body anyway."

"Hmmm."

"It was investigated, Roger. The verdict of hit-and-run came at the end, not the beginning. It means they couldn't find anything."

"It looks deliberate."

"It sure does."

But Phil was distracted by the game. Funeral director killed? Had the death of a man whose business was death seemed less in need of explanation? But Father Dowling's thoughts were such that, if he had expressed them, he would have been guilty of libel or slander or both. But it was a call from Amos Cadbury the following day that precipitated matters.

The patrician lawyer had represented the Wortman estate when the safety deposit box at the First Bank of Fox River was opened.

"It was filled with stock and bond certificates, Father Dowling. By a rough estimate, their value is some ten millions of dollars."

"Good Lord. Who is the heir?"

"That is why I called. Are you free anytime today?"

Father Dowling invited the lawyer to lunch and, after the noon Mass, they settled down in the dining room to Marie Murkin's pasta. No conversation was likely while the lawyer ate and praised what had been set before him. Marie, in a consternation of delight, came and went between kitchen and dining room like a figure on a clock. The surprising announcement came after Amos had sipped his tea and pronounced it celestial.

"She left everything after funeral expenses to the church, Father Dowling."

"The Church!"

"I believe she meant the parish."

"Oh no. Why would she leave such a sum to the parish?"

"She had no idea she was wealthy. Nor did I. The key to the safety deposit box showed up in her effects. She had never looked in that box herself."

"Had anyone?"

Amos cleared his throat. "Alex Sciacca."

8

"Of course I had a key," an unruffled Alex Sciacca said when Father Dowling spoke to him of the contents of the safe deposit box. "I had power of attorney."

"Andrew Wortman didn't sell off his stocks, did he?"

"Apparently not."

"Why did you think he had? Jill has no memory of it."

"You've talked with Jill?"

"What did happen to Andrew Wortman?"

"God only knows."

"Only?"

"What are you getting at?"

"I think you killed Will McDivitt because the two of you identified a derelict as Andrew Wortman. We know what McDivitt's motive was, but what was yours? How could you be so sure he wouldn't really show up?"

"The only speculation I care for has to do with the market."

"Your singleness of purpose frightens me. I can imagine that you would kill a man to prevent him from selling valuable stocks that would become more valuable."

Sciacca snorted. "You couldn't accuse me of theft though, could you?"

"With anyone else that might pose a problem. But you would have been content to know that they were locked up in the bank, increasing in value all the time."

Sitting beside the old man, Father Dowling told the story that he believed completed the one Iris Wortman had begun on her deathbed. Her husband had not deserted her. Doubtless he had intended to, and gone to his broker, who had prevented him from doing the unforgivable, selling off his investments. Alex would have been capable of using whatever means were necessary to stop that. When he heard of McDivitt's claim that

Wortman was in the morgue, he had known that was impossible. But he seconded the identification. Poor McDivitt had thereby put himself in a vulnerable position. Only he knew that Alex Sciacca had been willing to say that a redheaded derelict was the egg-bald Andrew Wortman. If that became known, the police would wonder why the broker had been willing to make such a misidentification.

"Are you going to tell this cock-and-bull story to anyone else?"

"Have you no remorse?"

Alex thought about it, as if the concept were unfamiliar to him. "You mean regrets? Of course not. I prevented a stupid, irrational deed. How much do you think those stocks are worth?"

"Ten million."

"More, much more."

"I meant regret for the deaths."

Alex Sciacca sat in his motorized chair, only a turn or two of its wheels from his own death, but his eyes were drawn to the monitor of his computer across which numbers endlessly moved. He struck a key and leaned toward his computer. Father Dowling felt that he had been dismissed. He watched the old man become absorbed in his transactions, and it seemed to be a kind of graveside ceremony.

"I'll be back," he said to Sciacca, touching his shoulder before he left.

The old man ignored him. Was that frail old man the murderer of two? And for what? How abstract a thing wealth is, evanescent numbers on a screen, certificates locked away in the vault of a bank.

"I'll be back."

And he would be, hoping against hope that he could awake the spark of conscience in the tireless investor. As a priest he owed him that. Besides, unless Father Dowling could convince the cardinal Mrs. Wortman had meant the archdiocese, Alex Sciacca was in his way a benefactor of the parish.

ASHES TO ASHES

1

Father Dowling sat with his visitor in the front parlor of the St. Hilary rectory.

"Russ wants me to just ignore the letter and I suppose he's right, but it preys on my mind, Father. What should I do?"

Julie Noonan was a beautiful young woman with ash-blond hair and violet eyes, but her face showed the ravages of the ordeal she had been through since her parents had met a bizarre end on a Caribbean cruise. It was a vacation they had dreamed of for decades but had postponed until the golden years of retirement. They had arranged for three days ashore on St. Thomas. The beach house they were occupying had caught fire and the Porters had apparently died in their sleep. The remains had been returned in closed caskets and Father Dowling conducted a service. Neither of the Porters had been Catholic but Julie was a fervent convert and seemed to think that a blessing could effect some posthumous change in her parents' status.

"Do you have the letter with you?"

Her hand trembled as she gave it to him. Obviously the letter had had a great effect on her and there seemed a danger of a relapse. Julie's faith had been insufficient protection against her parents' deaths and she was only now recovered from a nervous breakdown.

The letter was from a couple in Cleveland who had been on the boat with the Porters. They had not taken the St. Thomas option and sailed on and it wasn't until quite recently that they had learned what had happened to Julie's parents.

"Your mother and father both spoke so warmly of you," Mrs. Worley wrote, "and I can only imagine how you must miss them. My husband and I have only the happiest memories of them and that is how they come through in our videos. These are mementos of course, not professional, but you may want them. Perhaps when a little time has passed you will derive some consolation from seeing how they were enjoying themselves on a vacation that, alas, turned out so tragically."

"We have only photographs, Father. I don't know if I could bear to see them in a movie."

"Maybe Russ is right that you should ignore the offer. You have your own memories and photos."

Father Dowling was all but certain that it would unwise for Julie to subject herself to the sight of her parents cavorting in the sun when she knew what fate lay ahead for them.

"I'm not sure what to tell you, Julie."

"I have three days to go on my novena."

"Ah."

"Russ made me promise to make a novena before I answered Mrs. Porter."

Marie Murkin said she was glad that there were some young people who still understood the meaning of mourning.

"And don't tell me about the liturgy of hope and all that, Father Dowling. No one will ever convince me that a funeral Mass should be said in anything other than black vestments. When I die I want sadness, not a lot of empty chatter and smiling. And I want the Deese Erie sung too."

"The what?"

"You know what I mean."

He knew what she meant. But Julie Noonan needed less of the lugubrious, not more.

"I was just buying time," Russ Noonan said when he came by the rectory later that same afternoon after his wife told him she had broached the subject with the pastor of St. Hilary's. "No matter what I say makes it sound like a big deal. She couldn't stand it, Father." He looked out the parlor window and across the expanse of lawn to the parish center, where senior parishioners gathered during the day. The Porters had spent a day there, a trial to see if they would like it. They had, but before they accepted their senior status they wanted the final fling of the cruise.

"I blame myself," Russ Noonan said.

"Why?"

"I urged them to go. I made the arrangements, so they wouldn't change their minds, we drove them to O'Hare and put them on the plane to Miami." He shook his head. "I know Julie was thinking of that when . . ."

No need to finish. It must be awful for one spouse when the other falls ill, but a nervous breakdown would be particularly difficult.

Marie Murkin had followed the conversations with both Noonans and she had no doubt that Julie should have the video sent. The housekeeper waved off reminders of Julie's breakdown, but then Marie Murkin did not believe in the subconscious or any of the other fashionable explanations of human behavior.

"Did she think they were immortal?" Marie asked, looking from the pastor to Captain Phil Keegan, who showed little interest in the travails of Julie Noonan. Marie's appraisal of the grieving daughter wavered between approval and disapproval. "Does she think *she's* immortal?"

Marie was of the old school which held that a robust sense of the fragility of life was the best defense against adversity. Any other attitude was self-deception.

"And kicking against the goad."

Phil looked up from the paper. "I never understood the meaning of that phrase."

Marie stared at him and then turned to Father Dowling. But the pastor did not come to her rescue.

"Tell him, Marie."

It was clear that if the phrase was in Marie's standard repertoire, its meaning was not. She glared at Phil Keegan. "Don't pretend you don't know."

"I'm not pretending. Give me an analogy."

Father Dowling said, "It's sort of like punting, isn't it, Marie?"

The housekeeper rose, her face a mask of suppressed fury. If there was one thing she could not stand it was being teased. Father Dowling was filled with remorse.

"It sounds more like soccer," Phil said.

Marie left the room, arms straight at her sides, using a shoulder to push through into the kitchen.

"I think you're right, Marie," the pastor called after her, but from the kitchen came only the sound of a cupboard being closed, loudly.

2

Julie eventually decided that she did indeed want the video that recorded her parents' last happy moments on their Caribbean cruise. Father Dowling was reading Dante when Marie came into the study, eased the door shut behind her and whispered, "Julie Noonan."

"What about her?"

Marie put her finger to her lips. "She's in the front parlor. She wants to see you."

"Send her in."

"She wants to show you a video."

And there was a VCR in the front parlor. That was when the

pastor remembered Julie's last visit and the vacation video. He rose reluctantly but the one rule about difficult matters like this was not to postpone them.

Julie was seated in a hardback chair, looking out a window, but her expression suggested that she saw nothing. She was holding the video in her lap.

"I see it came."

She looked up at him. "It's the oddest thing."

To his relief she seemed calm. "Have you looked at it?"

"Father, it's not my folks. The Worleys got it all mixed up."

"They sent you the wrong video?"

"That isn't it. This is the one they meant. But the couple they think is Mom and Dad isn't."

"That is strange."

"In a way I'm relieved."

"I can understand that."

They put the video on and she fast-forwarded to the place where the Worleys had told her she would see her mother and father. But the couple who gradually became visible as they blinked against the bright sun and smiled into the video cam were definitely not Julie's parents. The man kept his hand before his face for the most part, shielding his eyes from the sun. In other pictures he wore huge sunglasses and a wide-brimmed floppy hat. "I knew it wasn't Dad before I could make out their features. He would never bare his arms."

"Oh?"

"He got a tattoo when he was in the navy and was mortally ashamed of it."

Julie was willing to let that be the end of it. She really did seem glad that there were no happy pictures of her parents taken just hours before they died. It seemed a sign of her relief that she forgot to take the video from the machine when she left, which is why Father Dowling was able to show it to Phil

Keegan later that day.

"The couple in Cleveland thought they had pictures of the Porters, but they didn't."

"That's a pretty dumb mistake."

"They meant to be kind."

Phil unwrapped a cigar and wet it down but left it unlit as he mulled over the strange story. They dropped it then, but Father Dowling knew that Phil found the story hard to forget. So did he. The next day, he closed the door of his study, made sure that Marie was not eavesdropping, and put through a call to Cleveland. Mr. Worley answered but his hearing was bad and he passed the phone to his wife. Father Dowling told Mrs. Worley who he was and said he had seen the video they sent.

"I found two photographs of the Porters, too, Father Dowling. In a roll I just had developed."

"You must have gotten to know them pretty well."

"We played bridge together. You find out a lot about people playing bridge with them."

He laughed. "And how did you rank the Porters?"

"Not everyone is meant to play bridge, Father."

"I thought he was pretty good." Good? Porter was much sought after for duplicate and had the equivalent of a black belt in bridge.

"Do you play, Father?"

"If you thought Mr. Porter was bad you wouldn't want to play with me."

"Should I send these pictures to the daughter, Father? She was rather strange about the video."

"Why don't you send them to me?"

He was giving her the address when he heard a receiver eased off the hook. "What's our zip, Marie?"

"What's that?" Mrs. Worley asked.

But the receiver was put down again. "Nothing. I'll look

329

forward to getting those snapshots, Mrs. Worley."

"You can decide whether to give them to the daughter."

The photographs when they came matched the couple in the video, but they were not the Porters either. Phil Keegan wrinkled his nose while he studied them.

"These people are strangers to Julie?"

"Yes."

"And the Worleys say it was this couple that died in the fire?"

The two men stared at one another, the implication of the video and photos stated at last. Father Dowling was wondering whose remains he had prayed over and buried a month ago. If the couple in the Worleys' photos and video were the people who had perished in the fire, then Julie's parents had not. It had passed beyond a mere curiosity.

Phil frowned at the snapshot. "This guy looks familiar."

"He's not much of a bridge player."

"Neither am I."

"Is that why he looks familiar?"

It was the kind of teasing remark that might have gotten a rise out of Marie, but Phil's mind was on the man in the photograph.

Missing Persons found no match for the couple in their current records. It was Agnes Lamb who had the idea of making use of the newer technology. A technician brought the photograph onto a computer screen and, prompted by Agnes, began to alter the face of the man. "Remove the hat and sunglasses," Agnes suggested. "Give him a mustache."

Lieutenant Cy Horvath and Phil Keegan looked on, the captain with an aloof look, until he was caught up in the exercise. "Thin out the hair," he said. "Make it gray above the ears."

"Glasses?" Cy suggested.

"Yes." And, when that was done, "Thick frames."

"Wow," Cy said.

"Peter Brady," Keegan said.

Agnes made an impatient noise. "He's dead!"

And so he was. He had been laid to rest in the ostentatious style preferred by members of the Chicago Underworld. Once they were beyond the reach of the law, there was no need for further lying low.

"Lying low is all he's got left."

Cy and Keegan looked at Agnes. She felt their eyes on her back and turned. "I thought that was pretty good."

"It was."

Brady, who had seldom been without a bodyguard and rightly worried that his enemies might bring him down before the police did, had met his death in the way fifty thousand other Americans did every year, in an automobile accident. His car had leaped a guardrail in Florida and plunged onto the interstate below, bursting into flames when it struck. The woman with him could not have been Mrs. Brady, because she was in the family home in Winnetka. The official story was that she was a bodyguard.

Agnes had attended the funeral, accompanying Cy. It was standard procedure to check the mourners at such events. Brady was the last of a line, an Irish "family" that had diversified after the repeal of Prohibition and now had a fleet of gambling boats on various Illinois rivers. The sons and grandsons of the deceased, generations removed from illegal activity, were the picture of respectability. Interment had been in a mausoleum modeled after Notre Dame in Paris, permission to copy the church on the University of Notre Dame campus having been refused, despite the generosity of Peter Brady and the three alumni among the departed's grandchildren. The police photographer had zoomed in on a diminutive gargoyle and then dissolved to a close-up of Cy Horvath.

McDivitt the undertaker had been in charge of the Brady funeral and Father Dowling decided to talk with him.

"I've invited Maurice McDivitt to lunch," he told Marie.

She froze. "The undertaker?"

"He prefers to be called a funeral director."

Marie had the spark of rebellion in her eye. Words of refusal seemed to be forming on her lips. Who knows what crisis might have been precipitated if the piercing whistle of her kettle had not called her to the kitchen? When she returned, she had had time to absorb the grim news.

"What would you like to have?"

"I think he's a vegetarian, Marie."

The emotions that had been quelled by a whistling kettle flared up once more in the housekeeper's eye.

"The Brady funeral was a McDivitt production," the pastor went on. "I wonder what we will find out from him."

Marie was transformed by the prospect of picking McDivitt's brain and she was not loath to say so.

"That's an unfortunate turn of phrase, Marie. He's a funeral director, not a pathologist."

But she was immune to teasing now. "I'll make a tuna fish casserole."

"Perfect."

Maurice McDivitt was waiting in the rectory when Father Dowling returned from his noon Mass. He was a dapper man, somewhere in his late sixties or early seventies, Marie would know, wearing a powder blue suit that gave luster to hair which had gone from black to silver to cotton white. He took Marie's hand and kissed it when she opened the door to him, holding that appendage a moment too long for Marie's comfort. She told the pastor later she was sure he was imagining a rosary entwined in her lifeless fingers. He greeted Father Dowling like a co-conspirator. Parish calendars were distributed at the beginning of each year, courtesy of the McDivitt Funeral Home, and the bulk of St. Hilary funerals were directed by McDivitt. Given the median age of the parishioners, Maurice could be forgiven if he regarded St. Hilary's with particular relish. Marie resented his air of being some sort of official of the parish. The man acted as if he were an assistant pastor.

"Or housekeeper."

"He couldn't stand the work."

But that was later. They settled in at the dining room table and Marie came sweeping in from the kitchen bearing the casserole. Cups of mushroom soup preceded the main dish, which was followed by fruit salad. McDivitt was suitably complimentary, even when Marie was in the kitchen, but of course she could hear him since she had drawn a chair up to the door for more comfortable eavesdropping.

"The Peter Brady obsequies were certainly well covered, Maurice."

"And so was Peter Brady, Father, if you'll forgive a little professional jocularity. Yes, it was. Photographs in both the *Sun Times* and the *Tribune,* to say nothing of the Fox River paper. The *Tribune* had an aerial shot of the cortege as we entered the cemetery."

"No St. Hilary's funeral could compete with that."

Maurice rotated his glass of iced tea, as if he were trying to get it properly positioned north and south. "No need to tell you the remote origins of the Brady wealth, Father Dowling."

"No." Some years before, Father Dowling had been consulted by Malcolm Brady, a grandson fresh out of college and of sensitive conscience.

"The family money was acquired illegally, Father. Doesn't that raise questions about my inheriting it?"

"How so?"

"Ill-gotten gains."

The received opinion was that it had been over a half century since the Brady family had been engaged in illegal business. Father Dowling was partially reassured on this point by Phil Keegan. "Gambling's legal now, Roger. All the crooks are now respectable businessmen."

Young Malcolm Brady's doubt was put to rest by reminding him of the family's charitable contributions over the years. It would be impossible to restore the money made in a wild era. Who precisely had been deprived of it? Recompense to the common good could continue to be made via charity. Malcolm was relieved.

"You should have scolded him about those gambling ships."

"Gambling is legal, Marie."

"Is it any less of a sin?"

Marie's moral theology was her own creation and did little harm, at least until she presumed to advise others. Thank God she hadn't had first shot at Malcolm Brady.

"It was a closed-coffin funeral, wasn't it, Maurice?"

"You might say that cremation had already occurred."

"None of the Bradys saw the remains?"

"It would have been like looking into an ashtray."

A faint scraping sound from the kitchen, as Marie shifted in her chair.

"I suppose those could have been anyone's ashes," Father Dowling said in a light tone. Maurice looked philosophical.

"Death is a leveler, Father Dowling. *Remember, man, that thou art dust . . .*" That out of the way, Maurice added in a less unctuous tone that, of course, if proof had been required, proof could have been given.

"Did you bury the popsy too?" Marie asked.

Maurice was puzzled until Father Dowling explained that Marie meant the woman who had been in the car with Brady.

"Popsy? Oh, she was at least your age, Marie."

Peter Brady, Phil Keegan informed Roger Dowling, had not emerged fully into respectability. In fact, the state's attorney had been presenting evidence against him before the grand jury and only death had saved Brady from indictment.

"These gambling boats are as bad as the rackets ever were," Phil grumbled. "And you'd think the rivers were international waters so far as local law enforcement goes."

"What would the indictment have been?"

"Kopicinski won't say. But he was certain he had Brady nailed."

That afternoon, while reading his breviary, Father Dowling was pestered by a question which he fended off until he had finished vespers. Then he closed the book and let the dates take shape in his mind. After a little figuring, he decided that the Porters had left on their vacation a week before the Brady funeral. He almost sighed aloud, but then the questions began again. There was an abundance of charred remains around and his imagination found that a fruitful fact. He wondered if his estimate of human nature was lower than it had been.

A call to the Noonans indicated that the Porters had planned their vacation with Simpson Travel.

Flo, the girl behind the counter, proved to be nearer Father Dowling's own age, despite the fierce redness of her hair and the heavy makeup. Large sparkling eyes looked out from flamboyant lashes. Contact lenses.

"Are you Father Walsh?" Her face arranged itself by stages in a smile.

"Father Dowling."

"Oh." The mask was restored. "I thought you were here about being chaplain on a cruise."

"Actually, I am here about a cruise."

His collar seemed to receive forty lashes when her eyes lowered to it. He explained that he was here about a couple that had gone on a cruise, the Porters. "Their son-in-law, Russ Noonan, made the arrangements." Her reaction was immediate. The great stack of hennaed hair swayed as she nodded her head.

"You're asking as a priest?"

"On behalf of the children."

She rolled back to a file cabinet and removed a folder. Scooting back to him, she displayed the records of the Porter travel plans.

From a jacket pocket he took the newspaper clippings that had featured Peter Brady and showed them to her. She looked at them impassively, then at him.

"Do you recognize him?"

"Oh, they didn't go on a cruise, Father." She closed her lustrous eyes, then snapped them open. "Florida. They went to St. Petersburg."

"Are you sure?"

"Absolutely."

He held up the picture the Worleys had taken of their Caribbean companions and there was definitely a reaction.

"But you have the pictures mixed up. This is the woman I sold a ticket to."

She was pointing to the picture of Brady and the unknown woman Marie had described as a popsy.

"She was Mrs. Brady?"

"That's what she said," she said carefully.

"Didn't you believe her?"

"I've learned not to get too nosy about the couples who book vacations together." Flo gave him a significant look. "Only they weren't going on a Caribbean cruise."

She managed to find the paperwork on the trip and Father Dowling asked her to make a photocopy of it.

"Didn't the Porters fly to St. Petersburg too?"

"That was a stop on the way to Miami. It's cheaper that way."

"Same flight?"

Flo frowned for a moment, then understood. She tapped at her computer and then looked up and nodded.

Maurice McDivitt flashed a professional welcoming smile as he looked up from his desk but then, seeing that his caller was Father Dowling, rose with a more genuine smile on his ruddy face.

"You said that the body of Peter Brady was not so burned it couldn't be identified, Maurice."

McDivitt rose and crossed the room to close his door. He returned to his desk and settled himself in his chair.

"He had a tattoo."

"On his arm?"

"How did you know that?"

"I thought everyone knew."

Maurice was anxious to learn what his answer to Father Dowling's question signified but the priest pleaded pastoral confidentiality.

"If I can tell you, I will, Maurice. You have been helpful."

"I wish I knew how."

Sitting on a bench beside a parish walk, out of earshot of Marie Murkin, Phil Keegan listened to Father Dowling's explanation of what had happened. Brady and his mistress had arranged to assume the identities of the Porters when the plane both couples had been on resumed its flight at St. Petersburg, headed for Miami. The unfortunate Porters, perhaps already dead, were then disposed of by Brady hirelings in a staged auto accident and Mr. Porter's charred remains had been the main attraction at a gangland funeral. Had the rivals who arranged for the death of Brady and his popsy in that fire on St. Thomas attended the supposed obsequies for Peter Brady? Mrs. Porter had been buried all but anonymously.

"McDivitt will know the location of her grave."

"And Mr. Porter is in that monstrous mausoleum Peter Brady put up?"

"Monstrous? It is an exact replica of Notre Dame."

"What are you going to do, Roger?"

This was the question he had been putting to himself since his guess had been corroborated by McDivitt. Cy Horvath had run a discreet check and ascertained that Peter Brady had not been tattooed. That removed the last reasonable doubt. Father Dowling was left with the knowledge that he had blessed the remains of Peter Brady and his mistress and that they now rested under headstones commemorating the Porters.

The problem he faced reminded him of the intricate but abstract puzzles they had discussed in seminary moral theology courses. He felt that he owed the truth to the Noonans, but he was tempted to kick against the goad. Punt, that is.

Three months later, Julie Noonan came to the rectory, her manner matching her loveliness. It was clear that she was reconciled to the loss of her parents.

"If only they had become Catholics."

"You mean before they died?"

She laughed. "I want you to say some Masses for them."

"I already have. But I'll be glad to say more."

In the interim, he had spelled out what had happened to Russ Noonan and together they had gone to consult with Maurice McDivitt. The funeral director's pink eyes widened when he realized that Mr. Porter lay in the ostentatious replica of Notre Dame while Peter Brady rested in more modest circumstances.

"Can it be done with discretion?" Father Dowling asked when McDivitt said that he could rearrange the bodies. The question pained Maurice.

"McDivitt's does everything with discretion, Father."

Whether to tell Julie was left to Russ and it seemed clear that he had not considered that necessary.

"All's well that ends well, Father."

"Indeed."

ADDITIONAL COPYRIGHT INFORMATION

ABOUT THE AUTHOR

Author and editor **Ralph McInerny** has long been acknowledged as one of the most vital voices in lay Catholic activities in
America. He is co-founder and co-publisher of *Crisis,* a widely
read journal of Catholic opinion, while finding time to teach
Medieval Studies at Notre Dame University and write several
series of mystery novels, one of which, *The Father Dowling
Mysteries,* ran on network television for several seasons and can
now be seen on cable. Scholars are rarely entertainers, but Ralph
McInerny, both as himself and under his pseudonym Monica
Quill, has been both for many years.